SPACE EMPIRES

The Rising Darkness

CALEB THOMAS SELBY

ISBN: 1507586590
ISBN 13: 9781507586594

Dedicated to my father

TABLE OF CONTENTS

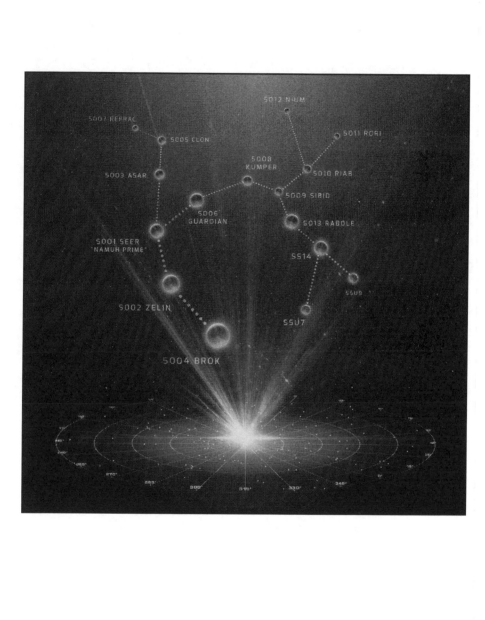

CHAPTER 1

DARK BEGINNINGS

The front left wheel of the cart squeaked as he trudged forward in the long line, but he didn't hear it. How could he? The squeaking wheel, the ever roaring coolant turbines four levels above, the rumbling flux generators just down the corridor and the unending grumbling of the men seemed to simply scramble in his mind into one monstrous symphony of chaos. Jamien had always cherished the quiet and frankly got quite agitated whenever there were loud or relentless noises about, making for a tough transition when his first child was born.

Yet, the overpowering and unrelenting noises and foreign sounds of the Navy dock sub-levels didn't bother him, at least not anymore. They had, of course taken their toll on his sanity when he had first started his monotonous job. But several grueling weeks of hard labor made Jamien realize his true enemy was not the deafening sounds; far from it. Rather, his true nemesis was the stifling, nearly unbearable heat that surrounded and permeated his body every minute of every day.

The solution to the problem seemed obvious enough to Jamien. Yet the industrial sized thermal reducer units that would be required to adequately cool the many corridors and rooms of the dock's sub levels were an expense that could not be justified, not that it was ever seriously considered by anyone. So what if a dozen workers passed out each day from thermal exhaustion?

Their labor was cheap and replaceable; two very nasty attributes to have for any position.

Jamien smiled a frustrated smile as he contemplated his own expendability and wondered if things would be better once the war was over. Surely they would have to be, right? How could they be worse?

"Next!" a voice from behind a counter called out, prompting the long line to inch forward.

"Hey! Watch it!" a portly man ahead of Jamien snapped as Jamien's cart accidentally brushed up against him.

"Sorry," Jamien quietly apologized and pulled the cart back and held it firmly. The man eyed Jamien sternly and then turned and pushed his own cart up to the counter.

Jamien rubbed his sleepy eyes with the back of his rough, oil stained hands. He glanced up at a clock fixed on the wall above the counter and then shook his head painfully. He was only halfway done with a solid three day shift and he was already well beyond exhausted. He didn't know how he was going to make it through another day and a half without rest and the thought was nearly more then he could endure.

He did his best not to think about the misery of his plight as he undid the strap on his thermos from the handle bar of the cart. He glanced down at the long line of sweaty, tired men behind him, shook his head and sipped some of the cheap lor. He cringed at the bitter taste but took several gulps nevertheless to help combat the fatigue.

"Next," the voice rang out again, indicating it was finally Jamien's turn, although he was in no rush.

He capped his thermos and tried hard to focus as he pushed his cart filled with worn tools up to the counter and peered through the open window. He was hoping one of the seasoned operators would be manning the counter, as they were usually more reasonable in assignments than the newer recruits. Jamien was disappointed when he spotted a young, preppy kid that had likely spent an hour on his hair that morning staring up at him with a disinterested gaze. Jamien tried to be optimistic as he leaned onto the aged, splintered counter, offering a forced smile.

The kid was half Jamien's age, perhaps younger, and was sitting down on an old, padded chair casually assigning the hard labor to the haggard maintenance crew. A small thermal reducer sat on his desk blowing fresh, cool air onto his highly pampered face. Jamien wished he could sit on the stool, just for a minute, to rest his weary legs and soak in some of the cool air.

"ID Card?" the kid asked curtly, waking Jamien out of his wishful daydream.

Jamien dove into his pocket and fished out his battered card and handed it to the kid, inadvertently reaching through the current of cooled air. As inconspicuously as he could, he left his hand dangling only for a few extra moments, thoroughly relishing even the smallest reprieve from the heat.

The kid glanced at Jamien's dirty hand and then looked up at Jamien cynically as he swiped the card though a reader.

"Ok, Jamien," he began as he looked at his data pad for job listings, "looks like we have a tertiary fuel pressure gauge malfunction deep in the southwest corridor, in section, oh let me see here, looks like section...D-three. Do you think you can handle that, Pal?" he asked smugly, as if he were a master mechanic that could fix anything and everything.

"Sure. I guess so," Jamien answered quietly, realizing that he had just received an assignment near the dock power core, the hottest spot in the sweltering facility.

"Get going then!" the kid ordered harshly, obviously loving the power he had over Jamien and all the others.

"Well, I actually was wondering..." Jamien nervously began, "...I was wondering if I could get a new polarity inverter. The one I've been using is shot to pieces and..."

"Jamien, Jamien, Jamien," the kid said as he sat back in his chair, placing his hands behind his head. "You know that we don't have brand new tools to hand out every time one of you clumsy idiots breaks one."

"Yes, but..." Jamien tried to answer, holding up his broken tool to show the kid.

"Don't you know there's a war going on?" the kid interrupted, nodding upwards. "Try to take better care of the things given to you! Understand?"

"Yes, I'm sorry," Jamien quietly said. "It's just that…"

"No more excuses!" the kid snapped. "Get a move on. Don't you see the line behind you? There are other people beside you that need their tasks. Hurry up before this whole facility falls apart under your feet! It's a wonder it hasn't already, with people like you fixing things. Next!"

Without another word for his case, Jamien dropped his polarity inverter back into his cart and obediently turned it around and started on his way toward the southwest corridor on the opposite side of the massive facility. The front left wheel squeaked as loud as ever.

Five years earlier a much more vivacious version of Jamien would have knocked the punk kid's head clean off. But that was then and this was now. The tumultuous events of the last several years did much to smother Jamien's once spirited persona. And besides, he needed this job too badly to be causing trouble with the management, even if a couple of them could use a good kick where it counted. Sure the hours were horrid and the pay was worse, but it was a job. He had a wife and two kids to feed back home and he didn't have the luxury to be picky. He was actually quite lucky to land one of the menial maintenance jobs at the docks, and he knew it. Out of the sixteen advanced level engineers that had escaped the heavy arms manufacturing plant disaster two months prior, only he had been able to procure another steady job. His former coworkers were being forced to rely on government welfare, a most unpredictable means (especially these days) for supporting a family.

Jamien thought on his cruel predicament as he silently trudged toward his destination. He had walked for nearly thirty minutes when he spotted another worker pushing a cart toward him. Jamien was pleased as he identified the man as one of the few friends he had made in his short tenure at the docks. He stopped his cart wearily and waited for the man to do the same but much to Jamien's dismay, he did not. Instead, he plodded right past Jamien as if he didn't see him, his dull, listless eyes not even glancing up to see who he was passing. Jamien watched for another moment before shrugging and returning to his clunky, squeaking cart.

He continued to push his heavy load down muggy, empty hallways and poorly lit corridors, the temperature rising slightly with every step.

During the two months of his employment he had only traveled this close to the core on one other occasion and he had not been anxious to repeat the long journey through the dirty and poorly maintained sub-levels of the massive facility.

He was nearly to his destination and getting hotter by the minute when out of the corner of his eye he spotted an open doorway down one of the restricted passages. The security door leading down the passageway was conspicuously opened, yet nobody was in sight. Jamien promptly turned his cart down the darkened hallway to investigate the matter and close the door, if needed. He parked his ever-squeaking cart right outside the opened door and approached.

"Hello? Is anyone over here?" he called out. There was no reply.

He timidly walked up to the room and peered in. The room was a standard monitoring station filled with pressure gages, monitors and scanners. Three large pipes ran along the ceiling bringing fuel from the depots buried far beneath the docks to the navy capital ships moored up on the surface.

Jamien took a step into the room and glanced quickly at a few of the gauges. Everything appeared to be in order. Jamien shrugged off the oddity and was just about to turn off the lights and close the door when he noticed it. A silver device, a little bigger then his polarity inverter, was tucked neatly just above one of the fuel lines. Jamien had been in enough of the monitoring rooms to know that this was not right. He curiously approached the device, wondering what it could be. The room was deathly quiet and he was just reaching for it when he heard the wheel of his tool cart squeak ever so softly, yet distinctly. Jamien jumped and quickly turned around and found himself looking straight into the eyes of a face that he recognized, but could not immediately place.

"What are you doing?" the man asked in a challenging tone.

Jamien stepped back awkwardly, unsure of who this person was but assuming he had some position of authority. "I was...I was just about to check on something," stammered Jamien.

The man glanced at the device and then back at Jamien and smiled...a wicked carnivorous smile. Before Jamien could react, the man transfigured into a hideous, blackened form resonating with evil in every inch of its being. An imposing monstrous visage with a large fang filled mouth and two menacing eyes materialized and looked at Jamien with insatiable appetite. The head was fixed by a stocky neck to a gaunt, shriveled torso that rested upon a cluster of writhing tentacles, seemingly having a life of their own, squirming this way and that, sensing their surroundings and preparing to strike if needed. The creature seemed part serpentine, part arachnid and nothing less than pure demonic. It was obvious from just a fleeting glance that the beast was primal evil and knew no good within its heart.

"What...what are you?" Jamien gasped in horror as he slowly backed away from the ghastly sight.

Jamien's words had barely escaped his lips when the creature lunged at him, enveloping him with the many powerful tentacles and holding him fast. Jamien tried in vain to free himself but it was no use. He was powerless in the creature's hold. The creature's mighty mouth opened. Jamien cowered away, trying to escape from the unhinged jaw as it slowly neared. It was useless. The heinous mouth formed a tight seal around Jamien's face and began the horrific act of sucking Jamien dry through his eyes, nose and mouth. Jamien died instantly but the beast continued do draw out what it could from the lifeless body. As it continued, Jamien's skin began to wither like aged leather and began to shrink around the fast drying bones as if his skeleton were being vacuumed sealed by his own skin. When at last there was nothing left to draw out, the creature dropped the dehydrated body unceremoniously to the ground.

The serpentine monster then slowly reassumed the countenance of a man. A slight trickle of Jamien's blood clung to his cheek, which he wiped off with a finger and licked clean. With a contented sigh, the creature posing as a man then made his way to the small device neatly tucked behind the fuel lines. It reached up and quickly pressed several buttons on the device's interface until a small screen came to life and began to blink red figures on the screen in synchrony. The countdown had begun. The creature then ran out of the room, down the hallway and toward the nearest emergency exit.

Fifteen minutes later, the preppy kid behind the counter was napping lightly with the cool breeze from the thermal reducer caressing his face when a rumble from the southwest corridor awoke him. His sleepy eyes barely had a chance to ascertain what was happening before he was engulfed in the ravenous flames of a powerful explosion.

⊿

Kesler tapped his data pad screen with an edger and then slowly looked back up at the massive, six-armed alien sitting across the table from him. The alien looked down at Kesler, two pairs of arms causally folded across his broad chest while he rested the other pair on the table. The alien's posture was poised, although he was obviously nervous.

Kesler had never liked the Branci race, and likely never would. Although humanoid in nearly every way, the differences between the Namuh and Branci were far more pronounced than the extra pairs of arms possessed by the Branci, at least in the minds of many Namuh. As a general rule, the Branci smelled bad, had poor manners, were physically repulsive and, in Kessler's humble opinion, were all dimwitted, devolved fools! Yet, what Kesler (and many others) hated most about the Branci were the entitlement programs created by his own government to set up the Branci with a worry-free existence at the expense of the Namuh. Housing, food, clothing and just about anything else that the Branci wanted, the Branci seemed to get, regardless of the cost. The few Branci that did work for a living, were handed positions and responsibilities through affirmative action and racial equality plans that should have gone to more qualified Namuh, or at least many thought. So the fact that Kesler was being forced to interview these creatures for an officer's post aboard a fleet warship was nearly unbearable for him. Kesler had spent five years of vigorous study and sacrifice to get such a post, and the fact that an inferior was going to walk right in with some flight time records and recommendation letters and try to land a comparably respected commission, made him sick.

"So, is everything ok there?" the Branci reluctantly asked after several minutes without a spoken word between them.

Kesler didn't answer. He tapped the data pad screen several more times, seemingly with no direction or intent. He had survived three such interviews already today and had managed to cause each candidate to withdraw his application after a half-hour of painstaking awkward silence and outlandish bureaucratic red tape that none of the Branci knew how to handle. This was the last Branci that Kesler had to see before his week and a half shore leave began. He could hardly wait. And the sooner he made this Branci leave, the sooner he could immerse himself in the infamous and oh so decadent Larep city nightlife. It was going to be great!

"Hey, listen. You don't have to like me or my kind, if you don't want to," the Branci suddenly declared after another minute passed, startling Kesler out of his daydream. "It's fine by me. Really. I just want to get my assignment and get settled on whatever vessel you want. If you want to put me on the most rundown frigate in the fleet because you hate me, that's your call. I just want to know sometime today!"

Kesler looked up from his data pad in a momentary loss for words. He had never before encountered a Branci that was assertive and wasn't quite sure how to respond.

"Well...you see...Mister," Kesler glanced back at the name on his notes.

"My name's Tarkin!" the Branci said with a hint of disgust in his voice.

"Yes, well, Mr. Tarkin, the thing is, I usually get a notice from the Branci embassy if they are planning on sending someone over for an interview. However, I don't have anything from them for your name and registration number today." Kesler finished and then nodded toward his opened data pad and shrugged. "So if you want to get in contact with your local delegate to get a sponsored interview, we'd be happy to take another look at your application. But I'm afraid without that official sponsorship, the Namuh Protective Federation Navy cannot consider you for candidacy at this time."

The immense alien rested all pairs of arms on the desk and looked Kesler square in the eyes. "Don't mess around with me! You know full well that under Article 16 subsections D and G of the Namuh Protective Federation Pact, all Branci can seek transfer of rank and position into the Namuh Navy if they have logged at least three thousand hours in interstellar travel. Sponsorship is only required for those without star travel hours!"

Kesler sat back in his chair, intimidated somewhat by the Branci's forward approach and uncharacteristic knowledge of the treaty bylaws. "Oh, did you have three thousand logged hours?" he finally said looking back down at the pad, already well aware that he did.

Tarkin nodded as he relaxed his stance slightly. "Two years with the Asar merchant fleet and seven months with Zelin Communications Satellite Drop Division. I'm an excellent pilot for smaller craft and a first rate executive officer for the big rigs. Both captains that I have served under have written letters on my behalf recommending me for a post in the fleet with an officer's commission."

Even Kesler momentarily realized the candidacy merits of Tarkin. Having overlooked the letters at first glance, Kesler humored Tarkin and opened the files and quickly glanced through them. "Exemplary character, loyal, quick learner, blah, blah, blah," Kesler quickly read to himself before nodding in approval and looking up at Tarkin. "Very impressive," he reluctantly said, offering a nod and a half smile.

Tarkin's rough face offered his first hint of a smile since the interview began. "Thank you. I've worked hard, very hard to get here today. Many of us Branci dream of serving in the fleet and defending our Federation from those who wish it harm."

"Oh I can tell," Kesler said with a hint of a condescending tone. "And in all honesty, you are an excellent candidate...as far as Branci go. But, unfortunately there are no open positions currently posted for entry-level officers in the Sixth Fleet. But I'll tell you what I can do for you. Because you have such an impressive portfolio, I'll add your name to the waiting list. How does that sound?"

Tarkin's momentary smile instantly turned to pure rage and he jumped to his feet, knocking over the chair behind him. "This is an outrage!" he yelled. "You and I both know that there are dozens of listed positions in the Sixth Fleet and that I am more then capable to fill any number of them!"

Kesler jumped back from the table, his hand reaching for his holstered lydeg. "Hold it right there big fella."

Tarkin eyed Kesler's weapon, carefully weighing his next move.

"Why don't you just get moving while you still can," Kesler said.

"If I don't?" Tarkin asked, still starring at the gun.

Kesler shook his head. "I'll make sure your name is blacklisted. Good luck getting a job cleaning toilets on the colony transports if that happens!"

Tarkin's many years of hard, and at times tedious work, flashed before his eyes. His dream of serving in the Fleet was being yanked away by a racist Lieutenant and he had no recourse. His helplessness made him angrier. It would have been quick work to kill the Lieutenant, even with him being armed, but the consequences of such an action were not worth it.

"Now that you've experienced my version of Affirmative Action, why don't you just saunter on out of here and head downtown and apply for a subsidized apartment and a food card. I hear we're still giving those away to anyone with six arms and a sob story," Kesler added, motioning toward the exit.

Tarkin didn't move.

"Do we have an understanding here or do you want me to defend myself from a perceived attack?" asked Kesler, once more patting his weapon.

Tarkin's mighty arms trembled with anger as he weighed the consequences of landing a few well-deserved blows on Kesler's face. He had yet to decide his course of action when a deep rumble followed by a series of deafening explosions, sent both men to the floor.

⚔

"Get up!" Tarkin said gruffly as he tried to prop Kesler up several minutes later. "Come on, we don't have time to waste!"

Kesler shook his head and slowly opened his eyes. "What's going on? What... what happened? Get away from me!" he shouted when he realized Tarkin was touching him up. "What did you do?"

Tarkin released Kesler and nodded toward the large window. "I did nothing...but someone sure has."

"What are you talking about?" Kesler said as he struggled to his feet and made his way to the window. The sight that met him caused tears to flood his eyes. "Help us all," he whispered as he looked down in horror as half of the Sixth Fleet was awash in flames, the other half struggling to break free of their gravity well anchors to escape the inferno.

Tarkin shook his head, unsure of what to say or do. Although not a member of the Navy, his heart had long been devoted to it and to see one of her fleets in such overwhelming tragedy was hard to watch.

"Lieutenant Ke......vara command," a crackly transmission sounded over the tele-link latched to Kesler's wrist.

Kesler immediately brought the tele-link to his lips. "This is Kesler. Go ahead, Iovara."

Another static filled transmission followed, "...is co...and wh...you?"

"Iovara Command, I can't make out your transmission," Kesler answered as he walked across the room to get a better signal. "I'm in observation tower three with a Branci. I was just conducting an interview when an explosion erupted somewhere down on the surface. I see fire shooting up everywhere. Please advise. Over!" Kesler looked out the window and spotted the Iovara though the smoke and debris. She was still in one piece. "I say again, Iovara, please advise! This is Lieutenant Kesler in tower three," Kesler yelled after several more moments of silence passed.

"Kesler, this is Fedrin," an authoritative voice finally replied clearly over the transmitter. "Get over here now! We need to take off before our hull overheats and cracks!"

"Admiral," Kesler said in a relieved tone. "I'm glad to hear your voice. What in the world is going on?"

"You know as much as we do," Fedrin answered. "Now get over here!"

"I have a Branci here with me," Kesler added. "What should I do with him?"

"You're call, Lieutenant. Leave him or bring him," Fedrin answered. "I really don't care. But you better decide fast!"

"I'm on my way!" Kesler answered and started toward the walkway door.

"You better hurry," Fedrin added. "We're pulling out of here as soon as we can with or without you. We have no choice."

"Don't wait for us!" Kesler said as he opened the access point door and then turned back and motioned for Tarkin to follow.

"You want me to go with you?" Tarkin asked skeptically. "I thought you don't like us Branci?"

"I don't!" shouted Kesler. "But, I'm not about to let you burn up here. That's no way to die, even for your kind. Now come on!"

"Your compassion is overwhelming!" Tarkin yelled back as he turned to follow his bigoted savior.

Kesler ran down the access shaft followed closely by Tarkin. The two were halfway to the ship when another explosion ripped through the walkway, just a few feet in front of Kesler. Kesler fell back to the ground and scrambled away from the leaping flames as they chased his feet.

"I hate fire!" yelled Kesler once he reached a safer distance with Tarkin. "I hate it!"

Tarkin brazenly walked up to the edge of the chasm and analyzed their predicament.

"I think we're done for!" Kesler shouted out from several feet behind. "There's no going back and forward just isn't happening!"

Tarkin's eyes scanned the obstacles for a few more seconds before nodding and walking back toward Kesler. "Can you jump over that?" he asked nodding at the leaping flames.

"Jump over that?" asked Kesler incredulously. "Not a chance, big guy! We're toast!"

"Didn't think so," said Tarkin as he grabbed Kesler with four of his mighty arms and held him tight.

"What are you doing?" Kesler yelled as he struggled to free himself. "Let go of me at once!"

"Shut up!" snapped Tarkin. "We're going to jump!"

"Whoa! I don't think so pal!" Kesler yelled as he tried to pry himself out of the Branci's overpowering arms.

"Trust me," said Tarkin in a calm yet commanding voice. "I can do this."

Kesler looked up into the gruff face of the Branci and reluctantly gave up his futile struggle. He then closed his eyes, and prepared to die. Never in his wildest dreams did he think his last moments of life would be in the arms of a Branci. Surely there were better ways to go.

Tarkin backed up the walkway a few extra feet and then shot down the corridor toward the gap. Just as he approached the edge of the chasm, he leapt up and through the ravenous flames. Kesler cringed as he felt the intense heat for a brief moment. Then it was over.

Tarkin released Kesler on the other side of the hole and then turned to continue down the ramp. But before they began their run again, Kesler grabbed at one of Tarkin's arms, prompting the Branci to turn around and face the Lieutenant. The edges of his beard and wisps of his longer hair had been singed and released a steady stream of smoke. The burning hair smelt awful but Kesler hardly noticed.

"Why did you do that?" Kesler demanded. "Why did you just save my life?"

Tarkin looked at Kesler's hand holding his arm and then looked back at Kesler. "Do you think a security guard on the Sixth Fleet's Flagship would let me enter unaccompanied, especially after these explosions?"

"Probably not," Kesler answered.

"Exactly!" Tarkin said and shook Kesler's hand off of his arm.

Kesler nodded slowly. "You saved me to save yourself?"

"To be honest, I did think about pushing you into the fire and then jumping myself," answered Tarkin. "But under the circumstances, it would not have been my most prudent course of action."

"I see," Kesler said as they once more started down the corridor.

The two finally reached the end of the ramp where they were met by a dull metal door outlined with thick rivets. A small circular window was set into the thick door, fixed at eye-level. Kesler pressed a small button on the door's face and then peered though the window, praying that someone would answer.

"Anyone that can rationalize that saving a Lieutenant is the best course of action to preserve their own skin as quickly as you just did, is someone I would want to work with," Kesler said casually as he pressed the button again.

"You don't owe me any favors," Tarkin answered. "You didn't leave me in the tower and I didn't let you burn. We're square, Lieutenant. No debts, no favors. I can make it on my own. I always have. You might say that it's my own version of affirmative action."

"We'll talk about it later," answered Kesler, pressing the button yet again, realizing they had only moments before the rest of the ramp would collapse.

Much to their relief the large door slowly swung inward allowing Kesler and Tarkin to dive aboard the Iovara, the prized flagship of the combined Namuh Navy. Kesler had just swung the large door back in place and was in the process of bolting it closed when a posted guard approached them with his weapon drawn.

"Halt right there!" he said gruffly facing Tarkin. "Non-uninformed Branci are not allowed on fleet vessels, especially not ones as ugly as you. Now get off!"

"He stays," Kesler said, turning from the door and coming face to face with the guard. "And if you ever talk to one of your superiors that way again, you'll be the one getting tossed out. Understood?"

"He is not my superior," the guard said with disgust, raising his nose in arrogance. "The Branci are scum and always will be!"

Kesler's eyes flashed in anger as he pointed to Tarkin. "He'll outrank you three levels by tonight! Now step aside before I look up your number and write you up for insubordination! Got it?"

The guard did not answer, but did relax his stance and allowed the couple to pass, yet giving Tarkin a disdainful look the entire time.

"Let's go Tarkin," said Kesler, motioning for the large alien to follow.

After several minutes, Kesler and Tarkin finally stopped their frantic run through the ship's corridors in front of a set of heavy reinforced doors. Kesler rapidly entered his officer verification code into a small entry pad on an adjacent terminal and the massive doors slowly slid apart, revealing a large, multi level room. The place was in absolute chaos.

Tarkin cautiously followed Kesler into the disheveled bridge and looked on in awe at the hundreds of monitors, operating consoles and stations scattered around the semicircular room, the literal beating heart of the Iovara.

"Coolant leak on reactor block sixteen!" someone yelled from one of the upper levels.

"Port thrusters seven, fourteen, and twenty-two are down!" yelled another. "Numbers three and four are sputtering."

"Tertiary ion reserves have ignited!" another officer announced. "Containment teams are responding!"

"All airlocks sealed and ready to go except for two on aft section G!" someone else shouted.

Other officers yelled back and forth from their command stations around the bridge in intolerable frustration, while ensigns scurried about the floor setting up the primary ship systems in preparation for the impromptu takeoff.

Leaving Tarkin at the entrance Kesler bounded across the floor toward his station. Snatching a headset and placing it over his head, he immediately went to work coordinating ship stations for the departure.

The bridge was in total pandemonium. Nobody seemed to know what to do or where to go. When Kesler made his way to his post, he noticed several untrained substitutes manning critical operating stations, testament to the urgency of the situation.

"What do you mean you won't deactivate the gravitational mooring lines?" Kesler heard Admiral Fedrin shout into a transmitter.

"Just that," said the calm voice of the traffic control officer. "As I've already informed you, I can not authorize your ascent until you've received full clearance from Larep flight control. Please stand by."

"Look out your window!" Fedrin yelled back. "Do you see those flames? Do you see all those burning ships? Do you see the smoke clouds so thick you can barely see the noonday sun?"

"There is no need to raise your voice, Sir," the voice answered.

"Raise my voice?" Fedrin yelled. "I'll raise more than my voice if you don't drop those gravity lines!"

"Please rest assured that we are taking steps to rectify your complaint promptly," the officer said.

"What is that supposed to even mean?" exclaimed Fedrin in exacerbation. "How are you going to rectify the fact that what's left of my fleet is sitting in a lake of fire? Answer me that!"

A warning signal sounded at Kesler's station. "Hull temperature is rising!" he spoke up and immediately started flipping switches and turning dials in an attempt to stabilize it.

An explosion somewhere outside shook the ship violently.

"What was that?" Fedrin yelled as he grabbed hold of his chair.

"Looks like the Triumphant just went up!" an officer replied. "She's gone, Sir!"

Fedrin slammed the arm of his chair as tears filled his eyes. "Did you see that? Another one of my ships just went up because you won't let us leave! Now order the docking authority to drop the lines before more lives are lost!"

"As I've already said, you need clearance to do that," answered the traffic control pilot like a drone.

"Temperature still climbing," Kesler announced as he adjusted several additional knobs on a power transfer panel in an attempt to redirect power to the shielding generators.

"Heat sinks one thru seven are maxed. Eight thru ten have already melted down!" an officer announced.

"Drop the lines now before I shoot my way out of here!" Fedrin yelled.

"I would advise against that, Sir," the officer answered calmly.

"Commander Drezden just signaled and said his shields can only hold another few minutes before they're done for," an officer shouted out.

"That's it," Fedrin said shaking his head. "Lieutenant Jonas!" he shouted out to the chief weapons officer stationed on a platform above the command chair.

"Sir?" Jonas asked peering over the railing.

"Charge all secondary particle weapons," Fedrin ordered. "Target the gravity line generators!"

"Your wish is my command!" replied Jonas, turning back to his computers.

"Admiral, please reconsider what you are doing before you do something we will all regret," the officer in the traffic tower said in a calm, controlled voice upon hearing Fedrin's orders.

"Shut up!" Fedrin yelled and terminated the transmission.

Fedrin tapped several keys on his command console and then looked up. "Kesler, have all ships that still have primary functions follow, our lead. Have them blast themselves free and get out of this death trap at all costs. Tell them that I will take full responsibility for their actions!"

Kesler nodded. "I'm on it."

"Weapons armed and ready," Jonas announced. "Target resolutions are locked and loaded."

"Traffic control fighter squadrons just came up on my scope!" Kesler called out. "They're heading this way!"

"They wouldn't," Jonas said in disbelief, gaping at his screen.

"Open fire on the generators!" Fedrin ordered.

"Firing port side particle guns!" Jonas announced as tremendous bursts of energy shot from the Iovara's turrets, smashing a row of generators on an already burning platform.

"Targets destroyed!" Jonas announced as the ship, now free of the gravity mooring lines, suddenly lurched upward.

Kesler nodded. "Confirm that. All lines have dropped and gravitational anchors have been severed! We're free to climb, Sir!"

"Atmospheric flight computer is not answering my orders, Admiral!" Kesler suddenly called out in alarm. "We're listing six degrees to starboard!"

Fedrin glanced around the bridge. "Who's manning the piloting station?"

"No one has reported in for it," Kesler answered upon glancing at the screen.

"We have seven atmospheric piloting capable officers and none of them are onboard?" Fedrin exclaimed. "Does anyone here have experience piloting a big rig in atmosphere?"

The officers looked amongst themselves earnestly, hoping someone, anyone would raise a hand. No one did.

Fedrin shook his head and was contemplating trying the difficult maneuver himself when someone spoke up behind him.

"Begging your pardon, Sirs, but I could do it," a strange voice sounded out near the bridge doorway.

The Admiral, followed by the other officers turned and looked on curiously as a Branci timidly stepped into the light.

"And just who are you?" asked Fedrin.

"My name is Tarkin," replied the Branci confidently. "I can pilot this ship out of the atmosphere without a computer."

The Iovara continued to list, prompting several of the officers to tether themselves into their stations or risk falling out of them.

"The Iovara is no ordinary ship," Jonas called down from his station. "She's the biggest atmospheric capable ship in the navy. She's not like piloting your average shuttles back home. So thanks for the offer but no thanks."

Tarkin looked up at Jonas and nodded. "I mean no disrespect, but I have flown bigger."

"There are none bigger!" Jonas snapped. "Didn't you hear what I said?"

Tarkin nodded. "I have flown freighter ships for the Asar Mining Company. They are atmospheric capable and are easily twice the mass of the Iovara. I have flown them unaided by guidance computers multiple times."

Jonas sat back in his chair with misgivings written all over his face but with no more comments to make.

"We either give him a try or risk punching our main thrusters in atmosphere," Kesler said. "Doing that would almost surely cover the ground in radiation."

"Thrusters aren't an option," Fedrin stated with authority and then reluctantly looked at the Branci standing uneasily before him. Finally Fedrin sighed and shook his head. "Ok Tarkin. Give us your best," he said motioning to the vacant piloting station. A murmur echoed through the bridge as the other officers exchanged looks about the bizarre scene they where witnessing.

"Everyone shut up!" Fedrin snapped. "He's your only chance at survival right now. So keep your comments to yourself until he's done!"

You could have heard a pin drop on the bridge as Tarkin promptly made his way to the piloting station. All eyes in the room were fixed upon him, a thought he pushed out of his mind. As he reached the station, he quickly looked at the input panels. The controls were more advanced then he had seen on the civilian ships but the layout was generally the same. With one last deep breath, he reached out for the multiple levers, his six arms making easy work of it, and slowly leveled off the mighty ship. As the list corrected, several officers clapped their hands in approval. Tarkin did not pay heed. He continued to slowly and expertly, guide the bow of the ship upward at a manageable angle and gradually increased the thrust from the secondary engines until she was moving at a solid pace.

Only as the ship ascended out of the atmosphere did Fedrin breathed again as the piloting was immediately transferred to automated systems that could operate outside an atmosphere.

"Who is with us?" Fedrin asked as he stood to his feet, the events of Tarkin's miraculous achievement already taking a backseat in his mind.

Kesler shook his head in stunned silence as he counted the ships that started to make their accent with them.

"Who is with us?" asked Fedrin again with more emotion in his voice.

"Only the Defiant and Bolter made it out," Kesler hesitatingly answered. "The rest are still on the ground."

"Signal the ones still on the ground!" ordered Fedrin as he dropped back into his chair and frantically looked at his own computer screen. "Ask them what assistance we can offer them?"

"Their transmitters are down," answered Kesler as he looked on in overwhelming sorrow and pity at the flames dancing upon the hulls of once mighty warships. "They are falling apart, Sir. It's just going to be us three. I'm sorry."

For a moment, it looked as if Fedrin's grief would overpower him and he would breakdown right on the bridge. But he quickly regained composure and looked up resolutely. "Have the Defiant and Bolter follow our lead and keep a tight formation. We're not out of the woods yet!"

Several dull sounds suddenly rattled the ship. Fedrin looked up and glanced at Kesler. "Don't tell me..."

Kesler nodded in response to Fedrin's assumption. "Traffic control fighters have opened fire on us!"

"Damage report?" Fedrin asked as he left his chair and walked over to Kesler's station.

"No primary systems damaged yet," Kesler replied, "but our shields have taken quite a beating from the fire already. If they keep it up, they'll rip through very soon."

"Lieutenant?" Fedrin asked, glancing up at his tactical officer.

Jonas nodded his head in agreement. "Our shielding is down to eleven percent. One more solid volley and they'll punch through with no problems."

"Commander Drezden is reporting that he is also being fired at by the patrol crafts and wants to know if he has permission to retaliate," stated Kesler.

Fedrin sat in his chair and rubbed his stubbly chin, all the while starring at the main screen shaking his head. He slapped a button down on his chair console and cleared his throat.

"This is Admiral Fedrin to pursuing patrol craft squadron. Disengage now, or I will order my gunners to take you out. I repeat, I will shoot you down! You have no chance against our weaponry. You must know this. Withdraw, or be destroyed!"

Several quiet seconds followed before another warning sounded at Kesler's station.

"Commander Drezden reports that his ship has sustained another volley and that his shields are now on the verge of collapsing," Kesler reluctantly voiced.

Fedrin shook his head. "Mr. Jonas!" he said, determination resonating in his voice. "Take them down!"

The turrets on the three fleeing war ships turned and roared to life, firing several rapid volleys at the pursuing patrols. The big guns of the fleet ships in the hands of experienced gunners were no match for the lightly armored patrol vessels. Moments later, they were all shot down.

Fedrin watched as the last of the ships burst into flames and spun out of control back toward the surface of the planet.

"We're clear and free," Jonas reported in a subdued tone, never having fired on his own ships before.

"Computers state that we brought down eleven patrol ships," Kesler added.

Fedrin's head hung low. "Survivors?"

"No life pods were launched," Kesler answered.

Fedrin nodded slowly. "Can we establish a tele-link with Larep?"

"I've tried half a dozen times already," Gallo, the chief communications officer, answered from his post at the front of the room. "The transmissions are going through but nobody's picking up. I've tried the capital building directly and the defense counsel building on multiple wavelengths. Nothing!"

"Maybe there's electromagnetic interference from the explosions?" Jonas suggested.

Gallo shook his head. "At this range, no amount of EM disruption could block out our primary transmitter. There's just nobody answering."

"We are however receiving dual transmissions from the Defiant and the Bolter," Kesler interrupted.

"Put them both on screen," Fedrin replied as he turned to face the large screen at the head of the room.

Two frazzled men, neither of which were in uniform, appeared on the split screen at the front of the bridge. Drezden, commander of the Defiant and close personal friend to Fedrin, looked shell-shocked, unable to speak. He had obviously been crying. Sanders, commander of the Bolter, looked furious.

"What just happened?" Sanders snapped.

Fedrin shook his head in a daze. "I don't have any answers for you."

"What's Larep saying?" Sanders asked. "I can't get through to anyone down there. And why in the world did they fire on us? That was the most messed up half-hour of my entire life! I just don't get it, Fedrin, I don't get it!"

"I don't know what to say," Fedrin repeated. "Our transmissions are not being answered either. We'll keep trying and I'll let you know as soon as they get back to us."

"How many people died?" Drezden quietly asked.

Fedrin shook his head and looked over to Kesler. "Any thought on numbers yet?"

Kesler shrugged. "It depends on how many of the crews were on leave, which I won't know for sometime. At the low end, I'd venture that at least twenty to thirty thousand lives were lost between dock workers and personnel aboard ships."

Drezden closed his eyes. "Thirty thousand," he whispered and shook his head.

"What of the fleet?" Sanders asked. "Surely it's not just us?"

Fedrin slowly nodded. "From the looks of things, the primary explosion occurred just under docking point four, right beside the main nuclear fuel depot for the fleet."

"It took out ten ships before we even knew what happened," added Drezden.

"So no accident?" Sanders asked, already knowing the answer.

Fedrin shook his head. "Not a chance. Today was the first time in two years such a number of ships were on the ground at the same time. Someone had this whole thing planned out, likely months in advance."

Sanders shook his head as he looked at images of the devastation on one of his own screens. "I wonder how they pulled it off?" he said, still in awe of the carnage.

"I bet it didn't go exactly as they were planning," said Drezden thoughtfully.

"What do you mean by that?" inquired Sanders.

Drezden shrugged. "Wasn't docking point number four the originally slated docking point for the Iovara?"

Fedrin shrugged and looked toward Kesler who nodded with affirmation.

"It was changed last minute by the traffic control authority to bay number seven due to several failed couplers in bay four," Kesler said.

"So what are you saying? You think the sabotage was intended to take out the Iovara?" Sanders asked.

Drezden shrugged. "I think it's safe to say she was the priority target, plus whatever else they could get with the ensuing blasts and secondary explosions."

"It's an interesting thought, but I doubt it," Fedrin said. "Other than the fact that this is the flagship, there really isn't anything overly significant about it."

"You're aboard her," Drezden said sharply.

Fedrin smiled and shook his head. "I appreciate the value you place on me but I am quite replaceable my friend."

"You'll have to pardon me Admiral," Sanders suddenly interjected after some commotion sounded out behind him. "There are a couple of issues that I need to address on my ship. Looks like two of our airlocks are swinging open in the breeze."

"By all means," Fedrin said, waving the commander off. "We'll be in touch."

"Do we have a heading I can plot in?" Sanders asked before signing off.

Fedrin glanced at the screen to his side and then nodded. "I think we'll head straight for sector eighteen and meet up with the Hornell Battle Group."

"Thank goodness the Hornell fighters weren't on the ground with us," Drezden added. "Loosing the teeth from a fighter carrier at this stage of the war could foreshadow the end."

Sanders nodded. "Agreed."

"I'll have Kesler inform the Hornell and her escort ships of our situation and have them hold position," Fedrin added.

"Aye, Sir," Sanders said and terminated his transmission.

"I need to run too," Drezden said. "We got pretty cooked back there and I need to make sure everything's ok."

Fedrin slowly nodded as he still struggled to gather his racing thoughts.

"You ok?" Drezden asked before signing off.

Fedrin looked up. "No...no I'm not old friend. But I don't have time for anything else right now."

"I'll be here if you need anything, ok?" Drezden said sincerely.

Fedrin looked up at Drezden and nodded before signing off. Fedrin sighed heavily. So much had happened that he had trouble processing it all. His head ached horribly as he tried to grasp on to the details and the sequence of events. Yet, his headache paled in comparison to the heartache he felt upon considering the deaths of the tens of thousands of crewmembers that had perished in a mere instant. He forced himself not to think about them. He had to appear strong and resolute on his bridge, now more then ever.

"Is my ship ok?" Fedrin asked rising to his feet and looking about his cluttered bridge.

Kesler gave his screens an once-over before turning around and offering a shrug and a nod. "Looks like all main systems are set to go. We've got a couple of things still being locked down in the secondary hangar bay but other than that, I'd say we're good."

Fedrin looked up above to the next level. "Jonas, how about it?"

Jonas nodded, and then looked down from his post. "Shield sensors appear to be showing inconsistent readings and will have to be worked on after the other critical systems are tended to. Until that is taken care of, we should avoid combat at all costs."

"And the weapons?" Fedrin asked stepping off the central command platform and making his way toward a monitoring station across the bridge.

"Most of the main weapon systems and particle defensive turrets seem to be intact. We did manage to burnout three secondary DEG placements on the port side but they can be repaired outside of dry-dock and as long as there aren't any glitches, that should be taken care of in just a day or two."

Fedrin looked up from the monitor and turned to Gallo. "Keep signaling Larep. We need to see what's going on down there as soon as possible. And Kesler, try and piece together exactly what went down chronologically. Look over the security cam feeds from all surviving ships and the docks. I want to know who did this and how."

"Then we can start some punishing!" said Jonas, patting his firing controls affectionately.

"Sure Jonas. What ever makes you happy," Fedrin said with a role of his eyes as he made his way back to his platform.

A high-pitched series of unique beeps suddenly sounded at Gallo's station, prompting Fedrin to look up sharply.

In well-rehearsed motions, Gallo flipped a number of switches and tuned in several sensitive dials, all the while intently watching a small screen. He nodded with approval when he was done. "Alright, Admiral. This is it. We are receiving a priority one coded transmission from Larep, the capital building to be precise."

Fedrin froze.

"It'll take a few minutes to initialize," Gallo said "but initial scans confirms this transmission is legitimate."

"Who is it?" Fedrin asked.

Gallo shrugged. "Not sure. Looks like it's being set up by an automated encryption system and the sending party is not ready to speak yet."

"I'll take it in my quarters," said Fedrin and made his way toward the door. "Kesler, plot a course to sector eighteen and inform the Commanders in the Hornell battle group of our situation."

"Right away, Sir," Kesler answered.

"Gallo, notify the Second, Third, and Northern Fleet Admirals of our circumstances and arrange a secure tele-link with them for this afternoon. We will have a lot to discuss."

"I'll get on it," replied Gallo.

Fedrin took two steps toward the door before abruptly stopping and turning toward the piloting station. "Tarkin, we all owe you a great debt. Your expertise saved the lives of everyone on this ship. Thank you."

Tarkin bowed to Fedrin graciously without saying a word.

"Keep her running gentlemen," Fedrin said with a lump in his throat as he began walked off the bridge.

Kesler let out a loud sigh as he went to work on his tasks.

"Well isn't this just lovely!" Jonas exclaimed from atop his post.

"You're not kidding," Kesler called back. "My shore leave was only few hours away! Goodbye Larep! Goodbye beautiful women I'll never meet. Goodbye happiness," Kesler finished as he waved out the window.

"So you think it was the Krohns?" Gallo asked when Kesler quieted down.

"It's got to be," Kesler answered. "Who else would do something like this? Who else would have the means?"

"Yeah but how?" asked Jonas. "If you haven't noticed, Krohns kind of stick out in a crowd, what with that whole reptile thing they got going on."

Kesler shrugged. "I really don't know. I don't even think I want to know. It's just too creepy."

"You said it," Jonas said.

Tarkin watched with great amusement as the officers talked amongst themselves. He himself was a man of few words and usually only spoke when spoken to, and this time was no different. Although riding high on his impromptu success, he still knew he had to be careful. Branci were not well liked at most places outside of their home world in the Federation but a fleet warship was an almost certain breeding ground for racism. He would have to watch his step and keep close to those friendly to him.

CHAPTER 2

THE PRESIDENT

Fedrin walked briskly to his room. He tossed his uniform jacket over a small table near the door and walked straight to his wall-mounted tele-link.

"Still initializing," he said to himself looking at the priority-one transmission blinking in red on his screen. He shook his head in frustration and then walked from the tele-link to the small window between his bed and desk. He leaned against the cold metallic hull and gazed out, as his world grew steadily smaller and smaller.

"When did it all go wrong?" he found himself asking as he gazed over the sandy, arid planet he called home. "When did the difference between right and wrong become clouded? When was shooting down his fellow servicemen a necessity in order to survive?"

He brought his hand up to rub his tired face and noticed that it was trembling, undoubtedly from the adrenaline surge of the past hour. He formed a fist to hold his fingers still, then suddenly slammed the cold unyielding wall. He slammed it over and over again, ignoring the pain. Tears of sorrow mixed with anger that he had valiantly held back while on his bridge, now flooded his eyes. Visions of his burning fleet and dying servicemen flashed through his mind. His grief was immense.

He stood there transfixed for a few more moments before forcing himself to look away, no longer able to bear the sight of his barren world. As he left the window he wondered when he would return. Perhaps he never would.

After again glancing at the idle transmission screen, Fedrin took a shaky step toward his bed, sat down on the edge and buried his face in his hands. The all too familiar feeling of helplessness began to creep back over him as it had done many times in the preceding weeks and months. He wasn't ready for this job, not by a long shot. He had only held the position for seven months, but it already felt like an eternity to him.

Although he hadn't known it at the time, his life as he knew it ended the day he accepted the Chief Admiralty. Of course, it didn't happen all at once, but by the time his wife left him, he had lost track of who he was and the people that he had once loved. He had become nothing more than a critical cog in the Namuh war machine but had lost everything else.

His torrent of thoughts prompted him to glance at a picture of his estranged wife on the near wall. He marveled at the fact that even with all the bitterness associated with her, he still couldn't resist a faint smile when looking at her. Her brown hair fell to her shoulders outlining her gentle face and her piercing green eyes, filled with vitality; they haunted him with memories of happiness that were once his.

He reluctantly looked away from her picture and let his eyes scan over his crowded wall. He shook his head as he pondered how important the many things mounted and framed on his walls once were. But the dust covered honors, merits, and certificates that he had amassed over the course of his distinguished career, now seemed hollow and meaningless. Who cared anymore that he had graduated at the top of his class at the Venter Military Academy? Who cared anymore that he had received every possible honor and recommendation during his training? For that matter, who even cared that he was Chief Admiral? Since his predecessor's untimely death, Fedrin had been hard-pressed to maintain a semblance of command within the fleets, as well as with his outspoken critics in Larep, the Namuh Protective Federation's Capital city.

After countless weeks of wondering, Fedrin had finally concluded that the reason he wasn't esteemed the way he assumed he would be as Chief Admiral, was his lack of commanding presence, an attribute gifted by nature, not learned or studied. He remembered vividly, the unwavering confidence and bold charisma that Nebod, the former Chief Admiral, always had when dealing with situations big or small. Every word Nebod uttered as Chief Admiral resonated with power, knowledge and strength and was treated as divine inspiration amongst his subordinates. These mannerisms were in stark contrast to Fedrin's more timid, passive approach to leading and this proved to be a challenge, in some form or another, on a near daily basis for Fedrin, not that be blamed his men. As a rule, men have a built in reluctance to lend their lives to those who have not earned the sacred trust that such a monumental act requires. Nebod had earned that trust and thus his men's loyalties. Fedrin was still being proved.

"Was it really only seven months ago?" asked Fedrin to himself, spotting the small picture of himself and Nebod nestled in the midst of Commander Recommendations that he stopped needing years ago.

Nebod had been the Chief Admiral over the combined Namuh Fleets for nearly a decade before Fedrin had assumed the position. Nebod had led the Namuh Federation with the utmost proficiency in its Second Great War for many years and he was justly credited with saving the Federation from the brink of demise on several occasions.

It was nearly two weeks after Nebod's celebrated victory, at the Battle of Zelin IV, when he was killed in what was called an 'unfortunate accident,' aboard one of the public transport pods in Larep. News of Nebod's death came as a great shock to the war weary Federation and his passing was mourned for many weeks, both by his own people and by the Branci race, which Nebod had done much for.

Thus it was that the then little known Commodore Fedrin of the Sixth Fleet became the acting Chief Admiral over all of the fleets. Although humbled by the grand task that lay before him, Fedrin was thrilled with the opportunity to lead the fleets the way he saw fit. The day he was sworn into his position, he determined in his heart to be a great leader, that would become immortalized with his success in battling the enemy, and ensuring a safe and secure Federation. But the overwhelming stress, responsibility, and anguish that Fedrin suffered in the first month alone, made it clear that the position was not nearly compensated for by the honor and glory that he had naively assumed came with the title. It was an unending, relentless, consuming, and thankless task that drained all other facets of his life and gave very little in return.

"Transmission initialized," a computerized voice suddenly announced from the console across the room, shattering the silence and bringing Fedrin back to the gloomy reality at hand.

Fedrin stood erect and walked immediately over to his tele-link, breathed out deeply and activated the transmission. No sooner had he done so when a massive headache came upon him and a voice echoed though his head. "Do not listen to their words," the voice spoke in a raspy but unmistakably distinct voice.

The unnerving terror Fedrin would have felt upon hearing an unknown voice in his head was overwhelmed by the growing pain that accompanied the ominous warning. So great was the pain that Fedrin thought he would collapse to the floor in agony. But as quickly as it had started, it subsided, leaving only a dull throb in its wake. The peculiar spoken words however, echoed through his thoughts loudly.

As the screen came to life, Fedrin was nearly overwhelmed by the sight that met his gaze. President Defuria sat in a high-back leather chair behind the imposing presidential desk, surrounded by the entire Defense Council and several other cabinet members. All had a look of profound sobriety upon their faces and all looked as if they would personally like to strangle Fedrin to death.

"Admiral Fedrin," a tight jawed, bitter looking man spoke up, taking a small step ahead of his companions.

"Minister," Fedrin replied, acknowledging Defense Minster Boide, one of Fedrin's most outspoken critics.

Boide continued. "By unanimous decision of the Defense Council, you have been relieved of the Chief Admiralty pending a thorough investigation into today's events."

"Investigation?" asked Fedrin. "Of what?"

Boide shook his head. "Of the charges brought against you," answered Boide.

"And just what are the charges?"

"Treason, sedition, sabotage, murder and espionage," replied Boide frankly. "You are hereby ordered to relinquish command of your vessel immediately and present yourself to the brig so that you can stand trial for your heinous acts."

Fedrin scanned the faces before him in complete shock. "May I ask on what grounds these charges have been brought against me?"

Boide had a disgusted look on his face as he once again took center stage. "The charges are based on your part in the destruction of the Sixth Fleet, your disregard for thirteen atmospheric traffic ordinances including opening gun ports in dock and lastly for your overt action against eleven of our traffic control fighters, resulting in eleven pilot deaths."

Fedrin shook his head in bewilderment. "Are you crazy? I didn't have anything to do with the explosions! And as far as the flight ordinance violations, the docks were on fire! I tried to get takeoff clearance and only blasted my way out when nobody would grant it! And I only shot down the control fighters after they opened fire on us. And I'd repeat each of my decisions in a heartbeat if I had to!"

"Spoken like a true psychopath," remarked Boide and shook his head.

"Excuse me?" Fedrin exclaimed. "What about the fact, that we were sitting in a raging fire, don't you understand?"

"A fire you caused!" another council member spoke up.

"I already told you, I didn't cause the explosions! Has the whole world gone mad?"

"We have video proof that you did it!" another councilman snapped. "There is no denying it Admiral! You are a traitor!"

"You are a murderer!" another yelled. "My nephew worked those docks for ten years! Now he's dead! You killed him!"

"Heed not their toxic words," the familiar raspy voice sounded once more inside Fedrin's head. "They speak lies for they are the children of lies. They know only how to destroy and corrupt. Now behold the deceivers for who they really are!"

The vindictive and scornful men standing around the President's office suddenly changed into hideous monstrous forms, the likes of which Fedrin had never seen before! The creatures filled the screen and crowded out the President's desk, obscuring the view of the seated man. The horrifying spectacle lasted only moments before the alien forms flashed back to that of the dignitaries, leaving Fedrin with vague images of large scaly heads and slithering appendages.

"Why did you do it Fedrin?" Boide then asked, apparently unaware that their true forms had been momentarily revealed. "Did the enemy promise you something in return? Lands? Spoils from the war? A safe haven for you when we lose? Something more? What Fedrin? What?"

"That is enough Minister," President Defuria said, standing to his feet. "I'll take it from here."

"But what about the..." Boide started to say, pointing at an open data pad.

"I said I got it," Defuria said firmly, motioning toward the door. "Now if you will all kindly step out, I will meet up with you in the situation room momentarily."

"Fine," Boide reluctantly replied, obviously put out. He then bowed to Defuria and then looked up at the screen to give Fedrin one more disdainful look before marching out of the room followed by the other members of the Defense Council.

Once they had left, Fedrin looked at the President suspiciously, not trusting anything he saw or heard.

Defuria casually crossed his arms and leaned against the front of his desk. His stance suggested he was relaxed and wanted to transmit that feeling to Fedrin. Fedrin kept his guard up all the higher.

"We've got quite a mess on our hands don't we," Defuria said, shaking his head. "Real shame about what happened, real shame."

"Sure is," said Fedrin coolly.

Defuria nodded slowly, seemingly planning his next words carefully. "There have been whisperings about outside forces interfering with our affairs Fedrin."

"Oh?"

Defuria nodded. "You haven't heard anything of this, have you?"

"Haven't heard a thing," answered Fedrin, unwilling to share the information about the strange voice or divulge what he had just moments earlier seen.

Defuria skeptically nodded before looking up at Fedrin with a sincere expression. "Fedrin, why don't you turn around, come back home and help us clear up this whole mess. Even if you are innocent and this whole thing is some elaborate setup, you look guilty by running. Don't you see that?"

"Don't go back," said the voice in Fedrin's head. "He is trying to beguile you."

Fedrin slowly shook his head. "From the sound of things, I've already been convicted. If I return now, I'll just be coming back for my sentencing. With all due respect, no thank you Mr. President."

"Fedrin, this is your last chance," Defuria said firmly, unfolding his arms and motioning to Fedrin like a wayward child. "Come back now and I promise I will protect you. Ignore this chance, and there is nothing more I can do for you!"

Fedrin thought for just a moment before waving to the president. "Thanks, but no thanks. I like my chances better up here."

"Don't be a fool Fedrin!" Defuria suddenly yelled. "Come back! Think of the Federation!"

"I am," replied Fedrin before reaching for the cutoff switch. As he did so however, he noticed an eerie glow begin to emanate from Defuria's hands and face. It pulsated as he breathed and gave Defuria a fierce and powerful presence that Fedrin suddenly feared. Without another word, Fedrin flipped the switch, ending the bizarre transmission.

Fedrin stood back from the tele-link and shook his head. What had just happened? He felt like he should contact someone...anyone about what he had just witnessed. But whom could he trust? He was now an outlaw. He tried to decide on a course of action. Nothing came to mind. Once again he felt lost and helpless. What was he to do?

Tarkin placed his three trays of food down on the table and sat down across from Kesler.

"Hungry?" asked Kesler, looking at the multiple trays piled high with food with amusement.

"A little," Tarkin answered honestly, missing the sarcasm of Kesler's tone completely.

Kesler smiled and then took a bite of his sandwich.

It had been nearly ten hours since the three surviving vessels had made their traumatic escape from Namuh Prime. The rendezvous with the Hornell Carrier Battle Group was still several hours away so Kesler had taken it upon himself to familiarize Tarkin with the Iovara's essential features.

Initially, Tarkin had received his fair share of nasty looks and snide whisperings from the various crewmen while roaming the halls with Kesler. But as the narrative of Tarkin piloting the Iovara to safety spread, he was treated less and less with bigotry and more and more like the hero he was. There were, of course, some crewmembers that didn't care what Tarkin had done, but they soon became the minority as his reputation spread.

"These are for you," Kesler said as he slid a silver data stick and a security access card over to Tarkin. "The stick has some training modules to get you familiar with some Navy policies and procedures. They will need to be completed before you are permitted to enter into active duty. It'll probably take you a few weeks to do all the modules and then take the exams. Normally this is all covered in basic training and classroom settings but under the circumstances…"

"I've already completed all of them," Tarkin interrupted. "It should only take me a few hours to take all the exams."

Kesler looked at Tarkin curiously. "You've gone through the Navy officer training program already? On your own time?"

Tarkin shrugged and nodded. "I didn't go to an academy so I wanted to be ready when I finally got here. I didn't want to be behind my Namuh counterparts when I started."

"But why?" asked a bewildered Kesler who had never picked up a textbook in his life unless absolutely forced to.

"Because, whether I like it or not, as a Branci serving in the fleet, I know that I will be under extreme scrutiny. I must give no occasion to my comrades to think of me as an inferior or less intelligent officer if I am to become an active and useful member of the crew."

Kesler sat back in his seat and shook his head slowly. A few minutes of quiet passed before Kesler thoughtfully spoke again. "The last Branci I interviewed before you, told me that the only reason he was interviewing was because he had to show he completed five interviews a month in order to remain on Federation welfare assistance. He told me that even if I offered him a position, he wouldn't take it. After he said that, he laughed and walked out."

Tarkin closed his eyes in deep sadness and perhaps, a touch of embarrassment.

"Tell me something Tarkin. What makes you so different from so many other Branci and how can we get more of you?" Kesler asked, looking intently at the finest specimen of the Branci race he had ever seen.

Tarkin smiled. "First off, I am nothing special. I am simply the product of my influences. Had my influences been different, I may have very well ended up just like so many others that seem anxious to take but never entertain the notion of giving."

"And what were your influences?"

"Two men," replied Tarkin simply. "My father and the former Chief Admiral of the navy."

"Nebod?" exclaimed Kesler. "You knew Chief Admiral Nebod?"

Tarkin nodded as a far off look filled his eyes. "In a manner of speaking. I met him briefly when I was but a boy."

"Under what circumstances?" exclaimed Kesler.

Tarkin took a sip of water and then sat back in his chair. "Before our alliance with your world was finalized, a terrible illness spread over my world, killing tens of thousands of my people. Although your people possessed the medicine to heal us, your government was hesitant to intervene for fear of contracting the disease themselves."

Kesler nodded, remembering even as a child, the outcry from many activists demanding that the Namuh government help the struggling Branci.

Tarkin continued. "Nebod disregarded orders from Larep and brought an entire relief fleet to our world."

Kesler chuckled. "I remember my folks watching that story unfold on the telecast when I was a boy. It caused quite a stir as I remember."

"His actions likely saved my people from extinction," Tarkin said emphatically. "If it wasn't for him, I likely wouldn't be here now."

"He was quite a guy," Kesler added.

Tarkin nodded and then smiled. "He personally came to my home during that infamous trip."

"Why?" asked Kesler in amazement, wondering why a Chief Admiral would have an occasion to make house calls on an alien world.

"To tend to my mother who was gravely ill with the plague," Tarkin answered.

"But why Nebod?" pressed Kesler. "Surely a medic could have handled it?"

Tarkin shrugged. "True, but the medic needed help carrying the supplies up into the smaller villages that could only be reached by foot. Nebod offered to help."

Kesler shook his head. "Incredible."

Tarkin nodded. "When they had finished, my mother was on the road to recovery and my father was weeping with gratitude. I remember him offering Nebod what few worldly possessions we had for payment but Nebod graciously refused, saying that our well-being was reward enough." Tarkin sighed before continuing. "That day changed my life Kesler. What Nebod and your people did for my family was more than I could ever repay."

"Incredible, simply incredible," Kesler said, marveling at the impact Nebod's actions had on a mere child.

"Nebod was the only ranking Namuh that ever saw value in our backward and at the time, primitive people," Tarkin continued. "He saw us as equals and treated as with dignity and respect." Tarkin shook his head. "His views were not shared by everyone however. A few bigots saw us as inferiors, good for nothing more than hard labor. Several asteroid plantation owners even had the audacity to kidnap some of us for use as slaves."

"That is when Larep instituted the compensation program to make up for their actions," commented Kesler with a weary shake of his head.

Tarkin nodded. "The program was intended to restore trust between our peoples but instead, it promoted a victimized mentality with almost all of my people overnight. As word spread that the your government was trying to rectify the wrongs done to a handful of Branci by a handful of Namuh, people flocked to the Namuh Consulate to file claims, mostly fraudulently. Only several hundred Branci were actually kidnapped and abused but almost every single Branci filed compensation claims with Larep for one grievance or another. Branci, who had never even met the true victims, demanded stipends from your government, which your overwhelmed and narrow-minded delegates agreed to. When it was done, almost the entirety of my world had become a welfare state and we were stripped of our dignity in the process. Forty years ago, you couldn't have found a nobler, or more proud people than the Branci. But now, unable to provide or care for ourselves without your people's help, we have become a parasitic sub-race indeed worthy of your loathing."

Kesler nodded slowly, surprised by Tarkin's scathing critique of his own people but also amazed by the eloquent way in which he spoke, making simple sense of the complicated social issues that had eroded away at the Federation for years. "So tell me Tarkin, how did you manage to avoid this trap that so many others have fallen into? You credited Nebod before, but what of your father?"

"Nebod was my inspiration but my father taught me honor," answered Tarkin. "He taught me that if something is worth having, it is worth earning. He taught me that taking something you did not earn fosters contempt for the very thing you have received and a hollowed out soul that always wants more but is never satisfied. Earning what you have is the greatest source of joy one can ever achieve. He lived by this and died by this."

Kesler shook his head. "I wish more Branci had father's like yours."

Tarkin nodded sadly.

Kesler was amazed by Tarkin's insight and by his character. Never before had he seen such devotion and patriotism from Namuh or Branci alike.

Kesler couldn't help but wonder how many equally zealous Branci candidates he had dismissed from service over the years due to his own bigotry. If even a tenth of them had Tarkin's passion, how much better would the fleets be today?

CHAPTER 3

PIRATES!

The room was unusually dark for midday. The deep blue drapes of the president's private office were drawn shut and all of the lights were off, except a small recessed light fixed within a tall bookshelf in the corner of the room. Behind the President's desk sat a lone figure clad in a stately black robe trimmed with a dreary gray. A silver box sat upon the desk and the seated figure held a hand firmly atop the box as if guarding it from an unseen assailant. He sat there perfectly still, staring at the door, waiting for the inevitable visit.

"Come in Minister Boide," Defuria said slowly when the knock finally sounded.

Light spilled into the chamber from the lit hallway as the Defense Minister entered the stately room. He wore a heavy cloak that concealed his face and hands from view. Boide carefully closed the door behind him and slowly approached the desk. "Did you manage it?" he implored anxiously, lifting the cloak and looking at the chair's occupant.

"No," Defuria replied coolly. "Fedrin is not coming back. He knows something is up. We'll have to handle him the hard way."

"My apologies," Boide stated nervously as he sat down in a polished wooden chair positioned in front of the desk. "I tried my best, I really did. I just don't understand how he could have managed to escape! I set the charge where the Iovara was supposed to dock and she moved berths before I realized it. I killed all her atmospheric pilots and yet they still found someone to fly her out of the atmosphere. I fed the traffic fighter pilots the story about Fedrin being a Krohn agent so they would shoot her down without objection but they were shot down first. I really don't know what more I could have done."

Defuria sat still, saying nothing, the scornful look on his countenance making up for his lack of words.

"I wonder if maybe he had outside help," said Boide reluctantly. "I wonder if our nemesis has once again interjected themselves."

Defuria looked at Boide critically, a single eyebrow raised. "You think the Sions helped him?"

Boide shrugged as he sat back in his chair. "I think it's possible. I mean, they swept in unannounced all those years ago and delivered the Namuh from the hands of the Refrac Empire when all hope seemed lost. Why wouldn't they help them again?"

"Because they've let them dangle so far in their war against the Krohns!" Defuria snapped. "If the Sions really had the resources to help save Fedrin, surely they would be able to stop the Krohns too!"

Boide shook his head defensively. "I'm not saying that they did help, only that it's a possibility."

"It's not a possibility!" Defuria snapped. "The Sions have no presence here! And blaming your complete and utter failure on a nemesis that hasn't set foot in this sector for well over a decade is in poor taste."

"I did my best!" Boide protested with arms outstretched. "Maybe if you had given me more resources I could have managed. You asked a lot from me, more than I could ever deliver."

Defuria raised his hand for quiet. "You are just embarrassing yourself Boide. Please...please don't make this harder than it needs to be."

"What do you speak of?" asked Boide, not trusting Defuria's sinister tone.

Defuria smiled sadistically. "Must I spell it out for you?"

Boide looked at Defuria uneasily and then stood up. "You told me I would get my share!" he shouted, pointing at the small box and glaring at Defuria. "You have no right to deny me what I've earned! No right!"

"Earned?" Defuria exclaimed and then laughed loudly. "You must be joking!"

"Give it to me!" Boide screamed as he suddenly leapt toward the box, snatching it up and retreating toward the door. "You can't stop me from taking what I've earned!"

Without protest, Defuria looked on as Boide fumbled with the latch to open the box. As the lid opened, a blinding burst of light poured out from the box and enveloped Boide who promptly fell to the ground in burning agony.

The whites of Defuria's eyes flashed a deep black and he stood to his feet and approached the thrashing figure on the floor. "It appears you were right," he commented with a twisted smile. "I can't stop you from taking what you've earned!"

"You...you deceived me!" Boide called out.

"It wasn't hard," replied Defuria with a sigh. "As always, you lack imagination."

"I...I did what you asked!" Boide screamed. "I've always done what you've asked!"

"No, no you really haven't," Defuria calmly replied as he knelt down beside Boide just as his assumed face faded away, revealing his true hideous self beneath. "Fedrin was the target," Defuria continued. "Not the ships, not the commanders, not the crews, not the docks. It was Fedrin, Boide! It was always Fedrin!"

"The pain is more then I can stand!" Boide yelled out to the deafened ears of Defuria. "Please, just kill me! I...I renounce my claim on my share! You can have it!"

"Oh, I know I can have it," Defuria answered with an evil smile. "I've already taken it as a matter of fact."

"Then just kill me!" Boide screamed. "Just kill me!"

Defuria shook his head, ignoring Boide's pleas. "Ships can be rebuilt! New commanders can be trained! Docks can be repaired, but leaders? Oh, leaders are a rare commodity indeed, Boide and point of fact, are far more deadly than a hundred ships!"

"How...how was I to know the Iovara would change docking points?" Boide pleaded in one last effort to sway his sadistic execution.

"That should never have been a factor!" Defuria snapped. "Destroying half the fleet to kill one man? Are you serious Boide? Why not just destroy the planet while you're at it, or the sun for the matter. It's like performing brain surgery with a dull axe with you around!"

"I'm...sorry," Boide said as he tearfully reached for Defuria's hand. "I'm sorry."

"Goodbye Boide," Defuria replied and stood to his feet.

Boide struggled to look up into the countenance of his assailant one final time. The light from the device saturated every shadow and crevice of Defuria's face and suddenly Boide's eyes grew with a great revelation. "You are...you are...a traitor," he muttered just as he succumbed to the burning light and melted away. When it was done, only a small pile of dying embers and blackened ash remained.

"You have complicated my job immensely," Defuria said as he kicked his foot through the pile, causing the ashen flakes to fly through the room like a sudden blizzard. Defuria then shook his head and casually walked back behind his desk and began to skim over several star charts already spread over the surface. "You have complicated everything," he muttered again as he located an item on a chart. "Computer," he said after reading the fine print on the chart. "Establish a direct tele-link with the NPF Tribulation of the Second Fleet, care of Vice Admiral Caton," Defuria paused pensively before adding, "And setup a secondary link with Commodore Tropnia of the same ship on an encrypted frequency."

"Transmissions initializing," the computerized voice replied. "Please standby."

Defuria opened a drawer in his desk and retrieved another silver box and sat back in his chair and stared at the transmission screen. He gently stroked the lid as he waited for the transmission to commence.

"It's a game of time now," he said aloud. "Who will get to our Chief Admiral first?"

⅄

"Status report?" ordered Kesler as he stepped onto the bridge floor followed closely by Tarkin.

"The outer satellite grid just picked up several rogue signals entering sector sixteen," answered Ensign Gallo.

"Refrac Pirates?" Kesler asked casually as he assumed his station and looked at the signals himself.

"Almost for sure," Gallo answered with a nod. "They must have evaded the Northern fleet and slipped in behind the patrols."

"They'll probably make a play for the shipping lanes again," remarked Jonas as he walked up behind Tarkin and Kesler. "They always run heavy with fuel and supplies this time of the year."

"I agree," Kesler said as he reached for a scanner switch at his station. "Do we have a breakdown yet?"

"Just came in," Gallo answered, looking intently at one of his screens. "Looks like two frigates and a small compliment of light star fighters."

"Carrier frigates," said Kesler, nodding to a string of numbers on a small screen next to Tarkin. "We haven't seen any of them in a while."

Tarkin glanced at the screen. "Will they be a problem?" he asked.

"Not usually," Kesler answered. "But considering the majority of our forces in this system have just been decimated, it'll be somewhat of a challenge to corner them."

Tarkin looked perplexed. "Why can't the Northern Fleet just come back and help hem them in? They have enough ships to do it."

"The Northern?" Jonas exclaimed followed by a laugh. "They can hardly maintain a steady orbit much less engage in coordinated tactical operations!"

Tarkin looked around the room for an explanation. None was offered. "I don't understand," he then confessed. "What is so wrong with the Northern Fleet?"

Kesler shook his head. "It's made up entirely of obsolete ships drawn from the dissolved First, Fourth and Fifth Fleets plus what ever else they could find. Most of the ships in it predate the Refrac War and haven't had much in term of upgrades or retrofits since."

"Their basically junk used for training," Gallo added.

Tarkin shook his head. "I knew the ships were old but I guess I had no idea the fleet was so impotent."

"They don't really broadcast that fact to everyone," Jonas said and then laughed. "Their presence alone is a good deterrent for smugglers and the occasional Refrac Pirate band."

"Until now," Tarkin jibed, nodding at main monitor.

Kesler nodded reluctantly. "It does seem they are calling our bluff more and more lately. Soon it won't even matter. The Northern is too slow to pursue anything faster than a freighter."

"They must be getting desperate for supplies," remarked Jonas, reaching in front of Kesler and pulling up a new data screen. He pointed at the readout as he spoke. "These are very old style Refrac frigates, probably leftovers from the war. They have no shielding and only basic armor components."

"So no threat then?" clarified Tarkin.

Jonas shrugged. "If we can close with them, it'll be a pretty one-sided engagement...my favorite kind!"

Kesler nodded as he looked over the data. "Is Fedrin still in the middle of his tele-conference?"

Gallo nodded. "He's been in there for the last hour! I did send a message down to him a little bit ago about the pirates so he should be aware but he hasn't sent any orders yet."

Kesler looked up from the screen and then shrugged. "Obsolete or not, these pirates could easily take out half of our freight lines in the sector if we don't get to them first. We need to act...and soon!"

"This is the last thing we need right now," Jonas added with a shake of his head.

"Agreed," said Kesler.

"The Refrac Pirates were not the only thing I wanted to bring to your attention," Gallo again spoke up.

"Oh?" asked Kesler, walking promptly back to Gallo's station.

Gallo pressed a button beneath one of his screens and then pointed.

"Well isn't that just lovely," Kesler quietly said. "From bad to worse."

"Just wouldn't be right otherwise!" commented Jonas from the back of the bridge.

⅄

The three Vice Admirals looked at Fedrin over separate tele-link screens critically, waiting to hear what their Chief Admiral, and at present, enemy of the state, had to say next.

"You have to believe me," Fedrin pleaded with the men. "I am just as much a victim here as anyone else! I've been set up to look guilty to erode my credibility with you. You must understand this! You must believe me!"

"Fedrin," spoke Caton, the Vice Admiral of the Second Fleet. "How are we to answer the questions set to us by our crews? Regardless of what we believe, the facts just don't add up in your favor."

"You say you saw the Defense Council appearing as aliens?" Nidrid, leader of the Northern Fleet and eldest of the active admirals, asked skeptically.

"Demons would be a more accurate description of them," said Fedrin as he recalled the horrific sight. "It was only for a moment but I saw them just as clearly as I see you all now."

"But why can't we see them as you saw them?" Caton pressed. "With each of these fantastic situations you narrate, it becomes harder to believe what you say, let alone convince others of your veracity."

"I don't know what you want me to say!" snapped Fedrin. "I'm only telling you what happened and what I saw. If that's not good enough for you I don't know what is!"

"We aren't challenging you Fedrin," Vice Admiral Sherman of the Third Fleet said in a reassuring tone. "We just need answers for our officers and crews. We must be able to answer their misgivings so that they can execute their duties with full confidence in their leadership."

Fedrin shook his head helplessly. "I can provide no proof for what has transpired other than my word. And I would hope that with you three, if with no others, that would be sufficient."

The three Vice Admirals looked at each other uneasily as Fedrin continued. "Something's going on at home gentlemen. Something darker and more sinister then I think we can imagine. At some point in the near future, we will need to return home and set things right. My forces, such as they are, will not be able to do this alone. We will need the combined forces of all the fleets when the time comes. Can I count on you?"

All of the Admirals sat in silence for several moments, contemplating Fedrin's request. It was a big request; of that there was no doubt. And the consequences for success or failure were both immense.

"Fedrin you are young and inexperienced when it comes to being Chief Admiral," Nidrid said frankly. "However, you were Nebod's choice to replace him upon his death. Based solely on that fact, I pledge the Northern Fleet when you call for it. I will be sure my men do not have any occasion to doubt you or your credibility."

"Thank you Nidrid," Fedrin said sincerely, nodding toward the elderly Admiral. "Thank you."

"I wish I could offer what Nidrid does," lamented Admiral Sherman. "Alas, my ships are tethered to our location by tactical necessity as you know all to well. But I do support you and your endeavor, whatever it may involve. I will lend any and all support I can in lieu of my fleet when the time comes!"

"And I thank you also," said Fedrin sincerely. "And don't think that just because of todays tragedies I have forgotten your supply problems. It is high on my list of priorities to address."

"I was wondering about it," confessed Sherman. "We'll need help within the week or these big ships will be nothing more than oversized coffins."

Fedrin nodded knowingly. "We'll be there, Sherman. Someway, somehow, we'll be there. I promise!"

Sherman nodded.

Fedrin then turned to face Caton, the most headstrong yet sincerely passionate of all his Admirals. "How about it Caton? Will you join us in freeing the Federation from our new assailants?"

Caton looked at all the Admirals and then slowly shook his head as if weighted down by something he didn't want to share but knew he had to.

"What's wrong?" Nidrid finally asked. "You don't look well."

Caton sighed and looked up. "About two hours ago, President Defuria appointed me as acting Chief Admiral."

Fedrin looked up in complete surprise.

"Defuria's first order for me was to immediately apprehend Fedrin and bring him and his command crew back to Larep to face charges," Caton added.

The other Admirals exchanged concerned glances before looking back at Caton. Caton in turn nodded and then offered a reassuring smile. "Rest assured, I have no intentions of assuming the Chief Admiralty or of arresting Fedrin," he said, causing everyone to let off a collective sigh of relief.

"But why lead us on then?" Sherman asked. "This isn't the time for games Caton!"

"You are quite right," said Caton solemnly. "This is not the time for games."

"Then what's this all about?" pressed Sherman.

Caton nodded. "When President Defuria appointed me Chief Admiral, he also charged my own Commodore with contingency instructions to replace me if I deviated from his directions."

"To replace you?" exclaimed Sherman.

Caton nodded. "He didn't use those words exactly but the idea was definitely implied."

"But she's just a Commodore!" exclaimed Nidrid. "She couldn't replace you. Surely your own men wouldn't stand for it!"

Caton shook his head. "I'm afraid it's not that simple."

"And why not?" asked Sherman.

Caton sighed. "Because Tropnia is no ordinary officer. She is a one of a kind leader. She is beautiful, she has the ear of the President and she has loyal following in the fleet. Add all that together and I have all the ingredients for a fleet-wide mutiny if she wants to start one."

"Well that's not an option," stated Fedrin. "I'd turn myself in before I'd allow something like that to happen."

Caton nodded. "Which is why I will feign obedience to Defuria for the foreseeable future. Commodore Tropnia will thus remain my supporter and

I will retain control of my ships. I can mismanage our movements and positions just enough to give you the time you need to figure out what is going on at home and put a stop to it."

Sherman and Nidrid slowly nodded as Caton's dangerous gambit became evident to all. Fedrin looked at Caton with profound gratitude, realizing the tremendous risk he was prepared to take upon himself. "Thank you Caton. Thank you so much. Your actions could very well allow us to restore the Federation."

Caton looked at Fedrin intently. "It's all I can do Fedrin. And I don't know how long I can keep the ruse up so let's all get to it!"

The other Admiral's echoed Caton's sentiment and then one by one they signed out of the conference leaving Fedrin alone in his quarters once more. He leaned back in his chair and closed his weary eyes. He was beyond exhausted but couldn't justify taking any time to rest. Big decisions had to be made and his sleep, just as every other thing in his life, was expendable.

He reluctantly opened his eyes and found himself looking at a picture of his wife and himself taken near the Ira Sand Dunes overlooking Larep on their honeymoon. The sunlight danced in both of their eyes and testified of love and unencumbered vitality. The more Fedrin looked at the picture, the more he felt as if he didn't recognize either of the people staring back at him. They were both seemingly too happy and carefree to be anyone he could know.

A knock sounded at the door.

"Come in," Fedrin said and looked up to see Kesler walk through the gray doors across the room. "What can I do for you Lieutenant?" asked Fedrin and then smiled. "Want me to assign that Branci to someone else? I hear Tenith doesn't mind them so much."

Kesler shook his head. "Tarkin is actually a pretty neat guy. Honestly, I wish he could have joined us years ago. He is going to be quite an asset."

Fedrin smiled. "I never would have believed you had befriended a Branci if I hadn't seen it with my own eyes. He must have made quite the impression."

"Anyone who saves me from being charbroiled alive at the risk of his own skin has my vote!" exclaimed Kesler.

Fedrin smiled and sat back in his chair. "So what is it that you wanted from me?"

"May I use your computer?" Kesler asked, followed by a nod from Fedrin. "Computer, replay telecast flash on Fedrin," said Kesler, speaking toward Fedrin's wall mounted screen.

An image of the docked Sixth Fleet prior to the attack came to life on the screen. Everything seemed as it should be when a sickening familiar sight of the first explosion ripped through the docking bays and proceeded along the row of destroyers, engulfing each of them in deep orange flames followed by billowing black smoke.

"As you all know by now, a terrorist attack on the Larep Navy docks was carried out earlier today," the familiar deep voice of a reporter solemnly said. "Initial estimates of the damage included the loss of multiple fleet destroyers and cruisers along with tens of thousands of servicemen, dock operators, and engineers making it the deadliest day for the Federation since the Brok III massacre."

Fedrin watched the telecast curiously, anxious to see what the reporter was going to say next but fearing he already knew.

"As has already been suggested by our Navy correspondent, the primary suspect in this heinous act is Chief Admiral Fedrin who fled the scene in a bloody spectacle shortly after the attack."

The view on the screen changed to show the Iovara blasting free of her gravitational mooring lines in her desperate effort to escape. The flames that had been eating away at her hull were conveniently cropped out of view.

A picture of Fedrin that was not at all flattering, then appeared on the screen as the reporter continued. "Not only did Chief Admiral Fedrin and his coconspirators flee the scene without offering assistance; it has also been reported that they ordered all surviving vessels to open fire on the docks prior to departure. There are also mixed reports suggesting that the Iovara and her two surviving destroyer escorts, the Bolter and Defiant, chased and gunned down nearly a dozen atmospheric patrol fighters that were arriving at the scene to help coordinate rescue efforts. Attempts to contact Fedrin and the other surviving Sixth Fleet commanders to this point have gone unanswered."

Another view of the docks appeared on the screen. Smoke and debris filled the sky, blotting out the sun and casting an eerie shadow on the burning ships. Several fire crews could be seen hosing down one of the cruisers with fire retardant in a vain attempt to cool them down enough for rescue crews to get in.

The reporter continued. "Our administration correspondent, speaking on condition of anonymity, was quoted a short time ago as saying, "In my opinion Fedrin, his command crew, and quite possibly the other surviving ship commanders, are the primary suspects in the horrific attacks that transpired today."

The view changed again, this time showing a handsome news reporter standing on a platform overlooking the remains of the smoking docks. "Our thoughts and prayers go out to the families of those killed in these senseless attacks. We will keep you updated on the situation, as more information is made available. Back to you Godown."

"Thank you Waren. In other news, the charred remains of Defense Minister Boide were found inside his burnt out Larep apartment late today. Officials are calling the fire that broke out in his kitchen a tragic accident and..."

"End playback," Kesler said and then looked up at Fedrin. "What's going on, Sir? Why are they doing this to us?"

Fedrin sighed. "Have a seat Lieutenant," he said, nodding to a chair in front of his desk. "There's a lot I need to fill you in on."

CHAPTER 4

THE FATE OF THE SECOND FLEET

He was a tall, well built man with wild, unkempt black hair and piercing blue eyes. His demeanor resonated with strength and cunning as if he should be commanding men by the legion in fierce battle on a far off world. But his situation at present was a far cry from such a place.

Standing knee-high in the waste-processing tank, he cranked down on the jammed outlet valve for all he was worth, his mighty arms bulging as he dedicated every muscle to the task. Slowly, ever so slowly, the valve succumbed to his unwavering strength and turned, allowing the buildup of refuse to once again flow steadily through the collecting pipes.

"Hard at work I see," an old man with a long white beard commented as he peered over a guardrail above the tank. He held a cane properly over one arm and held the guardrail with the other.

The man in the tank looked up, his blue eyes spotting the familiar face above him. He smiled cheerily; seemingly unaware that he was likely standing in the most grotesque spot in Larep. "Got to keep the system flowing!" he commented and then reached a gloved hand beneath the surface to adjust a pressure sensor.

"Most assuredly," remarked the old man and then chuckled, shifting his weight as he watched.

The young man stood up from his foul task, grabbed his tools beside him and slung them over his shoulder. "So, is it time?" he asked, once more glancing up.

The old man nodded slowly. "It is," was his only reply.

The stout man plodded his way though the sludge and over to a metal set of stairs that led out of the basin. Upon emerging from the stench, he walked toward the white-haired man and dropped his bag of tools on the graded walkway. He then leaned on the railing beside the other and looked out across the waste processing plant.

"The loss of the Sixth Fleet means that our enemy is in the final phase of their plan," remarked the older. "We need to check their progress and align ourselves with those we can trust...and quickly."

"It won't be easy," the younger commented.

"Fighting for what is right never is," remarked the old man. "But is must be done just the same."

The worker nodded and then stood erect. "Lets get to it then Professor. We have a lot to do."

"Surely we do Kebbs," answered the old man and followed the younger down the platform, the rhythmic rise and fall of his cane preceding his steps.

⚓

Etana tossed the suitcase onto the bed and began throwing items into it, seemingly at random. Fedrin watched her in complete confusion.

"Out of my way," she snapped as she opened a dresser drawer behind Fedrin and began emptying contents from it into the luggage.

"I don't understand!" Fedrin said again. "What happened? What's wrong?"

Etana slowed for a moment, looked at Fedrin with disdain, and then continued her task. "In two months the Idok is scheduled to form up with the Second Fleet for a week of training exercises," she said as she went to the washroom to retrieve her toiletries. "After the training week, we are heading to Kumper to patrol the sector for a three month mission."

"What of it?" answered Fedrin, well aware of the order set he had drafted for his wife's ship several weeks earlier.

"I have made a request directly to Defense Minster Boide to move the date for that mission to this week," she continued, speaking from the washroom.

"Why?" Fedrin implored. "What's wrong?"

Etana returned and stuffed an armful of items into a small bag, zipped it closed, and then looked up at Fedrin. "Because I'm done with you!" she snapped.

Fedrin was dumfounded. "What does that mean?"

"Guess!" she retorted and turned to walk back to the washroom.

She had taken only one step before Fedrin grabbed her by the arm and whirled her around. "Now I've had just about enough of all of this nonsense!" he snapped, glaring into her eyes. "I want an answer from you! What is going on?"

She shrugged off his hold of her and walked straightway to her data pad. She swiped through several screens before handing it to Fedrin in disgust.

Fedrin reluctantly took the pad and glanced down at the screen. The image that met his gaze nearly caused him to drop the device.

"She's pretty," Etana said indifferently and then walked to the closet.

Fedrin looked at his wife in shock and then back at the pad. The screen bore the unmistakable image of him and a beautiful woman, who Fedrin did not recognize, in intimate proximity to each other.

"What is this?" Fedrin exclaimed, waving the pad over his head.

"What does it look like?" Etana shot back.

Fedrin shook his head and pointed to the pad. "This isn't me!" he asserted tapping the image. "This isn't me!"

Etana looked at Fedrin incredulously. "Is that really the best you can do?"

"I'm serious!" he declared. "This isn't me! I have no idea who that is!" he said, pointing to the woman. "I've never seen her before! It must be a fake!"

Etana stormed back from the closet and pointed to a symbol in the corner of the image indigently.

"What's that?" Fedrin asked.

Etana shook her head impatiently. "It's an image verification stamp," she answered as tears began to fill her eyes. "I didn't believe it when I saw it, so I had the image verified for authenticity."

"And?" Fedrin asked.

Etana wiped her eyes. "It's not a fake," she answered. "The image is real!"

"Where did it come from?"

Etana shrugged. "It was sent to me over the cortex. I'm not sure from whom. Probably by a friend who just couldn't bare to tell me directly!"

Fedrin didn't know what to say. "It...it isn't me though," he stammered. "I never would have..."

"Save it!" said Etana as she reached for her luggage and shoulder bag. "I'll send for the rest of my stuff when I get back. You can pile it up in the front hallway closet if you want."

Etana reached for her data-pad, which Fedrin reluctantly released. She tucked it in her shoulder bag and then looked Fedrin squarely in the eye. Her tears were gone and her jaw was tight. Then, in smooth motion, she brought her clenched fist to cover her heart and clicked her heels in a proper salute. "Sir!" she said in good military order as coldly as if she didn't know Fedrin. "We'll contact the Iovara when we reach the Second Fleet. My Lieutenant will forward our flight patterns once they're plotted."

Fedrin wanted to say so much but the words didn't form in his mind correctly so he said nothing. Etana then turned, walked out of the room and out of the apartment without speaking another word. Fedrin stood in the empty room and listened as she opened the front door and walked out, changing his entire world in a matter of moments as the door closed behind her.

"You have one saved message from Vice Admiral Caton," the computerized voice in Fedrin's quarters suddenly sounded, waking him from his dream.

Fedrin slowly sat up in bed. Remembering the events of all those many months ago replay in his dream had left him disheartened. He sighed and reluctantly stood to his feet. Reaching for a robe, he wrapped it around himself and walked toward his desk. "Computer, start a fresh pot of lor and play back Caton's message."

"Orders received. Please stand by," the computer answered. A few moments later the lor unit in the far corner began brewing a fresh pot and the transmission screen came to life. The recording showed a very haggard looking Admiral Caton.

"Fedrin," Caton began uneasily. "There has been an incident. I'm not sure how, but Commodore Tropnia found out about my duplicity and challenged me directly with nearly a dozen of her most ardent supporters. Fortunately, I had several of my own men briefed on the possibility of mutiny and we fended off her attack with no casualties with the use of stun-guns. I've since locked all of them up, including Tropnia, in the aft escape pods. I did that rather than use the brig in an effort to keep the incident quiet. Obviously I won't be able to keep them in there forever. Once the rest of her following hears what happened, the Second Fleet may very well slip out of my control. If that happens, they will likely come for you. Get done what you can before that happens. I'll try to contact you again tomorrow morning with another update. I'm sorry. Caton out."

"End of message," stated the computer.

Fedrin sighed as he digested the implications of losing Caton and the support of the Second Fleet. He didn't have long to dwell on it when a beep sounded out on his tele-link.

"This is Fedrin."

"Evening Admiral. This is Lieutenant Tenith."

"What's happening Lieutenant?"

"Wanted to let you now that we should be joining the Hornell carrier group within the hour."

"Excellent," said Fedrin as he retrieved his fresh mug.

"I also wanted to let you know that our satellite positional update from the Second Fleet is overdue.'"

Fedrin froze, mug in hand, as he processed Tenith's words. "Did you run a network analysis?" he asked.

"Aye, Sir," replied Tenith. "I ran a quick check of the network and the initial results all checked out. I'm not really sure what the problem is."

Fedrin tried to convince himself that everything was fine and that his imagination was simply getting the better of him but he couldn't help but think the worse. "Keep trying to get the updates," he finally brought himself to say. "You can even try contacting the ships directly using the cortex. If that doesn't work, let me know."

"Aye, Sir," answered Tenith and signed off.

Fedrin had just set his mug down and picked up his data pad when yet another called sounded out on his link. "This is Fedrin," he said wearily.

"Hello, Sir," said Ensign Gallo.

"What can I do for you Ensign?"

"I need to speak with you, Sir," Gallo's timid voice crackled as he spoke.

"Isn't that what we are doing now?"

"In person, Sir."

"Is everything ok?"

"I'll be there in five minutes," was Gallo's only answer.

Knowing that Gallo wasn't a social officer, or one given to exaggeration, Fedrin felt uneasy at his request to meet. As the possible topics of conversation rapidly crossed his mind, Fedrin felt overwhelmed and promptly stopped thinking about it all together, knowing that dwelling on the innumerable 'what-ifs' would only drive him mad.

Realizing that he still wasn't dressed for the day, Fedrin got up and walked to his closet where he selected a freshly pressed uniform jacket. He slung the jacket on the doorknob of his washroom and rolled up his shirtsleeves. After splashing cold water on his face, he looked up into the mirror to see heavy eyes with dark circles beneath them. He splashed more water on his face, hoping to wash away his weary look. With his face still hung over the sink he reached for a small towel on a nearby hook. Having dried his face, he glanced up once more to see if there was any improvement. But as his eyes met the mirror, he instantly felt a familiar and overwhelming pain in his head. He stumbled back into the wall and struggled to look up but was horrified to see a faceless, red hooded figure in the mirror looking back at him.

"What...what do you want?" stammered Fedrin as he slid down the wall to the floor, grabbing at his throbbing head. "Who are you?"

"Open your mind," replied the ominous figure.

"What?" asked Fedrin.

"Open your mind," the figure said again.

"Go away!" moaned Fedrin in agony as his head felt like it was going to explode.

The figure began to dissipate but continued to speak. "There is much we need you for Fedrin. Open your mind," the figure said one last time and then disappeared.

Fedrin sat on his washroom floor catching his breath, all the while holding his aching head. He was trying to decide if what he had just seen was real or some sort of delusion when he finally heard a light knock at his door. He struggled to his feet and wearily made his way toward the chair behind his desk. He needed to sit down before he passed out. He sat there with his eyes closed tightly for over a minute when another knock sounded on the door.

"Enter," Fedrin called out feebly as he struggled to open his eyes.

The door slowly opened and Ensign Gallo entered the room, holding a data card carefully in his hand.

Ensign Gallo was an average man as far as fleet officers were concerned. He was short, slightly bald and looked like he was in his late thirties but was actually only twenty-six. He had served as the Chief Special Communications and Intelligence officer on the Iovara since the day she was commissioned. Most officers would use their tenure in such a visible post to position themselves into a First Lieutenant promotion or perhaps a commander candidacy, but not Gallo. He was perfectly content to stay in his position for the rest of his career. Listening to radio waves and starring into scanner screens was what he loved and no promises of promotion could lure him away.

"So what's going on?" Fedrin asked as he pushed the subsiding pain out of his mind and motioned for Gallo to sit.

"I think it'll be clearer if you simply played this," replied Gallo as he awkwardly held out the data card.

Fedrin's hand shook as he reached for the unlabeled data card and with some difficulty inserted it into a thin slot on the desk terminal. The screen came to life, flickering for a moment until the words 'Emergency Jettison Beacon Mark-478 NPF Tribulation' appeared. Fedrin's heart dropped. This was an emergency message sent from the Tribulation, Admiral Caton's flagship.

Fedrin looked at Gallo for a reassuring expression or nod. Gallo offered no such look. Fedrin shook his head and looked back up at the screen.

The first thing that Fedrin recognized in the recording was the burnt out hull of the NPF Driam, a heavy cruiser commissioned only eight months prior. All the running lights were off and half of the upper command decks were missing. A pair of hull breaches could be seen on her starboard side. Immediately above the Driam, was the wrecked frame of the NPF Lewison, a veteran destroyer escort. It too had several gaping holes along her hull and the main energy modulator platforms fixed on the fuselage were noticeably absent. The camera view from the beacon suddenly jolted and the screen went black.

"The beacon was hit by something," Gallo quietly explained. "Advance the transmission thirty minutes forward."

Fedrin advanced the transmission and looked on helplessly as the view now faced away from the Driam and Lewison derelicts. The new angle caused Fedrin to bring his hand up to cover his open mouth, for there on the screen was the rest of the Second Fleet, utterly destroyed! All twenty-one ships of the mighty Second Fleet were gone!

A veritable sea of debris floated aimlessly in and out of view of the beacon's camera. Mighty weapon turrets, armor plating, surface instruments, furniture, storage crates, and dead ship personnel all added to the horrific scene before Fedrin's eyes.

"They...they never fired a shot," murmured Fedrin, shaking his head in anguish as he studied the line of mangled destroyer and cruiser hulls. "Not one shot!"

"I thought as much," remarked Gallo quietly. "Looks like they ran into a minefield or something," he added as he nodded to the large distinct holes in many of the ships.

Fedrin rested his head against the back of his chair, his eyes closed. "How long ago did this come in?"

"About twenty-five minutes ago," answered Gallo. "But it was transmitting a good two to three hours before that. The signal was weak and the second-shift wave hunter didn't pick it up. Even I didn't notice it at first."

Fedrin shook his head slowly. "Half an hour after Admiral Caton contacted me."

"What was that, Sir?"

"Nothing," answered Fedrin. "Do you know if the rest of the fleet has received this?"

"I don't believe so," Gallo answered.

Fedrin nodded slowly. "Keep searching the sub waves for any possible enemy ships that could have caused this. If it was a minefield, something must have laid them. We need to find out where it is."

"Aye, Sir!" answered Gallo and saluted before promptly making his exit.

Fedrin exhaled deeply and then looked out his window as another wave of helplessness and defeat came over him like waves billowing through a collapsed dam. Two entire fleets had been destroyed under his watch without so much as a shot fired at the enemy; surely this was the beginning of the end for the Federation.

His listless gaze out his window fell upon the Defiant and he found himself examining her hull in detail. The sleek rows of decks, daunting cannons mounts and glowing relay grids resonated with power and authority. His wandering eyes drifted to the command deck two thirds up from the stern. Most of the lights were on throughout the decks and Fedrin wondered if Commander Drezden was sleeping or hard at work. He guessed the latter. As he sat there studying the Destroyer, Fedrin found himself wishing he were once again a ship's Commander waiting for someone else to make all the hard decisions for him. This Chief Admiral stuff was not for him.

⋏

"And that switch activates the main ship to ship relay transmitter," Kesler said, pointing to a small green switch buried in the sea of knobs, levers and buttons on the console.

Tarkin nodded. "And how do you differentiate the coded transmissions sent over homogenous frequencies by ships in the same grouping versus others?"

Kesler looked at Tarkin curiously, momentarily dumbfounded.

"He doesn't know what you said!" Jonas called down to Tarkin followed by a hearty laugh. "You're smarter than him!"

Kesler rolled his eyes, shook his head and then turned back to Tarkin. "The Navcom computer sorts out the transmissions automatically."

"How?" Tarkin pressed.

Kesler shrugged. "Unlike the civilian operated ships that you've served on in the past with individual networking, all commissioned fleet vessels are linked with the Navcom making communication and ship to ship monitoring and communication essentially effortless."

Tarkin scratched at his burly beard as he listened intently to every word Kesler said. He nodded occasionally and asked an insightful question now and then. He remembered every word imparted by Kesler and mastered the location of every switch, lever and button on the primary workstations without needing Kesler to repeat himself, even once. The only exception to this was one instance when Kesler made a mistake, inadvertently mixing up aft and bow stabilizer thruster switches. Tarkin caught the mistake himself and, in a humble tone, corrected Kesler at the first available moment away from the other officers.

"Hey, have you guys seen Gallo?" Jonas asked from his perch. "He's been gone for like twenty minutes. It's not like him to be gone this long when it's his shift. He starts to twitch after five minutes if he isn't starring into his signal screens."

"I think he went down to the Admiral's quarters to show him something he found during a wave hunt," Kesler answered.

Jonas looked down at Kesler and raised an eyebrow.

"My thoughts exactly," Kesler said and shook his head.

"What's that?" Tarkin asked, noticing the exchanged glances.

Kesler nodded to the empty communication station. "Gallo isn't much of a talker and he isn't very comfortable around people in general, especially the Admiral."

"So?" said Tarkin.

"So...if something came up that was important enough for him to walk down to Fedrin's quarters and talk with him face to face, it can't be good news," Kesler replied.

"Ah, I see," said Tarkin. "Well, we can always hope different."

"You'll be hoping for quite a while there buddy," Jonas shouted down. "Some things just don't change around here. Actually come to think of it, most things don't change around here."

"Like your loud mouth!" Kesler shouted up to Jonas.

Jonas was about to offer a comeback when a beep sounding at Kesler's station cut him off.

Kesler and Tarkin quickly turned and looked at the screen. "Looks like we've reached the Hornell," Kesler said pointing to a batch of blinking signals on a small screen. "Care to send salutations and offer the Commanders docking instructions?" he asked facing Tarkin.

Tarkin nodded and quickly tapped a series of keys and buttons, his extra sets of hands making short work of the task. When he had finished, he looked up at Kesler for approval, prior to sending the transmissions.

"Wow! That was fast," exclaimed Kesler, peering down at the commands to ensure their accuracy. "Very fast...and perfect. Well done!"

"I'm a fast learner," Tarkin said with a slight smile.

"I guess so," Kesler said as he nodded in approval.

"It also helps that I have these," Tarkin said, flaunting his extra arms and prompting a smile from Kesler.

"Gallo! Where have you been old buddy?" Jonas suddenly called out when he saw the stocky ensign slip back onto the bridge.

"Don't want to talk about it," Gallo said as he walked straightway to his station where he promptly placed his set of signal searchers over his ears and began once more staring into a computer screen.

Kesler glanced up at Jonas. They both shook their heads. It was bad. Real bad.

CHAPTER 5

THE SIXTH FLEET

The stately man walked confidently into the President's office without knocking. Sitting behind his desk, President Defuria looked up in surprise and then smiled. "Why Senator Trivis, how nice to see you," he said in a pleasant tone that didn't impress Trivis.

"Skip the pleasantries," the Senator snapped. "I'm three days late on my Grimsin share. It's usually in my delivery box by now. What's the big idea?"

Defuria shook his head. "Things have been busy Senator, or haven't you noticed?"

"Things are always busy," Trivis retorted. "Including me! And I can't stay busy and do my work without the Grimsin. You know this better than anyone!"

Defuria looked momentarily enraged by Trivis' aggressive mannerisms but he quickly regained his composure and nodded. "Of course Senator," he said and opened a drawer in his desk and retrieved a small metal box. "Your services are worth every drop."

"Now just to clarify, is this my Grimsin or are they going to have to take me out of here in a dustpan like Minister Boide?" Trivis asked, looking at the box suspiciously.

"I'm afraid I don't know what you are talking about," Defuria replied. "Boide died in a fire at his apartment. Tragic, tragic accident."

"Right..." Trivis said skeptically. "And I can fly. So can I have it?"

Defuria smiled as he opened the metal box and retrieved the contents within. "Your payment," he said as he handed the Senator a small vial filled with a crimson elixir.

Trivis relaxed his stance and took the vial from Defuria and slipped it into his breast pocket. "Is that the last of it?" he asked.

Defuria nodded. "I distributed final rations to everyone else yesterday and this morning. There will be no more until we complete our mission."

Trivis patted the pocket containing the vial. "Then we had all better get to work."

"Most assuredly," commented Defuria. "Time is not a luxury we have to work with."

Trivis nodded, turned sharply and walked out of the room.

Defuria watched until he had left before shaking his head. The upcoming events were going to have to be handled very delicately.

⚔

Commander Colby's shuttle had barely locked with the Iovara docking clamps before he lunged onto the landing; nearly slipping in the process and cracking his head open on the steel balustrade. He then skipped down the graded stairs until he reached the bottom of the platform and then bounded across the hangar floor in the direction of the main airlock.

After spending several minutes convincing the posted guards of who he was, a task made more difficult than necessary due to his lost ID card, he entered the ship proper where he proceeded to jog down the corridors toward his destination. In his left hand, he clutched a well-worn uniform jacket and in his right, a badly scratched data pad with instructions for getting to the meeting room. He had been aboard the Iovara for fleet meetings a hundred times over the years but he always managed to get lost in the massive vessel, her ever winding bowels and imposing levels; a test for even the most tenured Iovara personnel. Finally, with the help of an amiable lieutenant, he found the meeting room and burst through the doors.

He was momentarily relieved that most of the other Commanders were late too, but then the sickening realization hit him that they weren't there because they had perished. Colby, of course, knew what had happened but to come to a fleet commander conference, as they had all done so many times before, and notice over a dozen empty chairs, was something he hadn't prepared himself to see. He had just assumed they would always be there. Their absence was sobering and filled the air with a heavy emotional charge.

He walked past two empty chairs and took his usual place near the end of the long polished table. He sat back and stared at the empty places, still picturing their former occupants and hearing their voices in his mind. How could they be dead?

"Don't worry," Commander Kendrick said reassuringly, patting Colby's arm. "They're all in a better place now."

"He's right," Drezden added with a smile. "They're probably all looking down here feeling sorry for us poor chaps still stumbling around in this rat race."

Colby nodded and then looked up at Drezden with a forced smile. He then slowly scanned the faces of the other seated commanders, seeing each of them in a new, more thoughtful light in the wake of yesterday's events.

"So what do you all think about this business back home?" Commander Searle, the only female commander in the group, asked as she casually broke the awkward silence. "Pretty crazy right?"

"Still can't believe it," Kendrick said shaking his head in sadness. "Simply awful. And to think they are trying to blame Fedrin for this...this monstrous act. What is wrong with Larep anyhow?"

"What's right with Larep?" added Drezden followed by several agreeing nods.

"Still though, there is that recording of Fedrin in the docks," Commander Mick of the cruiser Corinthia and outspoken critic of Fedrin voiced up.

"Fake!" Drezden answered. "It's all fake!"

"Looked real enough to me," muttered Mick as he reached for his mug and sipped the hot lor.

"Did you guys hear the Hornell's Star Chaser fighters were replaced with the new Comet class?" Searle asked in an effort to lighten the conversation.

"No kidding?" exclaimed Sanders looking to Kendrick, Commander of the Hornell, for more info. "I didn't even know they were shipping the Comets already."

Kendrick nodded casually although all could tell he was very excited about his ship's new prize. "We received the first shipment of them last week. The Third Fleet should be getting the next batch in a couple of months and the Second Fleet should be receiving theirs by the end of the year!"

"Hope the Third Fleet is around long enough to get theirs," said Colby solemnly.

"Aye," muttered Kendrick with a weary shake of his head as he pondered the plight of the Third Fleet and their multitude of pressing problems.

Mick suddenly cleared his throat and looked intently at the seated Commanders. "So am I the only one who has misgivings about this whole thing?"

Kendrick turned sharply. "Thing?"

"Disregarding Larep and the Defense Council and going rogue," Mick retorted.

"Disregarding orders to sit in a burning dock is hardly what I would classify as going rogue," Drezden replied coolly.

"Better to be alive rebels then dead loyalists," Colby added.

Mick tossed his arms in the air. "So a few wires got crossed at the docks. That's to be expected right? I mean, they were on fire after all. Obviously no one intended for the ships to sit there and burn. But ignoring orders to return and set things right? That is what I don't like."

"There weren't wires crossed!" Sanders rebuked Mick harshly. "I was there on the ground yesterday, you weren't. Someone wanted our ships to burn. And when we wouldn't let them, they tried to shoot us down. It's pretty hard to misinterpret laser rounds smashing your hull, although I'm sure you could find a way."

Mick shook his head angrily. "All I'm saying is that we should let Larep sort this thing out. Giving full control of our ships to one man goes against the systems of due process. The Defense Council should be involved in leading us. Having Fedrin make his own calls with no accountability is a dangerous precedent to set...although this might have been his plan all along."

"Watch it, Mick!" Kendrick admonished sharply. "You're putting us all in an awkward position just by listening to you. Now knock it off!"

"What's he going to do? Court-martial me? Throw me in the brig? He can't afford to! There aren't enough experienced commanders to go around. He needs me more then I need him. That's for sure!"

"You shouldn't do this," Searle warned. "It's not good for the fleet!"

"Not good for the fleet?" Mick exclaimed. "I'll tell you what's not good for the fleet. Having that man as our leader without the Council having their leash on him! Drezden, you remember, don't you? The way he always sucked up to Nebod and the other politicians back in Larep? He was setting everyone up so he could get what he got."

"Which is?" Sanders asked.

"The Fleet!" answered Mick. "And with it, the ability to take control of the Federation himself. Before he's done, he might be calling himself Emperor. Who knows?"

"You really are delusional Mick," said Fedrin as he suddenly walked up, seemingly out of nowhere.

Mick looked momentarily shocked but quickly tightened his jaw and looked straight ahead with defiant arrogance.

Fedrin ignored Mick as he assumed his place at the head of the table. He then stood behind his chair in awkward silence as if considering what to say. His mannerisms showed nothing but anxiety and uncertainty. He was no Nebod.

"Approximately three hours ago we received an automated emergency transmission from the Tribulation's beacon drone," began Fedrin, the poignant words slicing through the already tense air of the room. Fedrin paused, the words he needed to say next seeming too horrific to utter. He shook his head and forged ahead. "The beacon has reported the utter destruction of the Second Fleet. This has been confirmed through the Navcom grid by my communications officer." Fedrin finished the distasteful deed and looked up. Commander Searle dabbed her eyes, morning the presumed death of her husband, a gunnery officer that had served in the Second. Commander Drezden stroked her back doing his best to comfort her, restraining his own grief, which was very great.

Commander Sanders shook his head slowly back and forth as his hands began to tremble. Images of his enlisted daughter flooded his mind. He refused to believe she was gone. He must be dreaming. With all his will power he tried to wake himself from the fast building nightmare. Nothing happened.

Commander Kendrick sat there in disbelief. "The Sixth Fleet disaster from yesterday and now this?" he said to himself.

Commander Mick shook his head from side to side with his eyes closed. He had lost one niece and countless friends. Commander Colby patted him on the shoulder, aware of his loss.

After the initial shock had been absorbed, Fedrin opened his data-pad and pressed play. The large light fixtures around the room dimmed allowing the ceiling to become a viewing screen.

The commanders looked up and gaped in disbelief at the raw carnage before them.

"How?" Drezden quietly asked, still comforting Searle. "How did this happen?"

Fedrin shook his head. "I don't know."

Kendrick and Colby looked up in awe at the former mightiest fleet in the Navy, both unable to speak. What was there to say?

"Is this it then?" Sanders blurted out. "Are we finished? Did we lose?"

The other commanders looked at Fedrin for his reply. Fedrin didn't know the answer. If entire fleets, the greatest fleets in naval history, could blink out of existence without a shot being fired, the war would indeed be over quickly.

"You know as well as I do that this is a major defeat made all the worse by the events of yesterday," Fedrin started bluntly. "Exactly how this happened, I couldn't begin to say. But I think it happened because I got a pledge of loyalty from Caton who reaffirmed his commitment to my leadership despite the baseless allegations coming from Larep."

Fedrin was suddenly interrupted by a squadron of Comet star fighters flying past the window, doing their customary welcome flight past all the ships in the fleet. Their roaring engines made it momentarily impossible to speak. The commanders, anxious to take their minds off the news even for a few brief seconds turned away from Fedrin and watched as the fighters made their impressive flyby. The first squadron was immediately followed by several others in rapid succession, each group flying a little closer and a little faster than the previous in a bid for the most impressive performance.

After the last formation had past, Fedrin shoved his data pad away and leaned onto the table. "Even with the catastrophic losses that we have sustained, we are still strong," he said motioning to where the fighters had just past. "The Krohn Fleet is still stuck in Brok and the Third Fleet is holding firm against them. Now that we've formed up with the Hornell Carrier group, we can secure our rear areas and protect the remaining shipyards scattered over our systems as they build new vessels. We can still do this!"

Fedrin cleared his throat and looked intently at his commanders. He could tell they weren't buying what he was selling but he proceeded full force. He had to buy their confidence in order to stem unrest on a broader scale. "We have good reconnaissance in all the forward areas right now and we are positive no Krohn fleets, other than the one in Brok, pose any imminent threat. So, although this is a major setback as far as trying to get back on the offense, we are by no means beaten. Far from it!"

Sanders timidly raised his hand. "I hate to be the eternal pessimist Admiral, but if our strongest fleet can be destroyed before even having a chance to launch their fighters, what's the point?" Several heads nodded with similar sentiment. "Maybe we can hold on for a few more months but to what end?"

Fedrin stepped back from the table and casually glanced out the window. "There is more at work right now than mere ships and fleets. Things have been happening that just don't add up. I don't know what they are, but they are big." He paused. "And maybe you're right Sanders. Maybe this is all just a waste of time. Maybe it is impossible." Fedrin smiled and turned back toward the table. "Then again, you remember what Admiral Nebod said when he took the First Fleet into Zelin to draw the line against the Krohn advance?"

Several heads slowly nodded.

"Conquering impossible tasks is what the Namuh do best," Colby quietly said.

Fedrin's eyes grew wide and he pointed to Colby. "Conquering impossible tasks is what the Namuh do best! Did you hear that Sanders?"

Sanders nodded.

"Who beat the Refrac when everyone said it was impossible?"

"We did," answered Drezden.

Fedrin looked to Kendrick. "Who stopped the mighty Krohn Fleet dead in its tracks when everyone said it couldn't be done?"

"We did," Kendrick answered.

"You better believe we did!" Fedrin said as he slammed the table with his fist, startling several. "And by Nebod, we can do it again! Yes, the odds are against us, but when haven't they been? And regardless of how everything turns out, I'm telling you all right now that I'll continue to fight on until the enemy is vanquished or I've died trying!"

"That goes for me too!" announced Drezden, rising to his feet in a much needed outward show of support for the Admiral.

"And me!" followed Kendrick, he too rising.

"They will regret what they did to my daughter," Sanders said as he stood, gesturing to the screen with vindication, tears now flowing down his cheeks as the realization of the moment became more and more apparent.

"Behind you all the way!" said Colby, joining the others.

Searle wiped more tears from her eyes as she too quietly stood. Drezden put an arm around her.

All the commanders had risen, save one. Mick sat in his chair stubbornly, looking cross as ever. An awkward feeling crept back over the room as the tension between Mick and Fedrin grew. After one last sip of his lor Mick finally, albeit slowly, stood up. "Guess there aren't any other choices. I'm in."

Fedrin glared at Mick. "I have not addressed your insubordination due to the horrors of the last two days. Please bear in mind, however, that after today there will be no such excuse for your behavior. And you had better dismiss this notion that you are irreplaceable because I know plenty of young and very capable officers looking for a ship commission, including an up and coming Branci. I won't think twice about giving any of them your ship if you make me. Am I clear?"

Mick stubbornly nodded his head.

Kendrick and Sanders exchanged uneasy glances. Mick had deserved worse but it was still awkward to watch him get reprimanded in front of everyone.

"Now as you are all aware, some dark things are going on back home," stated Fedrin, regaining everyone's attention. "It may require that we take some serious action to correct before everything is said and done. That said, I'm going to have to ask you all to trust me more than I've required of you in the past. We might have to face some challenges that you were not trained to confront and I will need you to be strong and face them head-on. Will you all be able to do that?"

The commanders all nodded their heads in agreement; except Mick, who stared out the window, seemingly ignoring every word.

Fedrin ignored his behavior once more and continued. "You have likely already heard that a squadron of Refrac Pirates evaded Admiral Nidrid's Northern Fleet and are now roaming freely in our home system. We will need to hunt these ships down and destroy them before we can undertake any other actions."

"Stinking Northern," Sanders mumbled.

"We'll split what's left of our fleet into three battle groups and sweep the system," added Fedrin. "My ship, the Defiant and the Bolter will comprise one group, the Revenge and Corinthia another, and the Hornell and Arbitrator III, the last. My flight officer has already sent these breakdowns to your command crews. By the time you get back to your respective vessels, you should be ready to head out. Clear?"

The Commanders nodded.

"I know it's asking a lot, but I would really like this operation to take no more than two days to complete. Satellite recon has already narrowed their whereabouts to a small section near the Asar shipping lanes. It should be a fairly basic mission but time is precious now, more than ever before. Once we secure our rear area for good, I will inform you of our next steps in the plan. Until then, please be patient with me."

"Let's get moving then!" Colby said. "The more time we waste here, the more time we're not killing Krohns," he finished as he started to make his way for the door.

"I guess that settles it," Kendrick said as the elderly commander chuckled at the impetuousness of Colby and followed after him.

Searle stepped away from Drezden and slowly walked over to Fedrin. She spoke quietly as to avoid the others from overhearing. "Is your wife ok?" she asked, speaking to him as a friend and not as a subordinate

Fedrin had been trying desperately not to think of his wife or of her fate. He now had no choice but to think of it and it caused his heart to ache. "She wasn't with the Second Fleet but I don't know anything more than that," he answered.

"I hope she is ok," Searle said quietly. "I know her ship was on deep patrol not far from there."

"Thank you very much for your concern Commander. I'm touched, really. And please allow me to offer my deepest condolences on the loss of your husband. I never met him but by all accounts he was a great officer."

Searle began to tear up again and quickly turned away. Fedrin shook his head, wishing he could help her but knowing she needed nothing but time.

The remaining commanders trickled out of the room somberly, but with more determination than when they had entered. On his way out, Mick stopped and locked eyes with Fedrin just for a moment. The look was less than pleasant. Fedrin ignored it, for everyone's sake. Drezden was the last one in the room when Fedrin turned to him and exhaled deeply.

"Well?" he asked.

"Well what?" asked Drezden as he gathered his things from the table.

"What did you think?"

"About what?" Drezden asked.

Fedrin rolled his eyes. "About what I said!"

"Oh that," Drezden said followed by a smile. "To be frank, I think you are a complete liar."

"I didn't lie, Drezden."

"You embellished the truth," Drezden corrected. "The Third Fleet is holding firm? Would you really call a bunch of ships that have no fuel, water and running dangerously low on morale a firm fleet?"

"I couldn't tell them all that," replied Fedrin defensively.

"Oh don't get me wrong my young friend. I totally agree with your methods. If your commanders feel like they've lost, then their crews will feel like they've lost. And if the crews feel like they've lost, they will. You have no choice but to paint the picture of imminent death with pastels," added Drezden as he looked up at Fedrin. "And let's be honest. We commanders aren't as stupid as we look. We know what's going on, but what we want is for you to tell us that the situation is under control, and that's what you did. We want to know that someone has done all the hard work of making the right decision and will execute that decision to the best of his ability. When it comes right down to it, a commander wants nothing more to do than sit on his fat butt in a comfortable chair and give orders to his crew that he got from the admiral. It's really the easiest job in the fleet when you think about it."

"I wish Mick would realize that," Fedrin said. "He wants my job badly."

Drezden shook his head. "Mick and Nebod were close. I suspect that when Nebod died, Mick assumed he was getting the job."

Fedrin nodded. "And when he didn't..."

"For all his shortcomings, and he has many, Mick is a fine commander," said Drezden. "But commander and admiral, let alone Chief Admiral, are much different things. I'd resign my commission and run a colony sewage freighter before I'd serve under him."

Fedrin sighed. "Sometimes I wish he did get the job."

"And why is that?"

"It's just that this, all this is way more than just a job," answered Fedrin, nodding toward the empty conference table. "The only way to do it right is to let it become your life. I don't exist as an individual anymore Drezden. I've gained the title and a lot of headaches but lost everything else."

"And that's why you will become great!" said Drezden sincerely. "And not that it matters much to you right now, but I'd rather be serving under you then any of the other officers in the Navy. You have something special when it comes to leading, even though you don't know it yet."

Fedrin nodded, not believing his friend at all. "I wish other people thought like you do."

"Give them time," Drezden said. "Seven months is hardly long enough to prove yourself to everyone."

Fedrin nodded.

A beep sounded out over Fedrin's tele-link. "I need to go," he said after glancing at his link. "I'm needed on the bridge."

"Duty calls," Drezden said with a smile.

"Could you stay aboard a few more minutes?" Fedrin asked. "There is something else I want to talk to you about."

"Oh?" asked Drezden with an eyebrow raised. "About anything in particular?"

"Yeah," Fedrin answered.

Drezden waited for an explanation that didn't come. "Do you want to tell me what it's about?" he finally asked.

"Not here," said Fedrin. "But let me take care of this and I'll meet you in my quarters in say, twenty minutes?"

Drezden shrugged. "Sure. That'll give me time to check in with my ship and make sure their flight orders are set."

Fedrin nodded. "Feel free to use my room's tele-link to contact your ship."

"Will do," answered Drezden as he walked out of the room.

Fedrin walked to the table and began to gather his things. As he did, he thought about the meeting. Although he had stretched his optimism for the sake of the commanders, he truly believed in his heart of hearts that that war could eventually be won. It had to be won, too much was at stake not to.

Another transmission beeped on his wrist. "Go ahead," he said with a sigh.

"Sorry to bother you Admiral," said Kesler. "I just wanted to let you know that you are no longer needed on the bridge."

"Everything ok up there?"

"Everything is fine," answered Kesler. "I had requested your presence for a transmission that I managed to establish with your wife's ship but the link just broke and it will take some time to establish another one. I think there is to much EM interference from the Second Fleet wreckage and the com-relay switch there."

Fedrin swallowed hard. "Before the link broke were you able to make contact?"

"I spoke with Commander Etana personally," answered Kesler with a smile. "She said that the Idok is fairing well and there has been no sign of hostile aggression in her immediate area."

Kesler's voice ran on and on but Fedrin heard nothing. His wife was ok, and that was all that mattered. She was still much too close to danger for Fedrin's comfort, but at least for now, she was safe.

"Thank you Lieutenant," said Fedrin sincerely. "Thank you so much."

"My pleasure, Sir. I'm glad she's ok."

"As am I," Fedrin replied with a relived sigh.

"Any new orders as long as I have you here?" asked Kesler.

"Yes," answered Fedrin. "Prepare to break formation with the fleet. The Bolter and the Defiant will escort us out. Our heading will be for Sector three-eighty-one."

"Aye, Sir," replied Kesler and left the transmission.

Fedrin glanced out the window once more. He looked just in time to see the Hornell Carrier begin to brake away from the fleet and head toward her assigned sector. The Arbitrator III combat destroyer followed behind in close formation.

Fedrin watched until the battle group was completely clear of the rest of the fleet and then made his way for the door.

CHAPTER 6

COMMANDER DREZDEN

"We had agents in the Second Fleet!" yelled Senator Trivis angrily as he glared at Defuria through his tele-link screen. "Why would you activate the minefield without warning them?"

"I had to act when I did," replied Defuria calmly. "The loss of our allies is regrettable, but I had no other choice. Admiral Caton made it clear where his loyalties resided and when my backup plan having Commodore Tropnia take over also failed, it became apparent that I had to act. For if they managed to combine forces with Fedrin, our job would be immensely more complicated and may have even put in jeopardy, our bid to acquire the Grimsin and finish this once and for all!"

"Be that as it may, your indifference to our continued collateral damage is starting to concern us," Trivis stated.

"Us or you?" Defuria asked directly. "I haven't heard anything from any of the other agents."

Trivis shook his head angrily. "I just want to remind you, Mr. President, that we all have a part to play in this masquerade. If too many of us meet a premature demise, there will be nobody left to finish what we've started and no one gets the Grimsin, yourself included."

Defuria chuckled, amused at Trivis' mistrust. "You fret needlessly Senator. For as you pointed out, we need each other if we are going to finish this. We have too many enemies and obstacles for any one of us to go it alone."

Trivis shook his head. "Speaking of, we still need to address Fedrin. He knows something is happening and if the Sions get a hold of him before we can finish him off..."

"The Sions are of no concern to us right now," Defuria said. "We are too far along at this point to become preoccupied with outside distractions. We must stay the course!"

"Perhaps, but we can't count Fedrin out until he's dead and gone," reiterated Trivis. "He will make a play to depose us once he is able, likely with Sion assistance. You can not deny this Defuria!"

"He won't have the time, even with the Sion's help," Defuria stated. "The Krohns will see to that for us!"

"When will they be here?" asked Trivis sarcastically. "Will they come before the Sions do? Will they come before Fedrin gets the Grimsin? Will they come before we are dead?"

"They are ready to advance on both fronts," Defuria replied confidently. "No matter what Fedrin does, they'll be waiting for him," he said flatly and then smiled. "He will die at their hands leaving the Grimsin to us!"

Trivis nodded slowly. "It's not that simple...Mr. President. We still need to find it and we can't find it until we locate the Origin Codex...as you well know! Without the ancient writings contained therein, we will have no way of finding the Grimsin."

Defuria nodded and spoke. "Of course Trivis, of course. It has all been planned for. The Codex, Fedrin, the Grimsin, it has all been taking into account. That's what I'm here for Trivis. I plan, you do. Got it?"

Trivis' eyes narrowed in mistrust but he held his tongue.

"What?" Defuria snapped. "Life not fair Trivis? Do you want to complain about your share again?"

"The shares aren't fair," Trivis mumbled. "We take all the risks and you get all the reward. How is that fair?"

"All the reward?" Defuria said in a shocked tone. "What do you call the Grimsin I give you every month?"

"A fix!" Trivis snapped. "It's just enough to keep us junkies coming back for more."

"Junkies?" Defuria exclaimed in a hurt tone. "Trivis, I've introduced the universe to you through the Grimsin's power! If it weren't for me, you'd never have achieved what you've achieved. You'd never have experienced what you've experienced!"

"You made addicts out of us!" Trivis yelled back. "You've indentured us to do your bidding with ever more dwindling rations of the Grimsin in return. And then, when we have outlived our usefulness, we are discarded without a second thought!"

"You are free to walk away anytime you wish," Defuria countered. "We'll manage just fine without you."

Trivis hesitated, wishing with all his might that he could have indeed just walked away. Alas, the Grimsin's hold over him was too strong and he reluctantly shook his head. "I don't want to walk away. I...I just want enough Grimsin from this job to be independent for awhile."

"The amounts are not negotiable," Defuria answered. "Take the share offered or leave it Senator. The choice, as always, is yours!"

Trivis slowly nodded his agreement to the terms, hating Defuria for his ruthlessness and hating himself yet more for being hooked on the Grimsin to begin with. How he wished the day that Defuria had approached him all those years ago had never happened. How he wished he was still a free being.

"When you are done feeling sorry for yourself, I want you to finish your task," Defuria said.

Trivis nodded like a drone, his fight all but gone. "I will soften up the ground forces in and around Larep in anticipation of the invasion."

"I assume you have a plan to do it?"

"I'll take care of it," Trivis answered flatly.

Defuria smiled, enjoying the power he held over Trivis. "Good. Because when the Krohns land, I don't want them meeting any undo Namuh resistance. I want them here to help us find the Origin Codex and then butcher the populace. If people are shooting at them, it'll take forever."

"I said I would take care of it!"

"I know you will," said Defuria snidely as he terminated the transmission. "You want the Grimsin too much to fail," he then added to the empty room.

⅄

Fedrin picked up the simmering pot and poured two steaming mugs of fresh lor. He walked over and handed one to Drezden who was seated in a plush armchair facing Fedrin's desk. Fedrin, mug in hand, then walked back over to a porthole and looked out. He sipped his hot drink slowly.

"So, how are you old friend?" Fedrin asked, turning from his window after a few minutes and glancing at his visitor. "We've been stationed in orbit together for almost two months but we've barley had the chance to say hello."

"Yeah, it's funny that we had to go out into deep space to get some time to talk," Drezden nodded in agreement as he sipped from his mug. "Too much going on at home I guess."

"You have no idea," commented Fedrin.

"Pretty bad?" asked Drezden.

Fedrin smiled and shook his head. "When I'm at Larep, everyone wants to talk to me about stuff I don't know about and involve me in meetings I don't belong in. It gets really tiring. All I want is to be in space, away from the politicians, bureaucracy and red tape. I just want to fly my ship and be left alone!"

"I can't imagine."

"If only you knew," Fedrin said as he walked to his desk and fell into his chair. He put his mug on his desk, sat back and rubbed his tired face.

Drezden had been the commander of the first ship Fedrin served aboard, the Purple Nova, a tired old freighter that made the circuit from the Zelin System to Namuh Prime. The Nova would complete the very dull task of ferrying raw materials mined from the asteroid rigs to the home world, and bringing back to the colonies such essentials as provisions, tools and occasionally weapons.

As part of Fedrin's officer training courses, he was required to intern aboard a civilian operated ship and monitor the goings on and then compare it with that of a navy ship and write a volume or two comparing the differences between his experiences and highlighting what the Navy could learn from the private sector and vice versa. It truly was an arbitrarily created assignment but one that had become so engrained in the fabric of the naval officer training program that it would never be done away with. And so it was that Fedrin found himself on the bridge of the Purple Nova, under the care of Commander Drezden, watching and taking notes so that he could write a paper he was sure would never be read. Of all ships to monitor, none could have been duller until that fateful day.

Halfway through his two-month internship, a rogue Krohn escort managed to blast through the Third Fleet blockade and penetrate deep into the system. Prior to being hunted down and destroyed by a small contingent of light cruisers dispatched from the Second Fleet, the escort stumbled upon the Nova and decimated it with several rounds of deadly laser fire. One of the rounds smashed through the bridge and killed the entirety of the command crew save Drezden and Fedrin. Several stray shots also managed to find their way to key systems in the vessel taking out engines, lights and three of the four life support generators. It wasn't until eight days later that fleet emergency ships managed to locate the Nova and rescue her survivors. For eight days, a crew of eighty survived on a generator intended to support twenty. For eight days, Drezden and Fedrin tirelessly kept up morale and strict discipline to keep the men and women of the Purple Nova alive. Between sleeping in shifts, militant rationing of food and water and enforcing a complete and total ban on speaking to conserve air consumption, the precious life support capabilities of the crippled ship managed to keep the entire crew that had survived the initial attack, alive until the rescue. The experience, needless to say, changed those involved forever, but none so much as Fedrin and Drezden, without whom the entirety of the crew would have surely perished.

"Looks like you haven't been sleeping again," Drezden commented after analyzing Fedrin's countenance.

"That obvious?" asked Fedrin, who knew that he must have looked awful.

"You should really cutback on the lor. It looks like it's taking its toll."

"Yeah I guess," said Fedrin as he instinctively reached for his mug.

A message suddenly beeped on Fedrin's data pad.

"What is it?" Drezden asked.

Fedrin set his mug down and looked at the screen thoughtfully. "Looks like one of the Hornell's squadrons located the Refrac Pirates."

"So soon?" Drezden exclaimed. "Is everything going ok?" he asked, leaning over to view the screen for himself.

Fedrin nodded. "Looks like the Hornell is pulling back and all fighter squadrons are launching."

"The Hornell boys in those new Comet Fighters will eat them for a snack!" Drezden said followed by a hearty laugh. "It won't even be a fair fight!"

"Indeed," Fedrin said with a smile. "I almost feel sorry for them."

Drezden raised an eyebrow. "Almost?"

Fedrin shrugged. "If they didn't raid our transports, attack our sentry ships and steal our reconnaissance satellites for spare parts, I might consider feeling sorry for them. But under the circumstances, I want them to all die a painful decompression death once their atmospheres vent..." Fedrin's voice trailed off.

"Well...that was dark," commented Drezden as he shook his head and chuckled.

Fedrin shrugged. "I've had a bad day."

"That you have," Drezden answered. "We all have."

The two men sat in stillness for several minutes. Occasionally Fedrin would glance at the pad to get an update on the skirmish while Drezden sat back in his chair sipping his lor and looking thoughtfully about the room. In the back of each of their minds ran thoughts about the dire situation they were all in, but neither wanted to discuss it.

Drezden finally broke the silence after looking at a picture on Fedrin's cluttered wall. "You miss him...don't you?" he asked.

"Who?" asked Fedrin, looking up from the pad.

"Nebod," Drezden answered as he nodded at the picture.

Fedrin looked up at the picture and then nodded slowly. "I wish he was still here. He would have the right answers for all this stuff going on...I just know he would."

Drezden sat back in his chair and looked thoughtfully at the picture. "So, what is going on Fedrin? What's really going on?"

"What do you mean?" asked Fedrin.

"You know what I mean," Drezden answered. "What's going on at home? You hinted at doing something big at the meeting. The only thing that I can think of that would require all the fleets, would be a coup. Am I far off?"

"I wish I was planning a coup," Fedrin said and shook his head. "If I was planning a coup it would mean I was planning something. As it is, I don't even know where to start."

Drezden looked at Fedrin like he was joking. "Come on Fedrin. I'm your best friend, maybe your only friend. Tell me what's up?"

Fedrin sighed and then looked Drezden square in the eye. "The War Council and the Presidency have both been compromised," he said frankly and then waited for Drezden's reaction.

"How so?" Drezden asked. "The Telecast hasn't pumped anything about that."

"That's because the Telecast doesn't know," Fedrin answered. "Or at least doesn't want everyone else to know."

"And you do?"

Fedrin nodded. "I got a glimpse of the Council's true selves yesterday. They were monsters Drezden. Horrid, evil looking monsters!"

Drezden looked at Fedrin in disbelief. "And the President?"

Fedrin shook his head. "I'm not really sure. He looked the same but he acted irrational and irresponsible when we spoke. He is not on our side, I'm sure of it."

Drezden shook his head and offered an uneasy smile. "I hate to say it Fedrin, but if you're right then I think our pessimistic Commander Sanders was right. We lose."

Fedrin reluctantly nodded. "The next few days will be challenging. There is no doubt."

"Challenging!" Drezden exclaimed and then laughed. "You're talking about an enemy that has cut down the Sixth Fleet and totally wiped out the

Second Fleet in two days Fedrin! Two days! Challenging doesn't even begin to describe the mess we're in!"

"Which is why I told you all in the meeting that we will not win this new war through the might of our ships and strength of our arms!" Fedrin reminded him.

"Then what are you planning to do?" Drezden asked with raised voice. "Send them flowers and ask them to leave?"

Fedrin shrugged. "Stay alive and learn more about what's going on."

Drezden shook his head as he tried to grasp everything Fedrin was saying. "So help me out here," he said as he raised his hand. "Just how are you going to learn more about back home while we're out here? Seems counter-intuitive to me."

Fedrin shook his head. "I haven't really figured that part out yet either."

"Uh huh," Drezden said skeptically.

"We'll think of something," said Fedrin with a sigh. "We always do."

"Maybe the Sions will rescue us again?" said Drezden sarcastically.

Fedrin rolled his eyes.

Drezden smiled and was just about to make another sarcastic comment but abruptly stopped as he spotted the Defiant come up into view in the large porthole behind Fedrin. He immediately stood to his feet and approached the window, awestruck at the sight.

"Sometimes I don't really appreciate how beautiful she is," said Drezden as he soaked in the sight of his ship, his home, his one and only true love.

"She is a fine vessel," Fedrin agreed, as he amusingly watched his friend's eyes dance over every contour of the craft as the orange glow of the Defiant's engines illuminated his face.

"Fine doesn't begin to describe her," Drezden said, not turning away.

Fedrin smiled. "She's a far cry from the Nova. That's for sure."

Drezden chuckled.

"How about those burn streaks?" Fedrin jeered, nodding at the black-ened marks inflicted by the explosions and subsequent fires at the docks.

SPACE EMPIRES

Drezden shrugged. "I kind of like them. It gives her more character...like she's actually done something in this war other than just fly around and look pretty."

Fedrin smirked and turned back to the ship. "Now she gets to fly around doing nothing while looking ugly."

"Her time will come," Drezden said, his eyes still fixed on her. "She'll show up all the other ships in the fleet. Just wait Fedrin."

"I'll be waiting a long time," Fedrin said in a patronizing tone. "Those destroyers really throw their weight around when the Krohn battleships are closing in."

A few moments of quiet passed before Drezden turned back to face his friend. "Fedrin, you're in a tough spot right now. I don't envy your position or the decisions you will have to make in the coming days. But I want you to know that I will back up any course of action you suggest wholeheartedly, regardless of the consequences. As I was to Nebod, I am also yours to command. If you say on to Namuh Prime, I'll be right there spear fronting the fleet. If you want to float around the system for a few weeks doing recon, we'll be there. Regardless of what you chose to do with your fleets, be sure to trust your instincts. Nebod chose you for a reason Fedrin. Although we may not understand why, he saw something in you that he knew we would all need when the time came. I believe that time is now and the decisions you are about to make will be the ones you were born to make."

Drezden finished speaking and the two men stood there for a moment longer not saying anything; nothing more needed to be said. After several more quiet minutes had passed, Drezden picked up his uniform jacket and left the room quietly, leaving his student, friend, comrade and now leader, alone at his window.

CHAPTER 7

THE SIONS

Tarkin removed his worn leather vest and tossed it over the rail of a vacant bed in his room. After kicking off his boots into a corner, he stretched all three pairs of his mighty arms before letting out a deep sigh and making his way toward his washroom to make ready for bed. He had had a long day and was most anxious to indulge in several hours of much needed rest before the intense learning program Kesler was subjecting him to was to start all over again in the morning. He had indeed learned much in his first few days but much more awaited him if he was to become an acting officer on the bridge.

After a quick shower, Tarkin climbed into the doublewide bed, a luxury he had cleverly arranged by pushing two of the single beds together, and let out another contented sigh. Once in bed, he glanced at the refurbished data pad he had been issued on his nightstand and then looked at the imposing stack of memory cards beside it. Each card contained required reading assignments selected by Lieutenants Kesler and Jonas detailing the standard ship operational procedures that all officers must master. Although having already studied much of the material on his own, there were still a number of classified training modules that he did not have access to prior to his impromptu joining of the Navy.

Although his first days serving in the fleet had been hectic, Tarkin had never been happier. Working aboard a Namuh Fleet vessel, let alone the Iovara of all ships, had been a dream of Tarkin's since he was a boy. The fact that he was finally acting on his dream was almost too much for him to believe.

"Don't set your sights too high," Tarkin's dad used to say when they'd be working together in the fields on their world. "Aiming too high will make you miss everything. But don't aim too low either," he would always add later, giving his son a reassuring smile. "You want to aim for what you can get. That'll make you the happiest." Tarkin smiled upon recalling his father's words. If only he could see him now.

He was just reaching for the data pad when he momentarily stopped and glanced around the large room filled with empty dressers, tables and beds. For the first time since his arrival he came to the harsh realization that the luxury he was enjoying of having his own room, had come at the expense of hundreds of men and women perishing or being left behind following the dock explosions just two days earlier. Dozens upon dozens of the ship's barracks were well below capacity, leaving the ship alarmingly low on personnel, forcing key officers to run mandatory double shifts just to keep the ship running. Although Kesler had yet to finalize his roll call, Tarkin had overheard in the mess hall that well over six hundred of the crew were missing and presumed dead including all of the atmospheric pilots.

Sobered by the realization, Tarkin picked up his data pad with renewed focus and determination. He was needed, maybe not wanted by all, but needed nonetheless.

Now ready to spend several hours studying when he'd rather be sleeping, Tarkin inspected the data pad in his large hands. The model was older and more archaic then the ones he was used to. He turned it around and around, up and down, side to side and back and forth. Eventually he began pressing every button he could find before giving up in frustration and reached for his tele-link.

"This is Data Tech. How can I help you?" a disinterested voice responded over Tarkin's link.

"Yes, hi thank you. I need help with my data pad please," said Tarkin in the nicest voice possible.

"What seems to be the trouble, Sir?" the technician asked in near robotic tone.

"Well...I seem to be having a small problem initiating primary applications," answered Tarkin as he continued to turn the machine over and over trying to figure it out.

The other end was quiet for a moment. "Do you mean you can't turn it on?" the technician finally clarified.

Tarkin cringed at how his problem sounded. This was not a great way to earn your place on a ship where eight out of ten crewmen were racist against you. "That's correct, Sir. I'm sorry. I've worked a number of data pads but never one quite like this."

"Is this that Branci fellow that was in my office earlier today?" the tech interrupted.

"It's possible," Tarkin said, knowing that he was the only Branci aboard. "I've been in a lot of offices today and I..."

"Stupid creatures," muttered the tech. "Ok. Bring it down. I'll draw some pictures to help you understand."

"Pictures won't be necessary, Sir," Tarkin said, holding his tongue back from what he wanted to say. "I just need to be shown how to turn it on and use the data card reader."

"Whatever," answered the technician.

"Great! I'll be there in ten minutes."

"Don't hurry," the tech said. "I just ate about fifteen minutes ago. If I see your face too soon I might lose my dinner all over my keyboard. Have you ever dug out processed food chunks from between keys before? It's not as fun as it sounds. Believe me!"

Tarkin ended the transmission and got out of bed. It was going to be a long, restless night.

⋏

"Is your mind open?"

Fedrin looked up to see the unsettlingly familiar hooded form standing in the middle of his room. Before he could respond or call for help, his room began to vanish before his eyes. First his desk faded away, followed by the accompanying chair. Next went his floors and then the ceiling and doors. At last, only the cloaked figure remained surrounded by a dreary gray mist.

"Is your mind open?" the figure asked again.

Fedrin tried to move but could not. "Who are you? Where am I?" he called out.

"Is your mind open?" the figure asked once more.

"You tell me where I am!" Fedrin shouted.

"You must calm yourself," the figure said in a tranquil, yet authoritative voice. "This neural interface already puts a great deal of stress on your fragile physiology. Prolonged agitation could harm you."

"That's just swell!" snapped Fedrin, still struggling to move.

"Please, do not be alarmed," the figure continued in a tone that tried to sound soothing but wasn't working for Fedrin. "Your corporal unit will endure no lasting damage during the short period the link is active. However, if you continue to be so frantic, you may potentiate the negative effects of the interface. Now, if you will be so kind as to wait just a few moments, the elders will be with you shortly."

The red hooded figure finished speaking, bowed to Fedrin and then turned and walked away, disappearing into the shadows of the surreal place.

Fedrin hadn't understood half of what the figure had said, but he did manage to get the message that he had to calm down, which he tried to do, although it was not an easy task. Going from sleeping soundly in his own bed one minute, to being brought to a strange foreboding place the next by a faceless creature was not Fedrin's idea of a calm evening.

The place he found himself in was massive. It appeared to be circular with multiple dim lights evenly spaced out on the floor near the wall. The walls themselves arched up mightily and formed an imposing dome, the breadth of which Fedrin could not guess.

In the center of the mighty room, mere feet from Fedrin, was a tree. It had long since died, evident by the dried and withered look of the branches. Yet it stood erect with the help of a few subtly placed supports and was protected from further decomposition by a glass case that had been carefully constructed around it. An inscription was engraved along one side of the case in symbols that Fedrin did not understand.

The place was old...terribly, terribly old and resonated with a peculiar air of sacredness and power.

The lights at the base of the dome cast an eerie array of shadows on the wall, which Fedrin found himself studying when he noticed one move, ever so slightly. He looked at it harder to see if his eyes were playing tricks on him. It moved again, this time he was certain. And then, before he could decide what was happening, it started gliding along the wall toward the floor as if it were descending an invisible staircase. No discernible figure could be made out, yet its movements were elegant and precise. Fedrin's gaze was fixed on it when out of the corner of his eye, he caught more movement. Another figure was descending along the wall in a downward fashion, again as if it were gliding down a flight of stairs without effort. Then he saw another, this time on his right, and then another on his left again. In all, nine figures emerged and slowly floated down the sloped walls, making their respective ways toward the rectangular lights at the base of the wall.

The first shadowy figure reached one of the lights and instantly morphed from an unformed essence, into a tall graceful figure clad in a yellow robe with a heavy hood covering its face and long wavy sleeves that covered the arms and hands so that no physical part of the figure could be seen. The figure stood on the light at the base of the room, perfectly poised and perfectly still, appearing almost lifeless to Fedrin's eyes.

Seven more of the figures found their way to vacant light pads and assumed similar forms and identical garments. A white sash was girded about each of the robed figures and clasped together by a large golden buckle at the front. Fastened to the sash was a thin sword sheathed in a rigid black case, which was ordained in intricate golden designs.

The last shadow descended slower than the rest. It gracefully descended onto the light fixture at the base of the floor in the center of the room and took on a similar physical form as the others but donned a deep black robe instead of yellow and could hardly be made out against the darkened walls of the room. He too had a white sash tied about him but had in place of a sword, a beautifully ornate dagger hung.

No part of any of the figures could be seen, their long robes and hoods covering them completely. All was quiet and tranquil and Fedrin was pondering whether he should speak when the red hooded figure again appeared from seemingly nowhere and took up position to one side of Fedrin. He raised a covered arm and gesturing to Fedrin, began to speak.

"Chief Admiral Fedrin of the Namuh Protective Federation's Navy, the High Council of Elders of the United Sion Star Systems, welcomes you and wishes you a long, and fulfilled life."

There it was! The word Fedrin was hoping and praying to hear ever since he could remember. Sions! They had returned! Feelings of excitement and relief built up like at no other time in his life. Surely they were here to help the Namuh once again! Perhaps all was not lost after all?

"It is my honor to represent both my race, as well as the Branci which are allied with us, to you," answered Fedrin, trying hard to restrain his newfound exhilaration.

The figure to Fedrin's side continued. "In attendance this hour are the eight system Chancellors of the United Systems, as well as our Sovereign Lord Chancellor, the servant of Yova, the great Trab who rules on high."

"All hail Trab, the servant of Yova," all the figures said in unison.

Fedrin nodded in the direction of the figure wearing the black robe with the dagger, assuming correctly that this was Trab.

The speaker faced the Chancellors and continued. "On unanimous decision, we have summoned this Namuh before us this hour as a representative of his people."

"All hail Fedrin!" the robed figures said together.

The speaker continued. "As is the will of all Sions and our Sovereign Lord Chancellor and servant to Yova, Trab..."

"All hail, Trab, the servant of Yova!" they said yet again.

The speaker kept on, unfazed by the interruptions. "As it is Yova's will, so is it our will, that all of Yova's created races honor and worship him."

The speaker's hooded head turned toward Fedrin. "Chief Admiral Fedrin, do you agree with this, our greatest order?"

Fedrin looked at the envoy and then scanned the room as if looking for an answer from the other faceless figures lined against the wall. When no answer came, he forced a smile and looked back at the messenger. "To tell you the truth, I have no idea what you are talking about," he sincerely said and then felt extremely stupid for appearing so ignorant before so great a gathering.

"We humbly apologize," the envoy said promptly, making a slight bow from his waist. "Our Namuh vocabulary is not perfect. I will attempt to redefine the Sion Order in terms that are hopefully more compatible with your..."

"That is enough!" a very deep voice from underneath the black robe bellowed out. "I will take it from here."

Without a word, the red-cloaked figure at Fedrin's side stepped out of the way, bowing at the waist toward Trab as he slowly made his way toward Fedrin. He came closer and closer until he stood directly before Fedrin. He raised one of his covered arms. A wisp of wind hit Fedrin's face and before he knew what was happening, the domed room vanished and for a brief moment he saw nothing but a deep empty blackness that seemed to swallow him up.

"Hello!" Fedrin called out, his words dissipating before they even left his tongue as if smothered by the permeating blackness. "Hello!" he yelled again, barely able to hear his own utterance.

The blackness gradually cleared and Fedrin found himself on a steep mountaintop overlooking a beautiful valley just before sunset. In the center of the dale was a sparkling city more magnificent and imposing then anything Fedrin had ever seen! Four colossal buildings, each at least a thousand floors high, marked each corner of the sprawling metropolis. Within the central parts of the city were all manners of other fantastic buildings, each beautifully designed with massive arches and geometric designs protruding out of them at all points. Many of the enchanting structures were made out of materials that glistened in the fading rays of sunlight more beautifully than the best, polished gems in all the Federation.

The various structures took hold of Fedrin's imagination and held it captive in a world of amazing accomplishments and mind bending wonders he could only dream of. Unlike the buildings of Larep and other large Namuh cities that were built first and foremost for function, with only a hint of aesthetic effort slapped on the superstructure as an afterthought, these buildings seemed to have been designed in the opposite direction. Beautiful designs, intricate harmony and natural forms gave the behemoth structures such exquisite grace that they needed no true purpose rather than existence itself.

"Magnificent, isn't it?" the deep voice of Trab asked as he walked up beside Fedrin.

"I've never seen anything more beautiful in my whole life," Fedrin replied gawking, his gaze still transfixed below, unable to turn his head even if he wanted to.

Both Fedrin and Trab gazed at the stunning city for several minutes in contemplative silence until Trab finally spoke again. "Do you know who created you Fedrin?"

"Created?" asked Fedrin.

"Yes," answered Trab. "Who created your people?"

"Well," Fedrin said awkwardly, "No one really created us. We exist because of the adaptive process of progression."

"Progressionism," said Trab quietly as if he'd heard of it before. "Don't tell me that you believe that you evolved from a single cell organism in a swamp somewhere?"

Fedrin wanted to change his answer but didn't even know how too. He instead said nothing and waited for Trab to continue.

"I knew it," said Trab in a disgusted, but not angry voice. "It seems that this is the favorite tool of the enemy. I've seen it used so many times over the ages and yet its potency never ceases to astound me."

"What are you talking about?" implored Fedrin.

Trab shook his head. "It astounds me that a relatively sophisticated people such as yours, can unanimously credit some illogical, astronomically improbable event with the creation of something as miraculous and beautiful as life."

Fedrin tried to look up and see Trab's face but gave up and looked ahead. "What else is there to believe?"

"What else?" Trab asked, his voice obviously trying to hold back his dismay. "Fedrin look over there, toward the upper right of the city," he said, pointing his covered arm toward a corner of the city below.

"What am I looking for?" asked Fedrin.

"The azure tower to the west side of the hovering waterfall structures," replied Trab. "Do you see it?

"I do," Fedrin said as he scrutinized what appeared to be one of the more fantastic buildings, boasting an array of architectural elements never before dreamed of on Namuh Prime.

"What would you say if I told you that structure came into being without an architect?" posed Trab.

"Come again?" asked Fedrin.

"What if that tower was just the lucky recipient of many cosmic and geologic accidents? What if the tons of materials and technology incorporated in its construction simply fell into place over a period of time until it finally took the finished form we see it as today?"

"Impossible," Fedrin answered, seeing where the exercise was headed but unable to steer away from it.

"But what if time was no factor?" Trab pressed. "What if enough constructive accidents and improbable events happened over the course of millions, billions or even trillions of years? Couldn't enough time eventually allow even the possibility that the building could build itself?"

Fedrin thought for a moment before reluctantly responding. "Even with unlimited time, the laws of the universe would not allow it."

"And you'd be correct in such a statement," Trab responded. "But, take what you just said to me about your progressionism belief Fedrin. Your very own body is a compilation of countless simultaneous chemical, physical and electrical-dynamic processes that operate in such amazing harmony that the best scientists in the universe will never be able to emulate it. By comparison, a single cell of your body dwarfs not only the accomplishment of that tower but of the entire city! And yet, you credit the miracle of life to chance?

A cataclysmic explosion followed by a series of genetic mutations over the course of eons? It makes no sense, Fedrin! In fact, it defies sense! It is contrary to the laws of entropy that govern the universe!"

"It does sound strange when you word it like that," Fedrin confessed. "And I mean no disrespect Trab, but what does our origin, or my belief of that origin, have to do with anything?"

"Everything!" shouted Trab, his strong voice echoing over the valley. "It has to do with why we brought your consciousness here! It has to do with why we must fight evil with good! It has to do with our purpose for even existing!"

Fedrin replied simply. "Tell me how."

Trab breathed in deeply and then exhaled. "Before the beginning, before time was time, before the planets were formed, before life was created there was only Yova, the creator."

Fedrin found himself rolling his eyes. "Creator? As in a god?"

"Precisely," answered Trab unfazed by Fedrin's lack of faith. "Yova saw fit to fill the emptiness of space with innumerable stars and planets which were his chosen medium to support the greatest of all of his creations, life. Millions of different forms he created, each one different, each one beautiful in its own special way."

"And why did he do this?" asked Fedrin skeptically. "To watch them torture themselves and be miserable? If so, this god is a pretty messed up guy!"

Trab walked in front of Fedrin and sat on a grassy bank beside him. The folds of his robe flowed in the gently breeze as he spoke. "Yova made these life forms for one reason and one reason only Fedrin."

"And that was?"

"Companionship."

Silence followed. "Companionship huh?" Fedrin finally said. "Sounds farfetched."

"It doesn't it all," answered Trab promptly. "Think of it this way. If you were the greatest painter in the world, would you not want others to see your work and comment on it? Would you not want galleries to be built and stories to be written about your pieces? Would you not want praise for what you had accomplished? Would you not be righteously angered for those who praised others for the work you had done? Although on a much grander scale, so too does Yova wish to be acknowledged as the great artist, architect and creator that he is! He desires his creations to love, honor and admire him for what he has done and in return for their praise, receive fellowship, love and blessings from him. For what glory is there in being a magnificent artist without an audience to display for?"

As Trab spoke, Fedrin thought back to his days at the Central Larep University where he studied for several years prior to attending the Military Academy. He vaguely remembered some gray-haired, university professor lecturing on the obscure theories of intelligent design and other equally bizarre superstitions of ancient days. At the time, Fedrin had shrugged them off as primitive folklore. But now, in the presence of this powerful and obviously more advanced being, the thoughts were becoming less and less primitive by the moment.

"Lets say for sake of argument you're right," Fedrin voiced up. "Lets say this universe was made for some god to brag about how awesome he his. If that really is the case, and I'm not saying it is, he really messed things up. Either that or you've got your fairytales confused because last time I looked around, there wasn't a lot of love and fellowship going on."

Trab turned his hooded face toward Fedrin and spoke sorrowfully. "The whole of creation has indeed been corrupted by a growing darkness Fedrin. It spreads from planet to planet debasing all it comes in contact with. Where it finds love, it introduces hate. Where it finds peace, it teaches war. Where it finds innocence, it brings corruption."

Their conversation paused momentarily as a large shadow slowly cast itself over the precipice on which they stood and a low but distinct rumble sounded throughout the valley growing louder moment-by-moment. They both looked up and watched just as an elegant, mighty craft flew stealthily overhead. The ship itself was like nothing Fedrin had ever seen before. It bore all the same elegance and beauty of the towers comprising the Sion city, while at the same time resonating with awesome strength and authority a hundred times more potent than that of the Iovara.

"The Conquer has returned from the front," remarked Trab, the word "Conquer" resonated deep inside Fedrin and nearly giving him chills.

"She's...she's beautiful," Fedrin stammered, imagining it flying side by side with his own ships battling the Krohns and whoever else dared challenge them.

"I'm sorry Fedrin, but we have no ships to spare," Trab suddenly said, as if he had been reading Fedrin's mind. "We need every last one we have for our own war."

Before Fedrin could reply, three more ships appeared overhead, rumbling loudly, following the same flight path as the Conquer. All had the general appearance of the former, yet they were each badly damaged. Large burn marks streaked across their hulls, huge indented explosive marks spotted their fuselages and small streams of smoke trailed behind their engine cores.

"What has happened?" implored Fedrin in awe.

Trab's voice was still filled with sadness as he answered. "They too have returned from the front...all that remains from a battle group of thirty such ships."

For the first time since he had heard fabled stories of them from his youth, Fedrin suddenly realized that the Sions were not omnipotent, near immortal beings as he had been taught and believed. These mighty and powerful beings were quite mortal, and their ships were not indestructible. The realization was sobering.

"With whom are you at war?" Fedrin earnestly inquired, almost not wanting to know of a race powerful enough to take out Sion warships by the dozen.

Trab paused before answering, as if the answer weighed on his mind. "We war against a dark power known to us as the Unmentionables," he began. "They are the legacy of terrible demons that once roamed these stars and now act as a scourge upon all of Yova's creations. Equipped with sinister abilities to deceive others and mask their appearance, they have started innumerable wars, wiped out entire civilizations and inflicted untold sufferings in their wake."

"Have they ever acted against us?"

Trab nodded. "Until recently, we have effectively stood against them in their efforts to openly attack you. But they have managed to reach you over the years by orchestrating the Refrac Conflict and more recently by stirring up the Krohns against you. And regrettably, they have also since infiltrated your society and are responsible for a number of recent travesties including the destructions of the Sixth and Second Fleets."

Dozens of questions began to race through Fedrin's thoughts. He wanted to ask them all but wasn't sure where to start. His head was beginning to hurt as it had done during the first Sion visit and he began to realize that the pain was a limitation of the communication system they were utilizing.

"You say they can mask their appearance," he finally stated as he tried to ignore the building pain. "Does that explain why my government has images of me in the dock security cams even though I wasn't there?"

"That is but a small sampling of what they are capable of doing," answered Trab. "They have used their chicanery with utmost proficiency to subjugate entire races to do their bidding. And in truth Fedrin, they have seeded many agents within your own Federation with assumed and stolen identities, just waiting for their time to act."

"But that doesn't make any sense!" Fedrin objected. "Why go through all this covert effort to undermine us when we pose no threat to them?"

"Aside from their ambition to dominate all of creation, your people possess something of great value that they earnestly desire," replied Trab.

Fedrin looked up curiously. "And what is that?"

"A tree," answered Trab.

A throb of pain suddenly erupted in Fedrin's head and it took all his willpower not to call out in agony. As the pain grew, the city began to fade from view.

"No!" Fedrin called out, realizing the link was ending.

"You have activated the failsafe," Trab announced, explaining to Fedrin why the session was abruptly ending. "Your physiology cannot maintain this link any longer."

"But I still have more questions!" Fedrin yelled.

"And we will provide answers," replied Trab. "But not now."

Fedrin's eyes immediately opened and he sprang from bed in near delirium as his faculties slowly returned. Once alert and calmed down, he sat down at his chair panting for breath and holding his head as the unbearable pain from moments earlier, slowly subsided.

"A tree?" he said to himself and then shook his head. He now had more questions then ever before and no foreseeable plan for finding any answers.

⋏

The officer burst through the door and ran down the cluttered hall, fiercely clutching a piece of paper in his hand. Packed boxes, cheap shelving units and stacks of near toppling paperwork created formidable obstacles for the young officer to navigate as he fought his way to the office at the end of the hall.

"General! General Darion!" he called out as he nearly tripped over a carelessly placed data card case outside the door. "General, we got it!" he finished and gasped for breath as he presented the man behind the desk with the wrinkled paper.

The man behind the desk was General Darion. He was as conceited as they came but not without reason. He was tall, good-looking and at thirty-two years, was very young for his position as Chief General over the combined land forces in Larep. He was generally popular with his men and even more popular with the ladies. When not in uniform, he wore clothes that were out of his price range and slightly too young for him. He held a reputation of being the "playboy general" which he enjoyed thoroughly as it made him the center of attention at every party and club that he attended (which was often). Gone were the days when being a general was synonymous with honor and valor. In the anemic realm of the Namuh Army, it was nothing more than a status symbol, which Darion flexed at every opportunity.

And so it was that the playboy general slowly looked up from his data pad where he had been chatting with several women for the last hour and slowly reached for the paper being thrust upon him by his young officer. His eyes quickly skimmed over the contents until a slight smile crept over his pampered face.

"What's going on in here?" Field Marshall Jarvik asked, appearing in the doorway. "Loson, you off your meds again?"

"Oh you're so funny!" replied Loson with a role of his eyes. "Check it out," he added with a nod toward the paper.

"Is that what I think it is?" Jarvik asked, his eyes suddenly gleaming with anticipation.

"Sure is!" Loson replied. "A senate courier just delivered it downstairs."

Jarvik squeezed into the small office. "Well, don't just stare at me like that General! What does it say?"

General Darion's smile grew and he turned back to the paper and began to read. "General Darion: on behalf of the Defense Expenditure Appropriation Committee, we are pleased to grant your increase of requested fiscal assets available immediately."

"Hoorah!" Jarvik shouted as he pumped his clenched fist in the air. "Its about time!"

"What's all the commotion about?" yet another officer inquired as he poked his head into the office.

"We were granted our budget increase!" Loson announced. "Who's ready to go shopping?"

"I'm going tonight!" Darion said and laughed loudly. "Then after that, it's party time!"

The officers cheered.

It was hard to believe, but it was true. After eleven months of lobbying and nearly begging, the Nineteenth District Army had finally received their increase in funds. General Darion, the interim executive officer over the district, had called in all favors and had even gone into debt on a few others to get the right result.

The result itself was an incredible feat: an increase in funds for a ground based military unit. It was the first time since the Refrac War that a tactical ground force had received an increase in funds outside of normal expenses. With the primary emphasis of defense focusing more and more in the extra planetary arena, the home world district forces had undergone extensive atrophy. There just wasn't the need anymore, or so the opponents of the bill had argued, to further fund a land based army when funds were scarce.

Darion opened a drawer in his desk and slid a tall bottle across to his men. "I've been saving this for you," he said and smiled. "You've earned it!"

Loson eagerly reached for the slender bottle but Jarvik quickly grabbed his arm and picked up the bottle himself. "Its for us Loson...not just you," he said followed by a roar of laughter.

"Whoa General!" one of the other officers exclaimed upon examining the bottle. "Real fruit juice? Where did you get it?"

Darion smiled. "It was a gift," he said not at all convincingly.

His officers smirked, knowing the costly bottle had most likely been part of a military contract bribe.

"Its bottled on the Branci home world!" Loson suddenly exclaimed as he pointed at the markings on the face of the bottle. "You better start upping your gift standards General. Now that we have the money I want to start seeing some real signs of affection from these contractors. No more of these Branci imports."

Darion smiled. "I'll pass your comments along."

"Hey, if you don't want any I'll have your share," Jarvik said.

"I didn't say that," Loson said as a he shoved an empty glass toward Jarvik. "I just hope the bottlers washed their hands this time. So help me if I find another Branci beard hair in my glass again..."

The other officers looked at Loson in bewilderment.

"You've got issues," Jarvik said with a shake of his head. "Serious issues."

Loson shrugged. "I'm just saying."

Jarvik shook his head. "To Senator Trivis!" he called out as he lifted up the bottle to the ceiling and began to pour each man a full serving of the juice...a rare delicacy in any quarter of the Federation but especially on the desert home world.

"Senator Trivis!" Loson repeated, toasting the air and then downing his entire glass. "I knew I should have voted for him!" he added followed by hearty laughs all around.

The revelry slowly made its way out of Darion's cramped office and toward the conference room at the opposite end of the cluttered hall. Darion smiled as he closed his door in a vain attempt to drown out the noise. It had taken all of them months of long days and sleepless nights writing letters, lobbying politicians and finding the right leads to get their bill approved. It wasn't an easy sell. The deciding factor finally came down to the seemingly all-powerful Senator Trivis. He had been convinced of their cause only three days prior, following a long conversation with Darion and the Defense Council immediately after the Sixth Fleet disaster.

And while the destruction of a majority of the Sixth Fleet would have seemed to spell doom for the bill, Trivis had masterfully turned the tragedy into stark realization of the vulnerability of the ground defenses, which led to a landslide ruling in favor of the bill.

Darion set the report on his desk and then glanced around his cramped little office. Rodent holes littered the floorboards of the yellowed walls and the ceiling sagged in several places due to a series of neglected roof problems. Cobwebs occupied the corners and dust coated nearly every surface. Yet, it was the best facility Darion could find with his bare-bones budget after the destruction of the Defense Complex nearly a year ago. He smiled at the thought of the nice offices he could rent with the money he was just awarded. He pictured a nice suite in one of the bigger Larep skyscrapers with a sprawling view of downtown.

"That would do quite nicely," he reasoned and then smiled.

CHAPTER 8

REVELATIONS

"We are receiving a transmission from the Hornell," Ensign Gallo announced after Fedrin stepped onto the bridge

"Transfer it to the main screen," ordered Fedrin as he made his way to his seat and looked up.

The multilevel main viewing screen in the front of the room came to life and Commander Kendrick's jolly, bearded face filled it up.

"Hello there, Admiral!" bellowed Kendrick, followed by a hearty laugh. "It's good to be back with the fleet! There's nothing quite like coming along side the Iovara's big guns to make a fella feel safe in bed at night!"

Fedrin smiled. "I heard you had good hunting?"

Kendrick chuckled. "If I had shot a tied up norpis calf in a pen at point blank range with a rocket launcher, it would have been better sport."

The Iovara officers laughed, a few clapped.

"But it was nice to get the pilots familiar with the new Comet Fighters," added Kendrick. "They've been itching to use them on something other than drones...though I still think our drones do better than those Refrac. I never saw a sloppier group of ships in all my life. Pitiful!"

"Well thanks for taking care of them just the same," said Fedrin. "Its one less thing we need to worry about."

Kendrick nodded. "Speaking of thanks, with your permission Admiral, I was planning on inviting all the command crews to join us for a small victory celebration this evening!"

The officers on the Iovara Bridge perked up and eagerly looked at Fedrin. Fedrin had a lot of work and planning still to do, but indulging in a party for a few hours wasn't going to drastically change any decisions he was going to make one way or the other. He reluctantly shrugged and nodded. "I suppose we could manage that," he said much to the excitement of his officers.

Tarkin leaned over and whispered to Kesler. "So do I count as command crew yet?"

Kesler smiled. "We'll get you there buddy! Don't you worry."

Tarkin smiled.

"Ok then," Kendrick said. "The meal will be ready in about two hours. Come over anytime before that."

"Sounds great," said Fedrin. "Are you going to break out some of the real food?"

Kendrick looked offended. "Of course we are!" he said and then, laughed. "Life is too short...and getting shorter all the time. We're breaking out everything we've got! Bring your appetites or stay home!"

The Iovara officers cheered, excited at the thought of real food and a chance to unwind, none more so than Tarkin who clapped his three pairs of arms mightily and let out a series of deafening shrieks.

"Better reserve two servings for Tarkin!" commented Jonas followed by a laugh.

"Will do!" said Kendrick with a smile. "Looking forward to meeting him!" he added and then ended the transmission.

"Lieutenant," said Fedrin promptly.

"Sir?" replied Kesler.

"Call up Second Lieutenant Tenith to staff the bridge this evening."

Kesler grimaced as he pictured Tenith, the punk officer that he had never gotten along with, having command of the Iovara. If even for a few hours, having Tenith get a command without a supervising officer aboard before himself, made Kesler rethink the Hornell party altogether. Alas, the allure of fresh food and the chance to hangout with the fleet pilots and his other friends for a few hours was more then he could he resist.

"This party had better be worth it," grumbled Kesler to himself as he reluctantly drafted Tenith's orders.

⤙

Kendrick was the eldest of the commanders in the Sixth Fleet by nearly fifteen years. Due to his seniority, he had a certain amount of personally appointed responsibility for the fleet's well being. He had been loyal to the core to Admiral Nebod when he was alive and was thus a staunch supporter of Fedrin when he was named successor to the Chief Admiralty. Kendrick knew the job was hard but did his best to aid the young admiral whenever and however, he could. With the recent events still weighing heavily on everyone's minds, Kendrick had decided to take the opportunity to defer some of the fleet's collective sorrow and stem any unrest in the disasters' wake. Even if it meant using up the Hornell's entire supply of real food, he was willing to do it in order to support the admiral and encourage his fellow comrades.

Light music crackled over the cheap dinning hall speakers while the Hornell cooks wheeled out large carts from the kitchen filled with all manners of delectable items. Roasted meats of several varieties, crisp vegetables, and even a small amount of fresh fruit adorned the platters that were placed before the wide eyes of the Sixth Fleet officers and Hornell fighter pilots.

"How did you manage to get fruit aboard your ship?" Commander Colby called out to Kendrick as he eagerly helped himself to a second portion. "I didn't even know that was possible!"

Kendrick laughed. "It helps when the dock supervisor is your nephew."

"He risks his position putting unlisted items on your ship just because you're related?" Colby exclaimed. "He must really love you!"

Kendrick shrugged. "It also helps when I pay him a hundred credits per pressurized container to store the fruit in!"

Colby shook his head and laughed. "You're one in a million, Kendrick!"

Forty-five minutes after the third course had been served, the celebration was still going strong. Fedrin smiled to himself as he passively listened to at least seven different renditions, each more magnificent than the one preceding it, of one of the encounters in the battle.

Commander Kendrick laughed as he heard one of the pilots from a different squadron argue about some trite detail that had occurred during the skirmish. "Come now, Mr. Cane," Kendrick said to a pilot sitting across from him. "Surely you and your Kormo wingmen can share some of the credit with Theda Wing?"

Cane laughed and shook his head. "Theda Wing couldn't hit a Krohn cruiser in the butt end with guided missiles if it was sitting still and had a big bull's eye painted on it!"

"Ha!" someone else shouted out across the dinning hall. "That Refrac gun ship is the only thing that Kormo Wing has ever shot down! Let them keep their story! We're better than them any day of the week!" the pilot said and laughed heartily.

Fedrin looked up from his plate and spotted Commander Sanders and Commander Searle in quiet conversation in a calmer corner of the hall. Having both lost close family in the Second Fleet, they felt an affinity toward each other in dealing with their grief. They shared pictures and stories of their loved ones and took turns tearing up. It was a touching, yet sobering sight.

In sharp contrast to the grieving Commanders, Mick, Drezden, and Colby sat at the far end of the commander table away from the commotion of the rowdy pilots and their stories. The men were thoroughly enjoying the meal prepared for them, talking little but eating much. It was indeed rare, even for commanders, to have the dishes being served. None of it was synthetic, not even the thick cuts of rare norpis, which was becoming a delicacy even in the affluent portions of Larep. The three hungry commanders ate more than their fair share and eagerly eyed the portions of others who didn't appear to be as hungry as they.

Kesler, Jonas and Tarkin sat at the other end of the hall with the command crews from the Defiant and Hornell, all seemingly having a grand time.

"Enjoying yourself, Admiral?" asked Kendrick as he walked up behind Fedrin.

"Yes, very much," Fedrin answered with a smile and nod.

"Excellent!" Kendrick said as he pulled up a chair.

"I really appreciate all this," Fedrin said as he nodded around the room. "I know this is a sacrifice on your part to host but I really do appreciate it."

"Oh, think nothing of it," Kendrick said, patting Fedrin on the shoulder. "I just do what I can, when I can."

"Well, thank you just the same," said Fedrin.

"My pleasure. Oh, if you'll pardon me Admiral. Looks like the pilots from Theta Wing are motioning for me again. Do you mind?"

"Not at all," Fedrin answered as he waved toward the group of rowdy pilots.

"Thanks. I'll be back momentarily," Kendrick said.

Fedrin's eyes followed Kendrick toward some of the loudest pilots in the room. He strained to hear what they were saying but couldn't make it out with all the other ruckus and laughter. He smiled and sipped his lor.

Halfway through the evening, Commanders Mick and Colby, stuffed well beyond their comfortable capacity, began debating about engagement tactics when battling certain types of Krohn heavy cruisers. Fedrin heard their differing arguments and disagreed with both, but didn't care to chime in. He just sat there, listening.

The party was winding down and Fedrin was contemplating his departure when an on-duty ensign walked up to him and saluted. "Admiral," the officer said. "We are receiving a priority-one transmission for you."

Fedrin looked up in surprise. "From where?"

"From Larep, Sir," answered the ensign. "Unknown party sending."

Fedrin nodded. "Where can I take it, privately?"

"Right this way, Sir," the officer said and motioned to a side room off of the main dinning hall.

Fedrin stood to his feet and promptly followed the ensign to a small chart room down the hallway from the dinning hall. Upon entering the room, Fedrin closed and locked the door behind himself and the ensign took up position outside to ensure the Admiral's privacy.

Once inside, Fedrin walked immediately over to the tele-link terminal and waited for the transmission list to populate. After a few moments, the screen showed several active transmissions taking place aboard the Hornell between various other ships in the fleet as well as between different stations amidships. The priority one message stood out with a bright red flashing border at the top of the screen.

Fedrin touched the blinking message and waited. He didn't know why but he felt very nervous. He wondered who could be contacting him and even more than that, he wondered why? Finally, the screen flickered to life and revealed a sight Fedrin had not expected to see.

Instead of a familiar face from the war council or the vindictive countenance of the President, an old man looked through the screen nervously. He had a long beard, wild unkempt white hair and wore little round spectacles that were balanced at the tip of his nose. Fedrin immediately recognized him as Professor Jabel, a premier scientist and the architect of the Clear Skies Missile Defense System...the last and strongest line of defense for the home world.

"What can I do for you Professor?" asked Fedrin.

"A lot," replied Jabel. "And I don't have a lot of time so you must listen to me very, very carefully. I won't have time to repeat what I am going to say. Understand?"

"I'm all ears," replied Fedrin anxiously.

Jabel nodded. "Last week every top level scientist, researcher and engineer that developed the Clear Skies system with me was killed or is now missing."

"Really?" exclaimed Fedrin. "I haven't heard a thing about it."

Jabel nodded. "And you won't. Someone is filtering the news outlets."

"I know how that feels," remarked Fedrin as he remembered the slanted portrayal he had received following the dock explosions.

Jabel shook his head. "Once I got wind of my colleagues dying, I went into hiding, fearing that it was only a matter of time before they'd catch up with me."

Fedrin nodded. "So why are you contacting me? Seems like you're still not safe."

"Because I need to warn you Admiral."

"About?" asked Fedrin as he readied himself for more bad news.

Jabel tilted his head to one side as if pondering what he'd say next. "Since I went into hiding, I've been keeping tabs on…things…trying to figure out what's been going on and who's responsible. Late last night, I discovered a virus buried deep in the Clear Skies Missile Defense mainframe."

"A virus?" remarked Fedrin. "What sort of virus?"

Jabel shrugged. "Near as I can figure, it overrides the firing protocols making the system effectively inert."

Fedrin nodded slowly. "So you're saying if an enemy ship approaches Namuh Prime right now, the missiles won't fire?"

"That's correct," answered Jabel.

Fedrin shook his head as he marveled at yet another horrific issue that needed immediate solving. "Can this virus be rooted out?"

Jabel sat back in his chair and stroked his beard. "The virus has rewritten a number of critical systems in the grid. At this point, nothing short of a total mainframe reinstall would fix it."

"Can you do that?" Fedrin asked frankly.

Jabel shrugged. "It can be done, but I need a non-infected copy of the program in order to do it. Reprograming from scratch could take years."

"And I take it you don't have a copy?" asked Fedrin.

"I did," answered Jabel. "It was hidden in a safe in my home which has since burned down…no doubt thanks to the same murderers that killed my colleagues."

"So where does that leave us?" asked Fedrin. "We can't exactly leave Namuh Prime to fend for herself without that grid."

"Quite right Admiral," commented Jabel. "Which is why you must retrieve the second backup copy of the program I created."

"Second copy? Where is it?" Fedrin asked, growing weary with the conversation.

Jabel smiled. "It is with Governor Onkil."

"Governor Onkil?" Fedrin exclaimed, his eyebrows raised. "As in the Voigt colony?"

Jabel nodded.

"Why? How'd you get it there?" exclaimed Fedrin.

Jabel shrugged. "When Governor Onkil was here three weeks ago for the annual Federation Economic Summit, I slipped into his shuttle and tucked it beneath one of the passenger seats."

"Why Onkil?" exclaimed Fedrin. "Why him of all people? He's half a dozen star systems away!"

"That's why," answered Jabel. "I wanted to send it somewhere safe. Somewhere far away from here."

Fedrin shook his head and then shrugged. "So have Onkil send the files in data burst through the relay system," suggested Fedrin. "You'll have them by tonight and we'll be back in business by tomorrow."

Jabel shook his head. "The relay system was destroyed when the Second Fleet went down."

"Of course," Fedrin said with a shake of his head. "Why wouldn't it be?"

"Besides, I don't know Onkil well enough to trust him with the task," added Jabel.

"But you trust me?" Fedrin asked.

Jabel shrugged. "With how much everyone keeps trying to run your name down and pin all our problems on you, I figured you must be legit."

"I see," replied Fedrin, unsure of the logic but satisfied with the conclusion.

"So as I was saying," said Jabel, "the files will have to be retrieved physically from the Voigt Colony and returned aboard ship until you at least recross the break in the relay system at which point you could send them by burst."

Fedrin nodded slowly as he decided a course of action.

"And incase you were considering sending a single ship to retrieve the device, you should also know that a Krohn Battle Fleet is in system thirteen, apparently tracking toward Voigt."

"Thirteen?" Fedrin exclaimed in shock. "There's no way a Krohn fleet could be in thirteen. It's impossible!"

"Impossible or not, it's there," answered Jabel. "And if you want to get the data device before it's destroyed, you better get there quick!"

Fedrin felt as if the wind had been knocked out of him yet again. The flood of bad news knew no limit.

"I'm sorry Fedrin," Jabel finally said in response to Fedrin's evident distress. "But I thought you ought to know."

Fedrin nodded in a daze. "I didn't want to hear any of this but I'm glad I did. Thank you for risking so much to contact me with this information. Many lives may be saved by your efforts today."

Jabel nodded solemnly. "I fear many lives will still be lost by acting on this information but the greater good must be sought."

"Indeed," said Fedrin. "You better stay alive and well in the meantime. You're the only man that can fix Clear Skies now and we need you in one piece when we send you the program files."

Jabel smiled. "Glad to hear you're so concerned about my well being. I will do my best to die only after I've repaired it," he chuckled. "You must know, however, the task that lays before me will not be easy just as yours will not be."

"Can anyone help you?" Fedrin asked. "Anyone you can trust?"

Jabel slowly nodded. "I know a few. Hopefully they'll be up to the task."

"One quick thing," Fedrin said. "I don't know much about what's going on myself, but I do have reason to believe that President Defuria and the Defense Council are not on our side."

"I've had my doubts about them myself but I do thank you for the tip," Jabel said. "I will keep it in mind."

"Anytime," Fedrin said.

"Don't send the data burst until I contact you" Jabel added. "If I'm not at one of the deep space transmitters when you send the burst, it'll just bounce off the cortex."

"Understood," said Fedrin.

"I must be off," said Jabel as he slowly stood to his feet. "It will be daylight here soon and I must conceal myself before the world awakes."

"Best of luck to you!" Fedrin said.

"And to you!" Jabel replied.

Fedrin exhaled deeply and stepped back from the console in a daze. It took all his willpower to reach down to his own tele-link and initiate a new transmission.

"Tenith," the voice of the acting officer sounded out on the link.

"Tenith, this is Fedrin. Plot a course to the Voigt colony in the Sibid System immediately and then forward it to all the ships in the fleet."

"Aye, Sir. Is that it?"

"We are going to have an emergency meeting here on the Hornell before I come back over. Look up Grider. I want him to join us."

"I'm on it."

CHAPTER 9

ONE LEGGED LEGEND

The celebration in the Hornell dining hall ended abruptly when Fedrin reentered the room followed by four guards who immediately took point at all of the exits in the room.

"I hate to spoil your fun," Fedrin shouted out, "but we have just been called to act on a very important operation. I need the room cleaned up and cleared out in five minutes for a private commander meeting. If you don't serve on the Hornell, please wait for your commanders in the waiting areas by your respective shuttles. I also need a warp-point network chart and a standard data pad in here straight away."

The officers, cooks, pilots, and commanders alike, swarmed the room and cleaned it up the best they could. There was electricity in the air as the officers wiped tables, swept the floors and moved dishes. They had been given combat orders, they were almost sure of it. Why else would Larep send a priority one message? Finally, they were going to kill some Krohns!

The room looked like there had never been a party in it when the last officers turned janitors, left the room. The commanders, together with Fedrin, remained in the room gathered around a warp-point chart strewn across a table.

"Let me get this straight," Colby said after Fedrin had presented a synopsis of the situation. "Whatever the things are back home that wiped out half of the Sixth Fleet and presumably the Second, have now taken over the missile defense network?"

Fedrin nodded.

"And the only way to fix Clear Skies is by getting a set of program files from the Voigt colony?" Searle asked, her voice filled with confusion.

"And a full Krohn battle fleet is baring down on the colony?" Drezden added.

"That about sums it up," Fedrin said, realizing how impossibly elaborate the situation sounded. "My contact didn't have time to give me all the details but those are the major points."

Mick shook his head. "What a load of junk! You didn't really believe him Fedrin, did you? Tell me you didn't!"

Fedrin slowly looked down the table to see Mick's scornful face looking straight at him. "That's Admiral to you Commander," Fedrin said sternly. "And yes, I do believe him. With all of the garbage that's been going down these last few days, it only makes sense."

Mick rolled his eyes and stood back from the table.

"I don't get how these Krohns think they are going to get all the way to Voigt," Searle said as she tapped on the star chart. "They have fuel and supply constraints just the same as us, just the same as always. That's just too far away from any known Krohn base."

"I agree," Sanders said with a nod. "Something here just doesn't seem legitimate. Could the satellite network be malfunctioning?"

"Is that even possible?" Kendrick asked. "I thought there were a host of safeguards to avoid getting corrupted signals?"

"They could be operating with new ship designs that can cover further distances between refueling," Colby suggested as he too leaned over the chart, trying to figure out how this tactical nightmare was happening.

"Or perhaps the Krohns have setup a supply depot right before system thirteen?" Drezden suggested pointing at the little known star system. "Our intel past thirteen is sketchy at best. Who knows what they've got in there?"

Fedrin raised his hands to quiet the commanders. "It doesn't really matter how the Krohns managed to pull this off at the moment. As far as I'm

SPACE EMPIRES

concerned they did, and we need to stop them from wiping out the Voigt colony."

"So you want to bring what's left of our ragtag fleet to stop a full force Krohn battle force?" Mick asked derisively.

"We wouldn't be alone," Colby corrected. "The colony has some defenses of her own too."

Mick tapped the chart and looked at Colby as if he were an idiot. "First of all, the colony's defenses are a joke. Counting on them for anything is nothing short of reckless! Secondly, even if we headed there right now, looks to me like we'd still get there several hours after the Krohn ships! Getting there after is fine, if all we are going to do is put people in body bags!"

"We'll be four hours and fifteen minutes late, to be precise," Fedrin clarified. "Assuming we leave within the next half hour."

Mick tossed his hands in the air. "You've already done the math I see. So are we just going to post some signs asking the Krohns not to attack the colony until we get there? I don't understand what your thought process is!"

"Great idea Mick!" Sanders exclaimed. "We'll post signs! Any other clever words you'd like to share with us or would you rather just shut up and let us sort this out like adults?"

"Ok, that's enough!" Fedrin said raising a hand. "It is true that we can only get to the colony once the battle has already begun but the battle will be far from over when we arrive. We will still have plenty of opportunity to engage the Krohns, save what's left of the colony and retrieve the data device. Granted it sounds far fetched, but I'm failing to see other choices at this juncture."

"And don't count out the Voigt defenses so hastily Mick," Kendrick added. "Between the Ilo Battle Station and the fighter squadrons stationed on the planet, she'll be able to hold her own for quite awhile."

"And what of the Idok?" the tactical wizard Colby added, pointing to the blue dot one star system above Sibid. "Maybe she could help during the initial attack to buy time for the rest of us to get there?"

Drezden looked up sharply at Fedrin, realizing the personal implications of Colby's suggestion. Yet Fedrin did not show any hint of emotion on his face. If everyone in the room hadn't known better, they would have never guessed that Fedrin's wife was the commander of the Idok. In contrast to his complacent appearance however, Fedrin was a wreck on the inside. He had known it was only a matter of time before someone would bring up his wife's ship.

"I was actually planning for the Idok to rendezvous with us once we enter Sibid and engage the Krohns with us," Fedrin replied. "It'll make our force that much more formidable when we engage them."

"Ha!" Mick exclaimed. "Doesn't mind letting everyone else die, but mention his wife's ship and suddenly he's all conservative and playing it safe!"

That was it! Fedrin had been patient, understanding, and even went out of his way to ignore the dissident commander. But this was the last straw! Before anyone knew what was happening, Fedrin had reached across the table, grabbed Mick by the collar, and slammed him down, face first, into the table. Mick struggled to free himself but was no match for Fedrin.

"You've crossed me for the last time!" Fedrin said before rolling him over the table and onto the floor. "Guards! Escort Mick back to his shuttle."

Two guards ran up from the doors and pulled Mick to his feet and held him firmly.

"Mr. Mick, as of right now, your rank and commission are withdrawn! You will be escorted back to your ship where you will surrender your command authority to your first lieutenant and then be placed in the brig!"

Mick looked at Fedrin with disdain, and then glanced around the room at the other commanders for someone to voice their objections or back him up. Only silence and hardened faces answered his pleading gaze. Without another word spoken in protest, Mick turned and walked out of the room, escorted closely by the guards.

"You did the right thing," Kendrick said after Mick had gone. "Mick has crossed the line once to often. It's about time someone put him in his place."

Several of the other commanders nodded in agreement.

Fedrin, too, reluctantly nodded and was just about to continue with his briefing when the doors leading into the room were swung opened by the two remaining guards posted outside. Coming through the doorway was the legendary former Admiral Grider. Several commanders gasped at the unprecedented sight of the one-legged, old man sitting in his hover chair as he approached the table. He pulled up to a place where he could see the chart and quickly spotted the Krohn fleet marker in star system thirteen. He instantly analyzed and understood the entire situation at hand and then looked up at Fedrin.

Grider was the oldest living member of the Namuh Fleet. He had been a commodore when the Refrac War began and finished the war as Vice Admiral over the Second Fleet. At the start of the Krohn War, he still held the rank of Vice Admiral. Due to health issues, extensive age, and generally acknowledged eccentricity, he was asked by the then Chief Admiral Nebod, to relinquish his responsibilities and serve as an advisor, a course of action that Grider initially resisted but eventually agreed to when faced with his other option, forced retirement. Although his position was more nominal then anything else, it was the least Nebod could offer the man that was credited with holding back the Refrac advance for the three critical months during the infamous 'Refrac Spring Offensive' and holding on until the Sions came to the rescue.

Although old and justifiably accused of being crazy by most commanders, Fedrin knew Grider was a true genius, which is why he had invited him to attend. Even though Fedrin had pretty much used up all of his own ideas, he wanted to try and tap Grider's brilliant, strategic mind once more. Perhaps with Grider and the other commanders, they could find an option that solved all the dilemmas currently facing them. It couldn't hurt to try.

Grider nodded again toward Fedrin and then gave an inclusive nod to the other commanders as he situated himself at the table.

Fedrin nodded in reply before continuing. "As I was saying, the Voigt defenses, weak or not, will hopefully take down several of the enemy capital ships and I'm optimistic that many of the Krohn fighters will be destroyed by the colony's own fighter squadrons, which will give the Hornell and Idok fighters reign over the battlefield once we arrive."

"What about the Ilo?" asked Sanders as he looked at the marker positioned atop the colony, representing the infamously obsolete battle station.

"At best, maybe the Krohns will waste some of their long range missiles shooting it down," Searle said sarcastically although she wasn't far from the truth of the situation.

"The Ilo will buy us valuable time by simply existing," Fedrin agreed. "She'll take a long time to bring down and may just be the extra thing we need to get to the colony in time to help."

Fedrin and the commanders talked on and on, trading points and offering ideas while dismissing others. Grider said nothing. His attention was lost in the chart draped over the table. He gazed at it, carefully scrutinizing every detail he could find. Several of the commanders inadvertently tuned out Fedrin and watched as Grider pointed to various star systems and planets and then squinted as if he were doing arithmetic in his head.

Fedrin was still talking about his plan of attack when he noticed the distraction and looked down at the former admiral. "Admiral Grider," Fedrin said, bringing the old man out of his trance.

Grider looked up, seemingly perplexed. "Everything ok?" he asked Commander Colby, who was standing beside him.

"More or less," Colby replied.

"Why is everyone suddenly so quiet?" he whispered.

"We are listening to the admiral's plan," Colby answered.

"The admiral's plan!" declared Grider looking terribly upset. "I haven't finished my plan yet so how can I be telling it to you?"

"Not your plan," Colby patiently said. "Admiral Fedrin's plan, remember?"

"Of course I remember you, you young punk!" Grider snapped back at Colby. "I know how the chain of command works and I think it's high time you did as well! You wouldn't have lasted a week in my Navy back when I was in charge. We had no room for disrespectful commanders when facing a fleet of Refrac warships!" Grider finished his rant and sat back in his hover chair and crossed his arms, still looking intently at the chart while periodically offering a disdainful glare at Colby.

Colby didn't mind the admiral's rudeness, and was rather amused by it. Grider had, after all, likely saved Colby and most of the other commanders in the room during the Refrac War in some way or another. There was no reason now to let the aged warrior know that his former subservient comrades were now his superiors.

Fedrin was about to begin again when Grider suddenly spoke up. "Admiral," he said looking at the map. "Why have you not committed the Idok to the colony's defenses yet? You and I both know it is the answer."

Fedrin looked at Grider at a loss for words.

"The Idok is powerful and her fighters are fast enough to distract any Krohn fleet of consequence for hours by simply running evasion tactics," Grider continued. "You could easily buy three to four hours that way, giving our fleet enough time to reach the colony in time to stop the massacre which is sure to ensue if we don't."

Fedrin thought for a moment before answering. "Sacrificing the Idok would not be prudent. We were, in fact, just discussing this before you arrived."

"What did you discuss?" Grider asked looking around the room as if he were just insulted.

"We discussed deploying the Idok over Voigt to help buy time for the Sixth Fleet to arrive," Searle said.

"That's not exactly what I had in mind," Grider said shaking his head.

"What did you have in mind then?" Drezden interjected on behalf of the Admiral.

"What I had in mind was to place the Idok directly on the warp-point leading into Sibid from thirteen," Grider said looking at Drezden and then back at the star map.

Fedrin turned from Grider and looked at the map. "Why?"

"I can see you know already by the look in your eyes," Grider replied. "You need to buy a few hours and cut this enemy fleet down to a manageable size."

Fedrin nodded.

"By placing the Idok on the warp-point, she'll engage the Krohn forces right out of the jump. The Krohns will be vulnerable and unprepared for battle. The Idok will buy precious hours for your ships to arrive and she will damage many of the enemy vessels in the process."

Fedrin looked at the Star Map and then back at his commanders. They quickly saw the merit in Grider's plan. The Idok and her fighters could destroy several of the Krohn capital ships and hold the rest in combat for quite sometime before being overrun. Such a course of action would allow the Sixth Fleet to get to Voigt before the Krohns caused too much, if any, damage.

Fedrin's heart broke as he put the pieces together that he had been trying so hard not to think about. He shook his head slowly, as if in pain as he looked at the map, desperately trying to come up with an alternative. There was none. Grider had found the best possible answer. It satisfied all the criteria; fewer Namuh ships would be lost in the long run, more colonists would be saved, and the odds of retrieving the data device would be much greater.

Fedrin clumsily turned to Grider in a daze. The two great warriors, one old, one young, looked at each other for several moments saying nothing and so much at the same time.

The other commanders awkwardly watched their Admiral suffer, not knowing what to do or say. Drezden badly wanted to say or do something not as a commander, but as a friend. He could think of nothing. Colby and Sanders carefully scrutinized the star map to find a flaw in Grider's plan, for the Admiral's sake. No flaw could be found. Kendrick replayed the strategy over and over again in his mind. It worked, plain and simple. Tears formed in Searle's eyes, the memory of her husband's untimely death in the Second Fleet still fresh in her mind. She missed his him so terribly. How much worse it would have been for her to essentially order his death like the Admiral was even now contemplating for his wife.

Grider finally broke the silence. "I'm sorry Fedrin. I truly am sorry about all of this. I'm sorry your wife is the commander of that ship. I'm sorry it's your decision to decide who lives and who dies. I'm sorry for everything your position demands of you." Grider's eyes began to get moist and he quickly looked out a nearby window to hide it from the others.

"At the peak of the Refrac Spring campaign, still several months before the Sion intervention, I had a similar decision to make," Grider continued, still facing away. "My son was the commander of the Drewin II, an old Constellation class frigate." He cleared his throat and continued. "Right before the battle of Asar, a unique opportunity arose to place the battle group he was part of in an asteroid field for an ambush of a strong Refrac fleet headed for one of the colonies," Grider paused and looked down at the table. "The ambush wouldn't have destroyed the entire fleet, but it would have cut it down and given my own ships the time to get into optimal position to defend the colony. The situations are remarkably similar actually."

"What happened?" Commander Searle asked when no one else did.

"Well..." Grider said and again cleared his throat. "I opted on forgoing the ambush because, although it would have certainly devastated the Refrac fleet, it would have also surely condemned all the ships that participated. And as I'm sure you've already guessed, I was not willing to sacrifice my son, even for the off chance of a solid victory."

Fedrin knew where the story was going but tried to focus as Grider continued.

"I ordered my son's battle group to stand down and join my own battle group over the colony in an attempt to engage the enemy there in force."

A tear escaped Grider's eyes and he casually brushed it away like it was never there and continued. "There's not much more to tell than that. You've all read the history books. You know what happened. The full strength of the Refrac Fleet entered Asar and headed straight for the nearest colony. When they arrived, they did something no one anticipated, myself least of all."

"They opened fire on the domes," Colby said quietly, recalling his military history.

Grider nodded. "They ignored our warships that tried so desperately to engage them! They didn't even turn to fire as we closed to point blank range with them! Those bloodthirsty monsters wanted the colony at any expense! Some of the nobler commanders in my fleet tried to save the innocent civilians by actually placing their ships in the line of fire to buy time for colonists to escape. All attempts were futile." Grider shook his head. "The colony was lost that day. We also lost two destroyers and one frigate commanded by the bravest men I have ever known." Another tear appeared on his cheek. Grider wiped it away, not as discretely as before, only for it to be replaced by several more, which he ignored. "My son died that day. He died bravely, saving the lives of thousands of colonists who managed to get to transports or bomb shelters. Fate, or god if there is a god, had decided that my son was to die that day regardless of the choice I made. Yet, had I chosen not to gamble and place my son's battle group in the ambush setup instead of trying to save it by merging forces, the colony could have been saved and thousands more could have been spared. I was selfish and got nothing in return for it, save a broken heart and a weighted conscious."

Fedrin held back tears of his own as Grider finished his tale.

"I don't envy your position Admiral. But know this. I would give my life to change that one decision I made so many years ago. I pray you have wisdom in your own decision."

And with that, Grider backed up his hover chair and made his way to the door leaving the Sixth Fleet commanders alone with their Admiral.

Fedrin paused for only a moment after Grider's departure before activating his link.

"Lieutenant Tenith," Fedrin said. "Set up a priority two coded transmission with the Idok, care of her Commander. Link it with my personal quarters and have it ready when I return," Fedrin finished and looked up at his commanders. "Please return to your vessels and prepare for a fast and hard journey. We will be running our engines hot. Be sure all safety precautions that can be made, are made. There is no time to lose!"

The commanders quickly began to file out of the room. Several thought of saying something to the Admiral on their way out but none knew what to say. Even Drezden just passed the Admiral in silence. What does one say to one that is about to say goodbye to his wife?

"Formations, battle protocols and contingency plans will be forwarded to your vessels when they are made available," Fedrin added followed by silent nods of acknowledgment.

Drezden had taken several steps out into the hall when he suddenly stopped and turned back. All the other commanders were gone as he walked up to his friend. "You knew," he said quietly. "You knew this was the only option, didn't you?"

Fedrin slowly nodded, obviously fighting an emotional battle. "Any third year strategy cadet could have found that as the only plausible option."

"But most cadets don't have their wives commanding the ship needing to be sacrificed," Drezden added thoughtfully.

"I...I didn't want to suggest it myself," Fedrin blurted out. "I wanted to tell my self that it wasn't me making the decision."

Drezden tried hard to smile as he placed a hand on Fedrin's shoulder. "I'm sure everything will work out. Etana is a capable officer and her pilots are the best of the best."

Fedrin shook his head. "Let's pray you're right!"

CHAPTER 10

JUST A PAWN

"**They're here!**" **Loson** yelled down the hallway. "Their transport pod just docked in the lobby!"

The other officers scampered around the hall, being sure that everything looked as nice as a rundown floor of a dilapidated office building could be.

General Darion looked up in his cracked mirror to be sure that he looked as impeccable as always. Trivis, the great and powerful Senator that had gotten Darion his funds, was coming to see him. The reason for the visit, Darion couldn't guess. But the uniqueness of such a high profile stop both alarmed and excited him.

He smiled as he donned his handsome dress coat and began buttoning it up. He looked quite dashing, or so he thought, as he examined himself in the mirror. A chime at the main door interrupted his appraisal of himself, his favorite task on any given day.

Three of Darion's officers dove for the door, all anxious to greet their newest idol. The door opened and Trivis, another seemingly important dignitary, and several imposing Sentinels, clad in full body armor, entered.

The Sentinels, an elite guard unit assigned to protect the president and other high ranking Larep political figures, wasted no time in crashing through the narrow halls, entering the small offices and securing the floor.

"Clear!" one called out after emerging from an office.

"Clear here!" yelled another.

After the Sentinels finished their quick, yet thorough search of the tiny offices and meeting rooms, Trivis and his companion walked in.

"Hello my friends!" said Trivis warmly as he saw the officers gathered around. "Nice to finally meet some of you," he said as he reached out and shook several of the officer's hands. "Pleasure, real pleasure," he genuinely said with a beaming smile as he firmly grabbed each hand.

"Right this way Senator," Jarvik said as he ushered the group toward Darion's office. "The General is expecting you."

"Thank you very much," Trivis said as he and his silent associate made their way toward the opposite end of the hall.

Darion stood in the narrow doorway of his office smiling brightly as he reached his hand out.

"Darion, it's good to see you again," Trivis said as he firmly took the General's hand. "I trust you're doing well?"

"Never better," answered Darion.

"Glad to hear it," Trivis said. "Allow me to introduce one of my good friends," he said, nodding to the well-dressed man at his side. "Darion, meet my chief advisor, Armid. Armid, General Darion."

"Pleasure," Darion said as they shook hands.

"I've heard a lot about you," replied Armid.

"Nothing good I hope?" Darion said and then laughed.

Armid chuckled. "They don't call you the playboy general for nothing as I hear it."

"Hey, you only live once! Am I right?" Darion said followed by another laugh, this one more obnoxious than the first.

Armid nodded with a smile but did not reply.

"Well hey. It's not much, but can I invite you into my office?" asked Darion as he nodded to the room behind him.

"Thank you," Trivis said as he followed.

"See that we're not disturbed," Armid ordered to the nearest Sentinel.

The armed man nodded and assumed a position in front of Darion's door, weapon at the ready, eyeing Darion's staff suspiciously.

"So what can I do for you?" asked Darion as he sat at his desk and motioned for his guests to sit.

"Well," answered Trivis as he sat in one of the chairs in front of the desk. "A couple of things have come up that Armid and I felt you needed to be informed of promptly."

"I'm all ears," said Darion as he propped his feet on his desk in apparent oblivion that it was a rude gesture to his guests.

Trivis looked at Armid to proceed who then pulled out a small data pad from his pocket. "Approximately two hours ago, recon satellites in the Brok system picked up a stray Krohn wave," he began, showing Darion a schematic of the southern star system on his pad. "This wave has just been decoded by one of our advanced code teams in the Third Fleet."

"What did it say?" Darion asked, wondering what this had to do with him.

Armid shook his head wearily. "It was a set of landing coordinates on Namuh Prime."

Darion was genuinely flabbergasted. "Landing coordinates? I don't get it."

"Its likely a prelude to an invasion," said Trivis, interpreting what should have been basic information for Darion.

"Invasion?" exclaimed Darion, setting his feet back on the floor and suddenly looking alarmed and nervous. "Where?" he asked, looking with genuine concern at Armid's data pad.

Armid tapped his pad and brought up an image of the barren desert world they all called home. He then rotated the view to the bottom of the sphere where the yellow and orange sands gradually gave way to small patches of white. "It appears they have chosen the arctic peninsula," he said, showing both Trivis and Darion the blinking red dot on their frozen southern continent

"Why there?" Darion asked. "Seems to be the most inconvenient spot on the globe for an enemy to land an invasion force? There aren't any cities or strategic installations anywhere near there."

"Perhaps because it is one of the few spots on our globe where the Clear Skies Defense Grid has no coverage," Trivis suggested.

Darion looked up in shock. "I had no idea there were any such locations. I thought the missile defense system was entirely inclusive?"

"There are just a few holes," Armid stated with dismay. "A few small areas over the arctic and a couple areas over the western dunes were neglected when designing the grid."

"The designers deemed that these places held no value to us and would be of little tactical advantage for an enemy to approach," Trivis said with a regretful shake of his head.

"And having a swath of solid ground big enough to land an army and establish a foothold isn't a tactical advantage?" Darion asked with disgust as images of Krohn soldiers interrupting his lifestyle of ease and luxury came to mind.

Trivis nodded. "It appears that there were some design flaws with the system. We are already launching an investigation into it."

"But how did these Krohns learn of the flaws? Or of the Clear Skies system at all?" Darion exclaimed. "I don't get it! This system was supposed to be our last resort. Now it sounds like it won't do a thing!"

"We honestly don't know how they got their hands on these coordinates," Armid answered. "Maybe it was Fedrin or one of his fellow traitors. Who knows?"

"But as bad as this news is, we have a lucky break of our own," added Trivis.

"And what's that?" asked Darion. "Sounds like were pretty messed up from where I'm sitting."

Trivis answered with enthusiasm. "By knowing the exact coordinates of the Krohn landing sight, we can prepare for them right where they'll touch down. We can set up anti-aircraft guns around the area and take down the ships one by one as they come in for landings through the narrow pass. It'll be a bloodbath, Darion!"

"We can also have sufficient men on the ground to engage any that do manage to successfully touchdown," added Armid.

"So are we assuming that the Third Fleet won't be able to stop these Krohns if we're already drawing up battle plans for the ground?" asked Darion.

"The Third doesn't have a chance of stopping them," replied Trivis. "That's not an insult on Sherman or the other brave men and women in uniform. I just don't think they'll be able to stop this Krohn fleet. It's massive. And thanks to Fedrin's defection, poor Sherman hasn't been able to cycle out his ships. They're in no condition to fight a Krohn battle fleet."

Armid reluctantly nodded. "The Krohns will most likely be here within a few days. With no fleet to count on, we need to prepare for them ourselves."

Darion looked at the two men curiously. "So what exactly is it that you gentlemen want from me? The arctic peninsula isn't exactly my jurisdiction you know."

Armid glanced at Trivis who proceeded to retrieve a rolled up paper from his suit pocket. He opened it up and handed it to Darion. "This is an authorization form from the Defense Council giving you temporary protective custody of the arctic region and surrounding areas."

Darion reluctantly took the paper and skimmed over the contents. "And what exactly do I do with this?" he said slowly after reading the form through twice.

"The Defense Council is hoping that you could front the resources to set up defenses around the Krohn landing sight," answered Armid.

Darion sat back in his chair and rubbed his chin, trying to think of a way to not get involved without looking like he was. "And just what kind of resources would this include?" he asked as he stalled for time to think of an excuse.

Trivis shrugged. "Three brigades including most of your big guns, hover tanks and special-ops."

Darion slowly nodded. "You do realize that that is essentially the entirety of my force?"

"We are keenly aware of that," Armid said with a somber nod.

"And you gentlemen don't see any problem with stripping the capital district of its defenses?"

Trivis shrugged and glanced at Armid for agreement. "It's not like the capital will be totally defenseless. Local law enforcement should be more than adequate to deal with anything that comes up in the few days that your army is setting up the defenses around the landing site."

"And if anything truly major happens, the other districts will be able to lend their troops to help out," Armid added.

Darion pointed to Armid and nodded. "Which brings me to why you've chosen my army as opposed to any of the others? Surely there are other districts that could afford to send their troops more than mine? I mean, the capital building is right down the street which is fairly important, or so they tell me."

Trivis smiled and shook his head. "Quite frankly Darion, I trust you more than any of those other fools. This could potentially be one of the most important battles in our time and there is no one I'd rather have at the front than you!"

A swell of pride came sweeping over Darion, a dangerous thing for someone who nearly worships himself. "If it means that much to you...I can make it happen," he said holding back a huge smile. "It will take some time to organize the deployment, but we can manage it."

"I hope you don't think it presumptuous of us General, but in anticipation of your cooperation, I had Armid draft up the orders for you already," said Trivis. "It should save time and effort on your part."

Darion smiled again, relieved that a lot of the paperwork and monotonous logistics had already been done for him. "I appreciate that but I really think that I should look over..." Darion feigned protest.

"And in the meantime we need to discuss your accommodations," said Trivis who then looked to Armid for an agreeing nod.

"What did you have in mind?" asked Darion, his imagination running wild.

Armid glanced down at his data pad and pulled up a new screen and then showed it to Darion. "Asar Stellar sold out to the Kumper Merchant Fleets last month and is leaving their eightieth floor suite in the Freedom Tower vacant."

"How's that sound, General?" Trivis said with a smile, feeding the fire he noticed already burning in Darion's eyes. "A suite in the Freedom Tower?"

"That sounds really nice," Darion confessed, picturing his own level of prestige rising even more.

"I know the owner of the Freedom Tower," said Trivis. "I'm sure I can get you in there right away. I'll have Armid draw up the lease papers tonight. I'm sure we can get you in there for a good price...not that price matters much for you these days."

Darion smiled.

"With any luck, tomorrow night you'll be looking over the city from your eightieth floor conference room," said Armid. "Let us know when you get settled and we can put on a little welcome party for you. Who knows, maybe even President Defuria would come?"

Darion's smile grew. Everything that he loved and sought in life was being handed to him one at a time. Fame, money, popularity, and just about anything else he could think of, he had. Life couldn't get any better!

A beep came from Trivis' wrist. "Looks like I'm needed back at the capital," he said after looking at his wrist. "You know how it goes."

Darion nodded as he stood to his feet. "Thanks for coming and sharing the news about Clear Skies and the Krohns. I'm honored that you prefer me to handle the problem, I really am."

"It's nothing that you haven't earned on your own accord," Trivis said patting Darion's arm approvingly. "Now I really do have to run. We're voting on some stupid clean air bill for the Branci home world and I need to make up an opinion about it in the next twenty-five minutes."

"Good luck with that," Darion said and chuckled.

Trivis shrugged. "The life of a politician I'm afraid."

"I will be in contact with you about the move," said Armid as he stepped in the hall and looked back. "Other than these offices, what else do you need moved?"

"Nothing," answered Darion. "This is all I have."

"But where are your records?" Armid pressed. "Where are all the files and archives? Surely you must have more than what can be stored here?"

Darion glanced around and then shrugged. "If it's not digital, it was probably lost when the defense complex burned down last year."

Armid glanced at Trivis, seemingly unsure of what to say.

"The defense complex had several high security vaults," stated Trivis, taking the lead from Armid. "I know their contents were saved from the fire because I saw the emptied vaults with my own eyes. I assumed the army took possession of the contents and relocated them, perhaps in a new vault or some other armed secure storage somewhere?"

Darion shook his head. "I have no idea what you are talking about. Is there something specific you are looking for? I could put out an inquiry at the base."

"No need for that," said Trivis quickly. "At least not right now. Maybe when things settle down we can revisit the topic."

"Most assuredly," said Darion. "I'll add it to my list."

"You need to go," said Armid to Trivis. "If you miss another vote, Defuria will have your head."

Trivis laughed. "Well we don't want that. Goodbye Darion. We'll be in touch."

"Take care gentlemen," Darion said as he watched the entourage quickly file out the door at the other end of the hall. As the last Sentinel left, Darion turned back into his office and closed the door. He glanced about the run-down room and then smiled. He wasn't going to miss this place at all!

"Do you think he suspects anything?" Armid asked Trivis as the group descended in the lift.

"Are you kidding?" exclaimed Trivis. "I'm surprised he can tie his own shoes in the morning without help! He doesn't have the intellect to suspect us of anything."

"So you think he'll go along with everything ok?"

Trivis nodded. "He will."

"What about the Origin Codex?" asked Armid.

"What of it?" asked Trivis.

"He doesn't know where any of the records are. How are we going to find it if we don't know where to look?"

Trivis looked at Armid incredulously. "We have an entire army en route to help us find it! I just wanted to make sure he didn't know where to look in case someone else solicits his help between now and when we kill him. From the sounds of it, he has no clue."

"He has no clue and we have no worries," said Armid with a smile.

Trivis nodded but did not smile. Although their plan was coming together, there were still many things that had to be accomplished before they would get the Grimsin. Until his share was in hand, he knew he must be vigilant. Although discounted by many, he feared their ever threatening enemy, the Sions, and knew they would do all in their power to prevent them from getting the Origin Codex and the Grimsin that it would lead to.

CHAPTER 11

COMMANDER ETANA

Fedrin walked from the aft Iovara hangar toward his quarters despondently. Even now, he tried to think of other options. It was useless. He knew before the impromptu meeting had started that this was the best option...his only option.

When he finally entered his room, he sat at his desk and activated the transmission that Tenith had already set up. The screen flickered a little and then, there she was. Her back was turned and she appeared to be holding a data pad. Fedrin opened his mouth to speak but paused. They hadn't seen or talked with each other directly in months. The false accusation of infidelity hung over Fedrin like a dark cloud and he wasn't sure how it would effect their conversation. He wished he could say something that would dispel her doubt but the evidence that she had been presented was daunting.

He had nearly worked up the gumption to speak but stopped again when images of Etana on the Idok Bridge surrounded by flames suddenly came to his mind. It caused a lump to swell in his throat and his hands feel weak. So strong were his feelings that he momentarily contemplated terminating the transmission and very well may have, if she hadn't suddenly glanced at the screen.

Etana looked at him curiously, as if she wasn't sure what to say.

Fedrin likewise was unsure how to proceed. He felt weak and frail, looking at his estranged wife wanting to say so much but not knowing where to start.

"Admiral," Etana finally said coldly, breaking the silence and setting a formal tone for the conversation devoid of all intimacy.

"Commander," he slowly replied in kind.

"What can we do for you?" she asked, avoiding prolonged eye contact.

"How...how are you?" Fedrin asked, giving his best attempt to initiate personal dialogue.

Etana nodded promptly. "The Idok is functioning splendidly. All systems are operating within parameters and there is no news to report, Sir."

Fedrin nodded awkwardly. "Glad to hear it. And you are doing ok?"

"Perfectly fine, Sir. What can I do for you?"

Fedrin nodded again as he struggled to gather his thoughts. He couldn't bring himself to ask the question yet. "So what is Kumper like these days?"

Etana looked at Fedrin as if he were joking and then pulled up her data pad with a subtle roll of her eyes and began to skim a list. "Let's see, finished stocking listening post eighteen last week. One of our recon drones found a mineral deposit in the asteroid ring orbiting McCabe VI the week before. We tagged it and sent the info to Asar Mining Industrial. Other than that, all's been quiet here, just as it's been for the last three months."

Fedrin nodded and began to realize that they were not going to be rebuilding any bridges this time around. The thought grieved him, as he did not want his wife going to her almost certain doom without reconciling.

"I don't mean to rush you Admiral, but I have a very important geological survey meeting coming up soon and I was hoping to make it," she said with a subtle hint of sarcasm in her voice that only Fedrin could have picked up on. "Is there something specific I can do for you or are you just checking in?"

Fedrin shook his head. "I can't go into all the details right now Etana, but I need you and your ship for a mission."

"Oh?"

"It's very complicated and very bad," Fedrin added.

She nodded slowly. "So what can the Idok do to help, Sir?"

Fedrin sighed. She wasn't going to make this easy. "Ok, here is the situation," he said, himself now avoiding eye contact. "The Krohns have a battle fleet in system thirteen," he stopped and breathed in deeply before continuing. "It is currently heading toward the Sibid System and likely the Voigt colony. In addition to the civilian lives in peril, there is a data device tucked away on the colony, which must be retrieved in order to secure the home world defenses. Now that the Second Fleet is gone..." Fedrin's words trailed off.

Etana nodded as she quickly put the pieces together. "So this Krohn fleet must be stopped or else Voigt is going to be wiped out?"

Fedrin reluctantly nodded. "That's essentially it," he said, looking out the reflective surface of the porthole behind her. "If that fleet isn't stalled and taken down to a manageable size, many of the Voigt colonists will die and the device may be lost which could lead to the loss of Namuh Prime itself."

Etana looked at Fedrin with uncertainty in her eyes. "Fedrin," she said, in her first hint of a personal tone. "I won't be able to stop an entire Krohn Fleet with my one ship. We're good but not that good."

"I know," Fedrin said softly. "I'm not asking you to take down the entire fleet. Just stall them and take out as many ships as you can while doing it."

Etana's eyes grew with understanding as she suddenly realized that she was receiving tactical suicide orders. It was a heavy moment.

"The more time you engage them, the less time they will be bombarding the colony. What's left of my fleet will arrive at Voigt roughly four hours after the Krohn fleet arrives as it stands now. If the Idok could buy us even half that time, countless lives could be spared and our chances of finding the data device will be greatly increased."

"I understand," Etana said.

For a brief moment Fedrin caught a glimpse of something in Etana's eyes that he didn't understand. Was it regret? Remorse? Love? He couldn't say. All he knew was that he missed her and wanted things to be like they had been.

"It wasn't me," Fedrin suddenly blurted out, referring to the incriminating photo that had acted as the catalyst for their separation.

"Not going there," Etana said stiffly, the transient look in her eyes now gone.

Fedrin shook his head. "You know, maybe I haven't always been there when you needed me Etana. In fact, I know I haven't. My job has often come before you and I am sorry for that, I really am. But I want you to know, whether you believe me or not, that I have never been unfaithful to you! Never!"

Etana looked at Fedrin incredulously.

"Say something!" Fedrin demanded.

A moment passed before Etana spoke. "You are unbelievable Fedrin!" she snapped. "Unbelievable!"

"What do you mean?" Fedrin asked.

Etana shook her head and laughed unpleasantly. "You call me out of nowhere after three months of silence, give my crew and I suicide orders and then tack on an apology afterwards? Are you serious Fedrin? How am I supposed to take that? You want me to forgive you now so when I die your conscience won't keep you up at night? Is that what you want Fedrin?"

Fedrin didn't answer. He didn't know what to say.

"If you were really sorry Fedrin, really truly sorry, you would have sent me a transmission the day after I moved out! You would have told me sorry for neglecting me, and that you really loved me! You would have told me that even though your responsibilities were paramount, you still cared about me!"

"I do care about you!" Fedrin yelled. "And I've told you I did!"

"You don't just tell someone you care about them!" Etana shot back. "You show it! You live it! Talk is cheap, especially from you!"

Fedrin shook his head. "We've been through this before Etana! The Fleets are the only thing between us and destruction. They require my full attention."

"Don't give me that old line!" Etana snapped. "I know full well the importance of the Fleets. I do. But would it have killed you to send me a note saying hello every few months? Do you think you could have sent me a transmission on my birthday just to say 'Hi?' How about a note saying that you were alive after the Zelin battle last year? You act as if I don't exist Fedrin but then get mad at me when I try to contact you to see how you are! I'm not a trinket you can put on a shelf when you are busy and take off when you want something. That's not how a marriage is supposed to operate and that's definitely not how I operate!"

Fedrin looked at Etana in a daze. Her speech was fast, full of emotion, and for the most part, true.

"Your job is tough Fedrin, I know," Etana continued. "But I also know that there is time in even the worse day for yourself. And since we were a team, I thought that I was entitled to just a small portion of that time," she finished and tears came to her eyes.

Fedrin sighed. "I don't know what to say other than I am sorry. And while my timing is awful, you're right that I didn't want you undertaking this mission without knowing how I felt about you and without affirming one more time that that picture was not of me. If you choose not to accept my apology, there's nothing I can do about it. It's too little too late I'm afraid, but at least you know how I feel."

Tears still flowed freely from Etana's eyes as she slowly nodded. "I need to go," she said as she wiped her eyes with the back of her sleeve.

Fedrin nodded and then glanced about his desk as if making sure there was nothing he was forgetting. "I'm sending you all the logistical information we have on the enemy fleet and the optimal location for you to engage them."

Etana nodded.

"I'm...I'm also sending you some recorded clips the telecast played after the dock explosions. They were only played locally so you haven't seen them."

Etana looked at Fedrin curiously.

"If you have time, review them. Not that I want to bring it back up, but the person in them appears to be me but isn't. There may be a connection with that photo but I really don't know. I just wanted you to see them."

Etana glanced down at her data pad and watched as the files downloaded. She then looked to Fedrin and nodded. "I guess I'll be seeing you then," she said.

"I guess so," Fedrin said solemnly.

"Goodbye Fedrin," Etana said with such finality that it seemed surreal to Fedrin.

"I love you," was Fedrin's reply but it was too late. Etana had already ended the link. His words echoed in his mind for sometime before he finally reached back at the tele-link screen.

"Lieutenant Kesler here."

"Its me. Instruct all vessels that no more ship to ship travel is permitted."

"Aye, Sir."

"And have all ships accelerate to fifteen percent above maximum speed and remain in tight formation."

"Will we be keeping the ships that hot for the duration of the trip?" asked Kesler.

"We have to," Fedrin answered. "We've got a lot of distance to cover and not a lot of time to do it in."

Kesler swallowed hard before continuing. "Sir, may I remind you that fleet regulations prohibit sustaining anything in excess of five percent over max speed?"

"If you haven't noticed, we haven't exactly been going by the book these last few days," Fedrin answered.

Kesler shrugged. "Point taken, Sir. I'll transmit your orders to the fleet at once."

"I'll be up there in a bit."

"See you then," answered Kesler and then turned to his station where he began inputting the orders.

"So, what happens when we run the ships too hot for too long?" Tarkin asked as he walked up behind Kesler, having overhead Fedrin's orders.

"The core melts down and we all die horrible painful deaths," Jonas answered from his perch at the weapon's station.

"That's if we're lucky," Kesler added.

"Lucky?" exclaimed Tarkin.

Kesler nodded. "Sometimes the radiation from the core just eats away at your internal organs making sudden death seem like paradise."

"The thing is though, at the point where you want death, you're too weak to actually kill yourself," Jonas added as he walked down the steps from his station and leaned onto Kesler's console.

Kesler shook his head. "So you just sit there and let the radiation eat away your body, hoping and praying that it will reach your heart or lungs to finish you off."

"How long can this last?" Tarkin asked as he held his three pairs of arms casually, trying to look like he wasn't nervous.

"It can last upwards of six days," Jonas cheerfully added. "Six days of living death. It just doesn't get better than that!"

The ship suddenly lurched forward as the new orders reached the engine room. Tarkin looked down at the console uneasily as he watched the power meter slower pass from the recommended maximum toward the fifteen percent above mark.

Kesler nodded solemnly as he too watched the meter. "But Branci are bigger and stronger than Namuh. So it stands to reason that the radiation would take longer to kill you than us."

Jonas nodded in agreement. "And in light of that, I'd appreciate it if, as a friend, you'd snap my neck or suffocate me should the situation arise."

Tarkin looked at Jonas in disbelief and then to Kesler.

"Tarkin you don't look so well," commented Kesler. "Feeling ok?"

Tarkin nodded. "I think I just need to grab some lunch."

"Go ahead," Kesler said. "We'll make do without you for a while."

Tarkin nodded and then slowly made his way out of the bridge. As the doors closed behind him Jonas and Kesler turned to each other and began to laugh uncontrollably.

⋏

The setting sun silhouetted Darion's figure as he looked out over Larep. The sky was painted in a myriad of soft orange and yellow hues that ushered in a peaceful end to a generally peaceful day. He soaked in the colors and breathed in deeply. His commanding view in the high priced, luxuriously furnished suite in the Freedom Tower was worth every taxpayer's penny.

"The anti-air batteries will be set up behind the hover tank units and sharpshooters," Jarvik said, pointing to a spot on a map of the arctic peninsula.

Darion nodded as he slowly walked away from his window and stood over the map sprawled over his desk. "And the infantry units?" he asked, feigning interest.

Jarvik nodded. "Several advanced engineer teams have already begun digging trenches and setting up laser dampening walls around the south-western edge of the purposed landing site. The heavy infantry squads will-ing occupy these forward positions here and here. Additional sharpshooters from the thirty-second airdrop battalion will set up in the high ground on the northeastern glaciers here and here."

Darion nodded disinterestedly and casually walked away from the map yet again.

"We should have them in a nasty crossfire," Jarvik commented as he made another notation on the map. "They won't stand a chance."

"It's a good plan," Darion said. "If I do say so myself."

Jarvik scratched his head. "Begging your pardon, Sir, but this isn't your plan, at least not the bulk of it. Most of the orders and notations came directly from Senator Trivis' office."

"Well the plan is good and I guess that's all that really matters, right?" asked Darion rhetorically as he walked over to his desk and grabbed his data pad.

"Yes, Sir," Jarvik answered wearily as he picked up the chart and started to roll it up.

"When will you be heading out?" asked Darion as he scrolled through screens aimlessly on the pad.

Jarvik slid the chart into a long tube and tightened the cap on one end. "I'll be shipping out with the third hover tank division as soon as they're ready to go."

Darion nodded slowly, appearing lost in thought and losing interest in the pad momentarily.

"Everything ok General?" Jarvik asked.

Darion shrugged. "I hope so."

"You don't sound so sure about all this," commented Jarvik.

"I'm not," said Darion, surprising Jarvik with his answer who assumed Darion had stopped caring long ago. "I know I'm not a good general," Darion then added. "I have no elusions about it. But sending away my army? Something just doesn't feel right about it."

"Can you change your mind?" Jarvik asked thoughtfully, himself having the same thoughts for much of the day.

Darion looked thoughtfully at Jarvik. "I'm really not sure. I seem to have been bought out by Trivis and the Defense Council. I feel that I owe them for what they've done for me."

Jarvik nodded thoughtfully. "It may not be my place to say, Sir, but that doesn't sound like a healthy place for you or your army to be in."

Darion nodded, knowing that Jarvik spoke the truth but not wanting to hear it. "You're right Jarvik," he finally said.

"Sir?"

"It's not your place to say," said Darion sternly.

Jarvik nodded. "Apologies, Sir."

"You better get going," Darion then said. "You still have a lot to do. And I'd appreciate it if you keep your misgivings about this operation to yourself."

"Yes, Sir," Jarvik answered and then offered a salute before turning and walking out of the room.

Darion walked back to his window. He thought of many things ranging from the threatening Krohn invasion, to the attack plans carefully crafted to crush it once they landed and all the details in-between. He didn't know how long he had been standing there when he heard a tap on his open door.

"I'm sorry General," a woman's voice spoke up as she stepped into his office.

Darion turned and looked at the lovely woman standing in his office and smiled. Her name was Reesa, a concierge of the Freedom Tower and person- ally assigned to Darion to assist him and his staff with the move. She was a lovely sight and therefore a major distraction for the playboy general that had every intention of asking her out the moment he felt he could get away with it.

"What can I do for you Reesa?" he asked, flashing his perfect smile in her direction.

"There's a representative of the Larep Waste Management Services here to see you," she answered with the same poise and professionalism she had expressed on every other occasion they had interacted. Darion smiled all the brighter, seeing her uptight composure as an alluring challenge and not as a deterrent.

"What should I tell him?" she asked.

Darion shook his head. "Tell him I'm busy talking to a beautiful woman."

Reesa was unfazed. "What would you actually like me tell him, Sir?"

Darion laughed and then shook his head. "Whatever you'd like Reesa. Be creative."

"He did say to mention that if you didn't want to talk to him that I should mention something about Kespa. I didn't really understand what he meant by that."

Darion frowned and then shook his head.

"Do you want me to have security usher him out?"

"No, that won't be necessary," Darion said. "I don't want to make a ruckus on our first day as tenants. Besides, we're the army. We shouldn't need private security guards right?" he said followed by a laugh.

"So what should I do?" Reesa asked once more, a subtle hint of impatience in her voice.

Darion sighed. "Send him in."

"He'll be right in," she said and then turned to walk out of the room.

Darion's eyes followed her graceful form as she left. He then shook his head and walked away from his window and waited near the door. As he waited thoughts of Kespa, the slum that he had grown up in, flooded his mind. Places where he had lived, things he had done, trouble he had gotten into, his first girlfriends, and so many other memories came and went in his mind. His fragmented thoughts were suddenly augmented a hundred fold when a familiar face entered the room.

He was dressed in a dark blue waste management jumpsuit that had holes in the knees and elbows. It was heavily stained by a wide variety of offending agents and a slight odor accompanied.

"Hello Darion...or should I say General?" the visitor spoke first and then smiled brightly.

"Hello," Darion hesitantly said, not reciprocating the smile.

"You remember who I am, don't you?" the man asked.

"I remember," Darion answered quietly. "When did you get out of prison Kebbs?"

Kebbs' smile faded and lowered his head. "I got out six months ago," he said with a touch of shame echoing in his voice. "I've been clean for all of it."

Darion nodded, not sure if he believed it.

"How about you?" asked Kebbs, anxious to change topics. "Looks like you're doing pretty good for yourself?"

Darion glanced around the office casually, as if he didn't realize how amazing his layout was. "Doing all right," he said in false modesty.

"I'll say," remarked Kebbs as he took a few steps deeper into the office.

Darion glared at Kebbs' filthy boots incredulously as they tramped across his beautiful hardwoods that had just been buffed the previous morning prior to their occupancy.

"I didn't realize the army had money for this kind of stuff?" Kebbs said in awe. "I sort of thought they spent what they had on guns and soldiers. Who knew interior decorating was also on the list?"

"Can I help you with something?" Darion snapped, already anxious for his uninvited guest to leave.

Kebbs thrust his hands deep into his pockets and plopped down on one of two leather sofas facing each other in the center of the room. He then looked back at Darion and smiled again. "Just stopping by to say hi to an old friend."

Darion sighed and reluctantly walked over and sat down across from Kebbs. "So, what have you been up to lately?" he asked as disinterested as possible, hoping Kebbs would get the hint.

"Oh this and that," Kebbs answered. "Trying to stay out of trouble," he said followed by a chuckle.

"So you've giving up killing children then?" jabbed Darion venomously. "I don't have any more brothers if that's why you're here."

Kebbs shook his head as old conversations and bitter grudges between the two men instantly came to the surface. "That's not why I'm here," he answered calmly.

"Then why are you here?" Darion shot back. "I thought I made it pretty clear last time how I felt about seeing you. None of that has changed!"

Without another word of protest, Kebbs stood to his feet and removed his hands from his pockets. "I'm sorry to have bothered you Darion. I'll see myself out."

"If I ever have issues with my trash service I'll know who to call!" Darion added sarcastically.

Kebbs smiled and looked over his shoulder. "Likewise if I ever see the streets crawling with Krohns or need my furniture reupholstered."

The door closed behind his unwanted guest and Darion struck the arm of the sofa in anger. How he hated Kebbs. After a few minutes he regained his composure and let out a deep sigh. He stood to go back to his desk but stopped short when he noticed a folded piece of paper on the floor near the sofa Kebbs had sat in. He picked it up and tugged the folds open. It was a message from Kebbs.

It read: "Chief: There are no holes in the Clear Skies System. Sending your troops to the arctic is a trap intended to empty the capital of the army. Meet me at the Refrac War Memorial fountain at noon tomorrow. We have to talk."

Darion muttered under his breath as he tucked the message into his pocket. He pondered his course of action for only a moment.

"Reesa," he said opening the door and stepping into the reception area. Upon entering, he glanced over and noticed his attractive concierge typing away feverishly on two different computers, taking notes and jotting down random numbers on a small pad.

"Have I really given you that much work already?" he asked, inadvertently startling Reesa who promptly closed down all her active applications with the press of single button and then looked up at Darion. "Ahhh" exclaimed Darion with a smile. "Doing a little shopping are we?"

Reesa glanced down at her note pad and then awkwardly back to Darion. "Sorry," she said coyly. "Its...my niece's birthday next week and I haven't gotten her anything yet," she said as she casually tucked the note pad into an attaché case beside the desk without Darion noticing. "I'm sorry, Sir. It won't happen again."

Darion shook his head and laughed. "Don't worry about it, really. I'll try to be louder when I come out of my office next time."

Reesa's cheeks were bright red and she was beyond embarrassed but she forced a smile. "What did you need from me General?"

Darion continued to smile. "I just needed to know what I am doing tomorrow at noon?"

"Just a sec," Reesa replied as she glanced at her monitor. "Looks like you have a meeting with the Joint Commission on Military Expenditures."

"Can it be canceled?" Darion asked.

"Umm...not really," Reesa answered. "It's the Joint Commission, Sir. It's sort of a big deal."

Darion shook his head and glanced back at the note. He sighed. "Do it anyways."

"Really?" exclaimed Reesa. "Everything ok?"

"I just have something important to take care of," answered Darion.

"More important than addressing six senators and eight congressmen about your financial plans with the money you asked them for?"

"Tell them I have the flu or something," Darion said. "Be creative."

"Anything you say General," said Reesa as she brushed a strand of blond hair out of her pretty face.

"Thanks," replied Darion. He was about to go back to his office when he stopped and looked back at Reesa. She had already busied herself typing the General's regrets and seemed oblivious that he was looking at her. He didn't stare long and was just turning away when she looked up.

"Did you need something else General?" she asked with a smile.

"Yes. Call me Darion."

"My manager insists we address all our tenants professionally," Reesa answered. "As an army general, you should be addressed as one."

Darion shook his head. "Do you want me to call your manager and tell him you aren't doing something I asked?" he said with a flirtatious smile.

Reesa looked momentarily flustered but quickly regained composure and looked up. "That won't be necessary...Darion."

"That's better," said Darion. "Now we're on a first name basis. Not bad for our first day together huh?"

She smiled politely but did not say anything.

"I can take a hint," Darion said and then laughed as he backed toward his office. "Why don't you take an early day and go shopping for your niece. I'll be fine here."

"But, Sir...Darion. It's my first day. I can't leave early on my first day."

"I say you can," said Darion. "Now get lost. I'll see you tomorrow!"

Reesa reluctantly gave in and after thanking Darion and apologizing once more for her temporary "indiscretion", she left the office, attaché bag in tow.

Once she was gone, Darion walked back to his office and casually walked to his window and looked out over the city. The sun had since set, but Larep was still bright as ever. Lighted transport tubes, skyscrapers, streetlights, and relay posts all did their best to combat the darkness that encroached upon the city.

CHAPTER 12

TREACHERY!

The lone figure paced back and forth in the cold, darkened hangar. He periodically glanced out the entrance anxiously. It felt like forever before the slender shuttle finally came into view. It slowed its approach as it crossed the field barrier and came to a steady hover as it made its way through the narrow confines of the hangar. Small stabilizing thrusters along the shuttle fired periodically, guiding the craft gently to its berth along the wall next to the other shuttles and smaller transports. The waiting man glanced over his shoulder and then quickly darted over to the shuttle, being careful to stay in the contorted shadows along the wall.

The shuttle let off bursts of steam as the cooling system went to work. Following a particularly large burst near the rear of the shuttle, a narrow ramp slowly descended and a door opened. The agitated figure walked up to the ramp and waited until a silhouette of another man appeared at the top of the ramp.

"I have orders to relieve you of your command and confine you to your room," the waiting man called up the ramp.

"We thought that might happen," the other said, cautiously hanging back from the ramp. "I assume you are going to disregard those orders?"

"Does that mean we are still on with the plan?" the man asked and then looked back over his shoulder.

"You better believe we are still on!" the other said, still from within the protection of the shuttle. "If we don't do something now, he'll kill us all for sure."

"Is Larep still with us?" the other asked nervously. "Because if they aren't onboard with this, I'm off right here, right now."

"Relax Neider," the man replied as he cautiously began to descend the ramp. "I've taken care of everything. My source in Larep has assured me that once Fedrin is gone, I'll have full command over the fleets."

Commander Mick's sneering face came into view as he stepped onto the hangar floor.

"Is everyone ready?" he asked as he noticed the apprehension and nervousness of his chief weapons officer.

"The command crew is set and we are ready to propagate your cover story to the rest of the crew as soon as you give the word."

"And the target?" asked Mick, as the two began to walk toward the doorway.

"All set," Neider answered. "The Iovara power relay grid is located between the two aft bulkheads on the port side. It's fairly close to the surface. One well placed round should be able to knock it out with minimal casualties but maximum damage."

"Excellent. You've done well Neider," Mick said patting him on the back. "I think a Commandership may be in your near future."

"I'm just doing my duty."

"And so you are," Mick said. "And in a couple of years from now, people are going to look back on this day and remember us as heroes!"

"Lets hope so," Neider said, as the two men went through the doorway and into the main ship. "These sorts of things have a way of making heroes or villains out of men that only history can decide."

"We'll let the history books have the luxury of naming us what we are," Mick said with confidence.

Neider nodded.

"Oh, when this is finished, make sure to send a team back to my shuttle," Mick said, nodding behind himself.

Neider looked at Mick curiously. "What for?"

Mick smiled. "To untie the two guards that I knocked out and stuffed in the luggage hold."

Neider shook his head.

Several minutes after they had left the hangar a faint orange glow illuminated from behind one of the other shuttles as Former Admiral Grider moved his hover chair forward. He shook his head sorrowfully and then made his way for the door as fast as his chair would go. There was precious little time to lose.

 ⋏

Fedrin was nearly to the bridge door when it happened. A tremendous explosion riveted his vessel, sending shock waves throughout the halls, blowing out capacitors and leaving many levels in total darkness. Screams of fear and panic filled the corridors as alarms sounded on every level compelling on and off duty personnel to race up and down the darkened halls toward their posts. Artificial gravity in several sections cycled on and off rapidly, tossing the crew about with violent affect.

Fedrin struggled to get to his feet, holding the wall fiercely to keep his barring. "What's going on?" he shouted into his link as he felt along the riveted steel panels as he slowly made his way to the bridge.

"The Corinthia just opened fire on us!" Tarkin yelled back.

Surely Fedrin had heard wrong. "What did you say? Is this Tarkin? Where's Kesler?"

"Kesler hit his head on the console," Tarkin answered. "He'll be fine in a minute."

"What you'd say about the Corinthia?" Fedrin demanded.

"She fired a single shot through our upper deck armor and took out the primary power relay grid," Jonas answered for Tarkin. "We can't raise shields or arm weapons without it! The ship is having a seizure with the power systems. Gravity is cycling."

"Casualties?" asked Fedrin as he approached the door.

"Not sure," Tarkin answered. "Probably upwards of several dozen."

"Life support systems?"

"Backups took over with no issue," Jonas answered.

Fedrin reached the door to the bridge and typed in his password on the illuminated number pad. The bridge was in an uproar. Officers ran back and forth to different stations and everyone was shouting. Above the room on the main screen, the Corinthia faced the crippled Iovara dead on. Her primary weapon port was open revealing the bluish molten plasma waiting to be released. Without her shields, the Iovara couldn't hope to survive a direct hit!

"What in the world is going on?" Fedrin demanded, still baffled by the situation.

"The Corinthia is hailing us," Ensign Gallo calmly spoke up above the noise.

"Mick," Fedrin said to himself as he walked to the front of the room. "On screen!"

The daunting view of the Corinthia was quickly replaced with Commander Mick's scornful face. A look of distain filled his eyes as he spotted Fedrin.

"Mick! What is the meaning of this?" Fedrin demanded.

"Meaning of what Fedrin?" Mick replied coolly.

"You just fired on my ship moron! What do think?"

"Oh that," Mick said nodding his head. "Well, that was just so you and your crew know that I mean business. Traitor!"

"Business? Traitor? What do you mean? What are you talking about?" Fedrin asked with arms outstretched in complete bewilderment.

"I'm talking about relieving you of your command and assuming the Chief Admiralty effective immediately," stated Mick.

"You can't lead this fleet!" Fedrin blurted out. "And even if you could, this is not the way to do it! What are you thinking?"

"On the contrary my dear Fedrin, this is the only way to do it," Mick said smirking as if he had just made some grand move in a complex strategic game. "You and your brainwashed officers would have me killed in a second if I announced a bid for the position!"

"You're mad!" Fedrin said shaking his head. "Completely mad!"

"Then, you'd agree that upsetting me is not the best course of action, wouldn't you? After all, I'm sure you've noticed that there's a charged plasma round currently locked onto your vessel. I don't need to remind you that one shot will be enough to destroy your ship and every man and woman aboard."

Fedrin turned and faced the back of the bridge in a daze. "Mick, we don't have time for this," Fedrin said in a near helpless tone as he turned to face the power hungry commander once more. "We need to get to Sibid before it's too late. My wife has orders to sacrifice her ship so we can save the colony. It's the only way we can save the Federation. Come Mick, you must understand this?"

Mick chuckled. "It is you, that doesn't understand. We're not going to Sibid, Fedrin. We're not going to the Voigt colony to get some stupid device. Quite frankly, we're just not obeying you anymore, about anything! Now in order to stay the deaths of your crew, I'm asking you to gather whatever honor you may have left and fly over to my ship where you'll surrender all Admiralty Codes to myself and then be incarcerated until we return to Larep. Once there, you'll stand trial for crimes against the Federation."

Fedrin looked to his command crew and then back up at Mick utterly dumfounded, unable to reply to the outlandish demands.

"Attention Corinthia," Commander Searle's authoritative voice suddenly rang out on one of the Corinthia's overhead speakers. "Disengage your aggression against the Iovara, immediately!"

"Searle!" Mick said in shock. "This is the man that killed your husband! Let me avenge him for you!"

"Mick, you're an idiot!" she replied promptly. "Disengage now!"

Mick tossed his hands in the air. "Target the Revenge too," he ordered his gunner. "She must be in league with Fedrin also. Pity."

"Corinthia, you have opened fire on the Iovara and have directed secondary batteries toward the Revenge. Please state the reasons for this action at once!" Commander Sanders voice sounded out next.

"Mick you numbskull!" Drezden's angry voice rang out moments after. "Stop it now before you kill us all!"

Mick appeared frustrated but kept his cool as he nodded to his communications officer. "My fellow commanders, I have been commissioned by the War Council to remove Fedrin from his position. He is a murderer and a traitor to his people. In light of this, I am assuming command over the fleet. You would all do well to follow my leadership."

Several moments of tense silence on all transmission lines followed Mick's statement. Fedrin swallowed hard and waited, unsure of what to say. How does one reason with a madman?

The ever-impetuous Colby finally broke the silence. "That's a negative. You have no authority to implement this action especially this way. Stand down or prepare to engage us along side the Iovara. Our gun ports are opening as I speak!"

"That goes for the rest of us," Kendrick followed. "Stand down now and you might keep your life Mick. My fighters are prepping to launch and they will not hesitate to open fire on your ship if I give the command!"

Mick looked confused and angry. Why were the other commanders not rallying around him? "Neider, open fire on the Hornell!" Mick finally ordered. "Kill everyone! None of them deserve to live!"

"Obey that order and it will be your last!" a frail, yet commanding voice sounded out in the back of the Corinthia's bridge.

"What?" exclaimed Mick as he turned around in shock to see Grider with a lydeg pistol held firmly in his hand.

"Well, well, well. If it isn't everyone's favorite senile admiral come to pay his new boss a visit," Mick said with a smirk.

Grider nudged his chair a little deeper into the room. "I'm not kidding around with you Mick," he said firmly. "Order your crew to stand down."

"And what will you do if I don't old man? Shoot me?"

"If I have to," Grider replied and then shook his head. "You're being manipulated Mick; If you really don't know that, then you're either more stupid than you look or just plain evil. My guess is a little of both."

"Manipulated?" shouted Mick, his eyes bulging with rage. "Me? I don't think so! It's all of you who are being played with by him!" he finished, pointing to Fedrin.

"No Mick," Grider said solemnly shaking his head. "Fedrin doesn't kill innocent people to prove a point."

"I didn't kill anyone!" Mick shouted back.

Grider closed his eyes and shook his head. "Let me get this straight Mick. You just punched a hole into the Iovara's hull and you don't think you killed anyone? Do you know what happens when you depressurize a starship in space Mick? Do you? Because I can tell you if you really don't know."

"If anyone died it was incidental!" Mick shouted back, as he waved his arm in the air. "They were but a small price that had to be paid to save the whole!"

Grider pointed a finger at Mick and shook his head. "A true admiral would never let a sentence like that come out of his mouth!"

Mick shook his head. "Wrong! A true Admiral must know when the collateral cost is acceptable, or have you forgotten how you let the Asar colonists get butchered because you wouldn't risk your son?"

Grider squirmed. "That was different! Now stand down before this gets uglier than it already is!"

"You'll have to shoot me old man because I'm not standing down. This is my fleet now!" answered Mick, tightening his jaw and looking as resolute as ever.

Grider raised his weapon till it pointed directly at Mick's chest. Mick stared down the barrel of the weapon as beads of sweat formed along his hairline. "You won't do it," he said as he slowly reached for the pistol fastened on his own belt. "You don't have the courage to pull that trigger. You've never had the courage to make the important decisions and you never will."

The Corinthia command crew looked on in awe at the situation playing out on their bridge, many beginning to wonder if Mick was indeed mad.

Mick continued to speak to Grider, all the while inching closer toward the handle of his own weapon. "Its a good thing your son died when he did."

"Why is that?" Grider asked with furry burning in his own eyes.

Mick shrugged. "Because he probably would have grown up to be a coward just like his dad!" he finished and grabbed at his gun and let off a shot, striking Grider in the chest but not before Grider had sent two of his own rounds into Mick.

Mick slumped to his knees and gasped as blood oozed from the gaping holes.

Grider too struggled to breathe as he rode up beside Mick and looked into his eyes. "My son...was not a coward," he calmly said and then leveled his weapon to Mick's temple and squeezed the trigger one last time. Mick slumped over dead. The rest of the Corinthia command crew looked on in horror as the leader of their short-lived mutiny lay dead in the center of the command deck.

Grider then dropped his weapon to the floor and mustered all of his remaining strength to look up at Fedrin. "Lead on Admiral," he struggled to say before slumping back in his chair, dead.

Fedrin turned away from the screen in a daze. He took several shaky steps toward the nearest operating station and rested against it.

"Sir, we are being flooded with transmissions from the commanders," Gallo hesitantly announced. "They all want to talk with you."

Fedrin slowly nodded. "Set up a fleet wide transmission. I want it played on all speakers in every corridor of every ship."

"Done," said Gallo promptly.

Fedrin swallowed hard and wiped his sweaty brow. "Attention crewmen of the Sixth Fleet. This is the Admiral," he began. "We have all just seen firsthand how our enemy operates. We should take heart in the fact that they are afraid...perhaps even terrified of us. They have beaten us badly these last several days, with the cost almost more then we can bare and yet they are still frightened of us! They are so scared in fact, that they are now resorting to sowing seeds of discord and mistrust within our very ranks with the hopes of destroying us from the inside out. I fear that they have already succeeded in doing this back home and today they nearly succeeded here! Yet Commander Mick's misguided treachery need not be a total loss for us. For with this audacious move by our enemy, take comfort in the fact that they fear us now, more than ever before! Now let's give them even more reason to fear us! Secure all equipment, retract all external instruments and divert full power to engine cores. We're going to Sibid and the Voigt colony!"

Darion walked away from the transport-tube ramp and made his way down the shaded stone path that led to the Memorial Fountain. He was dressed in civilian clothing, although he didn't really know why. To anyone that may have been tracking him, he must have stood out like a sore thumb.

The Memorial was located in the center of Liberty Park, a picturesque oasis in the otherwise arid Larep landscape. A few trees and a host of small, but well maintained vegetable gardens leased to restaurants and wealthy city residents filled nearly every free inch of the park's real estate. Circumscribed by these gardens was the famous Refrac War Memorial Fountain.

It was crafted out of a large asteroid harvested from the Asar system and hewn out to form a deep, watertight basin. A holographic star system hovered above the center. Embedded into the outer edge of the basin were hundreds of micronized water jets, which propelled tiny droplets of pressurized water through the holographic system. As the droplets passed though the hologram, they were reshaped by polarity beams to form the name of a casualty in the Refrac war. The name would display for only a few seconds before the form dissipated and rained back down into the basin.

An old man with a cane in hand stood nearby, looking intently as the names rained down. Every so often he would shake his head as a name appeared and then quickly vanished. A few kids, barely seven or eight years old, played on the other side of the basin each taking turns reaching their hands into the water and splashing the other, neither seeming to have any idea of the fountain's purpose or significance.

Darion sat down on a stone bench facing the basin and looked up at the raining names, all the while keeping a watchful eye for anyone or anything that seemed suspicious. The more he looked around however, the more he felt he stood out. This covert stuff was not his thing.

At least fifteen minutes had passed when a hand suddenly squeezed his shoulder. He quickly jumped to his feet.

"You shouldn't sneak up on a guy like that!" he exclaimed, holding his chest and then glancing around to see if he had attracted any attention.

"I see you got my note," Kebbs said and smiled. "Thanks for coming. I wasn't sure you would."

"I almost didn't," said Darion. "I didn't really want to see you again anytime soon."

Kebbs nodded awkwardly before smiling. "Then I guess double thanks are in order."

"Whatever," muttered Darion, not at all amused. "So what's this stuff about the Clear Skies system?"

"This isn't the best place for this discussion," Kebbs replied frankly, nodding toward the fountain and the people gathered around it.

"Then why'd you ask me to come here?" Darion asked rolling his eyes. "This place was your choice, not mine!"

Kebbs motioned toward a dusty path well beyond the fountain. "Walk with me," he said.

Darion glanced around before reluctantly following, having convinced himself that if he had come this far, he might as well go all the way.

They walked in silence for sometime, Darion wondering with each step what in the world he was doing while Kebbs suspiciously eyed every person they passed and made a point to walk on the harder paths. On and on they trudged until the lush oasis filled with water and pleasant little gardens was far behind them and nothing but dried up trees and unending sand mounds surrounded them. Tired and sweaty, Darion finally planted his feet after stumbling over a drift of sand and would be compelled to go no further.

"This is far enough Kebbs!" he said definitively. "Now do you want to tell me what's going on?"

Kebbs motioned for Darion to lower his voice and once more looked around nervously. "We are here because I don't want to take any chances," he said and nodded toward a cluster of withered trees, their deadened roots protruding out of the shifting sands.

Darion glanced up and then looked back at Kebbs in surprise and shock. "You mounted signal disruptors in the trees? You must be joking?"

"Like I said," Kebbs began "I wasn't going to take any chances."

"Chances about what? Your parole officer finding where you spend your time? Come on Kebbs! I don't have time to waste with all this cloak and dagger nonsense. You're a trash man for goodness sake! Now tell me what you have to tell me so I can go. I have a lot of responsibilities that I need to get back to...not that you'd know anything about responsibility."

Kebbs shook his head. "Some things never change."

"Apparently not!" snapped Darion. "You have three minutes! Make them count."

Kebbs raised an eyebrow. "Ok, then. Well, the reason I wanted you here instead of your office is because I believe your new office is bugged."

Darion momentarily looked surprised and then shrugged. "So?"

Kebbs shook his head; frustrated that his revelation didn't have the impact he had hoped but pressed on just the same. "I believe the same people who have bugged your office are the same people that are trying to make you their puppet now."

"Two minutes, thirty seconds," Darion replied, looking as disinterested as he could.

Kebbs eyes flared. "Don't be an idiot Darion! You know what I'm talking about!"

Darion leaned toward Kesler. "I have no idea what you are talking about. And if you have a point to make, I suggest you make it sooner rather than later. Your clock is ticking."

Kebbs looked at Darion in disbelief and then shook his head. "Darion, you have been set up to make our defenses as soft as possible, undoubtedly in preparation of a major landing by the Krohns!"

Darion looked at Kebbs and then turned to walk away. "You know what Kebbs, I don't have any time for this apparently. I'm sorry I came. Have fun at the trash plant!"

Kebbs held out his arms. "This isn't about your brother Darion! This is about the fate of the capital! Maybe the fate of the Federation!"

Darion froze in his tracks, still facing away.

Kebbs shook his head. "Don't be a selfish jerk! This is bigger than your feelings!"

Darion turned sharply and shook a finger in Kebbs face. "Try telling my brother that I'm a selfish jerk! Oh wait, you can't! He's dead!"

"Are you really going to start this all over again now?" Kebbs asked with disgust. "It was an accident Darion! I don't know how many times I need to tell you. It was just an accident!"

"You were responsible! You should have been watching after him more closely!"

"He wasn't a child, Darion!" Kebbs said sharply. "I couldn't hold his hand every step of the climb."

"Not a child? He was only seventeen!" Darion exclaimed. "Who brings a seventeen year old on the hardest climb on the continent? Who?"

"It was our third time doing it!" Kebbs yelled back. "He hit a bad spot and slipped. It was an accident Darion. And regardless of what you want to think, or whom you want to blame, at the end of the day, that's what it was! An accident!"

Darion tossed his hands up in frustration and turned once again to walk away.

Kebbs shook his head. "I'm sorry Darion. I've told you for years that I'm sorry. Isn't there anything I can do or say for you to forgive me?"

Darion slowly shook his head. "Nothing I can think of."

Tears nearly came to Kebbs' eyes but he fought them back and looked intently at Darion. "If I can't make you forgive me, please, please just let me help you! What I'm trying to tell you is important. I wouldn't have come to you if it wasn't. I wouldn't have risked reopening these old wounds for both of us if it wasn't important. I promise."

Darion reluctantly nodded, slightly moved by Kebbs' passionate appeal but not enough to show it.

Kebbs breathed in deeply, realizing he only had one shot. "There are no arctic holes in Clear Skies system, or anywhere else. The system was designed to be comprehensive. No enemy can approach the globe from any direction. But when the system is high jacked, it doesn't matter what direction enemy ships approach."

"What do you mean high jacked?"

"It's been reprogrammed by some sort of virus to ignore enemy ships and possibly even target our own."

Darion looked at Kebbs doubtfully. "The entire system has been reprogrammed?"

Kebbs nodded emphatically.

"And just how did you stumble onto this little nugget of information?" Darion quizzed Kebbs. "Do you study military mainframes when you're not at the trash plant?"

Kebbs shook his head. "I can't tell you how I know what I know, at least not yet. But trust me Darion, it's the truth."

Darion looked intently at Kebbs and then shook his head. "What if you're wrong?"

"If I'm wrong, the Krohns will land in the Arctic as you've been told and from there they will launch scattered attacks across the globe where the regional armies will battle them. It will be messy but manageable. But if I'm right, the Krohns will land in force right here in Larep, our capital city! If your army is not in the area when they land, our entire Federation will be crippled in less than a day!"

Darion shook his head as he began to fight an internal battle. The implications of making the wrong decision were suddenly tremendous. "I...I have to go," he said glancing at his link and then back up at Kebbs. "I will consider what you have told me," he said. "But I make no promises."

Kebbs slowly nodded. "That is all I can ask."

Darion nodded once more and then turned up the path and walked away.

Kebbs watched on until Darion was completely out of sight before turning toward one side of the path.

"Do you think he'll help us?" Kebbs asked as Professor Jabel appeared from behind a clump of withered bushes, his cane as always accompanying his strides.

"You've done what you could," said Jabel as he patted Kebbs on the shoulder. "That is all that matters."

"I just wish I could have gotten him onboard now, for sure. The longer he waits, the harder this entire thing will be for all of us."

"It's already too late," the old man answered and handed Kebbs a small data pad. "Got that post just a few minutes ago."

Kebbs glanced at the pad and then shook his head. "What do we do now?" he asked as he handed back the pad.

"We'll have to jump to plan C," Jabel answered and then chuckled, well aware that there was no plan C.

Kebbs smiled and shook his head. "I'll have to let her know of the change in plans then."

"She'll have to do it tonight of course," Jabel said thoughtfully. "If we wait much longer Darion will already be dead."

Kebbs looked at Jabel in shock. "You think they're on to us?"

"I doubt it."

"Then how do you know they will kill him?"

"Because after tonight, they will no longer need him," Jabel answered as the two began to walk down the path. "They have groomed him for this one decision for many, many months. Once it is made and acted upon, they will cast him away without a second thought."

"What if he doesn't go along with it? What if he changes his mind?"

"I doubt he will change his mind even after your passionate plea," answered Jabel. "Their hold over him is very strong and his own character is very weak. He will send the army away, with reservations perhaps, but he will do it."

"Then why continue to mess with him?" asked Kebbs. "He is the playboy general after all! This isn't news to us. Lets just wait for Fedrin and his ships to help us and leave Darion to deal with his own devils."

Jabel sighed. "We don't have time to wait for Fedrin. And although Darion has many faults, we need him. Like it or not, he is the key. We must convince him of his importance. Without him, we won't be able to restore Clear Skies. Without him, we won't get the Origin Codex. Without him, the Federation will be in jeopardy."

Kebbs smiled. "I thought you'd say something like that."

"Why don't you go ahead and contact her and brief her on the situation," said Jabel nodding to Kebbs' link. "Regrettably, she is our stubborn General's only hope for survival and thus our only hope."

Kebbs nodded.

"And I must presently return to hiding," added Jabel wearily, pointing with his cane back down the path. "It is not for cowardice that I hide but as the only one that can fix Clear Skies, I must remain alive until Fedrin fetches the program from the Voigt Colony and sends it to me."

"We have so much work to do," exclaimed Kebbs.

"We do indeed," remarked Jabel. "And time, as always, is not on our side."

"Do you have the adapters?" asked Kebbs.

"Right here," answered Jabel, presenting Kebbs with three small golden ringed-adapters.

Kebbs picked up the rings from Jabel's hand, thrusting two of them into his pocket but retaining the third. He held it between two fingers and looked through it, the sun illuminating the intricate inner workings of the hollowed device. "Its beautiful Professor. Simply beautiful."

"Regrettably, I only had materials and time enough to build three," lamented Jabel.

"Three is enough for now," Kebbs said contentedly.

A twig snapped in the dry underbrush a small distance away causing both men to turn sharply.

"We need to keep moving," said Jabel in a whisper.

"Couldn't agree more," said Kebbs as the two men quickened their pace in an attempt to avert a global travesty.

CHAPTER 13

TARKIN HAS THE BRIDGE

"This is Kesler," the voice sounded on Fedrin's link. "I just got a report from engineering confirming that the secondary power relay grid is up and running. All primary systems have checked out and we are ready to make full speed again."

"What was the total setback?" Fedrin asked, almost not wanting to know.

"We lost a little over two hours," answered Kesler and then cringed, realizing it was not what Fedrin wanted to hear.

Fedrin shook his head. The plan that had taken so many hours to perfect and that involved his wife's ultimate sacrifice, had been abruptly spoiled by Mick's misguided treachery. They were now hopelessly behind the optimal schedule that would have been necessary for a victory in Sibid. Now all that was left for them to do was try and clean up the pieces afterwards.

"Thank you Lieutenant," Fedrin finally said. "Would you also extend my appreciation to the mechanics that installed the grid. I know a job like that usually takes a day or more. Two hours is quite remarkable."

"I'll pass it along," replied Kesler.

"And I hate to ask it, but if we can squeeze any extra thrust from the primary engine core, please see that it's done," Fedrin asked wearily. "We have a lot of distance to cover and not a lot of time."

"I'll see what can be done," Kesler answered, knowing full well that the engines were already running well beyond their operating limits and that the chief engineer would never allow another increase.

"Are you sure about the Corinthia Kesler?" Fedrin asked. "By rights, she should be yours now. You are next in line for a commission based on ranked seniority."

"I'm happy to stay here if that's where you need me most," Kesler said honestly, but wishing that Fedrin needed him most in the command chair aboard Mick's vacated cruiser.

"I really appreciate that," said Fedrin. "I know what having your own command would mean to you, but I would be at a loss without you as my executive officer. You run this ship with extreme proficiency and I would hate to lose you, especially now."

Tarkin looked over and smiled at Kesler and offered six, enthusiastic thumbs-up in response to the Admiral's glowing remarks.

Kesler nodded less enthused. "My pleasure, Sir."

"And as far as the Corinthia herself is concerned, I assume Tenith has already taking command then?"

"Aye, Sir," answered Kesler, cringing at the thought of Tenith having a command before he did. "Commander Tenith arrived aboard the Corinthia half an hour ago with a new command crew hand picked by Commander Drezden per your orders."

"And Mick's old command crew?"

"The six leading officers actively involved in the conspiracy have been placed in the security brig aboard the Hornell. The rest of the unwitting officers were demoted as you ordered."

"Fools," Fedrin said under his breath.

"Sir?"

"Nothing Lieutenant," Fedrin answered. "Thanks for the updates. I should be up there later tonight to see how things are going."

"Actually my shift ends in a few minutes but I'll be happy to come back whenever you come though," Kesler answered. "Just drop me a quick link to let me know when you're planning on being here."

"No, no, no," Fedrin said, well aware that Kesler had been assigned more than his fair share of active duty hours over the past several days. "You take your rest. You've earned it. I'm sure we'll manage to find a way of getting along without you and Tenith for a little while."

"I was actually planning on asking Tarkin to cover the shift, if that's ok with you. The trip from here to the Guardian warp-point is a cake run...a perfect place for him to get a feel for things."

Tarkin perked up and looked at Kesler with such gratitude and humility that he looked silly. Acting officer of the watch, if even for a few hours, was an honor he hadn't dared to hope for anytime soon.

"You really think he's ready?" Fedrin asked skeptically. "You've only been teaching him the systems for a few days."

Tarkin's demeanor dropped.

Kesler looked at Tarkin and smiled. "Honestly Admiral, there's not much more I can teach him. He knows his away around these controls like he has been doing this all of his life."

"Your good opinion is not easily earned," Fedrin said. "If you really feel he's ready for this, I have no problem with it. Just make sure he knows what to if there are any issues."

"Jonas and Gallo are both on tonight," Kesler reassured. "They can help him if needed."

"Sounds fine then," Fedrin said. "Have a good night."

"You too Admiral," Kesler said and signed off.

Tarkin immediately walked over to Kesler's post and stood at attention. Kesler looked up and was about to speak but was stopped short when three pairs of strong Branci arms lurched forward and embraced him tightly.

⋏

He was lost in thought, trying to figure out what he should do when Reesa entered the doorway to his office. She was wearing a black skirt and light blue blouse, both of which complimented her figure (not that it needed complimenting).

"Knock, knock," she said with a flashy smile as she walked into the room holding a fresh pot of lor in one hand and a small platter of pastries and cookies in the other. Darion tried to smile as she filled his mug.

"It's been awhile since you topped off your lor so I thought I'd make sure you were all set in here."

"Thanks," Darion said, as the soothing smell of the fresh lor wafted up from the mug and momentarily calmed his mind.

"And these were sent up by the Kumper Mining Firm to welcome you to the building," she said, as she set the plate down. "I think they are on the twelfth floor or something."

"Please thank them for us," he said and sampled one of the cookies, more to be polite than anything.

"Already did," Reesa said with a smile.

"Thanks," Darion said and then looked down at his data pad.

"Everything alright?" Reesa asked, noticing the distracted countenance of the General.

Darion shrugged. "Not really sure."

"Anything I can do to help?"

"Not really," he answered with a sigh. "Just some issues going on with the arctic deployment that I need to figure out."

Reesa shrugged and then started to walk toward the door. Suddenly she stopped and turned back to Darion, offering a timid smile. "I'm not sure how appropriate this is Darion, but I was thinking that maybe we could do dinner somewhere? Since I'm not actually military, I thought maybe it would be ok?"

Darion smiled, his multitude of worries momentarily forgotten. "I knew you'd come around sooner or later. I must admit though, I didn't think it would be sooner. But sometimes even I underestimate the effects of my own charm."

"So downstairs in the lobby in two hours then?" she asked, not commenting on Darion's self-absorbed comments.

"Two hours in the lobby," repeated Darion with a contented smile on his face that made him look rather silly.

"Sounds good," said Reesa with a soft smile and then turned to walk out of the room, well aware that Darion's eyes were following her.

Darion's mind was momentarily taken off of his weightier issues with thoughts of Reesa's beauty gladly taking the place of invasions and conspiracies. The distraction didn't last. A beep on Darion's desk transmitter sounded. He glanced at the sender ID tag and then swallowed hard. It was from Trivis' office. Darion reluctantly activated the transmission, hoping it was Trivis and not his assistant Armid. He sat back in his chair and waited for the screen to show who the sender was.

"General!" Armid said loudly with a big smile. "How are you my friend?"

"Well..."

"That's great! Listen, I can't talk long. I just wanted to give you a heads up that there's some misinformation floating around about the missile defense system being offline and some other weird stuff. I just wanted you to know directly from me on behalf of the Senator, that it's simply not true!"

"Really?" Darion said, sitting up and trying to act surprised. "This is the first I'm hearing of this."

Armid nodded thoughtfully and then rolled his eyes. "It's been quite a hassle getting ahold of this story. We're still trying to find who has been starting the rumors but it's proving more formidable then we thought."

"So no truth at all to the rumors then?" Darion implored.

Armid reluctantly shook his head and then lowered his voice as if he were sharing a deep, dark secret. "Truth be told, there was a scheduled system core check the other day that took the system offline an hour or so longer than originally planned. Other than that, everything is and has been fine. So unless folks are taking that extra hour delay and letting rumors run rampant, we really don't know where this info is coming from. In any case, we wanted you to know everything is ok and to once again thank you for your cooperation with the arctic deployment."

"My pleasure," said Darion aloud but hearing Kebbs' passionate warning sound out in his head.

"Hey listen, I need to run," Armid said. "Trivis has a whole list of people I need to contact for more damage control. But if you do hear anything about this, let me know as soon as possible. We want to stop these rumors in their tracks. With no ships overhead, the last thing we need is everyone here getting all hysterical that we have no defenses."

Hearing the phrase 'no defenses' caused a chill to run up Darion's spine. "We wouldn't want that."

"Have a good night General. We'll be seeing you!"

"Night," Darion said and then fell back in his chair and covered his face. Why did everything have to be so unbearably complicated?

⚔

Admiral Sherman looked dismally at Fedrin and then to Admiral Nidrid. He shook his head. "I understand that we're all in a tough spot right now, but you must know we had no choice. My ships were running on fumes when I ordered the pull back last night."

"But if the Clear Skies system is targeting our own vessels, you won't get within deep orbit before they take you down," remarked Nidrid.

Sherman raised his hands in a sign of helplessness. "Don't you think I know that? I'm telling you, I have no choice! If we run out of fuel down here, we're as good as dead anyhow!"

Nidrid shook his head, knowing Sherman was right. "Do you think you could make it to Asar IV?" he asked as his mind rapidly sought for alternatives to walking straight into the jaws of death. "Half my ships topped off there two days ago without any problems."

Sherman shook his head. "We've already expended our reserves Nidrid. Getting to Namuh Prime is already a stretch. Asar is just too far away."

Nidrid shrugged. "What if we shuttled fuel down to you? One of the Asar Corp tankers just finished a run to the outer colonies. We could commandeer it and escort her down to you?"

"One tanker wouldn't be enough to fill us up," Sherman commented. "Not by a long shot."

"But it would give you enough to hit a different supply station on your own steam," Nidrid countered.

Sherman slowly nodded. "True. It is better then nothing I suppose and it beats getting shot down by Clear Skies. What do you think Fedrin?"

Fedrin looked apprehensive. "With your fleet off the Zelin warp-point the Krohns are now free to cross over into our territory. Your ships are no good to us without fuel but I hate surrendering territory to the Krohns that we have fought so hard for so many years."

Sherman nodded regrettably, himself burdened with a feeling of defeat.

"Did you leave EM decoy beacons behind?" Nidrid asked.

"We did," answered Sherman. "But I'm not sure how much good it will do. The Krohns challenge the warp-point daily. Once they realize we aren't there, they'll come across full force."

"Is there any danger of them overtaking you?" asked Nidrid.

Sherman shifted his weight before answering. "There is a very real chance that they could jump though and catch up with us. Their ships are faster than ours after all."

Fedrin looked uneasy.

"Reckon it wouldn't do much even if they stayed," Nidrid said grimly. "If The Second fleet can blink out of existence without firing a shot, I'd say the Third wouldn't stand much of a chance either."

"Speaking of the Second," Sherman spoke up. "Are you sure you want to bring your fleet that way Fedrin? You'll be flying right past where they all went down. How do you know you won't have the same thing happen to you?"

Fedrin shrugged. "I don't deny that it's crossed my mind. But the way I see it, we really don't have any other options. We need to set foot on Namuh Prime in order to set things in order, and we can't do that until we fix Clear Skies."

"And this Professor Jabel guy seems legitimate?" Sherman asked skeptically. "Sounds kind of sketchy if you ask me."

"Yeah, how do you know that this isn't just another elaborate setup to kill you and finish off the Sixth Fleet?" asked Nidrid.

"The simple truth is, I don't know for sure," Fedrin said. "But from what I could tell, Jabel seems like the real deal. Everything he has said has checked out. So unless you gentlemen have another idea, I see no choice but to head to Voigt as fast as we can."

"Nothing here," Nidrid said shrugging.

Sherman shook his head.

Fedrin nodded. "Then we'll continue with my plan then."

"And you just want us to hang tight in the meantime?" Nidrid asked.

Fedrin nodded. "After the Third has refueled and restocked with supplies, just stay ready and out of sight. My ships should be heading back this way in about a week. After you receive the signal from us giving the all clear, we'll converge on Namuh Prime and sort out the mess together."

"Think there'll be fighting?" asked Sherman.

Fedrin nodded. "These creatures have entrenched themselves in our ranks. They want something from us...something badly. They aren't going to just roll over and give up when we get back."

"It could get real messy," Nidrid said solemnly. "Lots of people could die."

Sherman nodded in agreement.

"We'll cross that bridge when we get to it," Fedrin remarked seemingly indifferent although he too had been tormented by the thoughts of the civilian lives in peril. "Now take care of yourselves and your ships," added Fedrin. "Once we cross into the Guardian System, we won't be able to communicate for fear of the transmission streams being monitored on the relay grid. So just stay safe and alive. Ok?"

Both admirals nodded and then terminated their respective transmissions.

Fedrin was just going to grab his data pad when a chime sounded on his wrist. "This is Fedrin," he said as he sat back in his chair.

"We're coming up on the warp-point," Tarkin's voice sounded out. "Less then an hour to go."

Fedrin glanced at the clock on his wall, keeping a mental countdown of his wife's encounter with the Krohn fleet. "And how's the fleet fairing?"

"All scanners and monitors are showing normal readings except on the Hornell," Tarkin answered.

"Oh?"

"Lieutenant Catrin reported elevated engine thermal readings about two hours ago. She said it's due to the coolant systems being overworked, undoubtedly due to our high and relentless speed."

Fedrin had been waiting for this, but he had hoped it could be postponed until after the fleet had warped into the Guardian System. "Can she hold out for the jump?" Fedrin asked.

"Not really my area of expertise," Tarkin answered. "I've sent a message to Commander Kendrick asking him his opinion but he hasn't gotten back to me yet."

Fedrin shook his head. "Even if Kendrick says no, I don't see how we have much of a choice here. We need the Hornell with us. She's our backbone. We're nothing without her and her fighters."

"I'll keep a close eye on her status window and inform you at once if anything changes," said Tarkin in a capable and assuring tone.

"Very good Tarkin," Fedrin said. "Thank you."

Tarkin signed off with Fedrin and then brought up the Hornell monitoring window and sat back in the command chair. He glanced about the Iovara Bridge and made sure all was as it should be. Navigation was calm. Tactical was quiet. Engineering was busy but under control. Communications seemed to be running smoothly. Everything was perfect. As he finished looking at the various stations he caught a glimpse of himself in a reflection on a nearby instrument panel. He paused and looked at himself, intrigued with the sight. He, Tarkin, a Branci, was sitting in the command chair of the flagship of the entire Namuh Protective Federation Navy. He smiled.

"This is for you Nebod," he said quietly as the mighty vessel sped full ahead into the night.

CHAPTER 14

THE LAREP CROWN

"**What should we** drink to?" Reesa asked with a gleaming smile as their waiter placed tall glasses of sparkling cava in front of them.

Darion reached for his glass, glanced up at Reesa and smiled. "To the future?" he said and raised his glass.

"To the future," said Reesa. "May it be a hundred times better than the present," she finished and brought the glass to her lips.

The Larep Crown was situated atop of the Asar Enterprises Building in the affluent western edge of the city. It was distinguished as the most luxurious restaurant in the entire Federation, edging out even the renowned Empress on the primary dome on the Asar II colony, and rightly so.

The Crown's rounded, reinforced glass walls facilitated a grand view overlooking the finer parts of the sprawling metropolis as well as the legendary Tharah River winding through the city. The once proud and mighty river that had, in days passed, been the life vein for a fledging community of settlers, now looked small and insignificant, besieged by the mammoth buildings and industry that she had spawned. Yet she was still beautiful and in the moonlight of that evening, she was nearly enchanting.

Yet, as grand as the view from the Crown was, it paled in comparison to the interior spectacle of the restaurant. Essentially one very large open room, the Crown's interior was a collection of suspended levels fixed at differing heights, much like large extensions of a giant spiral staircase. Circumscribed by the levels was a massive, cylindrical aquarium filled with an amazing variety of colored fish, rays, serpents and other unique marine oddities that occupied the two small seas of Namuh Prime. There was even a unique specimen of translucent nova fish taken from the southern ocean on Zelin IV.

At the topmost level of the magnificent staircase was a platform on which several musicians played soft, captivating music that seemed to take everyone away from the thoughts of war and doom outside the Crown's walls, if even just for a few hours.

"So, tell me more about yourself," said Darion as he put his glass down and leaned onto the table. "Have you always wanted to be a concierge?"

Reesa shook her head. "Its not exactly every little girl's dream. But then again, not everyone can grow up to be an asteroid princess now can they?"

Darion shrugged. "Could have fooled me."

Reesa rolled her eyes. "How about you? Have you always wanted to be in the military?"

Darion smiled. "Only after they said I couldn't be an asteroid princess."

Reesa laughed.

"So where did you grow up?" Darion asked. "You strike me as a big city girl. Maybe Larep or Corinth?"

Reesa nearly choked on her cava. "Lets talk about something else."

"Why? Got something to hide?" Darion asked with a flirtatious smile.

Reesa shook her head. "I just don't like to talk about it."

"No worries," said Darion with a shake of the head. "If it makes you feel any better, I grew up in Kespa."

"Kespa? Now where have I heard that before?" Reesa said. "Oh, isn't that what that trash guy mentioned the other day?"

"Yeah," Darion said with an unenthusiastic nod, wishing he could keep Kebbs out of his mind for just ten uninterrupted minutes.

"What was all that about anyway?" Reesa asked and took another sip. "He seemed so on edge. Everything ok there?"

Darion shook his head. "It was nothing really. He was just someone I grew up with. Nothing more."

"Friend?" Reesa asked.

"Hardly," said Darion.

"What did he want?"

"It's complicated," answered Darion with a shake of his head. "No need to worry yourself about it."

"I see," Reesa said hesitantly nodding. "So, what was Kespa like?"

Darion looked at Reesa as if she were joking.

"Did I say something wrong?" she asked.

"You don't know about Kespa?" he asked in disbelief.

Reesa shook her head. "Afraid not. I've not been in this area very long."

Darion relaxed and shook his head. "It's no loss for you believe me. Frankly, I wish I didn't know about it either."

"That bad?"

"Lets put it this way. Kespa is the slum that gives other slums a bad name."

"I'm sorry," Reesa said as she began to tinker with her menu buttons.

"Don't be. It's not your fault. It's just the way my cards fell," remarked Darion. "My parents both died when I was young and my kid brother and I were sent to live with my uncle." Darion took another sip of his drink and then leaned back. "Once the Refrac War broke out, he went away to fight and never came back. After that, we were pretty much on our own."

Reesa shook her head in sympathy. "How old were you?"

"I was twelve," answered Darion. "My brother was eight."

"That must have been hard," commented Reesa. "Taking care of your brother that is."

Darion nodded as a flood of memories, many of them bad, raced through his mind. "It wasn't easy," he finally said. "I didn't know what I was doing half the time but he always had complete confidence in me. He always trusted that I would take care of him. I wish I could have done better."

"I'm sure you did the best you could have," said Reesa. "That's a lot of responsibility to place on a child."

Darion shrugged.

"Do you two stay in touch?"

"He died when he was seventeen," said Darion somberly, picturing his brother and last living family member vividly in his mind's eye. "He would have been twenty-seven this year."

"I'm so sorry," said Reesa compassionately, aware from looking at Darion's face that the years had done little to dull the pain.

"Me too," said Darion with a far off look in his eyes.

The two sat there for several minutes starring blankly at the table saying nothing.

"I grew up on Voigt," Reesa finally stated and then peeked up to see Darion's reaction.

Darion's eyes grew with astonishment. "You're a colonist?"

"Is that so hard to believe?" asked Reesa.

"I'm just surprised I guess," confessed Darion. "You handle yourself so well."

"What is that supposed to mean?" Reesa asked harshly. That colonists aren't normal folk?"

Darion shook his head. "That's not what I meant at all. It's just that, you know, a lot of the colonists act different from home-worlders. I just never got that vibe from you. I wasn't trying to insult the colonists by any means. Hey, they're heroes in my mind. If it wasn't for them, where would we all be now?"

"On an overcrowded, overtaxed desert planet with not enough food or water to go around," responded Reesa harshly.

Darion lowered his head and looked at the table awkwardly, wishing he hadn't reacted as overtly as he had to Reesa's revelation.

A moment later however, Reesa shook her head and smiled. "I'm sorry I snapped at you. I'm just a little sensitive about it because a lot of people disapprove of us coming back to home world. Lots of people think that it's unpatriotic to leave our colony and they treat us like second rate citizens for doing it."

"I'm sorry," Darion said. "I wasn't trying to give you a hard time, really. You are anything but a second rate citizen to me."

"Thanks," she said and looked up into Darion's eyes.

Darion smiled and then took the last sip of his drink. "So tell me Reesa," he said placing his empty glass down. "As long as it's out now, how did you move back?"

Reesa shrugged. "It's a really long story and I'm not sure if even I know it all but basically it came down to my parents."

"How so?" prodded Darion.

"My parents signed up to go to Voigt when I was six years old. They thought it was their best shot to live a normal life, and considering where they were at the time, they made the right choice, at least that's what they've told me. But as I grew older, they both realized that they didn't want me to live the near slave-like conditions of a colonist's life. Sure it saved them from poverty, but they wanted something more for me than spending fifteen hours a day maintaining the colony domes or tending the crop wells."

"So they sent you back here? Just like that? I thought it was nearly impossible to leave a colony."

"It very nearly is," Reesa said shaking her head. "It cost them just about everything they owned plus extra work shifts for life to arrange it. And, as much as I protested at their sacrifices, they insisted on it." She finished and then looked down at the table, obviously fighting back tears. "All they asked for in return was for me to come back here and make them proud."

Darion had heard about how bad the living conditions were on some of the colonies, but he had never actually thought about it long enough to feel sorry for any of them before. He had always just assumed that they had asked for it by agreeing to be colonists in the first place. But the truth of the matter was that most of them didn't have a choice. They were too poor to live on the home world in anything less then complete poverty and their only chance at a halfway normal life was to sign on as a colonist and go to some forsaken rock and become a slave to the system that kept the colony one step ahead of collapse.

He was still thinking about it when he noticed Reesa still valiantly attempting to fight back tears. Not knowing what else to do or say, he reached his hand across the table till it met hers. She quickly looked up at him.

"I'm sorry I'm being such a wreck," she said as she looked around for something to dab her fast filling eyes.

"It's ok," Darion said as he gently rubbed the back of her hand. "You've been through a lot."

"No more than you have," she answered as she dabbed her eyes with her napkin. "At least my parents are still alive."

"Are you ready to order?" a tall man with a neatly trimmed mustache asked as he approached their table. "Oh, pardon me," he said after noticing Reesa's tears. "I'll come back later, yes?" the waiter finished and took half a step away.

"No, no," Reesa answered motioning for him to return. "I'm fine, really."

"The kitchen staff and I are in no rush tonight," the waiter said with an understating expression. "You are at the Crown," he added in a tone of earned pride mixed with warm invitation. "If you need some time, then time you shall have. If you need more cava, then cava you shall have. Any and everything we have to offer is yours for the asking. Do not be shy."

Reesa smiled. "I'm fine, really."

The waiter hesitantly returned to the side of table. "Very well. What can I..." the waiter started to say but was interrupted by a shriek followed by a loud commotion near the ground level, which caused the music above to stop abruptly. "Oh, what is it now?" he said frustratingly as he walked to edge of their level. "Please pardon the delay. I will be right back," he added and began to descend the levels.

Darion and Reesa looked at each other curiously and then peered over the railing just in time to spot half a dozen armed Sentinels in full body armor begin to ascend the levels. Two others were talking hastily with an irate manager and hostess while still several others ran across the floor to cover exits.

"Wonder what's going on?" Darion wondered out loud as he looked up at Reesa, who was suddenly white as a ghost. "You ok there?" he asked.

"They're on to me," Reesa said quietly, and sat back in her chair dejectedly. "I failed."

Darion smiled like Reesa was joking. "Oh come on. You can take them!"

Reesa shook her head. "I don't have time to mess around Darion! They'll be here in just a minute. I should have moved faster but there wasn't a good time. I saw them watching earlier and didn't want to risk it."

"Them?" Darion asked in disbelief pointing down the stairs. "What are you talking about Reesa? Those are Sentinels. There's nothing in the world they could possibly want with you unless you killed the President."

"Shut up and listen!" Reesa said, raising her hand for quiet. "We're all in danger! Everyone on the planet is in grave danger!"

"From what? Krohns?" asked Darion in bewilderment. "We can take them Reesa. My soldiers will be in the arctic under the hole sometime tomorrow. We'll all be fine. Relax."

Reesa shook her head in frustration, unable to convey all she wanted to. "Kebbs was right Darion! The Clear Skies System is compromised which means the Krohns can land an entire army wherever they wish! It also means it can target our own ships...including your transports! If you fly the army there it will get shot down!" She shook her head. "You've been used by our enemies to prepare us for an apocalypse! I know you didn't let it happen on purpose, but you did it all the same. Our only hope left is to stop the troops from leaving and even that may not be enough at this point!"

Darion looked at Reesa in shock. "You know about Kebbs and Clear Skies?"

"You there!" a Sentinel suddenly called out, pointing at Reesa from one level below. "Step away from the table and keep your hands where we can see them!"

Darion and Reesa hardly had time to react before three other armed men reached their level and gathered round the table, their weapons drawn and patience dangerously thin.

"No funny business now!" the Sentinel said from behind his face-concealing helmet. "I have a warrant for your arrest sweetheart. Now just stay calm, and nobody will get hurt. Got it?"

"What is the meaning of this?" Darion said, throwing his napkin to the table and standing to his feet. "Do you know who I am?"

"Yes I do General and that's why we're here," the lead Sentinel said as he took another step toward Reesa, withdrawing a pair of cuffs from a vest pocket and clicking them open. "This little devil here is wanted in a plot to feed you disinformation on behalf of our enemies. But don't worry, Sir. You're safe now."

Darion looked at Reesa and then back at the Sentinel. He wasn't sure what to believe.

Reesa looked up at Darion pitifully and then leaned over the table and kissed him on the cheek. "The enemy is amongst us," she whispered. "Stay alive! We need you!"

"I said back away from the General missy!" the Sentinel yelled.

Reesa stood erect, and slowly took a step away from Darion, all the while staring into his eyes.

"Now turn around slowly!" he commanded, keeping his weapon directed with Reesa.

It appeared as if she was going to quietly comply when she abruptly stopped. Before Darion knew what happened Reesa had spun around and kicked the weapon out of the lead Sentinel's hands, inadvertently causing it to fire a burst of laser rounds straight into the aquarium, instantly shattering the glass. Water, fish, and a dozen other creatures suddenly came pouring down, causing instant panic on the lower levels.

For the briefest of moments, the disarmed Sentinel flashed from his imposing form into a monstrous spidery figure with a collection of slithering appendages flexing beneath a sinister alien face. The glowing narrow eyes of the beast glared at Reesa with a lifeless gaze that resonated contempt while two rows of mighty teeth were revealed behind parted gaunt lips as if anxious to feed. Yet as fast as the horrifying sight appeared, it vanished, replaced once more by the form of the Sentinel.

Before Darion could process the surreal events being played out before him, Reesa sent another highflying kick into the Sentinel's head with enough force to propel him over the railing. He plummeted downward with the flow of rushing water until he violently fell upon the bar, several levels below, shattering glasses and bottles and adding a striking stream of red into the running water. Before Reesa could continue her rampage, several stun rounds from the accompanying Sentinel's struck her, bringing her to the ground in an unconscious thud.

Still speechless at the unfolding spectacle, Darion watched helplessly as the Sentinels tightly bound Reesa's hands and feet and began to carry her down the stairs, wading through flopping fish and ankle-deep water as they went. When they reached the bottom floor, they assumed a single file column and marched out of the door in good military order with two carrying Reesa between them and two carrying their dead team member recovered from the bar.

Darion was stunned. What had just happened? Just an hour earlier Reesa was a cute concierge in high heels and designer clothes that he was fast developing a crush for. Now she was kicking Sentinel's to their deaths prior to being arrested for reasons not entirely clear. Nothing was as it seemed.

Darion shook his head as images of Armid, Trivis, Kebbs, Reesa and the monster flashed in his mind. Who was telling the truth? Who could he trust? Was Clear Skies really compromised? Should his army stay in Larep or head to the arctic? Question after question flooded his mind. He had answerers for none of them.

He had just decided on filing a formal complaint with the Sentinel Service when he spotted something on the table beside Reesa's place setting. It was a small envelop bulging with something within. He pushed aside the napkin that half obscured it from view and picked it up. A hastily scribbled word on the face of the envelope spelled his name. Nothing more.

Darion glanced over his shoulder to ensure he was alone before quickly tarring open the package and examining the contents. Two items were inside the envelope and each perplexed the General to no end. The first was a folded piece of paper. Upon unfolding it, Darion read the words 'Origin Codex' scrawled across it. Having no clue what this meant and not having time to dwell on it even if he did, he refolded it and shoved it into his pocket. The other item within the package was equally peculiar, a lydeg firing adapter ring. Darion had seen many different lydeg adapters and accessories in his tenure with the military but never one that looked quite like this. The exterior was golden in color and contained three small black dials along the side, their purpose being foreign to Darion. Upon close examination of the band's interior, Darion was once again struck by the unique and bizarre design. A series of intricate lenses and precision cut prisms circumscribed a tiny transparent bladder that was filled with a glowing fluid of some sort.

Darion had no clue what the adapter was for and even less of a clue why Reesa would have it there with his name on it. These feelings of ignorance and confusion were beginning to feel commonplace. His mind began to go numb with the staggering number of absurdities and unknowns swirling about him. In his confused stupor he thrust the adapter into the same pocket as the cryptic note and without giving it much more thought, turned to leave.

His shoes splashed through the contents of the aquarium as he made his way to the top of the stairway. As he stood there preparing to make his decent a singular thought suddenly stood out in the chaos of his mind. He was alone.

◢

The massive swirling blue chasm shimmered with the enchanting blue luminosity that only a warp-point could produce. The color saturated every nook and crevice on every vessel of the Sixth Fleet as they approached, undaunted by the power before them. Electrical bolts shot out from the eye at irregular intervals, a testament of the tremendous power and at times, unpredictable nature of the spatial anomaly. Dozens of space buoys cluttered the approach, guiding Fedrin's humble fleet toward the jump.

Tarkin stood at the front of the Iovara's bridge and gazed out the main viewing screen with awe. Although having traveled through dozens of warp-points during his civilian career, Tarkin had never before had access to the awesome viewing screens afforded by a fleet battleship with which to truly appreciate a warp-point's beauty. It was mesmerizing.

"Approaching gravitational well of the Guardian warp-point!" Kesler called out, startling Tarkin.

"All engine operations and coolant temperatures check!" the technical advisor voiced from the upper command level.

"Tactical and defensive systems check completed. Locked, loaded and good to kill things!" Jonas shouted out.

"Emergency power injectors and life support systems all check!" reported an engineer after appearing from underneath his console where he was making last minute adjustments.

"G-lines and stabilizers good to go," another officer called out.

"All core operational systems check. We're ready to go," the propulsions consultant said after looking at his screen.

Kesler nodded and then turned to face Fedrin who sat patiently in the command chair. "All ships report checks on all critical systems. The only outstanding issues are the Hornell engines which are beginning to heat."

"What does Kendrick have to say about it?" Fedrin asked critically.

Kesler shrugged. "He is insisting that she'll hold together for the jump and does not want the fleet to slow down. He reiterated that point several times to me."

Fedrin nodded thoughtfully. "All ahead full Lieutenant."

"Aye, Sir!"

"Once we enter Guardian I want the Bolter to take up guard of the Hornell's port side and have the Defiant elevate her flight path directly above the Revenge. I also want the Arbitrator and three Hornell fighter squadrons to take up the right guard of the fleet. All shields are to be up and weapon ports open. I'm not taking any chances!"

"Aye, Sir," Kesler replied, rapidly typing out the orders as fast as Fedrin gave them.

"Gravitational pull of the warp-point will approach point of no return in just under two minutes at current speed," Tarkin spoke up.

The Iovara's hull began to shake as the pull on the ship increased from the deep blue hole in space. A stack of memory cards carelessly placed on the engineering computer counsel toppled over. Nobody cared.

Fedrin was scrutinizing his data pad, watching his ships tighten their formation in preparation for the jump, when out of the corner of his eye he noticed a white light begin to blink furiously at Ensign Gallo's station. Out of the thousands of lights, buttons and switches on the bridge, this particular one rarely turned on and its activation immediately caught Fedrin's keen eyes. It caught Gallo's attention too and he practically attacked the switch right below the light and looked intently into one of the screens at his station.

Fedrin had already dashed across the room to Gallo's side while the rest of the command crew officers stared on curiously.

Fedrin and Gallo looked at the screen, and then at each other. Fedrin then reached down and switched input from Gallo's station screen to the main screen in the front of the room while Gallo tried in vain to clean the quality. Something on the sending end of the transmission was wrong, seriously wrong.

All the commotion in the room stopped when the screen activated. Several jaws dropped, followed by multiple shaking heads, gasps, and horrified faces. In a burnt out bridge that very much resembled the very room they were all standing in, was Vice-Admiral Sherman of the Third Fleet!

Blood trickled down the side of his head from where an ear used to be. A deep gash ran from his forehead to the middle of his cheek, taking out his left eye and filling his beard with blood. His once handsome admiral's uniform was torn at the mid section and near the shoulder. Blood stained it all over. He held himself upright by resting against what was left of the piloting station chair, occupied by only half of the pilot's body. Blood was everywhere on the bridge, pooled where stations used to be and splattered against the walls and computer screens. Only one other person on the bridge appeared to be alive, the communications officer. As the transmission came into focus, he and Sherman were yelling back and forth to each other fervently. The communications officer desperately pressed buttons and poked at an open circuit panel beneath his station but to no avail.

"Their transmission apparatus is blown to bits," remarked Gallo. "From where the com-officer is fiddling, looks like the sound wave transmitters are destroyed."

The officer in the transmission slammed his station with both of his bloody fists in frustration and then looked helplessly up at Sherman. Sherman then yelled something to him and the officer jumped out of his chair and ran a data pad and script edger to him. Sherman took the pad and edger and painfully tried to look at what he was writing. His gouged left eye socket was gruesome so close to the camera. After a moment, he handed the pad back to the officer in frustration and put a small piece of fabric over his eye and pressed firmly while he began to dictate.

Fedrin's command crew stood gaping at the Iovara's one and only Victory Class sister-ship, the NPF Gemdon. It was a sight of surreal horror. Nobody quite knew what to say or do.

Sherman painfully and frustratingly spoke a few words, apparently choosing only the most relevant ones for lack of energy or time.

Fedrin wanted so desperately to know what was happening. Suddenly, a noise from behind him began beeping. The Sixth Fleet had entered the zone of commitment for the jump.

"Forty-five seconds before we jump!" Tarkin announced looking at a panel at his station.

"Reverse engines!" Fedrin ordered. "We need to contact Sherman!"

"That'll rip us apart Admiral," Tarkin humbly admonished.

"I don't care!" Fedrin snapped. "Do it!"

"It's called the zone of commitment for a reason Admiral," Kesler interjected, saving Tarkin from further objection. "I have already assumed the helm from Tarkin and I will not input your order."

Fedrin looked at Kesler in momentary furry before turning back to the screen just as a huge explosion on the Gemdon erupted, causing sparks to fall from the ceiling as power cables were ripped from their conduits. Ceiling panels and support rods came crashing down about the bridge, one smashing the communication station to bits.

The force of the explosion sent Admiral Sherman flying into what was left of the engineering station. Blood seeped up out his mouth and nose. He would never rise again.

The communications officer, who had been hurled to the left side of the bridge, recovered from the impact and returned quickly with the data pad. He shoved it into the camera's view.

It read: "Third fleet totally destroyed! Krohn fleet overtook us. They have entered the Zelin system and will soon be in Seer space."

The transmission screen then left the image of the Gemdon's wrecked bridge and was redirected to an exterior view. The screen was fuzzy but it was not hard to make out several Krohn vessels finishing off the remnants of fleeing Third Fleet ships. Missiles, laser fire and fighters swarmed the dead and dying cruisers and destroyers ensuring no survivors.

Tears came to Fedrin's eyes as he helplessly watched the Verhow Battle Cruiser get blown to pieces by a barrage of missiles. All seemed lost. The only hope left for the home world rested squarely on the planetary missile defenses, which would not be repaired for many days. He looked around the room at his officers. Each had complete confidence that their admiral knew what he was doing. If only he did.

"Thank you for having common sense," Fedrin said facing Tarkin and Kesler who both responded with a subtle nod but were too shook up themselves to say anything.

Fedrin then looked back up at the screen as it began to flicker and then go black as the Iovara slipped into the anomaly leaving the home world to fend for itself.

CHAPTER 15

GENERAL WITHOUT AN ARMY

The mighty Corinthia, now commanded by the newly appointed Tenith, led the Sixth Fleet with daunting authority through the jump. She shimmered beautifully, as did the rest of the fleet, with a radiant blue light that danced back and forth on her hull as it sped through the bridge-way between the two distant star systems. The jump was nearing an end and had been fairly uneventful, a good thing when it comes to warp-point travel.

"Status report?" demanded Tenith as he paced his bridge uneasily.

"Everything is still normal," his First Lieutenant answered wearily without even checking his screens this time.

"And what's our latest exit time?" Tenith asked.

His piloting officer rolled his eyes. "We will clear the jump in another two hours."

Tenith nodded anxiously as he continued to pace back and forth, a nervous habit he had developed during a bad jump experience in the past. The sooner he was out of the cursed system bridge, the better.

"We are receiving a transmission from the Iovara," the communications officer said, offering Tenith a much-needed distraction.

Tenith fidgeted with his hands until the Corinthia's screen came to life and First Lieutenant Kesler's face filled it up. Tenith dropped his hands to his side and tried to look cool and poised. He was delighted that Kesler could see him commanding the ship and wanted to come across as strong and resolute.

"What can I do for you...Lieutenant," asked Tenith, emphasizing the difference in their ranks by his tone.

"You look a little space sick...Commander" remarked Kesler, seemingly indifferent to Tenith's jab. "Is it the jump again? You never could handle them at the academy. Remember the time you puked all over our drill sergeant during zero-G training?"

"I'm fine!" Tenith snapped and then quickly regained his composure. "I'm fine Kesler. Now what do you need from me?"

"As long as you're not throwing up all over the bridge, Fedrin wants the Corinthia to take point once we clear the jump. If there's anyone on the other side of the bridge, we need to be ready for them."

"Understood," answered Tenith as he closed his eyes and tried to ignore the dizzying feelings coming over him. "Is that all?" he asked, opening his eyes and trying to fix them on the screen.

"That's all," Kesler said followed by a smile. "But you may want to relay the directions to your Executive Officer."

"And why is that?" asked Tenith with an unamused expression.

Kesler shrugged. "You may need to finish the jump in the infirmary. You don't look so good!" Kesler exclaimed and then cut the tele-link before Tenith could reply.

Tenith rubbed his sweating forehead while still trying to maintain the appearance that he was feeling fine when suddenly it hit him again, this time with a vengeance. He dove for the washroom off the bridge. His officers did their best to ignore the heaving noises as they smiled and shook their heads.

λ

The afternoon sun shown through his office windows and caressed his face with its warm rays. He felt cold.

He clutched the steely data pad with trembling hands, his reddened eyes unable to focus on the screen's content. Tears spotted his desk like the first raindrops on a dry rock soon to be lost in the deluge.

Darion had deployed the army to the arctic as prompted by Senator Trivis and Defense Councilman Armid. He had felt trepidation as he did it, hearing

Reesa's pleading echo in his mind as he gave the orders. Her impassioned words of warning now haunted him with deep regret and looming foreboding. She had sacrificed herself to warn him and he had given it no heed. Now she was gone and he was left alone with a decision that was not his own but rather purchased from him by men he began to realize he hardly knew at all.

The fateful decision gnawed at Darion the entire sleepless night and into the predawn hours of the morning. The thought that he may have been manipulated made him wonder why having the army in the arctic was so important after all. Why his army? Was it really his ability at leading men Trivis and Armid sought? Was it really his exceptional strategic skills? Hardly! The revelation of his manipulation slowly began to take form through the long restless hours of the night until he had had enough!

As he contacted his lieutenants and officers to cancel the deployment and bring the troops back to Larep, he no longer cared if Senator Trivis would withdraw his funding increase. He no longer cared if he held the favor of Armid or any of the others on the Defense Council. He was a General in the Namuh military, responsible for his army and for the first time in many years, he was ready to take the heat for a decision that did not directly benefit him.

Darion never would have guessed the ramifications of his change in heart. As he reread the telecast bulletin on his data pad tears again swelled in his eyes. It couldn't be true. He read it again, wiping the bitter tears out of his eyes as he did. He read it the same as every time before. He felt sick to his stomach and nearly had to hold onto his desk to keep from falling over in utter despair.

"General!" exclaimed Jarvik as the young officer burst into Darion's office without knocking.

Darion looked up in a daze, unable to answer his trusted officer.

"This can't be right!" Jarvik said fervently, pointing to his own copy of the bulletin clutched in his hand. "Tell me this isn't right! Tell me there is some mistake?"

Darion shook his head. "There is no mistake Jarvik. I've already received two independent confirmations."

"The numbers must be wrong!" protested Jarvik. "It can't be thirty-nine. It can't be!"

Darion nodded slowly. "Of the forty-two troop transports sent to the arctic, only three managed to make it. The rest were shot down somewhere over the delta wastelands by Clear Skies."

"But how?" Jarvik pressed. "You canceled the deployment! We spent all morning confirming the cancelation with the squad leaders and recalling the troops!"

"That is why they were killed," Darion said reluctantly, shaking his head in overwhelming grief and guilt. "Their death sentences were written out when I ordered the deployment. The sentences were carried out when I called them home."

Jarvik shook his head. "So Clear Skies just opened fire on our transport ships? It makes no sense General, no sense at all!"

Darion nodded slowly, hearing Kebbs and Reesa's warnings repeat in his mind and wishing he had come to his senses sooner.

"How could this happen?" exclaimed Jarvik once again. "Clear Skies is supposed to be our final and strongest defense, not our downfall! Who is responsible for this atrocity? They must be held accountable!"

"I am responsible," Darion answered despondently.

Jarvik looked at his General in surprise. "You, Sir?"

"Its a long story," answered Darion.

Jarvik shook his head. "Don't exactly have time for long stories right now sir. A Krohn invasion fleet is closing in on us and we need to prepare for it. What should we do?"

"What can we do?" Darion blurted out with tears streaming down his face. "There is no army left to mobilize! I've killed them all! Don't you understand? This was their plan from the beginning!"

"We can call up the cadets and local security forces," suggested Jarvik, ignoring Darion's hopelessness. "They may not be the best but it beats the alternative...of nothing!"

"You do it," Darion said as he slumped back in his chair. "You command what you can find. I'm resigning."

"You can't do that, Sir! We need you!"

Darion shook his head. "The army needs me like you need a hole in your head! I've done my damage Jarvik. It's time for someone else to give it a go."

Jarvik sighed as he shook his head. "I'll rally what forces I can, Sir, but I'll do it as a command from you. Mistakes or no, you are the still the highest-ranking officer we have right now. We can't lose you."

"Do what makes you happy," said Darion dismissively. "Now if you don't mind, I have something I need to do."

Jarvik looked at Darion uneasily. "Don't do anything stupid...with all due respect."

"You are dismissed Jarvik," said Darion sharply.

"But, Sir..."

"If you insist on keeping me as your General you had better obey me! Now go! Do what you can for our people! I'll do the same here!"

"Yes, Sir," answered Jarvik reluctantly, suspecting dark intentions on the part of the General.

Once alone, Darion sat back in his chair in misery and listened to the steps of his best and brightest officer fade away. He wanted so desperately to get up, shake off his self-pity and join him in the defense of his world but he knew that he had nothing left to offer. The revelation that he had been nothing more than a self-absorbed pawn in a grand plan orchestrated by the enemy no longer shocked him. He had somehow known in the back of his mind the entire time that he was being set up, but he never wanted to admit it to himself.

The more he thought about the last several months, the more he felt like a fool. He wasn't sitting at an expensive desk in a luxurious office suite because he had special abilities that set him apart from the rest. The reality of the situation was that he had been hand selected for his incompetence and manipulability. By who and for what ultimate purpose, Darion couldn't begin to guess, but what did it matter at this point? Reesa had been arrested, the Third and Second Fleets were destroyed, the remains of the Sixth were gone, a Krohn armada was on its way and his own army had just been destroyed.

With surprisingly little hesitation, Darion opened a drawer at his desk and removed a small pistol from its foam casing. It hadn't been fired in years and shimmered just as it did the day he had been issued it. He handled it gently, as if he feared it before suddenly turning the safety off. He slowly brought the weapon to his temple. He was about to do the unthinkable when an incoming transmission sounded. He didn't know why he did it, but he nervously tossed the gun back into the drawer and activated the transmission, shocked with what he almost did and yet lamenting the interruption. Armid's face filled the screen.

"What do you want?" said Darion, hoping he would once again be able to work up the nerve.

"I'm really not sure what to say," said Armid with an unpleasant smile.

"Try," muttered Darion.

"Well," said Armid, nearly unable to contain his excitement. "Before you kill yourself I wanted to thank you for all your cooperation over the last several months. None of what is about to happen could have without you. I am forever in your debt."

Darion shook his head as he realized that, true to Kebbs' warning, his office had been bugged.

"Not surprised?" Armid added, disappointed with Darion's lack of reaction.

"I put it all together last night after your people took Reesa."

Armid shook his head. "I'm surprised, I really am. After working with you all this time I had assumed you were incapable of independent thought. But I guess I can't be right about everything."

"What do you want Armid?" Darion muttered. "What more can you do or take from me than you already have?"

Armid shrugged. "Nothing. I just wanted you to realize that it was I all along. It gives a certain amount of job satisfaction you could say."

Darion didn't react. His fight had already been extinguished.

"Well, I guess I better run," said Armid in a disturbingly cheerful voice. "I need to finish interrogating Reesa this afternoon and organize a welcoming committee for the Krohns. So much to do and so little time."

Darion looked up in surprise. "She...is still alive?"

Armid smiled sadistically. "Reesa? Yes, for the moment," he said and then chuckled. "But I have very...shall we say, invasive techniques when it comes to interrogations. She won't last the night I'm afraid, although she is surprisingly strong for a woman. I have a feeling she wasn't always a concierge; I guess I'll find that out during our...chat."

"Leave her alone!" Darion yelled. "She has done nothing to you! Take me in her place!"

Armid chuckled. "Take you? You must be joking! At least this woman knows something! The only thing you know is where to get a really over-priced haircut! No thanks General. I don't want you!"

"I'll kill you! I'll kill you!" yelled Darion.

"You and what army?" said Armid mockingly. "Oh wait, you don't have one!"

"Trivis will stop you!" Darion said. "I have his personal link frequency. He'll know all about you within the hour!"

Armid smirked. "It is obvious your usefulness has reached its end Darion. Now do the planet a little favor and finish the job you started before I contacted you. Ok?"

"What...what if I give you the Origin Codex?" Darion suddenly shouted out, remembering the scrap of paper in his pocket and taking a rather large gamble that it was relevant.

Armid looked up at Darion in complete shock. "You...you have the Codex?" he stammered.

"Will you let her go if I give it to you?" asked Darion, realizing that he had just discovered a bargaining chip that he did not actually have.

"Where is it?" asked Armid.

"Do you want to deal or no?" repeated Darion. "Its not a trick question."

Armid looked at Darion critically before gradually nodding. "You better not be messing with me."

"And you better not touch Reesa," snapped Darion.

"Where and when?" pressed Armid.

Darion shook his head. "We'll be in touch," he then said and cut the link in what he hoped would be a show of confidence when it was really just the opposite. The moment the link was cut, Darion dove back into his desk drawer, reclaimed his weapon, tucked it in his belt and quickly made his way toward the door. The Sentinel response teams could reach any location within the city in mere minutes, meaning that he had precious little time to get out before it was too late.

As he ran out of the building and sprinted down the street, he marveled how he had been a mere finger squeeze from ending his own life. Now he was running through the streets trying to stay alive and hopefully save the life of a woman he had known for only two days!

⋏

Commander Sanders gazed forlornly out his window aboard the Bolter, his metal home away from home. Blue waves of translucent light flowed steadily past the circular window, taking his mind back to the horrific events of the last several days. The Sixth fleet had burned out from beneath him. His beloved daughter had perished with the Second Fleet, which dulled the otherwise disastrous news that the Third fleet had also been destroyed. The fact that a Krohn battle group was even now closing in on Namuh Prime hardly fazed him. He was so emotionally drained that he had nothing left to give, nothing left to feel. The critical past several days had given Sanders precious little time to dwell on his sorrows or grieve his loss. Quick actions and split second decisions were required to keep his ship and crew one step ahead of sharing fates similar to so many other ships and crews. His emotional distress was not a luxury he could indulge in.

In truth, Sanders felt guilty with how little he had mourned his daughter's demise. He had of course loved her dearly, but the distance created by serving in different fleets had a paradoxical soothing affect when he had heard the news, as if the displacement made the loss less real somehow.

Sanders shook his head and walked away from his window, tossing his shirt on the floor before collapsing on his bed. A wave of somnolence came over him almost instantly. He had nearly succumbed when he turned to his nightstand and looked at a picture of his daughter and himself when she was but a young girl of five. Sanders lay in his bed starring at the picture, marveling at the joy and contentment on his face all those years ago. His eyes then slowly turned to his daughter. She wore his uniform hat on her head, which came down and covered one of her deep brown eyes. She was smiling from ear to ear. How she had adored him.

Sanders looked at the photo thoughtfully for sometime as an avalanche of memories suddenly came upon him; places they had gone together, conversations long since forgotten returned in vivid detail and the strong bonds of fatherly love once again resounded in his soul. The emotional insulation of being separated for the last several months slowly slipped away as he carefully picked up the picture and held it close to his chest. A steady flow of tears followed him to sleep.

⅄

Twelve hours after arriving in the barren Guardian Star System, the Sixth Fleet continued to make good time toward their next jump. All had been calm since their entry, the first extended interval of calm the fleet had experienced since the attack several days earlier. Many used the uneventful hours to catch up on some badly needed rest or take care of duties that had been neglected during the more turbulent days following the escape from Namuh Prime.

The Iovara Bridge was particularly quiet, especially for the customarily commotion filled flagship of the fleet. The main officer contingent including Jonas and Kesler were off duty, their posts filled by young corporals in training. Even the ambitious and seemingly untiring Tarkin, was noticeably absent from the bridge. Only Gallo was present among the tenured officers and he wasn't much for company. He sat at his station adjusting knobs and fiddling with dials all the while staring into his multiple interface screens.

Fedrin yawned as he scrolled through screens on his data pad outlining the terrain of the Guardian system. Arguably, the most worthless system claimed under the jurisdiction of the Namuh Protective Federation, the Guardian Star System was devoid of habitable planets, useful mining sites, or frankly anything else of value. Nothing more then a few small asteroid clusters broke up the monotony of the otherwise barren star system.

Fedrin yawned again and glanced over at his empty lor mug. He picked it up and was just about to step off his command platform when a warning alarm suddenly sounded at Kesler's station. Normally the alarm would have been just one of many going off on the bridge at any given time, but with the sedated atmosphere, the alarm made everyone on the bridge jump. Ensign Gallo, whose station was adjacent to Kesler's, quickly darted out of his chair and investigated.

Fedrin placed his mug on his chair and also walked over.

Gallo rapidly tapped several keys on the main control panel and then looked up at Fedrin. "Sir, long range scanners just picked up a radio signature in the asteroid belt dead ahead."

"Do we have a fix on it?" Fedrin asked as he looked over Gallo's shoulder.

Gallo shook his head as he tried to clean up the signal. "No, Sir. It's fuzzy, probably due to the asteroid interference."

"Could it be a drone?" Fedrin asked as he looked at the radio waves.

"I don't think so, Sir, at least not any kind of drone that I've seen before. See here, these radio waves aren't packed the way a fleet recon drone's would be," Gallo said, pointing to a small box of wavy lines on his screen.

"Any idea what it could be then?"

Gallo shrugged. "Not really."

"Crud," Fedrin said under his breath. They had been making such great time through the system that he hated to take emergency action now, but he had no choice. "Alright," Fedrin said shaking his head as he walked back to his chair. "Have all vessels go to silent running mode. Kill all nonessential ship systems and order a ban on raised talking and recreational music."

"Aye, Sir," Gallo said as he began typing up the commands.

"Get Commander Drezden on the link for me," Fedrin added.

"Right away, Sir," replied the corporal at Tarkin's station.

"Pipe him over here when it's established," Fedrin said as he grabbed his mug and sat back in his chair.

A few moments later, Drezden's sleepy face filled Fedrin's private transmission screen affixed to his command chair.

"Hey Fedrin...I mean hello, Sir. What can I do for you?" Drezden said between several deep yawns.

"Sorry to bother you Drezden, but I have a job for you," Fedrin said.

"Oh?" Drezden asked as he rubbed his eyes and looked around his room for a clock. "Everything ok?"

"We caught a spook in the asteroid field but we can't get a fix on it."

"Any chance it's just a recon drone?" Drezden asked.

"My man here says no," Fedrin answered, shaking his head. "And my man is never wrong."

Gallo heard Fedrin's comments and suppressed a smile.

Drezden sighed. "You want us to investigate it then?"

Fedrin nodded. "You have the fastest ship in the fleet and we can't very well leave a radio signal this close to our home system unchecked, especially on a mission as delicate as this one."

"Understood," Drezden said. "We'll check it out."

"Be quick," Fedrin remarked. "I don't want you falling too far behind the rest of us."

"Got it," Drezden said.

"Oh, and if you need it, we'll be on page six," Fedrin added.

Drezden paused and then nodded casually. "Page six. No problem. We'll get the job done," Drezden said and then terminated the transmission.

"All ships in silent mode, Sir," Gallo said as Fedrin looked up.

Fedrin nodded. "Send a low frequency coded text transmission to the fleet."

"Ready, Sir."

"Page six," said Fedrin.

Gallo looked up. "You said 'page six', Sir?"

"You got it Ensign," Fedrin said as he brought his mug to his lips. "Page six."

CHAPTER 16

DANCING IN THE ASTEROIDS

"The party you are trying to reach is not available. Please try again later," the automated response of Senator Trivis's local link frequency said yet again. Darion shook his head and switched off his link.

The night air was unseasonably cool, prompting Darion to button up his jacket and pull up his collar. He then thrust his hands deep into his pockets, his fingers feeling the cool metal of the lydeg ring adapter he had recovered from the dinner table the night previous. Holding the adapter in his hand, Darion thought of Reesa, wondering if she was even alive.

Darion leaned against the tree and stared up at his darkened apartment windows ten floors up. The thought of his nice warm bed and frozen meals waiting to be tossed into the thermal radiator tormented him. More than once he nearly decided to walk across the street and take the elevator up to his room, but each time he thought it, images of Reesa being carried away by Armid's men flooded his mind and he held his ground.

"Hey bud," an old grubby man with an unkempt beard said as he appeared from seemingly nowhere.

Darion looked back in surprise, clutching his pistol in his pocket tightly. "Can I help you?" he asked, eyeing the man suspiciously.

"You got a stick?" the old man asked, eyeing Darion's pockets for any hints that he carried a pack.

Darion looked around uneasily before he shook his head. "I don't. I'm sorry."

"Don't be sorry lad," the old man said waving his hands and shaking his head eccentrically. "They're no good for you anyhow, just no good. Stay away from them, if you haven't started them already. That's what my father always said, but did I listen? Nope! I thought I knew better than him. Curse me for thinking so. You stay away from them and all the other wiles out there. You hear me lad? They're just no good for you!"

"I will," Darion said and nodded, hoping the man wasn't drawing any undue attention.

"Just no good for you," the old man said to himself as he continued to walk down the sidewalk. "Just no good at all. Should have listened to Dad. But did I?" The old man's ramblings trailed off into the darkness.

Darion shook his head and looked back up. He sighed heavily and watched as his breath formed a small cloud that quickly dissipated. A patrol craft flew over his building compelling him to step on the other side of the tree, just in case. After it passed, Darion cautiously stepped back out and looked up and down the street. He had done nothing wrong and yet was forced to feel like a fugitive. Half a day earlier he had been one of the most powerful and influential men in the city. Now he had nowhere to spend the night.

A beep sounded on his wrist and Darion glanced down and looked as his link flashed an incoming transmission from Trivis. "This is Darion," he said emphatically, relieved that he had finally gotten through to his last ranking contact in the city.

"Darion!" Trivis exclaimed. "I'm so glad you're ok. We've all been trying to find you."

"My army is gone!" Darion blurted out. "Armid orchestrated the whole thing!"

"He fooled a lot of people," said Trivis sadly. "We're looking for him too. Now tell me General, where are you now?"

"I'm...in my apartment," Darion hesitantly answered as he suddenly realized he had no great reason to trust Trivis anymore than he had Armid.

"Really?" exclaimed Trivis. "We stopped by there an hour ago and no one answered our knocks."

"I'm hiding from Armid," Darion quickly added. "He said he was going to kill me."

"He's not going to kill you General. Now tell me, where is the Codex?"

"Well actually I...I don't remember telling you anything about the Codex," Darion stammered, realizing sadly that Trivis was indeed an enemy.

Trivis paused briefly before answering. "We were monitoring Armid's transmissions," he finally said. "We overhead you tell him that you had it. Sorry for the breach of privacy General but it was for your own good. I'm sure you understand."

"Of course," answered Darion in what he hoped was a convincing tone.

"So where is it?" asked Trivis again. "We need to find it and secure it so Armid doesn't get it."

"Its hidden in the Larep Central bank," Darion lied. "Its in a private vault within the main bank corridor."

"What's the vault number?" asked Trivis.

"Forty-two," answered Darion, hoping that there was indeed a vault forty-two.

"Ok. I'm sending some of my people there now. In the meantime just stay put. Until we find Armid you could be in danger."

"I'm not going anywhere," answered Darion as he tried to think of his next move.

"Good," answered Trivis. "I'll see you soon."

Darion didn't even have time to take a step away when several enormous roars suddenly erupted from somewhere in the night sky. He looked up just in time to spot fire streams of two missiles as they effortlessly tore through the air until they smashed through his apartment windows. The tremendous explosion that followed nearly sent Darion flying to the ground.

As he regained his stance, he noticed multiple Sentinels in full fireproof combat armor, appear from seemingly nowhere and begin to storm the building. Their movements were rehearsed and eerily silent. Darion shook his head and began to step away quietly. He was way out of his league and he knew it. If it came down to a fire match, he and his pistol would be of little conse-quence against the highly trained tactical combat units matched against him.

He had just turned to walk away when he suddenly felt the muzzle of a gun press hard into his back.

"What are you doing out here?" a gruff voiced ask as he spun Darion around to see his face.

Darion looked into the darkened helmet of a Sentinel and shrugged. "Enjoying the night air?"

The Sentinel wasn't amused. With one quick strike he smote Darion across the head with the stock of his gun. Darion fell to his hands and knees, recovering from the blow and trying to fight off the urge to black out.

"I'll ask you again," the Sentinel said and lowered the muzzle until it touched Darion's temple. "What are you doing out here?"

"He already answered you," another voice suddenly sounded out from the darkness.

"Who's that?" the Sentinel challenged. "Show yourself now!"

Darion looked up and was surprised to see the same homeless looking vagabond he had spoken with minutes earlier appear from behind another tree and limp toward them.

"Its just me," the man said. "You wouldn't happen to have a stick on you would you?" he asked the Sentinel. "Its such a cold night and I thought you..."

"Get out of here!" the Sentinel barked.

The grubby man shook his head. "Now there's no need to get upset young man. I just wanted to know if you had a stick. If no, that's fine. They're no good for you anyhow."

"Well I don't! Now get lost before I start target practicing with your ears!" he snapped and raised his gun menacingly.

But the moment the Sentinel lifted the gun from Darion's head, the homeless man produced a weapon of his own from beneath a layer of his filthy clothing and without warning fired three rapid shots into the Sentinel. Darion closed his eyes in near agony with each shot, as they were by far the brightest things he had ever seen. When he could open them again he looked and noticed the Sentinel dead beside him. He then glanced up at his unlikely savior just as he was removing a fake beard and several textured strips of rubber from his face.

"Kebbs!" shouted Darion in relief and bewilderment. "What are you doing here?"

"I thought you'd be needing some help tonight," Kebbs answered and lowered a hand to Darion. "From the looks of things, I was right."

Darion took his hand and stood to his feet. After he brushed himself off he looked around and noticed additional Sentinels arriving across the street. "We're not safe here," he said and nodded toward a thick hedge several yards behind.

Both men retreated into the hedge and cowered down beneath the thick branches and leaves. They had barely taken cover within when an emergency response shuttle sounded out overhead and came to a steady hover above the building, sirens blaring, and lights flashing.

"They don't see us," Kebbs commented. "We should be safe for now."

"Good," said Darion looking at Kebbs intently. "Because I want to know what in the world is going on and why I am in the middle of it all?"

Kebbs chuckled, well aware that Darion's recent experiences must have been trying.

"This isn't funny!" Darion snapped. "This is my life we're dealing with here. Now what is going on?"

Kebbs peeked out of their hiding place once more before nodding and looking back at Darion. His expression told of a dilemma just trying to find the right place to start what must have been a very, very long story. He gave up the struggle and picked a spot.

"I got in some trouble Darion," he began and then wished he had started somewhere else. "After your brother...after he died I got pretty messed up. I did some stupid stuff trying to forget my problems and I eventually got locked up as you know."

Darion looked on without expression or comment as Kebbs continued.

"About six months ago I was allowed entry into an early release program that hooks up minor offenders with sponsors to help reintegrate us into society with some level of stability. My sponsor was this really terrific man named Professor Jabel. I honestly can say he has been the closest thing I have ever had to a father Darion. He helped get me a job, find my own place and teach me respect and the value of hard work. I really owe a lot to him."

"So you're living happily ever after," retorted Darion. "I don't care! What does this have to do with me?"

"Jabel headed up the Clear Skies Project," Kebbs said, regaining Darion's attention. "He knows about things that you and I have never heard of. He has insight into the forces around us and how to deal with them. He is a very special person and chose to sponsor me because I knew you." Kebbs paused. "He wants you."

"Because you knew me?" exclaimed Darion. "I don't get it. Why mess with you when he could have contacted me directly?"

Kebbs shrugged. "He wanted to use me as an intermediary between you and him that would not draw suspicion."

"For what?" asked Darion.

Kebbs smiled. "Originally he wanted your help get something called the Origin Codex."

"The Origin Codex?" exclaimed Darion.

"Yes! Have you heard of it?"

"Only in passing. But you said that was the original goal? What is it now?"

Kebbs reluctantly nodded. "Our priorities have now shifted to a more immediate concern, repairing Clear Skies. We were too late to divert the loss of your army but if we act fast, we should be able to destroy the Krohn fleet heading here now. Maybe not before it lands troops, but perhaps in time to help Admiral Fedrin reclaim our world when he comes back."

"And you know how to do all this?" asked Darion skeptically.

"Not a clue," answered Kebbs with a shake of his head. "But Jabel does. And we are going to meet him as soon as we rescue my cousin."

"Your cousin?" asked Darion.

"Reesa," answered Kebbs.

"She's your cousin?" exclaimed Darion shaking his head. "Is there anything else you want to tell me? Like are you really a Branci with two pairs of arms tied behind your back? Have I been in a dream machine for the last week? Come on! This is ridiculous!"

Kebbs chuckled. "I know that a lot of weird things have happened to you and I'm sorry. We had planned on easing you into a lot of this but unfortunately the enemy's timetable was not our own. But we don't have time to dwell on this. We need to get Reesa out. They'll kill her if we don't."

"Do you know where she is?" asked Darion.

"I do," answered Kebbs. "I was watching you two at dinner last night and I tracked them with her after they left."

"And?"

"They took her to your old office suite of all places," said Kebbs. "I don't know how we are going to get her out of there."

"I may have an idea," said Darion.

Kebbs looked up in surprise.

"Armid thinks I have this Origin Codex thing," explained Darion.

"Why does he think that?" exclaimed Kebbs.

Darion shrugged. "I spotted the word drawn on a piece of paper left behind by Reesa. I gambled that Armid knew what it was and sure enough, he seemed willing to trade Reesa for it."

"What do you propose?"

Darion shrugged. "An insane idea that probably won't work."

"Which is?"

"Divide and conquer," answered Darion. "I will contact Armid and tell him that I want to trade the Codex for Reesa and bring him on a wild goose chase through the city to find it. While I am doing this, you make a play to rescue her, which should be easier with half of his Sentinels chasing me added to the fact that they don't know you exist as a threat. Their guard will be down and hopefully you can rescue her safely."

"Hopefully?"

"Its all I got," said Darion with a shrug. "And unless you have something better, we need to move on this fast. The Krohns are on their way and once they get here, rescuing her will be impossible."

Kebbs reluctantly nodded. "Seems like the best plan we have at the moment. But before we start, I have one question for you."

Darion looked up. "What's that?"

"Why are you doing this for someone you hardly even know? Why are you risking yourself for someone who up to last night was putting on a charade for you?"

Darion smiled and then shrugged. "Two reasons I guess. One, I feel it's the right thing to do. I've been living for myself for a long time now and look where it's gotten me. You and Reesa seem to know something about how to fix what's going on and I want to be a part of it."

"And the second?"

"Reesa is really cute," said Darion as he tapped several buttons on his link.

Kebbs rolled his eyes.

"I've been waiting for your call," said Armid over Darion's link. "Are you ready to deal?"

"Depends," said Darion. "Are you guys going to blow up another building you think I'm in?"

"I'm sure I don't know what you are talking about," sneered Armid.

"Yeah sure," retorted Darion. "Ok. Here is how this is going to work. I'm going to give you the Codex and in return you are going to let Reesa go."

"Sounds fair," said Armid. "Where do you want to make the switch?"

"We'll meet tomorrow morning in the Kespa town square," answered Darion.

"Why not tonight?" asked Armid. "You really want Reesa to suffer through another night here with me?"

"Not really but I need to get the Codex before I can deal," said Darion. "Tomorrow morning is the first chance I'll have to get it from where I've hidden it."

"And I suppose you want to confirm Reesa is fine?" Armid asked.

"That was my next question," said Darion confidently.

A quiet moment followed before Reesa's voice sounded over the link. "Don't do it Darion! Don't give him the Codex!"

"That's enough!" shouted Armid as he once again came on the line. "You happy General?"

"Very," answered Darion. "Now you just keep her healthy until tomorrow morning and we'll both get what we want. Deal?"

"Deal," answered Armid and cut the link.

"Here goes nothing," said Darion turning back to Kebbs.

"Where will we meet up?" asked Kebbs.

Darion shrugged. "I haven't gotten that far."

"Do you still have the paper you picked up with Origin Codex written on it?"

Darion reached into his pocket and retrieved the small folded note and handed it to Kebbs. Kebbs took it and examined it carefully, using the light from the backlit link pad to see it. "There it is," he said waving the note. "She did it!"

"Did what?" asked Darion leaning in to see the note better.

"She hacked your mainframe and found out where the actual Codex is hidden. See these small numbers written in each corner?" he said, pointing at the note. "It's the address where it's stored, I'm almost sure of it."

Darion shook his head, remembering Reesa frantically working at her station when nothing seemed to be going on.

"Lets meet there tomorrow afternoon," added Kebbs. "Make sure you're not followed."

Darion suddenly ripped his link off his hand, taking with it a small amount of skin. He grimaced for a moment and then held it up. "I'll be there," he said confidently. "They'll be too busy chasing this all over the city."

Kebbs smiled and after wishing Darion luck, he redressed himself as the homeless man and slowly walked back out into the night in the direction of Darion's old office.

After he had gone, Darion crept out of the thicket and keeping to the shadows, made his way to a public transport platform. He had just reached it when the local pod pulled up.

"Everything ok there?" an elderly pod operator asked as Darion stepped aboard. "You look rough."

Darion didn't answer. He looked around the sparsely occupied pod before quickly walking to the last row of seats. After sitting down, he withdrew his torn off tele-link from his pocket and shoved it underneath a seat cushion and switched it on, allowing it to be tracked over the cortex.

He then sat back in a daze, trying to catch his breath all the while watching the opened door. He couldn't tell if he was followed or not, but he kept his hand in his pocket holding his last piece of security on the planet. It was a matter of great relief when the door finally sealed and the pod began to coast away from the platform.

The pod's single thrust engine was just coming on when Darion peeked out the window and watched in awe at his burning apartment building as it silhouetted itself against the blackness of night. Emergency personal were being lowered down from the small ship above, while several others already on the ground were trying to access the nearest water supply in order to combat the blaze.

He was just about to breathe a sigh of relief when out of nowhere, a Sentinel jumped onto the platform and came face to face with Darion. Darion looked at the Sentinel for just a moment before offering a large smile and pleasant wave. He knew that he couldn't be touched as long as they all thought he was their way of getting the Codex. He knew that rouse wouldn't last forever but he took comfort that it would work for the evening. He was terribly tired and needed some rest.

"Sorry back there," the pod operator called out to the Sentinel over a small speaker. "I got a schedule to keep. The number seven will back around in about twenty minutes or so."

The Sentinel stood still and watched as the pod picked up speed and headed down the tube.

✝

The Defiant slowly approached the outskirts of the vast asteroid field. Rocks, ranging in size from pebbles to the size of small cities, tumbled and turned as they trembled in the gravity field exerted by the distant Guardian star.

"Scanner results still coming back empty," Hoirs, the Defiant's First Lieutenant, quietly said again to Commander Drezden who was peering intently over his shoulder.

"Keep scanning," Drezden said and patted Hoirs on the shoulder. "Just a few more sweeps and we'll head back to the fleet."

Hoirs rested his chin in one hand as he looked blankly at his scanning screen. The pulses of scanner waves pushed back and forth through the rocks in search of the mysterious signal's source. Still nothing. Maybe the Iovara had just caught a random spook wave? It was possible. Stranger things had happened in the vast expanses of space than source-less radio signals.

He was just about to start another triangulation sweep when a shape suddenly appeared on one of his screens. It was too uniform to be a typical asteroid, but the lines were not well defined enough to accurately say for sure what it was. He blinked his eyes several times and looked again. Still unable to identify it, he sat up and focused the scan in the vicinity of the object.

"Commander!" he shouted out. "I think you need to see this!"

Before Hoirs could finish his sentence, Drezden was once again hovering above his shoulder looking down at the screen.

"What do you make of that?" said Hoirs, pointing to the irregular shape nestled snuggly behind one of the larger asteroids.

Drezden stroked his chin as he studied the shape Hoirs had identified. "Can we get a better look at it?"

"It will be hard operating the scanner in this field," Hoirs said as he tried to fine tune the sweep, only to lose the image. "To clean up the picture we'll need to get through some of this interference so we can raise the frequency."

Drezden continued to stroke his chin as he contemplated what his Lieutenant had told him. "How far in do you think we'll need to go?"

Hoirs shook his head. "It's hard to say for certain, but I wouldn't think too far. Really all we should need to do is get to one side of that big rock there to get a clean reading," he finished, pointing to the screen.

"All right then," said Drezden, exhaling deeply and looking around at his bridge staff. "Buckle up everyone! This might get a little bumpy!" he announced before occupying his own chair and securing his harness.

"Shields set to maximum, Sir!" the tactical officer reassured Drezden.

Drezden nodded. "Take us in Lieutenant, nice and slow. Maintain ship radio silence and keep down all internal sounds. If that is an enemy, I don't want to give it any warning of our presence."

"Aye, Sir!" said Hoirs as he began to plot the tricky course through the asteroids ahead.

"I want the crew to be on silent battle stations," Drezden said to his tactical officer. "And keep those shields burning at maximum and man all secondary turrets. If any of those asteroids get too close, I want them blasted out of my space."

"Got it!" replied the officer.

With battle stations manned and nerves on edge, the Defiant slowly entered a narrow channel within the asteroid field. Large asteroids, lumbering through space like drunken giants constantly threatened to fall into their course. But the plotted course was good and most stayed just out of the way. Just the same, the cannon gunners eyed them cautiously, hoping against hope they wouldn't fall into the Defiant's flight path.

Hoirs watched the irregular shape on his screen intently as the Defiant pushed deeper and deeper into the field, ready at any movement to make a drastic course correction.

After several tense minutes had elapsed, Drezden removed his harness and walked up behind Hoirs and looked down at the screen. "What do you think?" he asked after studying the forms for a moment.

"I can't say," remarked Hoirs. "Some of the lines are definitely becoming more defined but exactly what it is, I just don't know. It's possible that it's just an asteroid with a natural radio resonance and we are going through a lot of trouble for nothing. But still..."

"Keep on it Lieutenant," Drezden said cutting him off as he walked toward the front of the room and looked out the large main window.

Massive asteroids, just ahead of their flight path, tumbled out of the way as the vessel continually forged ahead. Drezden's searching eyes scanned the field ahead of them, soaking in every detail. A sudden movement to his right caught Drezden's attention. An asteroid, twice as large as the Iovara was tearing toward his ship with tremendous velocity! Before he could utter a command, a lone cannon blast shot forth from the ship's forward facing turret. The blast struck the asteroid dead on, blowing a portion of it off but not enough. Another round shot at it, taking off yet another chunk but leaving the bulk intact.

"Hoirs!" yelled Drezden. "Intensify forward fire power! There's a big one coming up off the upper starboard side!"

Before Drezden had finished speaking, a dozen other rounds fired, pulverizing the behemoth into scattered debris and dust. Weakened as it was, the Defiant still shook violently as she absorbed the subsequent wave of careening rock fragments and molten debris from the destroyed giant.

"Report?" barked Drezden as he held onto a nearby railing.

"We're ok, Sir!" answered Hoirs. "Just took some friction along the starboard shielding grid and...what in the world?"

"What is it?" Drezden demanded.

Hoirs shook his head. "The image we were maneuvering around is gone!"

Drezden walked briskly to Hoirs' station. "What do you mean gone?"

Hoirs shrugged. "Just that, Sir! It was there one moment but right after we fired at the asteroid, it disappeared. I have no idea where it went. It's off all my instruments!"

"Perform full area scan now. Fire up the sonar-locator. We need to find it!"

"If we use the sonar-locator, they'll hear us for sure!" Hoirs carefully reminded Drezden.

"Too late to worry about that now!" Drezden said, walking back to his chair.

Drezden had barely finished speaking when a tremendous explosion rattled the ship, sending him to the floor.

"What was that?" Drezden yelled as he struggled to his feet, ignoring a painful contusion along his arm. "Another asteroid?"

"We are under attack Commander!" Hoirs yelled out.

"Unidentified hostile ship in sector zero, zero, four has just opened fire!" the tactical officer announced. "Our shields are down twenty-eight percent but holding!"

"Bring us around to bear hard on sector zero, zero four!" Drezden said as he strapped himself into his command chair. "Fire port thrusters and charge the plasma weapon! Decelerate to mark two and invert primary thrusters! Realign the shielding modulator to focus in the bow quarter and have all batteries prepare to open fire on my mark! Signal the Iovara text only, 'Page six'!"

"Aye, Sir!" a dozen different officers answered as they picked out a command that was relevant to them.

"Hoirs, do we have anything on the attacker yet?"

"Nothing, Sir!" Hoirs answered. "Our scanners still can't get a solid lock on the ship's structure."

"What about visual systems?" pressed Drezden.

Hoirs shook his head. "Too much interference from the debris of the asteroid we shot down. Optical sensors will be down for at least another five minutes."

The large screen situated just above the main window came to life but only static and an occasional asteroid could be seen intermittently through the thick cloud of dust.

Drezden slammed the arm of his command chair. "We need to clear our view or we won't be able to fire back!"

Another blast rocked the ship, momentarily causing power outages on many levels including the bridge.

"Shields down another twenty-seven percent, Sir!" the tactical officer yelled.

"What do we do?" Hoirs asked desperately. "We need to take evasive action now or we're done!"

Drezden sat in his chair stroking his chin, seemingly deaf to Hoirs' pleadings.

"Sir?" pressed Hoirs again.

"Vent the forward plasma collecting chambers!" Drezden finally ordered, followed by hesitation from his officers.

"But, Sir!" Hoirs interjected. "If we vent the chambers we won't be able to fire our most powerful weapon!"

Another blast riveted the vessel and sparks rained from the ceiling as power couplers blew and resisters shorted out.

"We need the pressure built up in those chambers to blow away this dust so we can open fire with our secondary weaponry with a solid visual target! Secondary weapons are better than no weapons Lieutenant. Now do it!"

"Aye, Sir!" Hoirs said, hoping his Commander knew what he was doing.

The Defiant's hull rumbled as the plasma chambers voided their potent contents. As they did, the main screen in the front of the room instantly cleared just in time for Drezden to see a yellow burst of energy rip through the asteroid cluttered space and smash into his ship. The vessel jolted with the impact and the lights once again flickered.

"Damage report?" Drezden called out.

"Shields down to fifteen percent and faltering!" the tactical officer replied. "We won't be able to withstand another direct hit without sustaining hull damage!"

"We have acquired a visual target of the enemy vessel," Hoirs announced.

Drezden turned around and faced the main screen intently. "Let me see them."

The image on the screen centered on a cluster of larger asteroids to the upper left of the Defiant. Nestled in the midst of them was something that looked more like a jagged shadow than a ship. It was black, terribly black. Blacker than the deepest black any on the bridge had ever seen before. It bore no resemblance to any vessel the Defiant's crew had seen before. No effort was put into the vessel for aesthetic design, but rather was made to look like the killer it was. Sharp projections and protrusions scattered symmetrically around the hull carried with them an ominous and foreboding sense that resonated evil and death.

"You've got to be kidding me!" exclaimed Hoirs as his, and everyone else's, jaw dropped at the sight of the new enemy. The crew's gawking was cut short when a beeping noise started from one of Hoirs' panels.

"We are being hailed by the enemy vessel," stated Hoirs, looking up to Drezden for a reassuring look of confidence.

Drezden removed his chair harness, stood erect, and straightened his uniform. "Are the secondary weapons ready to fire?" he asked as he walked up behind Hoirs.

Hoirs looked at Drezden uneasily. "Yes. All operable cannons are armed and locked on the enemy."

Drezden nodded. "When I tap your shoulder, open fire. Understand?"

"Yes but..." Hoirs said hesitantly.

"Good," interjected Drezden. "Patch the transmission through."

A moment later the image on the main screen switched from the view of the enemy ship, to a blood red room with rows upon rows of small yellow lights covering the walls, ceiling and floor. In the center of the room was a cluster of stations arranged in a semicircle facing the transmission screen. In the midst of the stations was a large oval basin, filled with a variety of discarded bones and dried carcasses. Adding to the macabre spectacle of the room were a series of pens lining the outer wall. Half of the barred cages were conspicuously empty while the other half were filled with a variety of pitiful creatures eyeing the bones in the center of the room with foreboding.

The true terror of the room however came from the station occupants. At each, a menacing figure stood imposingly upon a host of tentacles, each one squirming autonomously. Brittle gray skin stretched over their gaunt, naked, insect-like frames making them look more dead than alive. Two glowing, un-blinking eyes contrasted against their otherwise darkened complexion, look-ing all the more threatening by their variance. One of the creature's mouths was partially open, revealing two rows of large, knife-like teeth that looked like they could rip through the armor of a hover tank without effort.

"Attention crew of the Namuh Protective Federation Navy Ship, Defiant," a frightfully deep and powerful voice, sounded out from the central-most creature, his eyes narrowing as he spoke. "You are hereby ordered to lower your shields and prepare to be boarded. Any deviation from this command will result in your premature extermination!"

Drezden walked to the front of the room and faced the screen head on. He had the look of one who held every card in the deck. His mere composure was enough to inspire his shaky crew.

"This is Commander Drezden of the NPF Defiant," he boldly answered. "We are in uncontested Namuh Federation space. Your attack is unprovoked and in violation of the sovereignty of the Federation. I hereby order your vessel to stand down or prepare to face immediate retaliation! You have ten seconds to respond!"

The creature looked at Drezden with indescribable distain coupled with what could only be recounted as a lustful hunger. "Commander Drezden," the creature finally said. "Your arrogance will cost you the lives of your crew."

Drezden slowly turned from the screen and walked back toward Hoirs' station. "You are going to kill us anyhow. Why wait?" he said and turned sharply to face his aggressor. "We have no intent of occupying your empty cages! If we are to die, we choose to die fighting!"

The creature laughed mightily, his eyes pulsating as he did. "You're ship is aptly named Commander, the Defiant! I feel compelled to tell you though; you are no match for our power! You will be taken care of just like the others. You are no threat to us and you never will be!"

"And just who exactly are you to be so bold?" Drezden demanded.

The creature's glowing eyes flashed brighter and his thin lips parted, revealing his weapon-like teeth. "We are your gods!" he snarled.

"Well nice to meet you!" Drezden said with a smile as he slowly placed his hand on Hoirs' shoulder and squeezed it.

Hoirs swallowed hard and released the firing control pin.

"Enough stalling!" the Unmentionable bellowed out. "Surrender your vessel and I promise your deaths will be swift..." his words trailed off as he watched a barrage of varying weaponry speed toward his ship.

"You'll come aboard my ship over my dead body!" Drezden yelled and then cut the transmission.

The cannon rounds smashed into the enemy ship, causing momentary hull shock but inflicting no appreciable damage.

Drezden jumped to his seat and strapped himself back in once more. "Full reverse. Realign the engine thrusters and get us out of here!"

"The path we took to get in has already closed in behind us!" Hoirs yelled. "We'll have to take the ship deeper into the field."

Drezden nodded. "Do it!"

The Defiant's engines roared to life as she cruised past the Unmentionable vessel and sped into the thicket of the asteroid field. Her weapon's batteries fired ahead continuously to clear a path.

The Unmentionable vessel in turn activated her engines and followed close behind, firing sporadically at the Defiant, barely missing but getting closer with each shot. The Defiant was just rounding a large asteroid when one of the Unmentionable shots finally found its mark.

"They've hit us again!" Hoirs yelled as the ship shook violently. The lights were off, for good now, and sparks sprinkled everywhere around the bridge.

"Shields are gone, Sir!" the tactical officer shouted out as he tried to route other power in the ship back into the shielding modulator.

"Damage?" Drezden asked.

"Computer indicates that we've sustained hull damage on aft decks six through ten!" Hoirs answered.

"Fire all rear guns at the enemy and don't let up!" Drezden shouted through the darkness of the bridge.

"Trust me, they've been firing!" the tactical officer replied.

Drezden looked around his darkened bridge. Only the lights of the control panels and screens showed the look of fear on his officer's faces.

Another shot ran out from the enemy ship, this time striking an enormous asteroid right in front of the Defiant's bow, blasting it to dust instantly.

"There's a clearing dead ahead!" Drezden called out, pointing to the newly formed void.

"I'm on it!" Hoirs answered and punched the main engine core booster.

The Defiant lurched forward in a last-ditch attempt to evade the vastly more powerful Unmentionable war ship.

"Hold on!" Hoirs called out as he swung the ship beneath one last clump of rocks.

Drezden gripped the arms of his command chair until his knuckles turned white as the ship vibrated under the strain of the difficult maneuver.

"And we're clear!" Hoirs called out as the Defiant finally burst out of the field.

"And they're right behind us!" another officer called out after another blast strafed the ship.

"Defiant this is Corinthia!" Commander Tenith's voice sounded out over the Defiant's main transmitter. "Pull hard to port and brace for shock waves!"

"Do it!" Drezden yelled to Hoirs.

The weary and battered Defiant pulled hard to the left, just as a series of plasma rounds and assorted laser fire from the entire Sixth Fleet roared past the main window.

"What in the world?" Hoirs exclaimed, standing to his feet in awe. "How did they know?"

"Page six," Drezden said.

"Page six?"

Drezden nodded. "It's a page from Admiral Nebod's book on tactic scenarios whereby a weak, yet fast ship, leads a chase by a stronger enemy into the firing paths of allies."

"Genius," Hoirs exclaimed. "Pure and simple genius!"

"Defiant this is Fedrin. Get your ship out of here! It's not over yet!"

"You don't need to tell us twice Admiral!" Hoirs answered as he quickly sat down and diverted all tactical power to the engine core.

Three of the five fleet's mighty plasma rounds found their mark on the Unmentionable warship, more than five times the firepower needed to take down a Krohn battleship, yet it continued, unabated.

"Initial plasma salvo ineffective!" Jonas called out in dismay from his perch on the Iovara Bridge.

"And now she's firing! Great!" Kesler announced followed by a powerful discharge from the Unmentionable warship that smashed the port side of the Iovara.

"Damage report?" Fedrin shouted out above sirens and alarms.

Tarkin looked at a nearby screen. "Shields holding at seventy percent, Sir!" he answered. "We're ok...for the moment."

"All ships, return fire with secondary weapons!" Fedrin ordered.

The capital ships of the Sixth fleet, together with the entire force of the Hornell's fighter squadrons, swarmed the Unmentionable cruiser, firing relentlessly but with no seeming damage scored upon the enemy ship.

Several fiery blasts from the enemy cruiser suddenly lashed out again, smashing into the Arbitrator with enough force to literally push it away from the battle.

"Is Colby alright?" Fedrin asked as he watched the destroyer try and steady herself.

Kesler nodded. "No casualties, Sir. Just got knocked around a bit and lost about half her shielding."

Fedrin shook his head. "Are we making any progress against the enemy ship?"

"Nothing, Sir!" Jonas called down to Fedrin. "Their shields go down each time we hit them, but following each reprieve from our fire, they build back up again."

"So we need to break her shielding threshold in order to score a hull hit?" Fedrin asked.

A loud crash followed by a tremendous jolt shook the ship.

"We've been hit again!" Jonas announced.

"Wouldn't have known that without your help Lieutenant! Thank you!" Kesler shouted as he tightened his chair harness.

"Jonas, will that work?" Fedrin asked, glancing above his shoulder up to the tactical perch. "Can we concentrate our firepower on her and overwhelm her shields?"

Jonas shrugged. "Seeing as how this isn't working, I'd say that it's worth a try, Sir. I'll program some firing resolutions now."

"Sure beats flying around in circles getting the crud beat out of us!" Kesler added.

Fedrin nodded and reached for a transmission switch on his chair. "Attention Commanders. The enemy ship appears to have a rapidly recharging shield technology that is not allowing us to score any damage. In order to beat this, we're going to try hitting her with all we have at the same time. My tactical officer is sending targets to you now. Stand by."

"The Bolter was just hit, Sir," Tarkin called out.

"Are they ok?" Fedrin asked.

Tarkin nodded. "She's pulling around the rear side of the enemy ship in hopes of evading those forward guns. She'll be ok, for now."

Fedrin nodded. "On my mark, all ships and fighters open fire and don't let up! Commanders, please override your weapon heat thresholds so we can keep it up!"

"How long are we going to keep that up?" Commander Sanders transmitted back. "There are heat thresholds on those guns for a reason."

"It'll take as long as it takes!" Fedrin barked back.

"Sounds like fun then!" Sanders answered.

"Oh yes it does!" said Jonas as he overrode the Iovara's thresholds.

"All ships, prepare to fire," Fedrin said.

"The Corinthia was just hit and the Bolter sustained another volley!" Tarkin announced. "I don't think they can take much more!"

Fedrin looked at his screen as the Unmentionable ship closed in on the weakened Destroyers at the back of the fleet. He nodded slowly as the enemy ship assertively paraded past what must have been perceived as impotent, albeit pesky, cruisers. "Steady...steady...set...fire! All ships fire! Fire! Fire!"

The big ships and comet star fighters of the Sixth, suddenly erupted in a display of firepower that would have rivaled a fleet twice their consequence. Plasma chambers, DEG turrets and EMOD batteries blazed away at the alien craft without mercy. They fired until the barrels of the turrets began to turn molten red. And still they fired!

"Guns are starting to overheat!" Jonas called out after attending alarms at his station.

"That goes for the rest of the ships too!" added Tarkin.

"Keep it up!" Fedrin yelled.

"There it is!" Jonas suddenly called down. "Their shields are faltering, Sir! I think we've got them! I think we've got them!"

"They're trying to pull away!" Tarkin voiced up from his station.

Fedrin threw off his harness and ran to Kesler's station. "Move us up to block her! She can't get away!"

The Iovara pushed ahead, cutting off the Unmentionable ship from escaping and turning her fight path right into three oncoming plasma rounds. The powerful weapons found their mark on the now naked hull and tore the ship in half.

"Cease fire," Fedrin said as he leaned up against Kesler's station, catching his breath. "She's ours folks. Well done!"

"Cease fire, all ships, cease fire!" Jonas echoed the Admiral's commands. "We got her!"

Fedrin breathed a deep sigh of relief.

"Now that's how it's done!" Kesler said, looking at Tarkin excitedly.

Tarkin smiled.

"Admiral, we're getting a transmission from the Defiant," Ensign Gallo spoke up.

"On screen," replied Fedrin.

A very relieved Commander Drezden appeared on the screen.

"Good work Commander," said Fedrin. "We just destroyed our first Unmentionable ship."

Drezden shook his head while smiling. "Next time you feel like sending one of your expendable destroyers to investigate a strange signal, don't send us!"

Fedrin chuckled. "But you're so good at finding trouble for us."

Drezden rolled his eyes.

"Hey, it's over now. We're alive, and we've taken down an Unmentionable Cruiser. What more could you want in an evening?" Fedrin implored.

"Sleep," Drezden answered immediately.

Fedrin chuckled again. "Well get to it Commander. You've earned it."

"Later," Drezden said. "Right now, we've got some serious repairs to attend to and a few bodies to count and identify."

Fedrin bowed his head, appreciating that their amazing victory was not without a cost. "Will your damages prohibit you from keeping up with the rest of the fleet?"

Drezden glanced at Hoirs who reluctantly nodded. "We're toasted but our engines and power systems are still operational. We'll keep up."

Fedrin nodded. "Good. Because if that's what we can expect from a single Unmentionable cruiser, we are going to need all the ships we can get!"

"You can say that twice!" Kesler said, glancing at Tarkin with a concerned look.

"You can say that a hundred times!" agreed Tarkin. "We are in big trouble!"

"We always are," remarked Kesler and shrugged.

CHAPTER 17

THE LOTTERY

"**S**top thirty-four, downtown Larep," the voice of the pod operator sounded out, waking Darion from his shallow sleep. He slowly sat up and took in his surroundings. He had ridden the pod network the entire night, jumping from one route to the next in an exhausting effort to avoid Armid and his Sentinels that had been sent to track him.

"Everyone out," the operator said as she opened the door and stood to her feet. "That goes for you too Hun," she said as she walked over to Darion. "Come on mister, you got to go. I got orders from the station that this pod is scheduled to start shuttling refugees to the city limits. No room for stragglers."

Darion glanced at the woman curiously.

The woman smiled and offered a hand to Darion. "If you plan on getting out of the city, you should line up outside and get a lottery ticket."

Darion took her hand and stood to his feet. "A lottery ticket? What for?"

The woman nodded sadly and headed toward the front of the pod. "There isn't enough time to shuttle everyone out of the city and there isn't enough room in the bunkers below the city for everyone to get a spot. So unless you're someone important, your only shot at getting out of here before the Krohns land is with the lottery. Doesn't seem right to me, but I guess it's the only way to be fair."

Darion followed her off the pod and onto the landing platform. The sights and sounds that met him there were enough to make him sick. Panic ridden throngs filled the streets, all seemingly trying to get to a heavily guarded stage erected in the main intersection where tickets where being handed out at one end and red tokens were being distributed to winners at the other. A podium in the middle of the platform was crowded with several frazzled looking men hurriedly puling tickets out of large buckets and calling out the winning numbers as fast as they could. It was total chaos.

"Good luck mister," the operator said as she patted Darion on the shoulder. "You're going to need it."

Darion thanked the operator and then turned and descended the graded stairs. Once off the platform, he made his way into the thick of the crowd. If the scene from the landing platform was bad, he hadn't seen anything yet.

Trampled corpses littered the streets. Mothers tried in vain to hush their terrified children. Half crazed men and women screamed and yelled at each other in the lottery lines fighting over tickets and the occasional token. Elderly citizens clutched fiercely to small parcels of belongings, suspiciously eyeing everyone that passed. Able bodied men and women with outdated weapons stood around in an unorganized fashion at different gathering points, seemingly waiting for someone to give them orders or direction. All seemed overwhelmed with uncertainty and an impending doom that felt thick and heavy on the air.

"Hey!" someone called out angrily after Darion inadvertently crossed in front of a line of people in an attempt to get through the throng.

Darion looked over his shoulder at an angry man standing in line to get a ticket. "You talking to me?" he asked.

"Yeah, I'm talking to you! No cutting! You need to get in the back like everyone else! Got it?"

Darion rolled his eyes and turned to walk through, inadvertently walking right into two Sentinels. Darion looked into their darkened helmets and hoped they didn't notice his shaking knees. He had no way of telling if they were loyal to Armid or just regular Sentinels trying to help organize the evacuation.

"Watch where you're going!" one of them said gruffly. "There's enough confusion around here without folks walking around with their eyes closed!"

"Sorry," Darion managed to say as he slowly backed away.

The Sentinels looked at him for just another moment before wandering away, much to Darion's relief. Once they were out of sight, Darion darted away from the commotion and headed down a smaller side street, which, although was still filled with people, wasn't as chaotic as the lottery stage scene.

"I hear ten thousand, who will make it twelve?" a man yelled from a top a large trunk as he held up a red token he had apparently just won.

"Sixteen! Sixteen thousand!" a man shouted frantically as he ran toward the seller, suitcase in hand, elated to have finally found another token for sale after the last several he had tried to purchase were bid up out of his price range.

"Is it for the bunkers or a trip pods?" another man called out as he too approached the seller.

"It's a pass into the bunkers!" the owner answered excitedly. "And it's yours if the price is right!"

"I'll give you seventeen!" a Branci woman suddenly shouted out, waiving her multiple pairs of arms in the air as she ran to the man, leading a young Branci girl with curly hair and a dirty face beside. "For her, please, Sir?" she begged as she retrieved her payment card from one of her tattered bags.

"Twenty-two!" the other man desperately interjected. "The kid will never make it down there all by herself! Sell it to someone who's got a chance!"

"Is that your last offer miss?" the man asked the woman coldly, waving the token tantalizingly close to her face.

Tears flowed down the mother's eyes as she shook her head. "She's just a child. Please...she is all I have! Please help her!"

"Maybe if you Branci scum spent more time working and less time leaching off of the Federation, you'd have more money!" the other man sneered.

The woman looked at the man, mouth wide open, at a complete loss for words.

Without hesitation the seller looked away and faced the growing crowd. "I have an offer of twenty-two thousand for this bunker token. Do I hear twenty five?"

The Branci woman began to sob as she picked up the little girl with two of her arms, and struggled to pick up her disheveled bags with another two.

"Do I hear twenty five thousand?" the seller called out again. "Its a small price to pay for life!"

"Forty thousand!" Darion yelled out, before he knew what he was doing.

The man with the token looked at Darion suspiciously. "You really got forty?"

"Right here!" Darion said holding up his card. "Take it or leave it! Right here, right now! No more bidding!"

The seller didn't think twice. He ran toward Darion, took his card and scanned it over his link.

"Looks like you're good for it. Here you are," he said, handing Darion the token.

Darion took the token from the man and straightway handed it to the tearful mother. "For her," he said, nodding to the girl.

The Branci woman didn't even have a chance to thank Darion when a shot from somewhere across the street struck him in the shoulder, spinning him around and sending him crashing into the ground.

Someone in the crowd screamed and others began to run chaotically.

"Get down, get down!" Darion yelled as he pulled the mother and daughter to the ground with him. "Stay low!"

Several more shots rang overhead before Darion withdrew his lydeg and with a great deal of effort, managed to squeeze several haphazard shots in the direction of the attack. Following his salvo he jumped to his feet and took off down the street, clutching his bleeding arm as he did.

He didn't know how long he had been running when he finally looked over his shoulder and realized that he was alone, or at least so it appeared. Taking advantage of the apparent reprieve, he crept into a darkened alleyway and sat back against the cool brick of a building and went to work dressing his wounded arm. Fortunately, the wound was nothing more then a graze that had been mostly cauterized by the blast itself.

He finished fashioning a makeshift bandage around his wound when a burst of powerful laser rounds suddenly smashed into the ground right before him.

"Get out here Darion!" a voice shouted out.

Darion had no options. His position was marked and he had no retreat. He slowly stood up and walked out into the open street. The sight that met him there was chilling. Armid stood in the middle of the street looking as malevolent as ever. Two Sentinels stood imposingly at each side of Armid, weapons in hand and pointed at Darion.

"Isn't this a bit overkill?" Darion asked, eyeing the men and then forcing a chuckle. "I mean, I know I'm good but is all this really necessary?"

Armid tossed a tele-link on the ground before Darion's feet. "You dropped this," he said with an amused expression.

"And you came all this way to bring it back?" Darion said reaching down and picking it up. "And they say the government doesn't do anything for you."

"Do you have it or have you just been playing games with us?" Armid asked furiously. "Because if it's the latter I promise you that words will not be able to describe how agonizing your death will be."

"Have what?" said Darion coolly. "I'm not sure what you're talking about."

"I'll start by removing every hair on your body...one at a time," Armid said coolly.

Darion shrugged. "I hate shaving so that works for me."

"I'll then peel off your skin starting at your eyelids. The screams will be deafening."

"Maybe you could make me into a sweet pair of boots? My skin is pretty tough."

"Enough!" yelled Armid with overwhelming furry. "You obviously care nothing for yourself but what of Reesa? You seemed to care for her yesterday. I have only to speak the command and she'll be dead before her body hits the floor. Now do you have it or no?"

Suddenly, without warning, a volley of blinding light beams came from across the street, striking two of the Sentinels, which let off unnatural roars and fell to the ground. Armid and the other two Sentinels immediately dashed back across the street for cover.

Without waiting for explanation, Darion promptly rolled back into the alley, inadvertently dropping his lydeg at the entrance as he tried to pull it out. He was just about to reach for it when a hand suddenly appeared from the shadows and picked it up. Darion braced for the end but was shocked when the hand twirled the gun around and handed it back to him.

"Don't drop this," the unseen figure said roughly.

Darion took the pistol by the handle and held it firmly. "Who are you?" he asked.

"Follow me," the voice said as it trailed off into the darkness.

Having no other options immediately available to him, Darion reluctantly followed the stranger deeper into the pitch-black alleyway.

"Slow down!" Darion called out after running into a wall. "I can't see where I'm going!"

An unseen hand promptly grabbed his own and began to lead him though the labyrinth of passages between the towering buildings far above.

How strange it felt, being led by an unknown, unseen hand through the dark and stinking alleys of outer Larep. His arm was bleeding. He had just given away all his money to an unknown little girl...Branci no less. He was officially homeless and at the moment friendless. The barrage of foreign experiences overwhelmed him, but he kept up his courage the best he could. What else was he to do?

The surreal journey finally ended on the other side of the city block. As Darion's eyes slowly became reacquainted with the light, he looked over to catch a look at his guide. "Reesa!" he exclaimed in shock as he noticed her unmistakable face emerge from behind a pair of night-sight goggles. "What are you doing here? Where is Kebbs?"

Reesa looked at Darion without expression and motioned for him to be quiet, a command Darion obeyed. She then withdrew a slender lydeg pistol from a holster strapped to her leg and held it up, ready to fire at a moment's notice. Darion noticed the same adapter fixed to the end of her gun that he had in his pocket.

"We were followed," she said nervously.

Darion glanced around. "By who?"

Reesa looked at Darion and rolled her eyes. "The Arts and Crafts Club!"

"It was just a question," Darion said as he peered back into the darkened ally.

"Keep your questions to yourself!" snapped Reesa. "I don't have time to baby you anymore! This is the real deal!"

"What is that supposed to mean?" asked Darion.

"That was a question," Reesa said coolly. "Now come. We need to keep moving."

The two traveled in quiet along the mostly empty street. Occasionally they would pass a few citizens frantically running the opposite direction but the further they walked from the city center, the fewer people they spotted until it was only them.

"Where is Kebbs?" asked Darion, having finally worked up the nerve to speak again. "Is he ok?"

"Yes," answered Reesa as she pointed down an intersecting street.

"You know, for someone that just helped save your life, you aren't being that nice to me," remarked Darion. "I think a thank you would be in order."

"You saved me, I saved you," remarked Reesa. "We're even. So I'll be as nice or as mean to you as I feel like."

Darion rolled his eyes and had just taken a step down the new street when a shot burned past his head, striking the side of the building right behind him and shooting up chunks of brick and motor into the air.

"Get down!" he yelled, as three more shots struck the building and ground around about them, each narrowly missing.

"Where are they coming from?" Reesa asked as she crawled toward Darion, gun in hand.

"I think it came from behind that loading platform," said Darion, pointing with his pistol just as two Sentinels stepped into the street with weapons pointing at them.

"Alright," said Reesa, poised to get up and run. "You hold their fire here and I'll circle around. And don't get killed!"

"I'll try not to," answered Darion as he crawled over to the corner of the building and peered back down only to be met with another barrage of laser rounds crashing all around. He quickly raised his pistol and fired two shots in the assailant's direction.

"General Darion!" one of the Sentinels suddenly called out. "We mean you no harm! Put your weapon down and let us talk with you!"

"After you!" Darion called out and fired another round in their direction.

"All we want is the Codex!" the other yelled. "Give it to us now or we'll kill Reesa!"

"Go ahead!" Darion shouted and fired again. "She's a jerk anyhow! You'll be doing me a favor!"

The Sentinels, enraged, began to run down the street boldly, relying on their armor to protect them from Darion's sporadic shots, several of which hit them with no affect.

Darion was just about to get up and run for cover further back when yet again, dazzlingly bright weapon's fire from multiple directions suddenly struck the Sentinels, brining them crashing down face first into the street. Darion rolled away from the corner and fired several more shots into the fallen corpses, just to make sure they were down. Once he was sure they were dead, he stood up and was about to claim their position when Reesa, followed closely by Kebbs, appeared from the other side and approached the fallen bodies.

"Disgusting," cringed Reesa as she kicked one of the corpses over.

Kebbs knelt and examined the other. "Incredible," he said and then stood back up. "Just like the others."

Darion walked beside Reesa and Kebbs and was just about to express his gratitude when he caught sight of the slain enemy. He nearly jumped back in disgust as he recognized the familiar monstrous form as that which had attacked Reesa when they had dined together at the Larep Crown. "What is it?" he exclaimed in astonishment.

Kebbs glanced at Darion and then back to the ground at the monster wrapped up in mangled tentacles. "Something very bad," he answered ominously.

Distant angry voices suddenly sounded out from somewhere further up the street.

"We have to go," Reesa said after holstering her pistol. "We still have time to get the Codex and fix Clear Skies if we act fast. You two coming?"

Kebbs nodded thoughtfully and followed Reesa's lead. "You bet!" he said and smiled. "And with the pods all tied up, it looks like it's going to be all by foot all the way there."

"At least I'm not wearing heels anymore," Reesa said tapping her boots reassuringly on the ground. "If I had to pretend to be a concierge for one more day I think I would have hurt someone."

"I think you did," commented Kebbs with an antagonistic smile.

Reesa shook her head. "They don't count."

Kebbs and Reesa took the lead as the trio began their arduous trip. Darion followed several steps behind the two cousins...in more ways than one.

λ

The battered Defiant slowly took formation at the rear of the single file row of ships preparing to enter the Kumper warp-point. Forty-two crewmen shorter than prior to entering the asteroid field and severely damaged from her encounter there, the Defiant retained function of all primary systems and had fully functional engines and dampeners.

Drezden stood in the front of his bridge in a melancholy daze looking out over the fleet before him. The warp-point painted the amassed vessels with blue light that made them shine like sapphires on black velvet cloth. Drezden watched in captivating awe as each ship slipped into the event horizon until only his ship was left.

"Full ahead Lieutenant," he said ordered as he left the window and walked toward the door. "Steady as she goes."

"Aye, Sir," Hoirs answered, followed by an unsteady lurch of the ship forward.

Drezden left the bridge and walked down the bare hallway toward his room. The thoughts of his recently lost crewmembers weighed on his mind. He continually relived the events in his mind, wondering if there was something else he could have done, or a decision he should have made faster.

"What does it matter now?" he said to himself dejectedly as he spotted a porthole and walked over to it. He leaned up against it and stared out into space. Blue and white streaks of light raced past the window so fast that it looked as if the Defiant was motionless on a sea of waves.

Drezden shook his head and stepped away from the window. As he continued to walk toward his room he thought about where the fleet was headed. On the opposite side of the jump they were in, lay something far more tragic than the loss of forty-two crewmen.

CHAPTER 18

KUMPER GRAVEYARD

Darion walked besides Kebbs, keeping a sharp eye for anything suspicious...which was essentially everything.

"You ok there?" Kebbs asked after Darion ducked in response to a transport pod passing overhead. "You seem jumpy."

"Why would I be jumpy?" retorted Darion. "I've only spent the last day dodging missiles, laser fire, Sentinels and aliens I still don't know the name of! Why would that make me jumpy?"

"Well as long as you're not jumpy," Kebbs said and chuckled.

"It would help if I understood more about these...these creatures we're matched against," said Darion. "As near as I can figure, they have the ability to appear as whatever they chose to be and can only be killed by weapons equipped with these adapters," he said holding up the ring.

Kebbs shrugged and glanced at Reesa. "That about sums up what I know."

"But who are they?" pressed Darion. "Why are they here and what do they want? And how did we get these adapters to fight them?"

"I don't know anything about them other than that they are bad news," said Kebbs. "They mean us some serious harm."

Darion shook his head, not satisfied with the answer. "And the adapters?"

"An invention of Professor Jabel," Kebbs answered. "They emit high frequency light beams that are apparently fatal to the creatures but harmless to you and I."

"Which makes our weapons useless against Krohns when the adapter is attached," Reesa spoke up. "So if you have a chance to pick up a secondary weapon it would be a good idea."

"Perfect," Darion said with a roll of his eyes. "A weapon one way and a flashlight another. Terrific."

"Its the best we can do," Kebbs said. "It's not perfect, but it's better than nothing. And believe me, our little skirmish back there would have ended a lot differently without them."

Darion looked at Reesa and then to Kebbs. "Who else knows about all of this? I mean, no offense, but it seems too big for just you guys to be working on this stuff. Where is the Defense Council in all of this? What about the intelligence agencies? Surely there must be more forces at play than us?"

Kebbs glanced at Reesa who just shrugged. "As far as I know it's just Professor Jabel, Admiral Fedrin, and us," Reesa said.

"Admiral Fedrin is in on all of this?" exclaimed Darion. "I thought he was a traitor. I thought he…"

"Blew up the Sixth Fleet?" Reesa interjected. "All lies!"

"Fedrin is one of the good guys," Kebbs reaffirmed.

"But President Defuria denounced him," protested Darion. "They had video of him doing it!"

"The clips were faked," said Kebbs confidently. "And President Defuria is compromised," he added gravely.

"The president too?" exclaimed Darion in disbelief.

Reesa nodded regretfully. "We can't trust anyone. If the enemy finds out that we know something is up, they will take concerted steps to stop us. As it stands, we may have an element of surprise. If we lose that, we simply can't win."

Darion nodded slowly as the magnitude of the threatening danger became more evident. He felt so small and insignificant as he imagined the might of the enemy forces stacked against them. How could they even hope to win? What point was there in even challenging such a machine? He tried to keep his pessimistic thoughts pushed back in his mind as they walked but it wasn't easy. Little did he know that his worrisome thoughts were also foremost in the minds of his two companions. They too felt oppressed by the evil at hand but unlike their General, they had a plan to combat it and the will to just maybe succeed.

The three walked on and on, crisscrossing and cutting through the massive city blocks in the direction of the identified safe house and archive storage center Reesa had discovered in her short but productive stint as Darion's concierge.

"So how exactly are we supposed to fix Clear Skies?" Darion asked when the group had walked in silence for sometime. "General or not, Clear Skies is, I'm afraid, out of my pay grade. The Codex maybe I can help you with, and I stress maybe, but Clear Skies? I think you two may have picked a bigger fight than you can handle with that one."

"It'll be a challenge but we do have a plan," answered Kebbs when it was apparent that Reesa had no intention of responding.

"Which is?" pressed Darion.

Kebbs glanced over his shoulder and then took a step nearer to Darion and spoke in a low tone. "Jabel is currently working with Admiral Fedrin to retrieve an unadulterated copy of the Clear Skies programming from the Voigt colony."

Darion closed his eyes and shook his head as if he had just missed a lot of back-story. "I'm sorry...what?" he asked.

Kebbs waved his hand and smiled. "That really is a long story and I'm not sure I know it all myself. But as for your role in all of this, we need someone with the proper clearance to be at one of the deep space communication towers at the right time to accept the data burst from Fedrin. It's really as simple as that."

Darion nodded slowly, knowing that the plan was anything but simple. "And just how exactly do you fit into all of this?" he asked glancing at Reesa as they continued to walk. "And no ignoring me this time. If you want me to help you the least you could do is talk to me."

"I used to be a special weapon's operative for a private security company," she answered reluctantly. "We operated in Asar space and kept tabs on the Refrac Pirates until about six months ago when the Northern Fleet took over all security of the sector. They fed us some line about "consolidating information and tactical readiness" but it's been one big mess since they did it," Reesa added with a shake of her head. "In our five years of operation, not one Refrac ship made a successful raid against our freight lines. Since the Northern Fleet took over, they've gotten through four times!"

Kebbs shook his head and shrugged. "The company was her life. When she was let go she was basically homeless. Since heading back to her real home wasn't an option, I asked her if she'd like to crash at my place, until she found her feet. She's been there since."

Darion looked at Reesa. "So what about all that stuff about being a colonist and your parents? Was any of that true or was that a lie too?"

Before Darion could respond or Kebbs could intervene, Reesa took hold of Darion by the collar and shoved him into a wall and thrust a finger in his face.

"Don't ever talk about my parents!" she demanded, her eyes flaring. "You don't have the right! You haven't worked eighteen-hour days for the last decade! You haven't known what it was like to sacrifice! You haven't had to decide which family member gets to eat for the day! The only amount of character you've been able to muster since I've known you came when you realized your gig as an overpaid do-nothing General was up and even then you had to be pushed to act! So don't talk about my family until you've earned it! Got it!" she said and then slowly relaxed her hold.

"What's your problem?" Darion yelled as he caught his breath and took a shaky step after her. "You know I didn't ask for this! I didn't ask to be in the position! I didn't ask to throw my lot in with you two! I chose to do it because you convinced me it was the right thing to do. Well guess what? I can change my mind anytime I want to! Got that! Anytime!"

Kebbs placed a hand on Darion's shoulder, trying to calm him down. "She heard today on the telecast that a Krohn Fleet is heading toward the

Voigt colony. She's scared about her parents and about the data device there. I know it's no justification for snapping at you that way but keep it in mind."

Darion looked at Kebbs' hand on his shoulder and then angrily shrugged it off. "Your words would have more power if I didn't see my brother's face every time you spoke," he said and then took a deliberate step away.

On and on the three walked, Darion trailing Reesa while Kebbs took up the rear. No words were exchanged by any for hours other than ones unavoidable to their task at hand and even those were spoken with harsh tones and unforgiving expectations. The distance between each of the sojourners increased until Darion could barely see Reesa ahead or make out Kebbs' silhouette behind. It was growing dark and the air began to fill with a cold sense of foreboding and loneliness, as the emptied city seemed to call out for anyone or anything to fill its vacant streets and desolate buildings.

It was completely dark when the three travelers finally met up again and made a makeshift camp in a vacant transport stop. During their walk, they had each gathered several small items to eat, some from overturned food carts and others right off the shelves of abandoned grocers. They piled their collected rations together and ate a hasty meal in complete silence. When it was done they each retreated to a corner of the stop and tried to sleep, although it would come to none of them. After an hour or two of listening to each other toss back and forth Reesa's voice broke the tense silence.

"I'm sorry Darion," her voiced cracked. "I've just got a lot on my mind right now and you were the nearest thing to take it out on. It wasn't fair to you. I'm sorry."

A pause followed. "Most of the things you said were true," said Darion in response. "But I'm working on it. Believe me, I'm working on it."

Reesa sighed contentedly before finding a position that afforded a modest amount of comfort and slowly drifted off to a light sleep.

"I'll take first watch then?" Kebbs said when he was sure Reesa was asleep so she wouldn't try to take a shift, knowing that her ordeal as Armid's prisoner had exhausted her beyond what either of the men had experienced.

Darion didn't answer. Kebbs looked over and spotted Darion huddled in a corner, his eyes closed and breathing rhythmically. He was already asleep.

"I guess I'll be taking both shifts then," Kebbs said to himself as he settled in for what would be a long, quiet night.

⋏

In turn, each vessel of the fleet burst out of the warp-point entering the Kumper Star System. As each ship decelerated and took position, their respective crews rushed to portholes, windows, and observation decks to look out at the site none wanted to see, but all were drawn to nonetheless. Some looked on in quiet horror. Some swore vengeance. Some were moved to tears at the sight of the ruins of the once glorious Second Fleet, the most powerful NPF fleet ever assembled.

Massive cruisers, carriers, and destroyers alike, some marred beyond any recognition by even the most astute officers, spilt their mechanical bowels into the cold emptiness of space. Some lay pitched to one side still relatively intact, while others were split into a dozen large sections, scattered about the sector like the pieces of a child's puzzle waiting to be assembled again.

"Launch all fighters," Commander Kendrick ordered immediately after receiving orders from the Iovara.

"Right away, Sir," replied Lieutenant Catrin as she turned to her station.

"Have Deta wing remain with the fleet but have the rest move into the debris field," added Kendrick as he walked up to the fighter squadron-monitoring platform.

"Clarification of flight orders, Sir?" a squadron relay control officer asked the Commander.

Kendrick nodded, his eyes piercing into the carnage before them. "Secure the area for the big ships to pass through. Whatever did this could still be out there," he said just as the first squadron flew past the main window. "Analyze any and everything that looks suspicious. We have no room for error."

"Aye, Sir," the officer answered and then turned back to his station.

Ten minutes later the entire Hornell fighter contingent slowed as they neared the devastation. They gradually broke formation as they entered the debris field and began their task of securing the area so that the bulky capital ships could pass safely. The sight of the devastation was moving for many of the pilots as thousands of dead servicemen could be seen floating in and amongst the wrecked warships, disfigured, mangled and bloated beyond any recognition. But the pilots forged on, ignoring their instinct to gather the bodies and dispose of them with dignity and respect. They had a job to do and the living took precedence. The dead could wait.

The lead pilot from Zeda squadron darted in and out of the wreckage, expertly dodging stray items and obstacles as he went about ensuring the safe passage of the Sixth Fleet. The nimble craft was just rounding what was left of the command tower of a mangled destroyer when something caught his attention near the stern of the Tribulation battle cruiser, the Second Fleet's former flagship.

The Tribulation was in better shape than many of the other vessels, which wasn't saying much for most. Her superstructure was still intact, although there were several large gaping fissures spanning several decks while other notable structures were completely missing, giving the appearance that someone had taken several bites out of her and then tossed her back.

The pilot adjusted a few instruments and then brought his fighter closer for a better look. He approached one of the larger holes, and then gently pulled the rear of his agile craft up in an attempt to peek inside the darkened crater-like hole.

"This is Zeda flight leader to other group pilots. I'm investigating something in one of the openings at the aft of the Tribulation. I'm going to try and get a better look at it. Over."

"Do you need help Zeda Leader?" a pilot from Kormo squadron asked as he too began to approach the location.

"Negative. Go back and keep scanning the rest of the debris. I don't want any accidents. Flying space is tight over here."

"Copy that," the other pilot answered and veered off.

Zeda Leader coasted to the other side of the hole and lowered the nose of his fighter again to get a better view. He still couldn't quite make out what he saw and he nudged his craft, ever so slightly, a little closer. He redirected his floodlights, until he could see it clearly. The sight sickened him.

A large, ten man escape pod lay pitched to one side and the thick hatch leading out of the pod was conspicuously opened to space. Through the opened hatch the pilot counted nine dead officers within, all still wearing their restraining harnesses. But unlike the scores of other dead, bloated bodies littering the area, these nine looked eerily different. Each appeared to have been completely emptied of every drop of fluid within their bodies giving them a dried, mummified appearance. Their skin stretched tightly over their skulls, outlining their eye sockets and jaws with such tautness that it looked as if it could rip through at any moment revealing the raw bone beneath. These men had not died of exposure to space, nor had they burned alive since their uniforms were not singed in the slightest. They had somehow gotten into the pod alive and had been killed by something from within.

The pilot quickly snapped a dozen images of the horrific sight and promptly uploaded them to flight command.

"Hornell Flight Command, this is Zeda Leader."

"Go ahead Zeda Leader."

"I just uploaded some images. I think the Commander will want to see them right away...maybe even the Admiral."

"Copy that Flight Leader."

"They aren't pretty," he added. "Something is very wrong here."

"Just three hours. That's all I'm asking for Admiral. Just three hours!" Searle pleaded with Fedrin across his tele-link screen.

Fedrin glanced around his room and then shook his head sadly. "I don't have three hours to give you Commander," he reluctantly replied. "I'm sorry."

"Just my cruiser then," Searle protested. "Take the rest of the fleet on and we'll undertake a system wide search and rescue."

"I need you and your ship with us in Sibid," Fedrin answered firmly. "We don't have firepower to spare and your cruiser's big guns could change the tide in a tight battle. I'm sorry."

"But what if my husband is alive out there somewhere?" she pleaded as tears began to roll down her cheeks. "Doesn't he deserve a chance to be found?"

"Searle, please," Fedrin said, in torment himself. "I would if I could. You know that, don't you?"

Searle wiped her eyes with the back of her hand and slowly nodded her head. "I know Fedrin. I know," she whispered. "It's just that..."

"I know," Fedrin quietly said, wishing he was with Searle to place a comforting hand on her shoulder. "Our job in Sibid is bigger then this right now. I'm so sorry."

"You're right," Searle said.

Fedrin looked at Searle compassionately and then shook his head. "I'll allow two shuttles from your ship to stay behind and search the debris, but that's it. Have them ready to launch in five minutes and be sure they have provisions enough to last several days."

Searle's face brightened a little. "Thank you Fedrin," she said as more tears flowed. "Thank you."

"I know it's not much but it's all I can give."

Searle nodded and terminated the tele-link.

Fedrin breathed out deeply, rose to his feet and walked back to his bridge.

"You doing ok?" Tarkin asked Fedrin as the two met outside the bridge.

"I've been better Tarkin," Fedrin answered honesty. "You?"

"No complaints," Tarkin replied.

"You off tonight?" Fedrin asked.

Tarkin nodded. "I've been up here for the last fifteen hours. I'm exhausted."

"Get some rest," Fedrin said, leaving Tarkin and going into the bridge. "You've earned it."

"We are going to pass very near my home world in a few hours," Tarkin said with excitement in his voice. "I'm going to stay up and watch for it."

Fedrin smiled. "What ever makes you happy Tarkin."

Tarkin saluted Fedrin then turned and walked down the hallway.

"We'll have to slow down if we are going to search the area," Kesler spoke up upon seeing the Admiral step on the bridge.

"Shall I give the order?" Gallo asked after Fedrin didn't respond.

"We aren't staying," Fedrin said as he sat down in his chair.

The entire bridge turned to look at him in shock as if he had just somehow betrayed them.

"Begging your pardon, Sir," Jonas spoke up. "But our instruments can't scan every crevice of all the ships. There could be survivors in air pockets all over."

"I am leaving two of the Revenge's shuttles behind to sift through the wreckage," Fedrin answered. "That's it."

"But the capital ships have stronger scanning instruments, Sir," Ensign Gallo quietly said. "They may find survivors that the shuttles can't."

"That's true," Kesler added. "Wouldn't it be..."

"This is not a discussion," Fedrin abruptly stated. "We are not on a search and rescue mission. Now please take us out of here Lieutenant, best possible speed."

"Aye, Sir," Kesler quietly answered.

CHAPTER 19

SUCKED DRY

"So what is this Codex?" Darion asked casually. "Is it really worth risking all our lives?"

"Not sure," answered Reesa.

"About which part?" asked Darion.

"Both," she replied.

Darion shook his head in frustration.

"The answers will come in time," said Kebbs reassuringly.

"Maybe sooner than you think," whispered Reesa after the trio crossed another street. "There it is."

The three companions looked up and down the long empty street. Rows of shops, boutiques, cafes, markets and salons filled the ground levels of the high-rise towers on either side. Many of the buildings had smashed windows and ransacked storefronts while others had bars and gates covering their wares and protecting their shops. Nestled between a quaint lor shop and chic hair salon directly across from the trio stood a nondescript looking office. It had two frosted windows flanking a plain wooden door with the title "Municipal Clerk" etched into a small plaque in the center. It was the sort of place that one could easily walk by on a daily basis for thirty years and never know existed. It bore no striking colors or flashy signs. Its architecture was bland. Everything about the place made it look dull and uninviting...just the way a secret military archive stash should look.

Darion looked at the place curiously and then glanced at Reesa who was busy studying the street and the darkened windows all around for signs of aggression.

"How did you ever find the place?" he whispered in bewilderment. "How did you even know to look for it?"

Reesa paused before answering. "The fire that destroyed the Defense Complex was no accident," she said intently. "It was theorized by some, Professor Jabel included, leading up to the event that someone was making a concerted effort to locate and presumably steal a number of manuscripts from a secured archive within the complex. In a very daring move that by-passed a host of standard protocols, the targeted archives were moved several weeks before the fire to a series of safe houses."

Kebbs pointed across the street. "And this one has what we want. This one has the Origin Codex."

"And it's your show now," added Reesa as she glanced at Darion. "There is a single occupant, biometric lockdown on the facility so you have to go in alone. Once inside you'll be challenged by an automated system."

"What will it ask me?"

Reesa looked at Kebbs who smiled and shook his head.

"No clue," replied Reesa as she faced Darion again. "All we know is that you need a level four clearance to gain admittance, and you do. What it asks you once inside I haven't a clue. I tried to find out but couldn't."

Darion nodded in disbelief. "Maybe a dumb question but has anyone thought that this thing might just be a trap for whoever tried to get the Codex last year?"

"I asked Jabel the same question," Kebbs said. "He said it was safe."

"Ah, but I don't know Jabel," protested Darion.

"But we both do," said Reesa. "We trust him with our lives."

"Its not your life I'm worried about at this moment," Darion grumbled.

"No one is making you do this," Kebbs said.

"Yes we are!" Reesa snapped. "Stop making excuses and go! We don't have time to mess around. The Krohns are on their way!"

Darion exhaled hard, shrugged and then turned to face the bland building that supposedly held one of the greatest secrets on the planet. He took an uneasy step toward the building when Reesa thrust something into his hand.

"Take these," she said, handing Darion a pair of solar glasses. "Jabel said you might need them."

Darion glanced at Reesa curiously as he took the glasses. As always, he had questions but, for once, he held back. What was the point? There were no answers.

The walk across the street was quiet. It was somewhat reassuring knowing Reesa and Kebbs were behind him with drawn weapons but the thousands of windows and alcoves above and around him did their part to unnerve him just the same. He reached the door and after seeing no other options available to him, took firm hold of the handle and pulled it open. He turned around and gave a quick wave to his compatriots before strolling inside.

The room Darion found himself in was not what he was expecting. Instead of an imposing security system and an array of aggressive automated protocols, the room was warm and inviting and much larger than he had guessed from seeing it outside. Bookshelves, filled beyond capacity with books and papers, lined all three walls from floor to ceiling. A single ladder was fixed on each of the walls with levitator pads to allow access to volumes out of reach from the floor.

Many of the books appeared incredibly old and used, their golden titles all but faded away and the leather covers faded and frayed. Others seemed to be quite new, their spines crisp and straight and their wording bright and fresh.

In the center of the room were two warn but well maintained high back leather chairs situated comfortably on a large bradded rug. The chairs sat partly facing each other with a small table between them, which was also stacked with books. There was a small desk with an accompanying chair situated in one corner but from the looks of it, it hadn't been touched in years. Books were stacked in piles ten deep over the desk's surface and the chair itself had long since been recruited for the task as well. Books and papers also occupied all the space beneath the desk so that if one truly wanted to use the table and chair as intended it would likely have taken an hour just to move the volumes.

The room bore a very cluttered feel but Darion remarked to himself that it was not messy. He could tell that whoever had organized and arranged the spectacle before him could at a moment's notice retrieve any one of the books without delay.

"May I help you?" a voice suddenly spoke up from behind Darion, startling him considerably. He turned around sharply and looked face to face with a man smiling from ear to ear. He was plump, sported a well-manicured beard, wore a knit black and white vest over a button up shirt, and looked as if he were a permanent fixture in the room. His countenance looked pleasant but Darion could tell that he was being sized up.

"May I help you?" the man said again, still smiling.

Darion paused for a moment, gathering his thoughts before he answered. "I'm uh looking for a book."

The man laughed. "This isn't the library son. Most of these are just zoning books, deeds and tax laws. Nothing a young fella like you would be interested in."

"I'm looking for a very particular book," said Darion uneasily, wondering why he wasn't just coming out and saying it.

"Oh?" the man said. "And just what might this particular book be called?"

Darion breathed deeply before answering. "The Origin Codex."

The words had hardly escaped Darion's lips when the room was suddenly filled with a pulsating white light that seemed to envelop and penetrate him so tightly that he would never be free of it. Darion fell to the floor covering his eyes, which he was sure, had just been blinded.

"Who sent you?" a deep voice suddenly echoed throughout the room. "Who has told you of the Codex?"

Darion lifted his head to answer but felt almost as if he were choking on the light and fell back over, holding back vomit as he did.

"I say again. Who has sent you?"

Darion lay on the floor covering his face and trying to find his bearings. He didn't know how long he sat there when he remembered the solar glasses

Reesa had handed him. He struggled to retrieve them from his pocket and place them over his eyes.

"For the last time. Who has sent you? Answer now or be destroyed!"

Darion slowly, painfully stood to his feet. The glasses dulled the light beams but didn't eliminate them. As he straightened, he looked into the eyes of the plump man who stood amid the waves of light nonchalantly as if oblivious of his surroundings.

"My name is General Darion!" Darion declared with authority, his voice cracking in pain only once. "I am here to gather the Codex on behalf of Professor Jabel! As General I have full authority to access classified materials in this district! Now hand it over!"

The overpowering light stopped. The pain stopped. The plump man disappeared. The chairs disappeared. The desk in the corner disappeared. The tall shelves and ladders disappeared. All of the books disappeared. In place of the cozy, cluttered office was a room as naked as could be imagined. Thick concrete walls overlaid with reinforced steel created near impenetrable barriers to outside incursion on all sides with force-fields set behind the window and doorframes. Aside from high-level military equipment, the room was virtually impregnable to all manner of assault. In the center of the cold, empty room stood a marble pedestal with a covered glass case on top. Within the case was a very thin, incredibly old leather-bound book. The binding looked worn but rugged. The words that once titled the book had since worn away. All that remained to differentiate the volume was a beautiful picture of a white tree embossed on the cover that looked as fresh and bright as the day it was made. The book seemed to resonate with power as Darion lifted the glass cover and slowly reached into the case. He picked it up and held it close. He pondered the significance of the event for just a moment before he took a step toward the door. As he approached the force-field dropped allowing his passage. He grabbed the doorknob and was just turning it when a voice once again sounded out behind him. Darion turned and looked at the plump man as he waved a pointed finger in the air dramatically.

"Be warned General," he spoke in an echoey voice. "The Origin Codex has untold power that can help you win your wars, solve your quandaries and bring stability and happiness to your lands. But should it fall into the hands of the enemy it will be your undoing! Guard it well. And if peradventure some evil besiege thee, know this. It would be better for you if the Codex was destroyed than for it to be taken by the enemy."

Darion nodded slowly, glanced at the all-important book in his hands and then walked out of the building. Reesa and Kebbs were waiting outside and eagerly approached when they realized Darion had acquired the prize.

"Not bad chief!" remarked Kebbs with a beaming smile as he produced a small cloth pouch and it handed it do Darion.

"Are you ok?" Reesa asked anxiously, noticing the haggard expression on Darion's countenance. "What happened in there?"

Darion shook his head as he slid the Codex into the pouch and tied the end of it shut. "It was tough," he admitted, downplaying the true challenge. "Thanks for these," he added as he handed the glasses back to Reesa. "Couldn't have done it without them."

"Thank Jabel," Reesa said with a smile. "It was his idea."

Darion shook his head and laughed. "Of course it was."

"Shhh!" Kebbs suddenly interjected, startling Reesa and Darion.

"What is it?" Reesa asked a moment later, lifting her gun and looking around anxiously.

"Shh," Kebbs repeated, raising his hand for complete silence.

All three stood still and listened as a faint rumble in the distance echoed across the sky.

"Thunder?" Reesa said, but knowing better.

Darion shook his head woefully as a sickening feeling began to build in his stomach. "Its a Krohn descender turbine. I've heard recordings of them at the academy."

"Descender turbine? As in landing ships?" Kebbs asked, although he didn't have to.

Darion tucked the pouch under his arm and withdrew his pistol. "We need to get out of the city. And we don't have much time."

Reesa nodded as she once again took the lead. "Couldn't agree with you more. Lets go!"

The three companions once again set out but this time they carried with them a package of unparalleled importance…though none of them knew why.

⋏

"It looks like they were tied down," Gallo commented as the Iovara command crew studied the enhanced images taking by the fighter pilot. "See how their hands are all obscured?"

"Like they are tied behind their backs," Kesler said as he spotted what Gallo had noticed and nodded.

Jonas shook his head. "I don't get it. Were these poor souls put in there forcibly?"

"Possibly," Gallo answered. "Or more likely, they got in legitimately trying to escape their dying ship and were overpowered when they arrived."

"But what could have done this?" Jonas asked in bewilderment.

"An Unmentionable," answered Kesler as he looked at the images in horror.

"But what did it do to them?" Jonas asked in disgust. "They look like empty water pouches."

"That's essentially what they are," commented the medical officer that Fedrin had invited to the bridge. "I think whatever did this, sucked them dry through their facial orifices. The mouth, eyes, and noses of each man are distended as if they had been sucked through like a straw."

Fedrin cringed.

"This stuff will give me nightmares for a week," said Jonas with a shiver as he turned away from the gruesome images. "Maybe two weeks."

"You and me both," remarked Kesler.

Fedrin shook his head. "What I want to know is who did this and where it is now."

The other officers nodded but had no idea how to start such an assignment.

"Incoming transmission from the Defiant," Gallo spoke up.

Fedrin dismissed the medical officer and gave Gallo a nod. "What's happening Commander?" Fedrin asked as Drezden's face filled the main telelink screen.

22

Drezden shrugged. "Nothing really. I just wanted to report an oddity that happened about ten minutes ago."

"Oh?"

"One of our external docking bay airlocks opened for no reason and then closed."

You could have heard a pin drop on the Iovara command deck as the other officers stopped their tasks and looked at the screen, each thinking the unthinkable.

Drezden continued. "Upon investigating it further, we realized that it had been opened using Commodore Tropnia's officer access code."

Fedrin's blood ran cold. "Drezden! You must go into lockdown mode now!"

Drezden looked at Fedrin curiously. "Why is that?"

"Just do it!" Fedrin snapped. "You haven't a moment to lose!"

Before Drezden could reply the transmission suddenly filled with static and began to flicker to other open channels.

"Drezden!" Fedrin called out, quickly standing to his feet. "Drezden are you there?"

A minute of tortuous silence passed before the transmission stabilized and Drezden could once again be seen clearly. Red lights on the bridge were flashing, sirens blared rhythmically and a large blast door could be seen sliding into place at the back of the Defiant's bridge.

"Something is very wrong!" Drezden said intently, his eyes showing fear, not for himself, but for love of his crew and ship.

"I know," Fedrin said calmly and then proceeded to tell Drezden about the escape pod filled with drained men and the missing aggressor. Upon finishing, Drezden shook his head.

"What should I do?" he said in a near helpless manner that unnerved Fedrin. "If it's aboard, it could be anywhere. It could appear as anyone."

Fedrin nodded slowly as he contemplated the tactical dilemma. "I would immediately make sure everyone aboard is accompanied by at least two others at all times. If this thing is Unmentionable, which I consider likely, it can appear as almost anyone. I would also not allow any corridor to corridor movement unless absolutely necessary."

"It'll be hard to run this ship for any length of time under those circumstances," remarked Drezden.

Fedrin shook his head. "I don't know what else to tell you. If an Unmentionable did get aboard your ship, it could mean disaster for you and your crew. We don't know how to find them, let alone fight them."

Drezden shook his head. "We need to think of something and soon. I want my ship back Fedrin."

"We're coming up on the Sibid warp-point," Kesler's voice sounded out.

"We will think of something," Fedrin said intently, looking at his friend. "I promise! For now, you must maintain the best control of your ship that you can. I don't know what else to say. We need you and your ship for the battle."

Drezden did not answer. He simply shook his head and turned back to his bridge in a near daze.

"Do you really think an Unmentionable is aboard her?" Kesler asked.

"I do," Fedrin answered with a nod.

His simple yet convicted answer sent chills through the fellow officers.

"Do we have a plan to help them?" Jonas pressed.

"No," answered Fedrin flatly.

Jonas, Kesler and Gallo looked at each other uneasily.

"Orders, Sir?" Kesler asked after a few moments.

Fedrin shook his head. "Orders haven't changed Lieutenant. Steady as we go."

"Aye, Sir."

CHAPTER 20

THE INVASION!

"There's another one!" yelled Kebbs, pointing toward a low-flying Krohn gunship before ducking under the next available cover.

The Krohn fleet had arrived and as predicted by Professor Jabel, the Clear Skies System never fired. Without Clear Skies, the Krohn fleet easily crashed through the lines of lightly armed freighters, transport ships and few fighter squadrons that dared to challenge the far superior force.

"Where can we go?" Reesa screamed as she watched the building in front of her turn into a massive fireball and then begin to rain down molten debris.

"That way!" yelled Darion over the roar of Krohn transport engines as he pointed down another street. "It looks clear!"

After defeating the pitiful attempt at stopping them from space, the Krohn warships descended into low orbit in preparation of planetary bombardment and a general softening of the ground defenses, as insignificant and uncoordinated as they were. Thus, with nothing left to oppose them, the Krohn Armada started the daunting task of landing troops on the surface in and around Larep. With the support of the Krohn fleet from above, Krohn fighter squadrons in the atmosphere and the overwhelming troop presence on the surface, the few Namuh positions and strongholds that had not been transferred to the arctic, were quickly overrun and destroyed.

Nevertheless, even as the paltry capital defenses burned, brave soldiers, civilian volunteers and even some noble Branci, rallied together and marched to face the Krohn onslaught as it closed in on the city. The resulting battle was quick and decisive. When it was over, only a burning field and charred skeletons remained as testament to the heroics of the Namuh and Branci defenders.

"Not going this way!" Kebbs said as he rounded a corner in the street and stopped cold.

"Why not?" asked Reesa as she ran up behind.

"That'd be my first reason," Kebbs said as he pointed to a Krohn landing craft that had just touched down and was releasing a squadron of heavily armed Krohn shock troops.

"Lovely," Darion said as he watched the reptilian creatures, their deadly tails waving wildly, as they made preparations to secure their specific objectives in the city; his city...the city he had been responsible to protect, and had failed so miserably at.

Larep citizens lucky enough to have won lottery places in the bunkers were tucked safely away, for the time being. Those who were shuttled out of the city now made their way to nearby mountain ranges and thick forests on foot in a desperate attempt to put as many miles between them and the city as possible. Still others chose to make their stand in their own homes and apartments, not wanting to risk the perils and uncertainties of nomadic refugees.

"Look out!" Reesa yelled as she watched a large piece of rubble come tumbling down the side of a nearby building.

Darion dove out of the way just as it crashed into the ground not far from where he had been standing. "Thanks!" he yelled as he scrambled back to his feet, clutching the all-important parcel in one hand and his weapon in the other.

"Don't mention it," answered Reesa.

"What's that noise?" Kebbs said as his eyes took to the sky once more.

"Sounds like engines," Darion said, as he shielded his eyes from the bright sun and looked up.

Kebbs shook his head. "They sound different than the others."

"Over there!" Reesa yelled, pointing to several fast moving black dots on the horizon.

"Fighters," Darion said knowingly.

"Hurry! In there!" Kebbs yelled pointing to a pile of debris that had once served as an ornate façade to a mighty skyscraper.

"Are you crazy?!?" Reesa shot back as she frantically looked around for alternatives.

"He's right!" Darion agreed as he ran toward the pile of stone blocks, motioning for Reesa to follow. "We need to get out of sight before those fighters strafe this entire area!"

Reesa and Darion followed Kebbs as he climbed up the pile and then disappeared into a small cavern within. Darion had barely squeezed in when the loud roars of the Krohn fighters flew overhead, followed by loud pitched laser rounds smashing the street and low level buildings all around.

"Sounds like they missed us," Darion said, several minutes later as he peeked out between two jagged blocks.

"Yeah, but not for long," Kebbs warned crouching up on his feet. "By nightfall these streets will be filled with Krohns looking for a snack."

"Incase anyone cares, I'm not down with that," Reesa said. "I have a particularly poignant aversion to being eaten!"

Darion shook his head. "Kebbs, how far to your place?"

Kebbs glanced out the opening and spotted laser and missile fire striking seemingly random locations all over the city, sending flames and ash high into the sky. He shook his head. "Too far with all that going on. But then again, I don't think we have a choice."

"We have to go now!" Reesa yelled after a blast smashed the street in front of them, spraying up rock and dirt all around. "Otherwise we'll be buried in here! And in case you were wondering, I have an aversion to that too!"

After another murderous pass overhead by the fighters, the trio hastily began their climb back out of their makeshift bomb shelter. Reesa, as always, took the lead with Darion right behind. It was a tough climb but Reesa and Darion managed to ascend the heap in good time. Kebbs, however, struggled on a particularly nasty and steep slab of polished stone and could not get a solid footing. Over and over again he tried but to no avail. He was just considering climbing back down and looking for another way when a hand was lowered from above.

"It's been awhile since I've climbed," Kebbs confessed as he reached for Darion's hand. "I haven't gone since…"

Darion nodded before Kebbs could finish his sentence. Kebbs looked intently at Darion for just a moment, but in the silent moment the two men spoke of many things; Darion's brother, their childhoods, the Krohn invasion, the Codex, and so much more than mere words would ever have been able to say.

"Are you two coming?" Reesa called from the bottom of the pile, weapon drawn, watching and waiting for anything.

"On our way!" called Darion after he had hoisted Kebbs up.

"Thanks," Kebbs said as he placed both feet on the top.

"Not a problem," Darion answered.

"We've got places to go boys!" Reesa prompted. "Lets go!"

"Right behind you," Darion said as he quickly began to climb down the pile.

"I think she's beginning to like you," Kebbs said as he climbed down behind Darion. "She hasn't threatened to kill you once today."

"I hope not," Darion said as he followed Kebbs.

"Why's that?" Kebbs asked with a chuckle.

Darion shook his head. "She scares me. She's not the cute secretary I thought she was. I don't think I could handle her like this."

Kebbs laughed. "I'm sure you'd manage."

The three companions continued on their journey out of the city keeping a watchful eye on the sky as well as the streets.

⚔

"We'll punch through the gravitational well of the warp-point in another fifty-eight minutes," Kesler said into his tele-link.

"All ships at tactical readiness?" Fedrin asked.

"You bet!" Jonas answered from his station. "Ready and waiting to kill things!"

Fedrin smiled and shook his head. "Glad to hear it."

Kesler flipped a few switches and turned back to his transmitter. "I'll contact you when we're a few minutes from entry."

"Thanks Lieutenant. I'll be there!" Fedrin finished and cut the transmission.

"Am I the only one a little freaked out about this jump?" Jonas asked. "I mean, we all know what's waiting for us on the other side, right?"

Tarkin looked up from his post and nodded. "Not too thrilled here either, but we've got to do it."

"But shouldn't the fact that we know what's on the other side make us adjust our moves?" Jonas implored to anyone that would listen. "Granted, I'm no tactician. My job is to sit here and blow things up that Fedrin doesn't like. But this just seems ridiculous! An enemy fleet twice our size is waiting for us. What about this isn't making sense to anyone?"

Kesler leaned back in his chair. "The situation stinks but Tarkin is right. We have no viable alternatives. We need to get to Sibid and there's no other way to get there than straight through the jumps."

Jonas sat back in his chair and folded his arms. "Well I'd like to officially protest this action."

Kesler sat up and pretended to type. "While I log your whining, how about you see to it that the weapon systems are primed. After you do that, feel free to sit there and wait to die."

"You have such a poetic way with words," Jonas answered. "It's a wonder you didn't get into politics."

Tarkin chuckled.

⋏

Fedrin glanced at the faces of his commanders in separated sections of his room's transmission screen. The pressure that each face unknowingly placed squarely on his shoulders was staggering. He wondered if they knew.

After glancing down at a few hastily prepared notes, Fedrin cleared his throat and began to speak. "Sometime yesterday afternoon, the automated telecast broadcasted these images over the Cortex Network," he said, as a parade of images appeared before each of the commanders. "As you can see, the Krohn Fleet has successfully reached and attacked Namuh Prime."

Searle gasped as she saw the horrifying images of Krohn warships in orbit over her world.

Commander Colby sighed as he looked at several pictures of Larep in flames. It was a demoralizing sight.

"So does this mean we lose?" the ever-unabashed Commander Sanders asked. "We all knew the Krohn Fleet was going to reach home before we were able to return, but this? I thought the Unmentionables were essentially in control of both sides here. Why would they need to do this?"

"Because they're the bad guys," Kendrick answered.

"And they're hungry," Colby added as an image of a Krohn hunting squad appeared.

"I think there's more to it than that," Fedrin remarked.

The commanders looked intently at their leader.

"How do you mean?" Kendrick asked.

"I can't explain it fully," Fedrin said shaking his head. "But something tells me that the Unmentionables don't want us just crippled as a military force. Why would they? We pose no tangible threat to them."

"Then what?" asked Searle.

"I think they want us exterminated, as a people, as a race," answered Fedrin somberly.

"But why?" Tenith, the youngest of the Commanders asked impetuously when nobody else did.

"I think is has something to do with what Trab said to me before my link with the Sions was severed. Something that we possess that the Unmentionables desperately want and, yet, also fear," he said pensively.

"Sounds like a good reason for genocide," added Searle, followed by several solemn nods in agreement.

"I don't mean to always sound like the voice of doom and gloom," spoke up Sanders, "but at the rate our ships and cities are falling, I don't think there's going to be anyone left to capitalize on what we possess, whatever that may be."

The other commanders slowly nodded in agreement and then looked up at Fedrin for an answer.

"All the more reason to keep our focus and be true to one another!" Drezden declared. He held out his hand and continued passionately. "Friends, our enemy fears us! If they must resort to butchering civilians from space and using their Krohn pawns to murder our people on the ground, it means they are desperate! Take their fear and draw courage from it, not doubts!"

Fedrin nodded slowly. "I agree with Drezden. Our enemy fears us for reasons we do not yet fully appreciate and won't unless we stay the course."

The other commanders again nodded, albeit this time reluctantly. They trusted their Admiral, but the stakes of the game were growing higher and higher with each tragedy endured by the wounded and bleeding Federation.

"Sibid is fast approaching," said Fedrin resolutely, aware of the subtle misgivings of his subordinates. "Be vigilant and strong and we will prevail."

The other Commanders nodded and smiled, more for Fedrin's sake than their own, as one by one they cut their links until only Drezden remained.

"You ready for this?" Fedrin asked as he buttoned up his uniform jacket and glanced at the lone commander still connected in the transmission screen.

Drezden smiled. "I'd feel better if there wasn't an Unmentionable aboard my ship."

Fedrin shook his head in anguish.

"Don't worry about it," Drezden quickly shot back, noticing Fedrin's distress. "We'll be fine. The real question here is if you're ready?"

"I guess we'll see in a few minutes," answered Fedrin as he made his way to the door.

"Do you think Etana will be there?" Drezden asked as Fedrin stepped into the hall.

Fedrin froze in place for just a moment. "I'm not counting on it," he answered flatly and then walked away.

Drezden shook his head. "I hope she is for your sake," he said to the empty room.

∧

"Status report?" Fedrin called out as he entered the bridge.

Kesler turned in his chair and looked back at his instruments. "We are preparing to enter Sibid."

Fedrin nodded in response and began checking his own monitors.

"Are all fleet system checks completed?"

"Aye Sir," Tarkin answered immediately.

"And?" Fedrin asked promptly.

Kesler pulled up a screen. "All vessels are faring well except the Hornell's engines which have reached critical overheat. She will be forced to decelerate or risk a meltdown if they are not given rest within the next few hours."

Fedrin shook his head and closed his eyes. "Will she be ok for the entry?"

"Kendrick's officers are promising me that she will," Kesler said doubtfully. "They know her better than me, so… I'm saying yes."

Fedrin breathed a sigh of relief. The Hornell Carrier was the backbone of the humble Sixth Fleet. Without her and her fighters for support, the other ships in the force didn't stand much of a chance.

A series of alarms and sirens began to blare at multiple stations.

"Activate dampeners," Kesler ordered to the propulsions engineer. "This is it!"

An officer in the front of the room rapidly flipped a series of switches on his console. "Dampening thrusters engaged," the office announced as the ship slowly stabilized.

Fedrin's gaze was absorbed in the growing star filled hole at the other end of the warp-point. Random bursts of energy emitted from the eye of the jump, but were quickly pulled back into the anomaly.

"Ten seconds to warp exit!" Tarkin announced, trying to sound brave and calm but in reality was anxious to the point of being sick.

There was complete silence on every bridge of the Sixth Fleet. Each officer focused intently on their respective stations making sure everything was just right while inwardly relying heavily on their shipmates to care for their own tasks with the same level of attention. All the commanders looked out their viewing screens as their ships prepared to enter Sibid. On the other side of the jump was the Voigt Colony, the Krohn Fleet, the Clear Skies program and their destiny.

CHAPTER 21

One Less Hero

Row upon row of the tall, subsidized housing towers stretched as far as the eye could see. Each identical, hideous gray tower reached toward the hot, unforgiving sky in a vain effort to escape the filth and moral decay clawing at their foundations. This was Kespa, the pinnacle of a noble program to provide free housing to all, but now arguably the worst slum in all the Federation, and a blight on the socialist record.

"I sure don't miss this place," Darion exclaimed after the three companions rounded a corner and took in the full view of the depressing sight.

"I wish I could miss this place," Kebbs retorted, nodding to the dumpy shops, streets in disrepair, and dilapidated facades that lined the tower's street level floors. "Maybe when this stupid war is over I can get a place in Larep somewhere."

"What? And miss all of these wonderful neighbors of yours?" exclaimed Reesa as she pointed to a group of wild men and women running around the street laughing loudly, seemingly oblivious that their world was under siege.

Darion shook his head. "Disgusting."

"Makes me sick," Reesa said with abhorrence in her voice as she watched several teenagers throw stones through a convenience store's front window and then climb in. "There are people all over the planet right now just trying to survive, and here you have people taking advantage of the situation and stealing from their neighbors."

Kebbs looked at the scene in profound disappointment, rather than contempt. Having been in their situation prior to his incarceration, he felt an affinity toward them, regardless of their heinous actions.

"Look!" said Darion in awe. "There goes someone with an armful of new data pads. Hope he doesn't trip over the curb and hurt himself."

"I hope he falls and breaks his neck," Reesa said.

"And look over there," Darion said pointing. "She has more shoes then she'll be able to wear in a lifetime!" he said, watching the woman struggling to haul two heaping bags filled with shoes, purses, and other novelties taken right off of the racks of a nearby store.

"I have half a mind to walk right over there and..." Kebbs said as he took a step toward three punks trying to break the front windows of a music boutique.

"Wait!" Reesa said, grabbing Kebbs' arm before he got too far. "Do you guys hear that?"

Kebbs and Darion stopped and listened.

"Hear what?" Kebbs asked.

Reesa didn't have to answer. A blood-chilling scream from somewhere much further down the street rang out, followed by another, and then another. Each sounded closer than the preceding one.

"Something's going on," Darion said, as he pulled out his gun.

"You think?" Reesa shot back sarcastically as she withdrew her own weapon from the holster and removed the adapter.

"Krohns?" Kebbs asked.

"Not sure," Darion answered, "...but probably. Let's stick close to the buildings and keep our eyes open, eh?"

"Well, I was going to close mine but thanks for the tip," Reesa said.

"She likes you," Kebbs quietly jeered and gave Darion a light elbow.

Darion rolled his eyes.

"You keep this close now," Kebbs reminded, patting the pouch tied around Darion's waist.

Darion nodded and checked the pouch. "We're good," he said reassuringly.

A dozen mighty roars suddenly trumpeted all around, but still no Krohns were in sight.

Kebbs swung his lydeg automatic from off of his back, slammed down on the primer, and removed his adapter ring. "I'm ready for them," he said as he eyed the street.

They had only taken several more strides when it all broke loose. Krohns, from multiple directions, suddenly charged the exposed looters who didn't stand a chance. The reptilian beasts bounded over each other in a vicious frenzy to reach the fresh meat that was so obligingly vulnerable.

"We should do something!" Darion exclaimed as he brought his weapon up.

Kebbs grabbed his arm and held him back. "There's nothing we can do for them Darion. We have to think of protecting ourselves, for the sake of our mission, if nothing else."

"I can't watch," Reesa said, turning away from the screams and thrashings offered by the plunderers, now victims.

"What are we going to do then?" Darion asked, reluctantly stepping back into the shadows. "We can't fight our way through that."

"Hurry! In here!" Kebbs said, pointing to an open door of an already trashed clothing shop.

Without protest Darion and Reesa piled through the doorway behind Kebbs as quickly and quietly as they possibly could.

"Did they see us?" Reesa asked as she helped Darion lean a heavy cabinet against the door.

"I don't think so," Kebbs said as he peered out the front window. "Looks like they're preoccupied right at the moment," he added while he watched in disgust as Krohns, their snouts covered in fresh blood, continued to feed on their still living prey.

Darion and Reesa joined Kebbs in the front room and looked out.

"The door is secured," said Darion.

"Well, at least a little more than it was," Reesa clarified. "It wouldn't really take much to knock it over still."

"Let's hope they don't go building to building then," Kebbs said as he lowered the butt of his rifle to the ground and leaned against a counter.

Reesa sat down near a corner of the large front window and withdrew a small canteen from her belt. "There's something I don't understand," she said after taking a small sip.

"What's that?" Darion asked, taking the canteen from Reesa and resting up against the sill, being careful to avoid a direct line of sight with the Krohns.

Reesa motioned out the window. "These Krohns seem like a bunch of wild animals, not a race of space-faring imperialists. Am I missing something?"

Kebbs nodded in agreement. "I was actually wondering the same thing. I was expecting at least to see them dressed in some sort of combat gear with actual weapons, transmitters, and stuff. These things are just a bunch of overgrown, hungry lizards."

Darion nodded. "Every time we've ever faced the Krohns in a land battle, we've lost. So there's not been a lot of information gathered on their tactics and strategy. But one thing we have learned, or at least formed reasonable theories on, is that there is a sub race of Krohns that that goes into battle first."

"I take it that these are the lower versions?" Reesa asked.

Darion shrugged. "They're like attack dogs, expendable scouts meant to stir up trouble ahead of the main, more sophisticated force of Krohns...or so the theory goes."

"I see," Reesa said. "And do they..."

"I hate to interrupt story time but I think they're about to stir up some trouble," Kebbs said as he quickly hoisted his rifle back in his hands.

Reesa and Darion turned back to the window and nearly fell backwards at the sight of a massive Krohn standing frightfully close to the large and painfully thin pane of glass.

Seeing a Krohn so terribly close was terrifying! Of course, each had seen images of the bipedal reptiles in the past, but seeing edited images broadcasted over the cortex in the comfort of one's living room and staring up at one through a storefront window were night and day differences that no one had ever wanted to compare.

"Stay still," Kebbs whispered. "Their eyes respond more to movement than to shape...or is it the other way around?"

Reesa looked at Darion with a terrified expression. Darion wished he could calm her but he was pretty sure that he was more terrified than she.

The Krohn's ugly snout rubbed against the window, leaving a path of moist residue on the previously clean pane. It stood there staring in for several moments longer before it turned and slowly tromped away.

All three breathed a collective sigh of relief.

Darion offered a nervous smile. "That was ridiculously unsettling."

"You think?" Reesa said turning sharply to Darion. "That was the most horrifying thing I've ever had to do! Even worse than wearing heels for two days!"

Darion smiled.

Kebbs chuckled and shook his head and was just about to add a smart comment when the departing Krohn turned sharply back toward the window and charged. Before any knew what was happening, the reptile effortlessly leaped through the glass, and in smooth stride, chomped down on hard on Kebbs' chest with a resounding 'crack' that echoed throughout the room.

Reesa screamed at the sight of spraying blood and the massive creature attempting to feed on her cousin. "Kill it! Kill it Darion!" she yelled over as she tried to reach for her own weapon which had been knocked out of her hand by the creature's flailing tale.

She didn't have to repeat herself. The creature had barely touched the glass before Darion's pistol was already drawn and firing. Over and over again he shot the beast at point-blank range and shot after shot seemed to have no effect. He didn't know how many shots he had poured into the creature before it finally released Kebbs and turned to face the nuisance.

Without thinking twice, Darion raised his gun to the reptile's neck, which appeared to have thinner scales than the rest of its body. He squeezed the trigger once more. The pile of colossal muscles encased in armored scales dubbed a "sub race" of the Krohn war machine, slumped to the ground in a 'thud.'

"Kebbs!" Reesa yelled as she ran over to her bleeding cousin. "Are you ok?"

"Get it together, Reesa!" Darion yelled, pulling her up by the shoulder. "They're coming!"

"We're going to die!" Reesa yelled back. "We're finished!"

Darion turned to Reesa and grabbed her face with both of his blood stained hands. "Listen to me! We're going to be fine! Let's get through this and we'll be on our way. We'll be fine!" he finished and handed her a pistol.

"Just aim for their necks," he added as if he had done this hundreds of times before. "Their scales are the weakest there," he said, followed by a clean shot that brought another of the vicious beasts down. "See, nothing to it," he said and fired at another, missing horribly.

Reesa looked back at Kebbs, locked her jaw and fired a salvo into the midst of several advancing Krohns striking two in the chest slowing them for just a moment before they continued their hunger driven charge.

"It's ok," Darion said trying to encourage her. "Just be patient and place your shots."

"Shut up!" yelled Reesa. "I don't use patience when things are trying to eat me!" she screamed as she motioned to the charging Krohns. She brought her pistol back up to the window in anger and fired two more shots in rapid succession, each round finding their intended target and bringing down two Krohns.

"Not bad," Darion said nodding at the dead Krohns in the street.

"Look out!" Reesa yelled as a Krohn leapt from several yards back, toward their position.

Darion had barely turned to see the blitzing Krohn when a burst of firepower from behind smashed the Krohn squarely in the chest, nearly ripping the beast in half and sending up a spray of hot blood.

Reesa and Darion turned to see Kebbs propped up against a beam, with his rifle in hand. He was obviously in a great deal of pain, but managed a smile before bringing his weapon back to his shoulder just in time to kill two more charging Krohns.

One by one the three companions picked the reptiles off with sniper like proficiency until the last one fell in the middle of street letting off a terrible roar. The charge had been stopped.

"Nice work boys," Reesa said as she stood to her feet. "Now let's get out of here before their friends come looking for them."

"Get down!" Darion suddenly yelled, pulling Reesa by the arm.

Reesa landed hard on her knees. "What's your problem?" she asked harshly.

"Here's where it gets bad," Darion whispered, looking out across the street.

"Worse than this?" asked Kebbs, nodding to his gushing chest wounds and then chuckling. "I need to reset my expectations I guess."

Reesa brushed a strand of greasy, sweat soaked hair out of her face. "We need to get him stabilized," she said followed by a laser shot smashing into the wall above her head.

Darion quickly looked around the room. He knew Reesa was right, but he was fast running out of options. A moment later, a barrage of laser fire from alcoves, roofs, and windows across the street compelled them all to cower close to the floor for dear life.

"I think they're moving up on us," Darion yelled as he noticed the massive creatures running back and forth in the hazy smoke outside. "Reesa, four on the left! Four on the left!"

"I see them!" she answered and fired at a group of Krohns carrying shoulder-mounted rockets trying to get a clean shot into the storefront. "Take that you ugly dinosaurs!" she screamed as she brought down one after another with perfect shots.

"Look out!" Kebbs struggled to yell after spotting a rocket launched from somewhere across the street.

Reesa ducked just as the rocket hit the ground in front of the store, sending up a wave of fire, smoke and debris.

"Everyone ok?" asked Darion between gasping coughs.

"I'm fine!" Reesa said as she crawled over the dead Krohn and back to the two men. "I thought I got them all but I guess one got lucky."

"Kebbs, you all right?" asked Darion.

"Shoot!" Kebbs screamed.

Darion turned abruptly and saw a Krohn soldier, tail waving wildly, as it stood in the window. Lines of saliva dripped from the creature's open mouth. The beast brought a rod type weapon to its shoulder and was about to fire when a single shot hit him in the chest, startling but not seriously hurting him. His reptilian blood red eyes looked up in rage to see Darion standing several feet away holding a smoking pistol.

"Hey, Ugly!" yelled Reesa as she too trained her gun on the Krohn. The Krohn turned to face her just as she fired a clean shot into the creature's fleshly neck, sending it falling backwards out of the store and into a pool of blood outside

"Darion drop!" Kebbs yelled as he brought the rifle up.

Darion fell to the ground just as a Krohn lunged at him from outside. Kebbs planted a solid shot into the creature's head with his powerful rifle, nearly severing it.

Another Krohn jumped in behind and took a snap at Darion's foot but was brought down quickly by a well-placed shot from Reesa.

"There are too many!" yelled Darion as he climbed over the fast piling Krohn carcasses in an attempt to retreat deeper into the shop. "We need to get out of here!" he shouted and then fell backward over a thick rug, dragging it with him.

"Look!" exclaimed Reesa as she pointed to a hatch on the floor that had been previously obscured.

Darion quickly shoved the rest of the rug away and yanked the door open. "A service hatch!" he announced with hope building in his voice.

Reesa fired several shots blindly out the window before looking back to Darion for direction.

"Go down and see if there is a way out," said Darion. "I'll go get Kebbs."

Without hesitation Reesa lowered herself through the hatch.

Darion crawled back to the front of the shop firing blindly through the front window as he went. "Ready to go?" Darion asked as he fell to the ground beside Kebbs.

Kebbs grabbed Darion's arm and held it firmly.

"No, no," Darion corrected, repositioning Kebbs hands. "Put your arm around my neck like this..."

"I'm not going with you," Kebbs said, holding tighter.

Darion looked at Kebbs in dismay.

"Looks good!" shouted Reesa as she reemerged from the shaft. "There's a way out!"

"Of course you're coming with us!" said Darion as he once again tried to prop Kebbs up.

"No!" Kebbs said, pushing Darion's arms off. "I'm dying Darion. I've already lost too much blood to stand on my own. It's only a matter of time before I lose consciousness too."

"Then we'll carry you!" Darion answered. "Reesa get back up here! We need to carry Kebbs down the shaft!"

Darion had barely finished calling for Reesa when another Krohn jumped through the breach and let off a terrible hissing roar. In the blink of an eye, the Krohn pounced at Darion, throwing him against the wall. He was about to take a bite of Darion's arm when a shot from behind struck the creature in the face, sending him to the ground in a loud thrashing thump. Darion picked up his own gun just in time to fire a shot into another Krohn's neck as he, too, was preparing to jump in through their fast deteriorating fortress.

"We've got to move!" Darion said as he struggled to get to his feet. "Come on!" he said as he tugged on Kebbs arm. "Reesa where are you?" he called back out.

"I'm right here," Reesa answered after firing several more shots out the window. "I'll get his feet and you get him there under the arms. Careful of his wounds."

"No!" Kebbs yelled as he pushed Darion's hands off one more time. "You won't be able to make it ten feet down that shaft dragging me!"

"Then we stay here and die together!" Reesa announced and turned to fire several more shots out the window, bringing down another Krohn by chance.

"I'm not about to let all the work we've done be wasted by a meaningless shootout!" Kebbs protested. "We can't fight the entire Krohn army ourselves! We have the mission to think of! We have our people to think of!"

"We aren't going!" Reesa screamed as tears filled her eyes.

"Listen to me!" Kebbs said, grabbing Reesa's arm and pulling her down. "There are bigger things at stake here than my life. Make me proud and finish what we've started," he entreated and let go of her arm.

Tears were flowing freely down Reesa's face as she threw her arms around Kebbs' neck and kissed him on the cheek. "I love you," she said as she stood to her feet.

"I love you too, kid," Kebbs said as he held her hand. "Take care of Darion ok? He's helpless on his own," he added, managing a smile.

"Watch your self!" Darion yelled as he fired two quick shots out the window to scare off several Krohns contemplating the tradeoffs of jumping in and eating a fresh Namuh or getting killed.

"Yeah that's right you ugly lizards!" Darion yelled. "You stay out!"

"You need to go," Kebbs said patting Darion's leg. "Take care of Reesa for me. She's not a bad person once you get through her armored exterior."

"I'll do my best," Darion said touching Kebbs' shoulder.

"And Darion," Kebbs added, as Darion stepped away. "I am sorry about your brother. Perhaps someday you can find it within your heart to forgive me."

Darion froze in his tracks; momentarily forgetting that Krohn weapon fire was racing passed his head. He turned and locked eyes with the bleeding man he had once had called friend, many years ago. "I already have," he answered before following, Reesa who was already descending the rungs of the service hatch, tears flowing all the way.

Kebbs sat back against the beam, weapon in hand, blood flowing freely and a serene expression on his face.

Darion lowered himself through the hatch, closed and bolted the access door, and descended down the shaft. Lower and lower he went until his boots hit the damp floor of a subbasement. Rats scurried away as the companions tried to make their bearings in the dark room. Only a few scattered rays of light streamed in past the slow moving blades of an air vent fixed near the top of the wall. The rat's squeals and the squeaking of the vent's blades were drowned out beyond recognition when shots from Kebbs' rifle, followed by Krohn roars, and subsequent laser fire rang out. The sounds were horrible and intense for several minutes before the noises abruptly, and unsettlingly, stopped.

"Come on," Darion said as he made his way toward a small opening across the room. "We've got to keep moving."

"I'm going to miss him," Reesa whispered.

"Me too," said Darion as he took Reesa's hand and led her down the service tunnel and away from the murderous Krohns.

They had only walked for several minutes when Darion suddenly froze. His face turned white and he felt ill.

"What's wrong?" Reesa asked, her voice still cracking with emotion.

Darion didn't answer. He didn't know what to say.

"Are you ok?" Reesa pressed, looking intently into Darion's eyes.

"The pouch," Darion said weakly, holding up a severed cord fastened to his belt. "It's gone."

Reesa brought her hands up to cover her mouth in dismay and horror.

"I'm...I'm sorry," Darion blurted out, feeling as if he had already betrayed Kebbs' memory and Reesa's innumerable sacrifices. "It must have gotten torn off during the fight. I'll go back and get it," he said and took a step back down the tunnel but stopped when Reesa grabbed his arm.

"You'll do no such thing!" she snapped. "It's just a book, Darion! Going back now would only be handing your life to the enemy."

"But what if the enemy gets it?" Darion protested.

"Then they get it!" Reesa answered. "We still have another job to complete and I can't do it without you. Don't let his sacrifice be in vain! He would have wanted you to go on."

Darion reluctantly nodded and turned back down the tunnel. They walked side by side in silence for what seemed like hours. As they walked, Darion couldn't help be replay the warning of the well-dressed plump man at the archive.

"...*Should it fall into the hands of the enemy, it will be your undoing!*"

CHAPTER 22

SIBID

Tarkin hovered over Kesler's shoulder, staring into the star system screen curiously and then glanced out the main window just to confirm what the screen said.

Gallo frantically adjusted scanner dials and focused intently at his station's multiple viewing screens.

Jonas' finger hovered over the primary weapon's trigger, waiting, watching, and listening for a command from Fedrin to release the pent up power of the Iovara's impressive arsenal.

Kesler checked his array of instruments and then rechecked. He glanced back at Fedrin who was pacing back and forth.

"So where's the Krohn Fleet?" Tarkin finally asked, vocalizing the question that was foremost on the minds of each of the officers.

Following the dramatic entry of the seven ships into the Sibid star system, nothing had happened. No Krohn Armada was awaiting their arrival. No distress calls from a burning colony reached their receivers. No damaged from the wrecked Idok battle carrier or Ilo defense station cluttered the sector. There was simply nothing out of the ordinary.

"Status report?" asked Fedrin for the third time as he paced past Kesler's station, suspiciously eyeing the seemingly vacant star system screen.

Kesler pulled up several data screens and began to list off the reports... again. "The Hornell blew three power couplers during the jump. She'll need some repairs before the trip back home."

Fedrin nodded as Kesler continued.

"Commander Searle is reporting that the Revenge lost several external receiving rods during the jump but she's insisting that it won't impede her ship's combat ability."

Tarkin tapped Kesler's shoulder and pointed to another data file.

Kesler nodded and maximized another screen. "And it looks like the Bolter is reporting a small power outage on decks two and six. Commander Sanders said that the problems should be fixed within the hour and that no major systems were damaged. Other than that, all ships are faring well and holding in steady formation."

"Fighters?" asked Fedrin as he turned from the window and walked back toward the interior of the bridge.

"The last wings are being launched now," Jonas answered from his perch. "Hornell fighter control is reporting that all fighters are green-lit. All the guns at our disposal are good to go, Admiral. We just need some targets."

Fedrin nodded as he leaned up against Gallo's station. "So what's out there?" he asked, glaring out the massive observation window as if he could see the millions of miles between them and their target.

Gallo removed a set of headphones and shook his head. "Latest broad stroke scan coming back right now," he said as he pressed several buttons on his station. "And it still looks empty," he added several moments later. "Other than our ships, and the Hornell fighter squadrons, there are no other capital ships in this system. The only other signals I'm picking up are from a few communication satellites above the planet, about a dozen drones over the colony and the old Ilo defense station in high orbit. That's it, Admiral. We're alone."

Fedrin shook his head. Where was the Krohn Armada? By all rights, the Krohns should have beaten his small squadron to the planet by several hours and gone to work dismantling it from space. But the system was clear of all ships, including his wife's battle carrier. Where was everyone?

"I assume the colony is fine then?" inquired Fedrin as he ran a hand through his already unkempt hair.

"The colony appears perfect," Kesler answered. "All three dome transmitters are reporting normal structural parameters and there is no sign that they have been attacked."

"Peculiar," Fedrin said shaking his head. "Very peculiar."

"We are receiving a transmission from the Corinthia," Gallo spoke up. "Commander Tenith wants to know how to proceed."

Fedrin walked back to his chair. "Tell Tenith to keep his pants on. I'll clarify our orders when I know what's going on myself."

"Aye, Sir," Gallo said turning back to his station.

"Kesler," said Fedrin as he assumed his seat.

"Sir?"

Fedrin nodded toward the image of the defense station orbiting in geosynchronistic orbit above the planet. "Have we received any direct communication from her?"

"The Ilo?" Kesler clarified.

Fedrin nodded.

Kesler turned to his station and then looked back at Fedrin "We received an automated friend or foe transmission the moment we jumped in but we haven't received anything else since."

"And they haven't answered our manual hails yet either," added Gallo.

Fedrin stroked his chin. "Did the transmission bounce back?"

"No, Sir," Gallo said. "Ilo definitely got them. They just aren't answering."

Fedrin fidgeted in his chair, looking at various screens and reports over and over again. "And we are sure the Idok isn't out there somewhere?"

Kesler shrugged. "The Idok is a big ship with a massive EM signature. If she were here, we'd be able to pick her up."

Fedrin sat back in his chair and slowly nodded his head in acceptance.

"You ok?" Kesler asked.

"Of course, Lieutenant," Fedrin said as he put a stern look on his face. "Keep trying to contact Ilo and start transmissions to the colony. I don't like it, but we're going in. We're here for the data device and if the Krohns aren't here to challenge us, all the better I suppose."

"Very good then," Kesler said and turned back to his station.

"Gallo," Fedrin called out. "Keep scanners up. I don't know what's going on but I don't want to get caught unprepared."

"Will do," Gallo answered.

Fedrin turned around and looked up at Jonas. "Lieutenant, keep all weapons hot, shields at full and see to it that all other ships do the same until instructed otherwise."

Jonas nodded. "My favorite orders...other than fire at will."

"Tarkin," Fedrin called out facing the six-armed crewman. "Monitor the colony. Keep an eye for ships, weapons, or anything out of the ordinary. I want to know the moment you see anything. Clear?"

"Yes, Sir," Tarkin said emphatically and went straightway to an open terminal to beginning his task.

Fedrin glanced around his bridge and then nodded slowly. "Very well gentlemen, bring us in."

⋏

The battalion of Krohns marched boldly down the main street of Kespa, their reptilian blood red eyes scanning side streets, alleyways and buildings as they went, always looking for the rare foolhardy soul or the occasional abandoned animal that hadn't already fled the city or been devoured.

Reesa timidly peered out the darkened window of her late cousin's sixth floor apartment as the battalion passed below. She shook her head in sadness as she watched them march down the street without any fear or concern, as if they owned the city, and always had.

Seated behind her, in the middle of their makeshift war room, Darion sat at a table strewn with maps, charts, graphs and papers. Notes were jotted everywhere and just as many of them were scribbled out. More than once, Darion pondered the irony of how just several days earlier he was in command of thousands with near limitless resources at his disposal but without an enemy to flex them against; how things had reversed. Now, he felt the entire weight of the Krohn Consortium upon his back; his manpower was all but gone, and he had as many assets to his name as a Kespa soup kitchen patron.

Hearing the ominous stomping outside Darion leaned away from table and glanced at Reesa. "How many?"

"At least ninety," Reesa answered without turning around. "Maybe a few more."

Darion shook his head and looked once more at the daunting pile before him, unsure of how to proceed.

"You ok?" Reesa asked as she returned from the window and set a comforting hand on Darion's shoulder.

Darion grabbed her hand and held it tightly. "I'll be better once I figure out what your cousin's plan was," he said tapping the table with his other hand.

"I know most of it," Reesa said assuredly. "I'm just fuzzy on some of the finer details."

"Those finer details are what's worrying me," remarked Darion. "We don't have a very large margin for error."

"We'll make it work," she said confidently and released Darion's hand, "I'm sure of it."

A distant scream suddenly rang out followed by an unsettling silence.

Reesa winced and sat down, feeling helpless and isolated from all she knew, and had known. She folded her arms on the table and rested her head upon them, fighting the urge to close her eyes.

Darion stood and walked over to the window. The Krohn battalion had since passed their building and was now some distance further up the street.

"Where are they going?" Reesa asked, following a yawn and giving into the urge to rest her weary eyes for a moment.

"Looks like they're passing the warehouse district," Darion answered, nodding toward the large gray and black buildings near the river. "I've seen several battalions head in that general direction in the last hour or so," Darion added. "I wouldn't be surprised if that's where they have set up a local base camp seeing how they're the largest buildings this side of Larep. I guess it's kind of a good thing they're all heading down that way. Hopefully, it'll make the next step in our plan a little easier," he remarked and looked over at Reesa. She was fast asleep. He glanced around the room and spotted a tattered quilt in a corner. He picked it up and gently laid it over her. "Sleep well," he whispered and kissed her forehead affectionately. He watched her for another moment and then walked back to the window. He leaned on the sill and gazed back out into the darkness. Another battalion was coming down the street. He shook his head.

A

A cool breeze blew through the courtyard as Armid and Senator Trivis approached the imposing figure standing beneath the magnificent archway of the capital building. Lit torches lined the stone walls painting the marble floor with warm yellows and oranges.

As they made their way nearer, they noticed Defuria with a hand extended directly into the fire. He turned his hand back and forth curiously, observing the flames as they danced around his ghostly white fingers.

"The Sion fire that we have feared for so long is dying," Defuria said sinisterly as the two joined him. His hand slowly left the flame and slid down to the base of the torch. "Soon, very soon, the torch will be passed from them to the Namuh."

"And when that happens, we will be there," stated Trivis.

Armid nodded enthusiastically. "And the Grimsin Tree will be ours!"

Defuria nodded reservedly. "You forget that we do not know where the garden is. Until we do, we can do nothing!"

"I have three Krohn regiments tearing the capital city apart looking for the Codex," Armid said with pride. "If it's in the city, they'll find it!"

Trivis shook his head. "Unless it's been hidden by the Sions...or destroyed."

"It wasn't destroyed," Defuria stated confidently. "The Sions put it somewhere where it would be safe and protected in the event they died before they could tell the Namuh of the content themselves."

Trivis looked at Defuria curiously. "How do you know so much about the Sions and how they think?"

"Its my job to know!" replied Defuria brusquely. "Its my job to understand how the forces of the universe operate so we can take advantage of them!"

Trivis raised a hand to indicate he didn't't wish to continue the tangent.

"What Defuria says does make sense," said Armid, nodding to their leader. "And if the Sions are indeed waning, we must be in a position to act swiftly when we do find the Codex!"

Defuria nodded. "Exactly! If the Namuh have been told of their destiny and beat us to the Tree, all will be lost!"

Armid suddenly looked concerned. "Do you think this likely?"

Defuria shook his head and chuckled lightly. "Hardly. I just don't want to take any chances. The Grimsin will be ours sure enough. The fleet will ensure it for us!"

Trivis glared at Defuria and raised an eyebrow. "The fleet?"

"Every single ship that bares our banner," answered Defuria with a touch of egotism. "They'll be here in a matter of days."

Armid couldn't help but smile at the revelation. The whole of the Unmentionable Armada had not been assembled in one place for a millennia; now it was coming here! What glory, what majesty there would be for the Unmentionables, and none more so than for the operatives involved in bringing down the Namuh. Surely this event would be a new dawn for the Empire!

"But what of the Sions?" the ever cautious and conservative Trivis asked. "They may not have the same power to tout as they once did, but they still cannot be ignored."

Defuria sneered. "The Sions will not be able to do a thing about it this time. What is left of their pitiful forces is currently locked in a magnificent battle over their last stronghold. They have no ships to spare without dooming what is left of their own territories! We have effectively won!"

Several roars, followed by a series of loud hissing and clicking Krohn tongues, suddenly sounded out from a chamber further down the hall. Defuria closed his eyes and shook his head. "It appears I must go. Before I do, I want you to remember that, although the fleet is coming, we still have much to accomplish ourselves. Armid, you must do all that is in your power to find the Codex! Kill, torture or destroy whatever or whomever you need to in order to find it. Nothing is more important than getting it. Understand?"

"I do!" Armid answered quickly, followed by a devilish smile.

Defuria nodded optimistically. "And Trivis, be sure the trap to kill Fedrin works...or you'll have much bigger issues to deal with than dividing Grimsin shares."

Trivis looked at Defuria uneasily, not saying a word.

"Don't feel threatened," said Defuria in a tone meant to be reassuring, but had the opposite affect. "You have already done all the hard work. Now just make sure you finish what you have started."

"What of the Northern fleet?" Trivis pressed, ignoring Defuria's statements.

Armid laughed. "That antiquated collection of scrap metal? You've got to be kidding Trivis! Loosen up!"

"What of it?" asked Defuria, his demeanor becoming more and more agitated at Trivis' many misgivings and challenges.

Trivis shrugged. "I'm just concerned by the fact that it still exists; maybe it's not made up with the most advanced ships in the Namuh arsenal, but it's still there. I just don't think we should be overlooking loose ends, especially at this stage."

Defuria shook his head, once again dismissing Trivis' notions. "Our forces don't have the time to go gallivanting around star systems looking for outdated war ships for target practice."

"What if they challenge us?" Trivis pressed.

"Then we will kill them!" Defuria answered sharply. "And if they don't, we will kill them after we've retrieved the Grimsin. Either way, they'll die on our terms and on our timetable, not theirs!"

"Very well," Trivis said with a small amount of hesitation in his voice as he begrudgingly bowed to their leader. "For Yova's disgrace, and for the Grimsin."

"For Yova's disgrace, and for the Grimsin!" Armid repeated as he, too, bowed to Defuria.

The two Unmentionable lieutenants then turned to walk back down the corridor leaving their leader play host to the invading army of reptiles.

"I can't believe the entire fleet is coming!" said Armid excitedly when they were some distance down the corridor. "It's over for the Namuh. Over! They don't stand a chance!"

Trivis nodded but did not answer. He was deep in a maze of troubling thoughts. The entire Unmentionable Fleet was coming? Why? It made no sense. Of course the objective of securing the garden and the Grimsin Tree therein was critical, but calling up all the forces in the empire when a mere fraction would suffice. And how would the Grimsin be divided amongst the entire Unmentionable Armada when certain shares had already been promised to the operatives currently on the assignment? Trivis was certain he would not take a smaller share and was confident his immediate comrades felt likewise. It just didn't add up.

CHAPTER 23

BATTLE OVER VOIGT

Commander Searle moved briskly down the hall, half jogging, and half walking, toward her bridge. She had only been gone for a minute, returning from a quick consult with her tactical engineer when a rather frantic sounding ensign called her back.

"Commander on deck," an officer called out as Searle walked through the doors.

She motioned for the officers to be at ease as she made her way directly to the monitoring station.

"What's happening, Ensign?" she asked the small framed officer standing at his station in the center of the room.

The officer looked up and then quickly pulled up the star system screen; he then sat back in his chair, arms folded with a contented smile on his face.

"What exactly am I looking at here?" asked Searle as she leaned in for a closer look.

"It's the Ilo," the officer answered confidently.

Searle looked at the officer for explanation. "I can see it's the Ilo," she said patiently. "What's important about it?"

The officer shook his head, leaned forward and tapped several buttons on another screen. "See here? This is an image of the Ilo Battle Station taken four months ago."

"And..." said Searle, getting annoyed with the delayed presentation being put on by the officer.

"And this is the Ilo image our scanners compiled five minutes ago," stated the Ensign as he sat back once again with a look of accomplishment and pride on his face.

Searle leaned in closer, studying the screen intently. Suddenly she saw it! "Help us all," she whispered. "Get Fedrin on the link! Now!"

"Aye, Ma'am!" the communications officer answered promptly.

Searle walked straightway to her command chair and strapped herself in. "All stations prepare for battle," she announced over a ship wide announcement. "Secure all lose articles, lock all connecting bulkheads and prepare for immediate combat! I repeat, prepare for immediate combat!"

"You're on with Fedrin," the communications officer announced.

"Patch it here," Searle said nodding toward her personal transmitter.

"What's happening, Commander?" asked Fedrin, paying more attention to his own commotion filled bridge than to hers.

"We found them," was Searle's reply.

"Yes that will be fine," Fedrin said to one of his officers and then looked back to Searle and shook his head. "I'm sorry. What was it you said?"

"I said we found them," she repeated patiently.

"Found them? Found whom?" Fedrin asked, nodding in response to an engineer trying to ask him a 'yes or no' question.

"The Krohn Fleet," Searle answered.

Fedrin was just about to pass out another order but froze and looked straight at Searle. "You found the Krohns?" he clarified.

She nodded.

Fedrin raised his hand for silence, which was immediately obeyed. "Where?" he asked, looking to another screen fixed on his command chair.

"Zoom in on the Ilo's lateral axis, sector sixteen by thirty," Searle answered.

"Kesler, lock visual scanners on Ilo and zoom in tight on sector sixteen by thirty," ordered Fedrin.

"Aye, Sir!" Kesler answered as he dropped his dozen other pressing tasks and immediately obeyed Fedrin's order.

A strange stillness filled the Iovara Bridge as Kesler worked on the scanner. Officers, who just moments earlier were running important errands in preparation for a possible battle, found themselves standing completely still, waiting the result from Kesler's unique order.

"How we doing there?" Fedrin impatiently asked after a few moments.

Kesler looked at one screen and then turned to face another. "Coming back right now," he answered.

Fedrin glanced at Searle and raised an eyebrow. "On main screen."

Fedrin, together with the rest of the Iovara command crew, looked up in awe as the massive floating hulk of metal, more than a hundred times the size of the Iovara, stood before their eyes.

At one point in time, the massive station had been the primary forward post for the Namuh Federation expansion. Used at first for launching scouting runs to nearby systems, it was eventually retrofitted to function as a low yield shipyard and supply depot for the fleets. Shielded better than ten battleships, and armed with nearly as many DEG turrets and EMOD batteries as the entire Second Fleet, the Ilo was truly the most advanced technological achievement of its day. But a mere five years after its commission, the Great Krohn War began on the opposite side of the Federation, forcing the high maintenance station to become an unacceptable liability to maintain. The mighty Ilo was therefore all but disbanded, leaving a skeleton crew of a mere four hundred souls to operate a station that once took the combined efforts of more than twelve thousand.

The last time Fedrin had seen the station, it was still in full-scale operation. He remembered how the near thousands of lights and beacons dotted over the structure made it shine like a star. He was shocked, and a little disheartened, at the sharp contrast that now faced him. The floodlights that once proudly shown over the bold Ilo name were absent. The dozens of docking bay lights were out; even the flight warning towers were disengaged. The only portion of the station that still hinted at a remnant of life, was a small face on the upward hemisphere, where the remaining crew resided.

After a quick inspection of the station, Fedrin turned to Searle perplexed. "I'm looking at it."

"You're not looking hard enough," Searle commented.

Fedrin reluctantly turned back to the screen and studied the image. He was nearly about to ask Searle for a clue when he spotted it. "Kesler, tighten image around the lateral axis!"

The image on the screen changed from the full station view to a small shaded section on the station's surface.

Kesler's jaw dropped.

"Would you look at that?" Jonas exclaimed from up in his station.

Tarkin looked at the screen and then to Kesler. "I don't see anything."

"It's a Krohn Battle Cruiser," Gallo said quietly, starring at the screen. "It has somehow latched onto the Ilo in hopes of blending in."

"Which it very nearly did," remarked Fedrin. "Good work Searle...fantastic work!" he added. "You may have just saved a lot of lives!"

"It was actually my Ensign that deserves credit for the find," Searle clarified. "I never would have found it either."

Fedrin nodded to the officer and then turned back to the image. "So they've been here the entire time."

"But why?" Searle asked. "They could have easily destroyed the colony. Why just sit around playing hide and seek?"

"Maybe they knew we were coming and wanted us more than the colony?" Fedrin suggested. "After all, they have no idea of our intentions to get the data device. Perhaps their plan all along was to lure us here and they feared that if they destroyed the colony too soon, we wouldn't come."

"So you think this entire thing was a trap, for us?" Searle asked.

Fedrin shrugged. "If it was, I intend to mix things around a bit for them."

"How do you want to proceed?" Searle asked.

Fedrin rubbed his chin as he thought. "We'll continue on our normal course toward the planet...for now," Fedrin answered. "We'll take it nice and easy until we're just outside the range of their missiles. Once we're there, we'll turn hard toward them and get a few shots off before they break away from the station. Their shields are obviously down as are their main weapon systems evident by the lack of EM waves flying around. We should get them totally by surprise."

Searle let out a long sigh. "Here goes nothing then," she said and waved a quick goodbye.

Fedrin nodded. "Good luck, Searle!"

"You too!" she answered as the transmission ended.

"All right, gentlemen," Fedrin spoke up. "Looks like we've just gotten our first break in a long time. Let's take advantage of it."

The officers looked at each other and then turned to Fedrin, all ears.

"I want everyone on full battle readiness but whatever you do, don't make it look like we're battle ready. I want our formation to be easy and causal. I don't want the plasma weapons charged fully until I say. And don't sound the alarms!"

"How to do my job without looking like I'm doing it?" Jonas said to himself curiously. "I'm usually trying to do the opposite."

Tarkin and Kesler looked at each other and shook their heads.

⅄

Commander Colby stared out the window, as the Ilo station grew larger and larger with each passing moment. They were close enough now that several of the bigger Krohn ships were easily identifiable on basic scans.

He glanced behind him and eyed his command crew. They nodded in unison to his unspoken inquiry of their readiness. Colby then turned back to the window and continually watched as his ship inched still closer to the tens of thousands of Krohns that wanted to make him, and his crew, their supper. The thought was less than pleasant.

He had just turned from the window and was making his way back to his seat when he heard it. Loud hisses and gurgling tongue clicks sounded over the fleet-wide broadcast channel. The alien utterances were chilling and vile, even though they were not understood.

"What in the world was that?" Colby yelled as he ran to the side of his communication officer.

"It came from the Defiant!" his officer yelled.

Colby shook his head. "Drezden, what is going on over there?" he said to himself.

"The transmission keeps repeating," the officer announced. "And it's an open link. Anyone in the system can hear it!"

"Someone has just given us away," said Colby under his breath. "Any chance one of the Hornell fighters could target the Defiant's transmitters?"

The officer shook his head. "No need. The Defiant is pulling out of the system!"

"She's what!?" Colby yelled.

The officer pointed at his screen. "She is heading back toward the warp-point!"

Colby glanced at his own screen and then shook his head. "What is going on?"

"This is First Lieutenant Kesler to all ships," the overhead intercom suddenly sounded out. "Launch the attack! I repeat, launch the attack!"

"Here we go!" the officer announced.

"Hard to starboard!" ordered Colby followed moments later by an unnatural lurch in the ship directly toward the Ilo station.

"Picking up Krohn EM signatures," the lieutenant announced. "They're waking up!"

Colby shook his head as his ship centered on the massive station. They were being forced to spring the trap much, much too soon.

⋏

The ships of the Sixth Fleet, minus the Defiant, which had indeed abandoned the fleet with no warning or alarm, promptly changed course from the planet and headed toward the battle station simultaneously. Weapons were hot, shields burned at maximum, and nerves were on edge.

The anonymous tip from the compromised Defiant had barely finished sounding out when Krohn ships began dislodging from the station and prepared for the imminent attack.

Hornell fighters swooped into defensive positions around the capital ships while the small squadron of tactical bombers remained close to the Hornell for protection, waiting for their chance to strike.

Fedrin's ships had yet to reach weapon's range when the Krohn force had assumed their battle formations and opened all gun ports, effectively nulling the 'would be' surprise counter offensive Fedrin had quickly planned.

For several more painstaking minutes, nothing happened. The Krohn fleet grew closer and closer while the Sixth Fleet pressed onward.

"Where are Voigt's fighter squadrons?" Fedrin yelled out when he noticed the skies begin to fill with Krohn fighters pressing hard on their position. "We're going to need them!"

"No answer from the colony on that," Tarkin answered. "My transmissions asking them to launch aren't being answered."

Fedrin shook his head. This wasn't going to be pretty.

"What are they doing?" Catrin asked Commander Kendrick as she pointed to the advanced Krohn fighters brazenly entering the range of the point defense batteries. "They must know they stand no chance this close to us!"

"They want blood at any cost!" Kendrick answered knowingly. "Life is cheap to them."

"Well let them try!" Catrin answered resolutely as she brought up the tactical transmitter to her lips. "All point defense batteries, fire at will! I repeat, fire at will! Light up my sky!"

The point defense turrets on the Iovara, cruisers, destroyers, and mighty Hornell roared to life. They cut down the Krohn fighter groups as fast as they came into range, blasting dozens out of the sky in mere moments. The magnificent barrage of yellow point defenses, orange glow of engine cores, and the Krohn fighters' blue energy weapons made such a dazzling display of light, color and sound that it was nearly impossible to tell what was going on. So many ships, near innumerable fighters, and such firepower turned the scene into momentary chaos, until the first wave of Krohn fighters had been destroyed.

"Commander," Catrin spoke up as the last of the nearby enemy fighters careened out of control and exploded near the Corinthia heavy cruiser. "Interceptor squadrons are requesting that we coordinate their attack formations and organize pursuit."

Kendrick shook his head. "The Krohns want to be chased. Have our wings set up protective positions around the fleet and guard for flanking runs by Krohn gunships. Do not give pursuit clearance."

"Sir!" yelled Catrin, looking up at the main screen. "Look!"

Kendrick looked up just in time to see multiple bursts of white light, followed by tiny streams of grayish smoke, come streaming from the Krohn capital ships in the far distance. Missiles!

"This will not end well," Kendrick said shaking his head. "All hands prepare for impact. Divert all nonessential power to the forward shields and hold on!"

Catrin nodded as she typed out the orders and held her breath. The missile launch was on its way!

⋏

"Forward point defense batteries prepare to fire on my mark!" Searle ordered as she watched helplessly as the deadly missiles approach the fleet.

"You're receiving a transmission from Commander Sanders," Searle's first lieutenant called up from his station.

"On screen!" Searle ordered.

"Searle!" Sanders exclaimed when he saw her. "Fedrin wants you to drop back and cut to your port side. We're going to move ahead and veer to starboard so we..."

"So we can maximize the number of batteries that can fire at the missiles," Searle said aloud as she gave the go ahead nod to her lieutenant.

"Exactly!" Sanders said.

The missiles were nearly atop the fleet when the ships suddenly broke formation, half veering hard to port and the other half hard to starboard. The remaining point defense batteries began to open fire, releasing another powerful display of intercepting weaponry.

"Don't let up!" Searle ordered as she saw the rate of fire from one battery slow down.

The missiles came closer and closer. A few exploded violently as point defenses got lucky; but most kept coming, unimpeded by the counter measures valiantly thrown up by the vessels of the Sixth Fleet.

"The Bolter has been hit!" Searle's lieutenant announced. "A direct hit was scored on her transmitter station."

"You ok, Sanders?" Searle called out through her transmitter.

A static ridden transmission filled her personal screen. "The missile… no…penetrate…hull…out…main transmit…"

"Be careful!" Searle yelled, hoping Sanders could hear her better than she could hear him.

"You...too!" Sanders called back and cut the transmission.

"Got to go!" Searle shouted as she spotted more missiles coming in hard and fast, dodging the point defense rounds and seeking their targets with a fiery rage.

"Oh no," Searle's lieutenant said in trepidation as he spotted five missiles bearing down hard on the Corinthia.

"Tenith get out of there!" Searle yelled into her transmitter. "Punch the main engine core!"

"They aren't going to make it," Searle's lieutenant remarked sadly as he watched the missiles simultaneously impact the hull of the mighty cruiser.

The massive vessel stopped dead in space as if hitting a brick wall. The huge hulk of masterful engineering and precision craftsmanship then sat in space for a moment, uneventfully. All running lights were out and only sputtering activity emitted from the engine cluster in the rear. All exterior signs made it look as if someone had simply pulled the plug on the mighty war machine. Just when it seemed that perhaps she was not as bad off as first supposed, it happened.

Tears filled Searle's eyes as the mighty vessel began to explode near the engine core. The explosions were small at first; but as they moved in synchrony up the fuselage, they grew larger and larger, each one blowing out larger fragments of twisted metal and armored plates into the surrounding space. The fiery explosions finally reached the plasma weaponry core causing a single, tremendous fireball to signify the end of a vessel that had taken three years to build, and only twenty seconds to destroy.

Kesler had never liked Tenith. Since their days at the academy, they had been in fierce competition for varying positions, promotions and even once, a romantic interest, with one barely edging out the other at every turn. Their rivalry had culminated in the fact that Tenith had received his own command first, a fact Tenith had been sure to rub in over the short course of his appointment. How it had irked Kesler, having Tenith think he was better than him, even though Kesler had been asked directly by Fedrin to forgo the promotion in order to help him run the Iovara.

Yet now, watching the stray fragments of burning hull and blackened ash floating where the Corinthia had, just moments earlier, been flying proudly, Kesler instantly felt juvenile and trivial forever wishing Tenith anything but the very best. Kesler couldn't even remember if he had ever shared one kind word with Tenith in the eight years they had known one another. Now, he would never get another chance to do so.

Fedrin gawked at what was left of the Corinthia, astonished and speechless. One of the most powerful ships of his fleet was gone before it had fired a shot. He hardly had time to process the loss when more alarms started to blare and the tactical display began to flash. More missiles were on their way; willing and eager to inflict more damage upon the ever humbled, and shrinking, Sixth Fleet.

"Move us up!" ordered Fedrin as he spotted Commander Colby and his destroyer in trouble. "Get between the missiles and the Arbitrator!"

"Too late!" Kesler called back as he watched the Arbitrator take two missiles back to back on her port side.

"It's not too late!" Fedrin yelled back. "Take us in!"

The Iovara shot forward just in time to take the full brunt of a solo missile bent on destroying the now vulnerable destroyer. Fedrin held the arms of his chair tightly as the missile smashed the topside shields of his ship.

"Commander Colby extends his thanks," Gallo voiced up.

"Tell him to get out of here," Fedrin said. "There's no use having him here that weak. He'll just be a liability."

Another alarm sounded. Fedrin looked up and shook his head just as three missiles slammed into Hornell Carrier, crippling her aft secondary fighter bay.

"We're getting eaten alive out here!" Searle shouted out to Fedrin over a transmission.

More alerts sounded as two other missiles came swooping down beneath the Revenge, and then back up to smash into the Bolter.

"The plan is a bust!" Commander Kendrick called out over a transmission. "We have to pull back now or we're as good as dead!"

"Searle lookout!" yelled Fedrin, switching transmissions to the Revenge cruiser.

"I see them!" Searle answered. "They're going to hit us Fedrin. There's nothing I can do!"

The missiles came hard and fast toward Searle's cruiser. Fedrin winced as they crashed into her starboard side, one after another, wearing the shields down so much that the last one pierced right through the ship, coming back out the other side and exploding some distance away.

"You ok?" Fedrin called out.

"We...fine...breach...locked," Searle answered in a choppy transmission.

Fedrin turned to Kesler. "Do you think can we hang on till we get into firing range?"

"I can't see how," Tarkin said on behalf of Kesler who was tied up in a transmission with the Bolter. "This is a disaster!"

"It's how most battles start in open space!" Jonas shouted down to Tarkin. "The Krohns have the superior long range weapons and always wreak havoc on us like this from afar. But once we get close..." Jonas smiled and patted his control station.

Kesler ended his transmission and shook his head. "I agree with Tarkin. I don't think we can win this time. Our plan was compromised and we're outnumbered four to one. Even if we get a couple good shots in, they'll still have plenty of ships left to finish us off."

Fedrin sat back in his chair and reluctantly nodded. "Then take us out of here."

"We're almost in weapon's range," Jonas called down. "Be a shame not to fire what we have loaded before we hit the road."

Fedrin reluctantly nodded. "Let's fire our rounds and then get out of here then."

"What of the data device?" Kesler asked.

"We'll have to think of something else," Fedrin answered. "Something less overt."

Kesler looked at Fedrin skeptically.

Fedrin shrugged. "I've got nothing right now."

Kesler shook his head as he turned back to his station.

"I think..." Tarkin started to say but was interrupted when a tremendous surge of energy riveted through the ship.

"Plasma rounds away!" Jonas called out.

Fedrin nodded. "Take us about, best possible speed!"

The remaining ships of the sixth fleet fired their primary weapons and turned away sharply; their plasma rounds continued to burn toward the enemy vessels to help cover their retreat. The molten plasma shots struck multiple Krohn warships, destroying several of them, but not enough to dent their overall superior force.

A fresh series of warning alarms sounded at Kesler's station. "More missiles on the way!" he shouted out, much to everyone's dismay.

"Do you ever have any good news to report?" Jonas called down to Kesler.

"We need to move faster!" Fedrin shouted out. "Those missiles will rip us to pieces if they get to us!"

"Engines are running at maximum!" an engineering consultant answered. "There's no more to give, Sir!"

"Have Commander Kendrick divert all fighters to our rear!" Fedrin ordered, ignoring the engineer. "Have them try and target the missiles the best they can!"

"Aye, Sir!" Kesler answered, knowing full well that the fighters had little chance of shooting down one missile, let alone a dozen.

Fedrin felt helpless as he watched the formation of missiles close the distance with his fleeing ships and then proceed to slam into the Bolter destroyer. He winced as one after the other, the deadly projectiles pounded down the Bolter's shields until she was exposed and vulnerable. The final missile easily pierced through the naked hull and passed through several decks of the ship before it lodged itself into a bulkhead somewhere deep amidships. Fedrin turned his eyes, not wanting to see what was to happen next.

The resulting explosion tore the humble destroyer in two halves; the engines and secondary hangar sections forming the mass of one; and the bridge, life support generators and primary hangar comprising the bulk of the other. Bodies, furniture, personal effects, and various storage boxes and containers slowly spilled into space confirming the totality of the ship's demise. It was hard for the Iovara officers to watch as the frigid, murderous space slowly killed their comrades, their friends.

"That ship was home to a lot of good people," Kesler said, blankly staring at the screen while the ship continued to spill its life's blood into space.

"Commander Sanders is with his daughter now," Gallo said quietly.

The Iovara command crew hardly had time enough to absorb the shock of yet another catastrophic loss when two more missiles crashed into her. The first missile grazed off the top of the ship, taking with it several exterior instruments before spinning off behind the ship and harmlessly exploding. The other slammed into her side, ravaging the shielding but inflicting no major damage.

"Report?" Fedrin called out.

"We're ok," Kesler quickly answered, "...but I'm guessing those eight missiles heading straight for us will leave a fairly large dent!"

"Seriously? Enough with the cruddy news!" Jonas shouted down. "Is your job to depress us all the time?"

Fedrin looked up to the main screen in time to see the missiles parade past the scanner heading toward his ship.

"Here they come!" Kesler announced, prompting the command crew to brace for impact.

The missiles were mere moments from smashing the Iovara into space dust when a tremendous burst of red light slashed before their flight path, causing each projectile to explode ineffectually.

"What was that?" Fedrin yelled as his ship shook violently from the nearby shock waves. "I want to know what that was!"

"We're alive!" Jonas yelled out and clapped his hands. "Being alive is my favorite!"

Kesler rapidly looked at several of his instruments and then shrugged. "I have no idea Admiral!" he said. "It looks like something intercepted the missiles before they hit us but I have no idea what it was!"

"Any idea where it came from?" Fedrin asked.

"Working on it right now," Kesler answered. "It'll take the combat computer a minute to triangulate."

"Better work fast," Gallo said, gazing into a monitor. "Looks like the rest of the Krohn fighters are coming up followed by more missiles!"

"Admiral!" Tarkin suddenly yelled.

Fedrin looked down at Tarkin.

"There's a big ship coming up from the planet!"

Fedrin immediately looked to Kesler who was already scanning the surface of the cloudy planet below to confirm Tarkin's sighting.

"Enemy fighters closing in!" Gallo updated.

Fedrin nodded as he considered his options. "Move all fighters to intercept!" he finally ordered. "Keep their formations loose and able to adjust to advances on their flanks. Have the Revenge and the Hornell cut hard to port, and offer a few broadsides of their DEG guns to the fighters. Everyone else, hard to starboard!"

"Whoa!" Kesler exclaimed as he spotted what Tarkin had noticed.

Fedrin shed his harness and jumped to Kesler's side. "What is it?"

Without a word, Kesler inputted his screen data to the main viewing screen. What Fedrin saw made his jaw drop.

"What is it?" Tarkin asked, who was unsure of the significance of the sight before him.

Kesler gaped at the screen in stupefied disbelief. "It's...it's the Idok!" he stammered.

"It's about time you came up with some good news!" Jonas yelled down. "See, it's not so hard!"

Tarkin looked at Kesler slightly confused and then nodded in understanding. "The Admiral's wife's ship?"

Kesler nodded. "That it is."

A spontaneous cheer went up on the bridge as the mammoth battle carrier came into full sight, followed closely by her fighter squadrons. Fedrin hadn't had time to process the significance of what he was seeing when the Idok let loose with several sweeping motions of the same powerful weapon he had witnessed moments earlier. The beam instantly destroyed a wing of Krohn fighters, and three formations of inbound missiles.

"Hail them!" Fedrin said.

"They've already hailed us and have instructed us to join them in a counterattack!" Gallo announced.

"All ships come about!" Fedrin yelled, activating the fleet-wide transmitter. "I repeat, come about! Open gun ports and let loose with everything we have! We're going to win this thing after all!"

Kesler looked up at Fedrin and held his ear. "I'm right here, Sir!"

Fedrin laughed, slapped Kesler's shoulder, and then leapt back to his seat. "Divert all surplus power to prow shields and keep them steady. Let's do this!"

"Aye, Sir!" Gallo answered.

The surviving Sixth Fleet vessels collectively turned around together and followed the Idok's brazen attack toward the superior force of Krohn warships.

"Would you look at that?" Jonas exclaimed, gazing with unbridled envy as the Idok fired her new and mysterious weapon at a batch of three Krohn cruisers, destroying all of them almost instantly.

"Stop your drooling and coordinate our firing resolutions!" Fedrin called up to Jonas. "It's not done yet!"

"Right, right," Jonas said as he looked to his own station.

Moments later, another surge of energy riveted through the ship as two more plasma rounds left the confines of the Iovara and burned toward the enemy.

Kesler pumped his fist in the air as he watched the two rounds make contact with twin Krohn destroyers, utterly destroying both.

"Nice shot!" Tarkin called up.

"It really was," Jonas said. "But thanks for noticing. It's nice having your work admired."

Tarkin smiled and shook his head.

A beep sounded at Kesler's station. "Looks like three Krohn Cruisers have broken away from the main fleet body and are coming full speed toward our left flank."

"Arm DEG guns and ready EMOD turrets," Fedrin ordered.

Jonas nodded as he flipped the switches to activate the Iovara's host of secondary weaponry. "DEG guns armed and ready," he announced.

"And the EMOD's?" Fedrin pressed as he looked at his own tactical scanner.

"Coming on-line now," Jonas answered. "Give me a target in range and I can offer discounts on cremation...calling hours and service included!"

"I don't think we're going to need them," remarked Kesler as he watched the three inbound Cruisers fall prey to the ever-impressive attacks from the imposing Idok.

Fedrin looked on and realized Kesler was right. Nothing but unorganized fighter squadrons, and hundreds of escape pods now stood where one of the greatest Krohn fleets ever assembled had been just moments earlier.

"Receiving transmission from the Idok," Gallo said, hardly able to control himself from shouting out in excitement.

A young Lieutenant, Fedrin did not recognize, appeared on the main screen.

"Lieutenant Commander Pertikone of the NPF Battle Carrier Idok reporting, Sir!" the young man said emphatically, following a proper salute.

"Where is your Commander Lieutenant?" Fedrin asked bluntly.

The young man relaxed his stance and shook his head. "It's a long story Admiral."

"Get on with it then!" said Fedrin sharply. "Is she there? Is she ok?"

"Admiral!" Gallo suddenly called out.

Fedrin turned to face his ensign. "What?" he asked harshly.

"I'm getting some strange EM activity coming from the planet," he answered ominously.

"Confirm that," Tarkin added. "And it's coming up fast!"

Fedrin hardly heard what was being said when a small, familiar looking ship came bursting out from the cloudy atmosphere and gracefully flew under the Idok.

"Whoa there," Kesler said in awe. "What do we have here?"

"This has got to be the weirdest day of my life," Jonas said with a shake of his head. "And I've had some weird days."

"A transmission is forcing its way into our network!" Gallo spoke up with alarm. "It's routing its way to the main screen. I can't stop it!"

Fedrin turned to the main screen as the image of the Idok Bridge was slowly replaced by a cloaked Sion figure.

"Trab!" Fedrin exclaimed. "What is going on? What is happening?"

"Fedrin," Trab answered in a very reserved, yet pleased tone. "All will be explained in time."

"But how can you be here?" Fedrin asked. "You told me that we would be on our own! You told me that the Sions could not afford to help us!"

The hooded form nodded and spoke in an ominous tone. "Things have changed Fedrin."

"Such as?" asked Fedrin.

"Many of your ships are damaged, are they not?" Trab asked, ignoring Fedrin's question.

Fedrin nodded. "Some of us got beat up pretty bad. Some much worse," he added sadly.

Trab nodded with understanding. "Allow your ships to come into high orbit and begin repairs. My ship and crew will lend assistance to your repair teams and install Sion components as we have done with the Idok. In the meantime, we must meet on the colony."

"Meet on the colony?" Fedrin asked. "As in you and I?"

Trab nodded.

"For the device?" Fedrin clarified.

Trab nodded. "Amongst other reasons."

"I already have a Raider team prepping to go down," Fedrin said. "I've told them where the device is and how to get it. That'll be our fastest and most efficient option."

"They have her," said Trab calmly.

Fedrin looked confused. "Have who?"

"They have your wife."

"Who has her? Why?"

Trab waved his arm activating a recorded video message that played in the lower right corner of the main transmission screen. It showed a darkened room with a single hanging light fixed above a metal chair in the center. In the chair sat Commander Etana, head down, stripped of her uniform, wearing nothing but rags. She was tied to the chair with composite chains that dug deep into her flesh. Blood seeped from where the bonds wrapped her legs, chest, and arms. Only the faint rhythmic rise and fall of her chest indicated she was still alive.

Gallo, Tarkin, Kesler, Jonas and the other Iovara officers looked at the video in horror and then slowly turned their collective gazes to their Admiral. Fedrin sat resolutely in his chair, undoubtedly distraught, but in full control of his emotions. His jaw was tight, his fists clenched, and his eyes fixed on the horrific spectacle before him.

"Fedrin," a vile sounding voice from off screen spoke. "If you ever want to see your little tramp again, come to the Voigt colony before the setting of the sun," the voice trailed off and the image dissipated from view.

"Is that it?" Fedrin asked, looking intently at Trab.

Trab nodded. "That's all we've received."

"And it's genuine?" Fedrin asked.

"It is," Trab answered gravely.

"It's a trap," stated Fedrin frankly, looking for Trab to dissuade him.

"Undoubtedly," replied Trab.

Fedrin nodded with resolve. "I guess I'll see you there!" he said firmly and immediately stood to his feet. "Kesler," he then said promptly. "You are promoted to the rank of Commodore, effective immediately."

Kesler looked at Fedrin stunned, unable to respond.

"My standing orders are to coordinate with the Sions to repair the fleet. With any luck, I'll be back here tonight with Etana and the data device."

Fedrin stepped off of the command platform, motioned toward his chair and then nodded to Kesler. "Take care of her Kesler. I want her back in one piece. Got it?"

"Got it," replied Kesler solemnly.

Fedrin looked once more around his bridge and offered a satisfactory nod. "I'll be seeing you!" he said in a tone that seemed, to some, as a way of saying goodbye. He had only set one foot into the hallway when he turned sharply and faced Tarkin. "Tarkin, you're with me!" he called out, much to everyone's surprise, and then walked briskly off the bridge.

Tarkin awkwardly stood to his feet and looked at Kesler for affirmation.

"You deaf or something?" Jonas called down to Tarkin after he didn't move.

"You heard him," Kesler added and nodded toward the door. "The Admiral called you. Get going!"

Tarkin nodded promptly and started after Fedrin.

"Tarkin," Kesler called out just as Tarkin reached the doorway.

Tarkin turned.

"Be careful," Kesler said and offered a nod.

Tarkin nodded in return and offered a smile to his friend. "You too."

"And punch something for me!" added Jonas. "With all six fists!"

Tarkin offered a slight smile as he followed quickly after the Admiral. He didn't know it as he walked, but he was preparing to undertake the most important mission of his life.

⋏

A loud rumble sounded outside, followed by several deep Krohn roars.

"What is it?" Reesa asked, looking up from the table.

"Looks like they're breaking into some more buildings on Fifth Street," Darion answered after glancing out the window.

"I think they are looking for the Codex," remarked Reesa.

"Think so?" asked Darion as he studied the Krohns carrying boxes of old books and papers out of one of the buildings and begin loading them onto a support vehicle nearby.

Reesa shrugged. "Why else would they be spending so much time sifting through archives, libraries and museums? They want it. I'm sure of it."

"Lets hope they spend all the their time looking in banks and museums and not in ransacked clothing stores," commented Darion with a shake of his head.

"Don't think about it," Reesa said. "What's done is done. We can't move forward if we keep looking back."

"Speaking of looking forward," said Darion returning to the table with two bottles of water and setting one in front of Reesa.

Reesa took her bottle and nodded at a sheet of paper filled with notes. "There really aren't a lot of options as I see it."

"That's what I think," said Darion, opening his bottle and taking a long swallow.

Reesa nodded. "We know that we need to get to a deep space transmitter to receive the Clear Skies program from Fedrin."

Darion nodded.

"Of the nine deep space transmitters on the planet, only three of them are in proximity to our location," continued Reesa.

"The Capital Building, the Defense Complex, and the Clear Skies Research Center," Darion said with a sigh, having already gone through the details multiple times.

"The Capital Building and the Defense Complex are in the heart of Larep and are probably crawling with Krohn foot soldiers," commented Reesa.

"Which leaves the Clear Skies research center," said Darion with a nod.

Reesa nodded. "It's the only one I see happening. It's an empty building on the outskirts of the city limits with no real strategic or tactical value to the Krohns. They might not even have a troop presence there."

Darion shook his head. "But it's so far away. How can we possibly get there in time?"

"I think that's why Kebbs left this," Reesa said as she slid a paper across the table.

Darion picked it up and shook his head. "You've got to be kidding me!"

"Afraid not," Reesa answered.

"These are trash-line schematics," protested Darion.

"And Kebbs was a trash man," retorted Reesa. "Makes sense to me."

"Is it to late to trade jobs?"

Reesa stood to her feet and patted Darion's arm affectionately. "Get some rest, General. You have a long night ahead of you."

Reesa retired to the apartment's only bedroom to catch some needed rest. The task she had in store was no picnic either. Traversing the lizard infested city, making her way to Professor Jabel in the bunkers, and keeping him safe until Darion obtained the data device, was a mission that an entire legion of elite troops would have a hard time completing; but a single woman?

Darion watched as she walked away and then glanced at the table covered with their notes and plans. He shook his head. What they were about to undertake was so outrageously improbable and so brazenly stupid that it nearly made him laugh at the thought; what were two isolated individuals going to do against the Krohn war machine? The answer would be evident soon enough.

Defuria stood in the silence of his empty office, soaking in the fading rays of light as the sun gradually set behind the distant mountains of Larep. He smiled cruelly.

The Federation was in turmoil, by all accounts on the brink of collapse, if not already plunged over the side. Krohns occupied the skies above Namuh Prime and her capital city, with no formal opposition in sight. The last mobile fleet of any consequence in the combined navy was in the furthest star-system under the Namuh flag, unable to offer assistance and hopelessly outmatched even if they could. Everything was unfolding just as he had masterfully orchestrated. Nothing could stop him now.